MANEATER

THE MAVENS
BOOK 1

MORGAN ELIZABETH

PLAYLIST

Maneater - Nelly Furtado
    Her - Megan Thee Stallion
    Guy on a Horse - Maisie Peters
    Super Graphic Ultra Modern Girl - Chappell Roan
    Blank Space - Taylor Swift
    The Feels - Maren Morris
    Womanizer - Britney Spears
    Not My Fault - Renee Rapp
    Bang Bang - Jessie J
    The Man - Taylor Swift
    Come and Get It - Selena Gomez
    Manchild - Sabrina
    Vigilante Shit - Taylor Swift

A NOTE FROM MORGAN

Hello, Mavens!

I'm so excited you agreed to take this mission with me—I mean, read this super fun book with me.

The Mavens were created as a silly text to my group chat where I said *Charlie's Angels but she fucks Charlie*. While no one hooks up with the Maven's mysterious owner, Gabriel, in this book, it did start an idea in my mind I couldn't ignore. When I finished writing Tourist Trap and decided I wouldn't be going back to Seaside Point until next summer, I knew this was the Mavens' time to shine. And *damn* did they shine.

I love this story and Josie and the Mavens SO MUCH. I knew I would have fun writing this book, but I didn't expect to have this much fun, which is why it's my longest book to date. Between trying to make sure the mystery plot made sense and kept you on your toes, and making sure Rowan and Josie got plenty of time to banter, and for the enemies to turn to lovers, I needed lots of words.

I hope you love this wild ride as much as I loved writing it! A few housekeeping things before we move on, though. I am not a super hot spy, much to my own disappointment. I don't have any stealthy skills, nor do I hold much knowledge of how actual spies or PIs work. While I did some liberal Googling, please remember this is a work a fiction and I took some artistic liberties when it came to how things *actually* work. If you're a PI or a super cool undercover spy, first off, amazing, cool, so jealous, and second off, maybe skip this book in case any of my inaccuracies annoy you.

Next, this book contains adult language and situations, sabotages that involve bodily harm (nothing gruesome, or on page!) and the mention of infidelity or just general assholery (not the main characters, but she's a super hot spy who flirts with men to get them to tell her their secrets). Reading is supposed to be our happy place, and if at any time that feeling fades, feel free to stop reading. Mental health always comes first!

Love you to the moon and to Saturn!

Morgan

ONE

JOSIE

Sometimes, I feel bad about ruining the lives of men.

Sometimes, I catch glimpses of a different version and see past the carefully crafted one meant to pull unsuspecting people into his web. Those days, despite the research we've done to ensure our client is in the right and that the man I'm currently trying to pull evidence from is, in fact, a piece of shit, I feel the tiniest niggling of guilt about deceiving them to get their deepest darkest secrets with a simple smile and a bat of my eyelashes.

Not this time.

"I have a bitch of an ex-wife. Well, not quite an ex-wife yet, but we're in proceedings."

I smile and nod, remembering that the file says he had filed for divorce while his wife was away, taking care of *his* sick mother, claiming she hadn't been *meeting his needs*.

And now he's trying to claim he doesn't have the money to pay her a good amount of alimony. We already gathered evidence that he's cheating on her, but we're pretty sure he's hiding money to conceal it for the divorce proceedings.

"That must be really hard," I say with an apologetic frown. This is probably the worst part about my job: having to win over the grossest specimens of men and stroke their egos just enough so they slip up. He takes another too-large bite that makes me want to gag before I smile and nod.

"And now she's trying to sue me outta house and home for alimony. The bitch has never worked a day in her life!" My mind flashes to the file I left at my apartment, which declared she was climbing the corporate ladder before he told her he didn't want her to work—insisted on it, even.

I let my eyes go wide, and my lips drop into a shape of disbelief. I know I sold my faux-shock to him when his eyes shift to the full, pink lips I lined in the car on the way here, when he nods and continues.

"But don't you worry," he says, a small, proud smile on his lips, now greasy with his dinner. "I've got that handled. Won't let that bitch bleed me dry."

God bless her for leaving, because I don't know if he knows how to call a woman anything *but* a bitch. I don't plan to stick around long enough to find out, not when he's already so pliant in the palm of my hand.

"Oh?" I ask, an elbow going to the table, my head tipping as I rest it on my hand, dark hair spilling as my tits come together, making my cleavage nearly ludicrous.

"My accountant's been protecting me for years, making sure something like this wouldn't happen. You know...diversifying." There's a knowing twinkle in his eyes like I'm just supposed to know what that means, and, as is my specialty, I play dumb.

Evidence is only good if it's direct and straight from his own mouth. We could go after the accountant, probably get a warrant and find the money he's hiding, but something tells me this asshole would claim ignorance, say he had no idea all along and still find a way to duck out of paying his ex-wife.

"Diversifying?" I ask, brows together, lips pouting. "So like, all of your money is tied up in stocks or real estate or whatever?"

His eyes are locked on my tits, and in that moment, I know I won.

Even more so when he leans in a bit, his tie falling into his plate of red sauce. I fight the grimace that wants to win.

"No, no, putting money in overseas accounts. Untrackable, untraceable, unable to be used against me."

"Oh, wow," I say. "That's so smart!" I twirl a lock of my silky, dark hair around a finger and smile at him.

"Well, that's what I am, you know. Smart, rich, and good-looking." He's already batting zero for two, and when I look over his shoulder to see Rory nodding, indicating she got the recording, I know he's about to be zero for three.

That admission was exactly what I needed, my assignment for the night complete.

As an investigator at Mavens Investigations, it's my job to get whatever evidence our client needs. This time the plan was simple: I was to bump into our target, Jackson Wilson, on the street, and flirt my way into a date where I could talk to him more. Then on that date, I was to bat my eyelashes and flip my hair and flirt with this scumbag all evening, plying him with liquor and a great shot of my cleavage until he confessed he was hiding money from his soon-to-be ex-wife.

After barely five minutes with the man, I quickly became aware of why he was an *ex*. He's a terrible human.

Eager to get out of his presence, I glance over his shoulder, spotting Rory in the server's uniform that we got, her long blonde hair pulled into a tight bun, and give her the signal: a flip of my hair and then a roll of the stud earring in my right ear. She nods before she puts on a fake smile, grabs a tray filled with water, and makes her way to us as *Jackson* continues to babble on and on about his accounts in various countries, the homes he owns, et cetera, making a further attempt to impress me.

"Is there anything—oh my goodness!" Rory gasps, stepping back as all of the glasses—and the large pitcher of water, because Rory never does *anything* half-assed—come tumbling down onto the table —and me. The rush of freezing cold water chills me to the bone because, apparently, she had to be more realistic by making it *ice* water. Pushing my chair back with a loud screech, I stand, brushing the ice cubes out of my lap. The very corner of Rory's lips tips up, and I have to fight the all-consuming urge to roll my eyes.

"What the hell!" my date yells, a dark glare moving to Rory before staring and reaching for the ice cube that fell in my cleavage. I step back, swiping it out before he can put his grimy hands on me.

"'Oh, I am *so sorry*," Rory gushes, reaching into her apron for some napkins and handing them to me. The flimsy cocktail napkins don't do anything, and she sets the tray onto our table over our meals. This is over, anyway.

"I want to talk to your manager," Jackson says.

"It's so okay; I—" I start.

"It absolutely is *not*," he roars.

"Of course, I'll get you my manager right away," Rory says, her blue eyes turning to me.

I give her a smile and then a tight one to my date before announcing, "I'm going to the bathroom to try and dry off."

"I can come help—" Jackson attempts.

Ew.

"No, I think I can manage," I say, grabbing my bag and my cell before moving towards the back of the restaurant. Once I'm in the dark hall, I go left to the kitchen instead of going right towards the bathrooms.

"Hey, Josie!" the chef says, then takes in my drenched clothes. "Looks like Rory got you good."

"It was iced," I grumble, moving towards the staff rooms as their laughs echo behind me. We use this location, owned by a friend of our boss, Gabriel, often, so the staff know what to expect when we're here. Once in the break room, I grab the outfit Rory left for me and change, pinning my thankfully dry hair up with a clip before shrugging my bag over my shoulder.

Then I'm out the back door.

With my phone to my ear and keys in hand, I beep the lock to my car as I make my call. When he picks up, I don't wait for a response before speaking. "Mission accomplished. We'll have a debrief and audio proof to you in..." I check my watch. "...four hours? Rory has the recordings, and her shift is still two more hours." I smile at that, because at least I get to leave. She has to make her shift as a waitress seem *realistic*.

"Good job, Maven. Go dry off. You'll have your next assignment tomorrow."

TWO

Rather than go home, I go to Opal, a high-end bar and nightclub in downtown Hudson City, to brush up on my skills. Going to an expensive bar to sit there, flirt, and see what kind of free drinks I can get from stupid men is far more entertaining than sitting at home.

An hour later when I'm two glasses into the most expensive champagne the bar carries, courtesy of the older man sitting next to me, I know my skills are working. He's in the middle of explaining some golf game he had with some politician that's supposed to impress me when his phone buzzes. He looks at it quickly before setting it back face down with an apologetic grimace.

"I'll be right back," he sighs, tipping his chin to the phone whose screen he has diligently hid from view since I sat down. "Work."

"Hurry back," I say, a sexy purr in my words. "I need to hear how the rest of the story goes." He gives me a wide grin in response before walking off, though with the way he took his jacket with him, I can almost guarantee he won't be returning. I shift my body to fully face the bar once more.

"Wife or girlfriend?" Carrie, the bartender, asks once he's out of earshot. She's seen me play this game more times than I can count, seeing as how this bar is closest to my condo.

"Wife for sure."

Carrie rolls her eyes and scoffs, wiping down the already pristine bar. "Gross."

I shrug. "At least my drinks are on his tab."

"Amen to that, my girl," she says with a smile.

"You really don't have to do that, you know," a familiar deep voice says. It's a good voice, the kind that rolls through you—a little dangerous like thunder in the distance, but bringing with it a warning of what's to come.

When I turn, the lights behind him cast him in shadow, but I still know what—or rather, who—I'm dealing with. The man who keeps bumping into me at bars and restaurants across Hudson City while I'm on jobs and who has started to make a game out of riling me up. If I didn't know better, I'd think he was stalking me or something, but fortunately, I'm a Maven, and I do know better. If I had a stalker, Gabriel would be on it in a flash.

Rowan.

I've bumped into him a dozen times while on missions over the last year or so. Once, he was having dinner at Coastal with a group of men while I was determining if a stockbroker was being truthful on his resume, and another time, he was sitting at the bar when I was investigating fraud at a high-end pub. A good half dozen of those times, he's come to the table for a while and made small talk with whoever I'm investigating, making me think he knows everyone in the upper crust of Hudson City. With his perfectly tailored suits and expensive watches, I think it's safe to assume he is part of the upper crust himself.

I've never wanted to know much more than his name, though, not with the way he always looks down his nose at me, with the way he always gives the tiniest barbs that stick a little too deep. And with how my body responds to him in a way completely opposite to how my mind does, he could easily blow my cover on assignments.

"I'm sorry?" I ask, exasperation in my tone, though part of me is excited for the banter I know is impending.

He approaches, putting his hands on the back of the chair my company just vacated, before explaining. "Flirting with men to get your drinks paid for. You don't have to do that."

I give him an easy smile.

"I know," I say with a tip of my head. "I can afford to buy my own drinks. It's just more fun this way."

The flicker in his eye—a mix of intrigue, heat, and irritation—is reminiscent of the time I had the unfortunate experience of almost having an entire dinner with him three months ago. He happened upon me on a prearranged date with a man we were pretty sure was embezzling from his company. My date invited him to stay for the meal, an offer Rowan accepted. He spent the entire night glaring at me, only taking the time to speak directly to me when we were alone.

"He's married, you know," he had said, when Stephen, my date and target, stepped away to use the bathroom.

I was aware of that, a fact I had been documenting in my spare time and creating a file to send to his wife when we handed over the proof of embezzlement to our client.

A little pro bono work, if you will. Girls supporting girls and all that.

"I'm well aware," I had said. He hadn't been good at hiding it, so it was easy for a highly skilled private investigator like myself to pick up on the signs.

"I guess that fits my understanding of you," Rowan had said.

I fought every instinct not to let my jaw go tight, not to snap at him, instead keeping my pristine mask on and giving him a soft, angelic smile.

"Oh?"

He took a slow sip of his drink, a satisfied smile spreading on his lips as he sat back in his chair.

"It's just that every time I see you, you're on a date with some new

rich or powerful man." He looked to the side to where Stephen had disappeared before returning his look to me, now tinged in pity I didn't need or want. "It's been that way since college."

College, because the first time I met Rowan was in my junior year, when I was running an underground business of testing girls' boyfriends to see if they were cheaters and would fall for my flirting.

Spoiler: so, so many did. At that point, I was targeting different frat boys and trust-fund babies almost every week, using my unique skills to help out my friends and friends of friends.

He judged me back then, too, though I'll admit, it probably did look strange that I was always out with some other guy.

"And?" I asked, raising an eyebrow.

"You're a gold digger. Always trying to lure some poor schmuck into falling into your trap."

I sat on that assumption for a moment, deciding that it was an okay one, one that would be far safer than the truth, and shrugged.

"Sure," I said, unwilling to give in to whatever trap he was so obviously setting for me. He raised an eyebrow.

"Sure?"

"You can think whatever you want about me," I said, leaning back with my wine glass in hand, gently swirling the liquid like I had not a care in the world. His jaw was tight as he looked over me, and I did my own personal thorough onceover to ensure every muscle in my body remained loose and unaffected.

"So, you're a gold digger?" he pressed.

I shrugged one shoulder before taking a small sip of the expensive wine. I was on a job, which meant this glass had to last me all night, though with the man sitting across from me I could use the whole fucking bottle.

"I don't owe you an explanation for what I am or am not doing."

"You're not going to deny it?"

"Again, I owe you nothing. Not an explanation, not a denial. Nothing. You're clearly very intrigued by me and my happenings, *since this is what? The third time you've found a reason to talk to someone I was having dinner with?" His jaw tightened, proving I had hit a nerve. "And, really, I can't blame you—I have a mirror, after all. But just because you so desperately wish you were the one wining and dining me doesn't mean you have to be a dick to me."*

He opened his mouth to argue, probably to lie and tell me he wasn't into me, but then Stephen returned, and his mouth shut. He only stayed a few minutes after our talk, but it didn't deter him from stopping by anytime he happened to be at the same place as me, chatting with my date and, if not taunting and prodding at me subtly, then completely ignoring me.

This, though, has never happened.

He's never bumped into me and started a conversation when I was off the clock.

I'm startled when he pulls the chair next to me out and sits down, though I don't bother to argue and tell him that it's taken. If I'm being honest, I'm...intrigued by him.

"Seems a little insincere, doesn't it? A pretty woman flirting with a man she has no interest in just to get a free drink and have some fun at his expense?"

I shake my head.

"If you're trying to make me feel bad about conning him out of two hundred bucks, you've got the wrong woman, babe. I don't feel bad for a man who is clearly married and hitting on women at a bar. And I definitely don't let random assholes like you make me feel bad about any decisions I make in my life."

I can feel rather than see his gaze burning into me, and then I hear his laugh. It's even better than his voice, warming me like a shot on an empty stomach. At the sound, I can't help but turn fully to look at him. The light shifts as he also moves to look at me, and I'm reminded once again that despite his horrific attitude, the man is hot.

He has a sharp jaw that I imagine is typically well groomed but now sports a thin layer of a five o'clock shadow, and thick, dark eyebrows that show off hazel eyes with thick lashes. His dark brown hair is longer on top and neatly combed back like always, and like always, I feel the undeniable urge to muss it up. He's in what I assume is his daily work uniform of slacks and a button-up, the sleeves of which are rolled up to his elbows to reveal tanned, toned arms, a thin dusting of dark hair, and the very edge of a tattoo.

"You know, I think in an alternate universe, we could be friends. You with all that sass, absolutely no filter, and—"

I cut him off before he can continue. "And you with your dry personality and clear obsession with me?"

He smiles again, and this time it's more genuine, with all his straight white teeth and full lips.

"Yeah, something like that." He looks me over, top to toe—or at least what he can see from where I'm sitting—and that smile goes lazy in a way I feel through my whole body. I could convince myself it's the two glasses of champagne, but I know in my gut it's just *him*. "How about a truce?" he asks, and I raise an eyebrow.

"A truce?"

"Yeah. We play nice for the length of a drink. But next time I see you out with some man twice your age, I'll still stop by and attempt to irritate you."

"I thought you were stopping by to say hello to colleagues and the like?" He turns to me a bit, just enough so the lights of the dimly lit bar hit his smile, and I jolt when heat runs through me.

Oh, god, this man is dangerous. Not because he clearly is an ass or is making assumptions about me, but because that smile could be absolutely catastrophic if used correctly.

"Watching you get pissed while I'm there is a nice perk."

"I don't get pissed," I say quickly.

"Then nervous, maybe?" he asks, assessing, and I don't like it.

Still, I deflect, my lips tipping a bit with a cocky smile that is more facade than anything and give him a slight shake of my head.

"I definitely don't get nervous."

He holds my gaze for what feels like a long stretch of time, though I know it's just seconds before he decides to let that one go.

"Clean slate," he responds, putting out a hand to me. "Hi. Nice to meet you. I'm Rowan."

THREE

JOSIE

Josie

I assess his outstretched hand closely. It feels like a test, a challenge, and I'm not the kind of girl to back down from one. I put my hand into his, holding firm as we shake, our eyes locked like we're in some kind of battle as we shake.

"Josie," I manage to say, without sounding incredibly breathy. Heat rolls through me at the sensation of his firm grip in mine, and when it's over, I miss it. Afterward, he sits back, putting an arm on the back of my chair and takes me in. With the move, the white button-down he's wearing stretches over his shoulders in a way that would be concerning to the integrity of the stitches if it wasn't clearly a high-end, expensive piece.

"So, Josie, is this your idea of a fun Wednesday night? Sitting and flirting with men to get free drinks just to see if you can? Seems a bit too easy for you, like shooting fish in a barrel with your...skills."

I put on my most catlike smile. To others, this would be a violation of our truce, but, I take it as a compliment.

"If you're trying to make me feel bad for playing that guy, you're out of luck. He flirted first, and he was married."

"How do you know he was married?"

I roll my eyes but explain all the same, ticking off the reasons on my fingers.

"He couldn't bother to take care of himself, but his suit was expensive, perfectly fitted, and the tie matched the entire ensemble perfectly. A woman picked out that outfit. He sat with his phone face down the entire time, and even when it rang, he looked at it and then placed it back face down. I'd guess his background screen is kids or his wedding picture, and I can guarantee that was his wife calling before he left. Plus, he paid in cash."

Rowan laughs then, shaking his head, and the sound of it warms me.

"Paying in cash doesn't mean anything. Maybe he wanted to impress you."

I shake my head. "Or maybe he didn't want the charge to show up on his credit card, the statement of which goes to his house."

"Or—"

He continues to try and argue, but I proceed to drop my most convincing pieces of evidence.

"His cuff links were engraved J+K, and while his name was Joseph, I doubt the 'K' was for his last name. And to top it off, he had both an indent on his ring finger and a tan line. The man is married. Trust me, I know these things."

There's a beat of silence before he speaks again.

"You got all that in that short amount of time?" If I'm not mistaken, there's a hint of awe in his words. He's impressed, and I can't help but preen.

"You can get a lot of information from someone if you take a moment to read them."

Carrie comes over to where we're sitting after filling a large order.

"Hey, Rowan, what can I get you?" she asks. There's friendliness in her tone, meaning he's passed the pretty strict test she gives all customers at the bar.

"A whiskey neat. Macallan."

Typical, I think. I know the type, of course. They're often my target. Uptight, expensive drinks, judges everyone and anyone around him.

Sounds about right.

"What about me?" he asks.

"You?"

"What do you get from me?" I stare at him, trying to see if he's playing a game, but I think he's being serious.

So I do what I do best: assess.

Okay, so maybe it's what I do second best, because flirting is truly my specialty.

"No ring, no tan line, no indent, not married. You're here at," I check my watch and smile. "Seven-thirty on a Wednesday, so you're either here for travel or are single. You give major only child energy, though that one is harder to confirm or deny. There's a tattoo peaking from the sleeve of your shirt, so a rebel, but not enough to fuck with your chances of working in...." I tip my chin towards where the sleeves of his button-down are rolled to his elbows and continue to take him in... "Corporate, for sure. Business, I'd guess. High end." Some things are just instinct, and this is mine working in real time.

"Pretty good," he admits with a smile.

"Unfortunately, you have shit taste in liquor," I say, tipping my chin towards where the bartender is reaching for the bottle of his far-too expensive top shelf whiskey.

"Not a Macallan fan?"

"Not a whiskey fan." I smile then, genuine and wide, before shifting once more to face him. "So how close was I?" A beat passes before he smiles, and fuck, his smile is good, especially now that I can see the full force of it, how it crinkles at the corners of his eyes, how it stretches across his cheeks.

"You've been on dates with colleagues and business partners of mine, so how do I know you didn't get info from them?" I tip my head to the side and give him a pitying pout.

"Aww. It's so cute that you think I'm asking about you while on a date with another man. I guess I can add a big ego to my list, huh?" His jaw tightens, but there's a spark in his eyes, the slightest tip of his lips that tells me he's enjoying this back-and-forth joust as much as I am. "So does that mean I was right?"

"Pretty dead on," he says, a bit of a laugh in the words. He's entertained by me. It fuels me, wanting to push it further.

Carrie slides the whiskey to him, and he thanks her, sliding a black card across the bar back to her.

"Put her other drinks on here. Keep the previous payment as a tip. And a fresh glass, if she wants," Rowan says.

Something about it is undeniably hot in a way that doesn't usually do it for me. The smoothness of the card slide, not only insisting on paying for my next drink, with the assumption I'll be enjoying it with him, but my previous ones as well. Not ordering me another glass, but instead offering it. I smile at him, genuinely, then at Carrie.

"Why not?" I say. "I'll have another." Carrie nods, then she shifts her back to Rowan and gives me a thumbs up that makes me smile. She's saying *he's a green flag, good luck girl!* in a way only women can silently communicate. When I have a new glass, I turn back to my bar-mate.

"What do you do for fun?"

"What?" he asks, clearly thrown by the question.

"Fun. Personal enjoyment? Things that make you happy? Hobbies?"

His brow furrows in clear confusion, and it's almost cute.

"Why are you asking?" I let out a loud laugh that I know draws attention to me, but the only attention I'm interested in right now is his. It's so heated and exact, so targeted, I feel like the only woman in the room.

"God, have you ever just made small talk with a woman before?"

He hesitates before a lazy, hot grin slides along his face, and I feel it in my belly.

"I don't typically need small talk."

I force myself to talk instead of melting under the mere presence of this man. He surely doesn't need the ego boost.

"Because you're so boring, you need to rely on only your looks to get women, got it." I nod, taking him in exaggeratedly. "That tracks." We stare at each other, waiting to see who will break first. I win this battle when he lets out a sigh before answering my question, finally.

"I don't have hobbies. I work." I give him a raised eyebrow, not buying it, but he shrugs. "You were right: I work in high-end corporate. I enjoy my job, so I do it a lot. Climbing the ladder doesn't leave a lot of free time for other things."

"What a way to live," I scoff, and he shrugs. "Okay, if you weren't working, what would you be doing?" I say, sitting back and taking a small sip of the bubbly, crisp champagne.

"Not flirting with men in order to get a free drink, that's for sure."

"You know, the whole grumpy asshole thing is kind of hot, but I bet you'd get laid more if you dropped it." It's a bit of a lie because, unfortunately for me, assholes have always been my type.

And worst of all, I think Rowan could also be my type. Because fuck, just look at how his arms look in that button-down. The fabric is literally straining. I have to actively fight against the urge to fan myself. Add in the fact that his bared forearms are thick with veins and sinew and muscle that make my mouth water, along with the edges of a tattoo I desperately, in my tipsy state, want to see in its totality, and I'm lost to common sense.

With my words, his gaze goes molten.

He drops the indifference that I now realize was an act and turns his body to me fully, taking me in over the rim of his whiskey glass. His eyes roam my face, pausing at my lips, then move down, burning over the cleavage I have on display, then the curves of the skin-tight olive-green knee-length dress I'm wearing. When his eyes shift back to mine, his tongue peeks out, wiping possibly non-existent droplets of liquor from them, and I think I almost come right then and there.

"A real man doesn't need to play some dashing gentleman to get laid."

"What does he need then?"

He smiles. It's devilish and shoots lust through me. It's probably a mix of adrenaline from a completed assignment earlier, drinks on a nearly empty stomach, and banter with this man who drives me mad that is creating an undeniable cocktail of desire to shift through me, but for once, I don't care. For once, the tight rein I normally hold on my restraint and common sense is loosening.

"Skill," he states simply.

"I'm assuming you think you have the skill?" I ask with a laugh that's breathier than I intend.

"Oh, I definitely have the skill."

It's an arrogant remark, the kind I should hate. It's the kind of remark men who rarely have the skill to back up that kind of promise love to say, but for some insane reason, I believe him.

And for some reason, some psychotic reason I can't quite fathom, I smile. "I've found that actions speak louder than words," I say. It sounds huskier even to my own ears, and for once, it wasn't intentional, not part of some intricate scheme to win someone over, to convince them to tell me what I want to hear.

This is so far out of character for me. Usually, I'm all talk, no action. All flirting with no payoff. God, I can't remember the last time I went on a real date that wasn't set up for work, much less the last time I kissed a man.

But right now, I want Rowan Fisher to prove to me he has the skill.

His gaze burns on me for a long moment before finally breaking, reaching for his phone. He taps on it a few times, then waits until it dings once before tapping the screen and sliding it into the pocket of his pants. That's when he stands up, pushing his chair in. His chin tips towards Carrie. "Mind watching my seat for me? I gotta go into Dante's office for a bit."

"Not at all," she says with a smile. Disappointment fills me, since by the time he gets back, I know I'll have made the big girl decision of heading out and going home because tomorrow will be a busy day.

"It was nice to—" I start, but then his hand is on my wrist, thick, long fingers wrapping around it. I gasp as he tugs, pulling me up and out of my chair. His breath coasts along my lips as I stand, our bodies mere inches apart from one another before he speaks.

"Come with?"

I can't think of a good response, not when barely two words and the feel of his skin on mine has my mind short-circuiting and heat spiraling through me.

"Okay," I whisper, and then I'm following Rowan through the bar.

We move quickly as he pulls me past a small dance floor and tall tables in dark corners towards a part of the high-end bar and night club I've never ventured. "Do you work here or something?" I ask with a laugh. It might just be the lingering rush of endorphins from a closed case or the liquor, but either way, I feel giddy.

"Or something," he says, looking over his shoulder at me. I lift an eyebrow. "The owner of this place is a friend of mine."

Finally, we move through a door, and he closes it behind us before pushing me against the solid wood with his body. There's a low light on the desk, but that's it, leaving both of us cast in shadows.

"Is that supposed to impress me?" I ask, and his face is close to mine. He stares at me hungrily, his gaze moving between my eyes and my lips, a small smile tipping the edges of his own.

"I feel like you're not an easy woman to impress, Josie."

"Seems like all of your obsessing over me has paid off a bit."

"I'm not obsessing over you," he lies.

"Sure you aren't, baby." I don't have much time to revel in the flash of pleasure and heat that lights his face at my words because then his lips are on mine, and the world slows. Every bit of my focus drops to where we meet, to where his tongue glides along my bottom lip, a polite request to open, which I oblige too quickly.

When his tongue touches mine, my arms lift, looping around his neck as I groan. It's a full body experience, the way he feels pressed against me, the way my mind quiets, the way he tastes, the throaty sound of approval that comes from his chest as he kisses me. His hand moves, gripping my hip and pushing his hips into mine.

He breaks the kiss, his lips move to the spot beneath my jaw, and he presses them there before nipping my ear. My head falls back with a light thud, my eyes drooping with pleasure.

"How's that whiskey you hate so much taste now that it's on my tongue?"

I groan, my hips shifting to try and get some kind of relief from the need quickly building in me, and a deep chuckle rumbles through him.

"It's an acquired taste, I suppose," I murmur. "I haven't quite decided yet how I feel about it."

"Give me a few minutes, I can guarantee you'll love the taste when I'm done with you."

I roll my eyes and force back another moan as his hips rock into mine.

"You're so fucking obnoxious," I say as his lips move down my neck. "And I don't do arrogant."

"Is that right?"

"Yes." But still, I groan as his lips latch onto my neck, sucking at the sensitive skin over my pulse. My dress hikes up as my leg lifts to wrap around him, moving to press my hips tighter against his, to grind and get some kind of friction, get closer when I feel it.

He's already hard.

Fuck.

I want him.

"Fucking wet," he groans, his hand sliding over my ass and under my dress before his fingers shift between my legs, sliding up and along the seam of my panties.

"Please," I whisper, my eyes fluttering shut, shock rolling through my system at how turned on I am. It's never like this. I've never been so turned on by a man that I lose all common sense, let him pull me into a room in a bar, and beg him to ease the ache inside of me.

I don't have time to overthink it, though, because his hand is moving to my front before his fingers tuck behind the seam of my underwear and back down until he's cupping me. My leg falls to the ground to steady myself, though he's holding me in place, and I moan again, my hips pressing into his hand.

"Is this what you want? You want my fingers inside of you? Or do you want my cock?" I bite back another please and smile up at him with hooded eyes.

"You have to prove yourself worthy before you fuck me, Mr.—" I pause, realizing I don't actually know his last name.

"Fisher," he says, then slides a finger into my wet pussy. "But you can call out Rowan when you come." Then the finger moves out, and I mewl at the loss. A low chuckle leaves his lips as he shifts his hand out of my panties. Before I can protest, I understand his purpose: his hand is shifting up to my hip, hooking under the band of them. Then he's bending to tug down my thong, silently instructing me to lift one foot and then the other to step out of them before tossing them somewhere behind him.

Finally, he's pressed up against me again, my dress up to my waist now as his hand shifts back to my wet center. I hold my breath, my eyes fluttering closed as he slides a single finger into me before tightening around it as he crooks it inside. He gifts me with a few exquisitely slow pumps before sliding out to rub my clit in slow, unrushed circles.

"Fuck, I'm so close," I moan, hoping I keep the shock of that development from my words. "Make me come, Rowan." His fingers tighten on my hip at the use of his name.

"Is that what you need? Me to prove myself before I get the pleasure of fucking you?" I smile then, all drooping eyelids and satisfied lips, before nodding.

"Exactly. I'm not wasting my time with a man who doesn't know how to make me come."

"Challenge accepted," he says, lips moving to my neck to suck. He slides two fingers into me and starts fucking me, the wet sound of my pussy and our heavy breaths the only sound in the room. It comes quick, the pleasure of it, heat starting in my belly, then blooming in my back as he works me as if he already knows everything about my body, every move that will pull me closer to the edge. When he adds his thumb to my clit, my back arches, my hands on his neck pulling him closer, needing purchase as I call out his name and come on his fingers.

It rolls through me, fast and hard and his fingers continue to move inside of me as it does, pulling every last drop of pleasure from my body.

"Okay," I say once they slow, panting and with a bit of a disbelieving laugh in the word. "Skills proven."

And then some. My body is still singing with bliss, my heart still racing, and despite the orgasm, I already want more.

He lets out a dark chuckle of his own, a shake of his head that has my entire pussy tensing once more.

"That was just the start, Josie." His hand lifts, wet fingers moving to my lips as I stare at him with lust and need. "Clean these."

The idea of tasting myself on a man has never been something I thought was hot, but my fucking god when he slides his fingers between my lips, when my tongue tastes the salty, musky flavor of myself on his thick, calloused fingers, remembering how they stretched me and made me come quicker than ever before just moments before, I moan.

His arrogant smile comes out again, and heat rips through me at the mere look. This doesn't normally do it for me, this thinking he's got me figured out, thinking he has me in the palm of his hand, but for some reason, with Rowan, it doesn't feel like a show. Instead, it's like a game.

But two can play, and god, I love to win. With a cat-like smile, I shift down to my knees, keeping my eyes on his.

"What are you—"

"Your turn," I say, eager for this almost more than I was for him to touch me. The groans he made while making me come were hot: I can only imagine the ones he'll make when he's halfway down my throat.

My hand moves to the bulge in his slacks, palming the thick, hot length of him. He's hard and huge, that much I can tell. I want to unzip and free him, but with the way he's looking at me, I want to tease him even more. Moving my hand down, I cup his balls through his slacks before leaning forward and pressing a kiss to where the head of his cock is.

"Don't tease me, Josie," he murmurs, his hands moving to my hair, pushing it back behind my shoulders. "Be a good girl and take my cock out and then wrap those pretty lips around it."

My pussy tightens again despite just having come and I know my breaths are coming though parted, kiss-swollen lips. I want that. I want his cock in my mouth, his hands in my hair, his praise filling my ears. Eagerly, I move a hand to his zipper and start to move it down.

And then his phone rings.

"Fuck," he groans, his body stilling.

"What?" I ask, my hand continuing to move the zipper down. The phone continues its shrill call from his pocket, and his head falls back to look at the ceiling with another pained groan.

"I have to get that." My eyes snap up to him, and like a child who knows she's about to not get her way, I put my hand over his dick, palming it once more. It twitches beneath my hand.

"What? No. No, you don't. Ignore it."

"Unfortunately, I can't. It's my emergency line." His fingers slide out of my hair, and he steps back. Without thinking, I mewl in protest, shoulders dropping as I pout.

Pouting.

Me, Josephine Montgomery. Pouting for a man.

What the fuck is happening to me?

"Trust me," he says. "I hate this even more than you do." The ringing stops as he steps away, and I give him a hopeful look. My body is humming with need, and I think the only person who will be able to sate it is standing right in front of me. Maybe the emergency is over, maybe—

But then the ringing starts again, and his hand is in front of me, offering to help up. I don't miss that it's the one that was in me not long ago as I take it with a defeated sigh.

At least I got an orgasm out of it.

FOUR

ROWAN

The first time I met Josie, I was enamored.

The second time I was annoyed.

This is the twenty-second time I've bumped into her. Each time I left feeling slightly different, but this is the first time I'm leaving with blue balls.

Never in my life have I regretted my job or the way I've pushed every personal want and desire aside to continue to climb the ladder, but there is a first time for everything. Because right now, my phone is sounding off with the ringtone for the line my assistant is only to use if and when there is an emergency. Sutton is probably pacing her apartment right now, sending every curse she can think of my way for not answering immediately, but I can't find it in me to care.

An extra minute in this woman's presence isn't going to impact whatever the issue is. So instead of answering, I reach over to the desk and grab Josie's panties that I threw there earlier. I have to send Dante a bottle of something really nice for letting me use his office as I kneel before her, stretching them for her to step back into.

I've never been on my knees for a woman, but my fucking god, the way she looks down at me like she knows she could own me if she asked nicely makes my already hard cock throb. She lifts a leg, placing it into the underwear before repeating the move with her second, and slowly, gently, reverently, I slide the fabric up her legs, making sure to graze my thumb along her pussy as I do.

Yeah. Still wet.

Fuck this job.

I make sure the black lace thong is situated perfectly on her hips before tugging the hem of her dress back down, all the while ignoring my phone, and standing. Then I pull her into my arms, taking in her sweet, floral perfume. I've smelled it a dozen times when I've interrupted one of her many dates with colleagues and acquaintances, the scent of it haunting me each time.

Just like the woman now in my arms.

"Your number," I murmur, pressing my lips to her neck, her pulse thrumming against my skin. I haven't ever felt such a pull to a woman like this, this undeniable need to touch her, to taste her. Considering that no woman has interested me enough to make me put my work aside for even a moment, this feels monumental.

Despite myself, I want more of her. It feels like an idiotic move to let this go. I like the way she pushes my buttons, and the way I can push hers back without her getting offended. I like the way that she's clearly attracted to me yet doesn't throw herself at me like some women I encounter do.

The truth is, I could get any woman I wanted, but I never jump at the offers. That would be far too simple. Instead, I want the one who incites a violently possessive need in me each time I see her sitting across some other man I know is an ass.

"Give me your number. We'll finish this another time. We'll have a real dinner and drinks."

And then I'll take you home to a real bed and fuck you until you're out of my system.

"No," she whispers, a bit of a tease in the word before she steps back. The room is dim, but I can see a smile playing on her lips as my phone continues to ring shrilly. Each one is a reminder that normally,

I'd push whoever I'm with aside to answer it, but for the first time since I started working at Daydream Resorts, someone else holds the priority.

"No?" I ask, confused. Her smile widens as she takes another step back, her hands moving to her clothes to straighten the skin-tight dress I would do just about anything to be able to tear off of her.

There's something so magnetic about her, something that pulls me so when I saw her sitting across from Stephen Jones months ago, I knew I needed to talk to her. Josie is nothing like the women who fawn and faint around me, batting their lashes and pouting their lips. Instead, she challenges everything I say and practically begs me to argue with her, instantly knowing how to press my buttons in ways I shouldn't like, but I do all the same.

"If you want me bad enough...a big, powerful man like you... you'll find me." The words, like everything about her, are so unexpected, they stop me in my tracks.

"Find you?" She's fluffing her hair as she reaches for the bag I didn't realize had slid to the floor when we entered, a playful smile on her lips. That's when it hits me: she's really going to leave without giving me her number.

She shrugs before responding. "Yeah. If you want me, find me."

"I don't chase women," I say, my mind muddled with the incessant fucking *ringing* and the way she's staring at me and the throbbing of my cock that should be deflating but my god, she's still in the room. I can still feel the ghost of her on my fingers, still hear her breathy moans in my ears.

"Well, then, thank you for the orgasm, Rowan." That smile has gone wide as she reaches for the doorknob. Despite my better thinking, I stand quickly, reaching her and pinning her to the wall beside the door before she can leave. That smile is still playing on her pink lips, and it takes everything in me not to kiss her again.

"You're really not going to give me your number?"

"You're really not going to put in the effort to find me?" she counters in a whisper.

"I'm a busy man, Josie. I don't have time for games." Something flashes in her eyes, and then she moves, dipping under my arm, smiling, and pulling open the door for good this time.

"Then it sounds like you're too busy for a woman like me. Thanks again."

And then she's gone.

I stand there in shock for long moments before coming to my senses. I'm already annoyed when I answer my phone and sit down in Dante's chair. But when I finally take a moment to look at the screen of my phone, I realize it's not Sutton calling. Instead, it's the emergency line for the resorts. My stomach drops as I tap the screen to answer and bring it to my ear. "Hello?"

"Hi, Mr. Fisher, I'm so sorry to bother you," the voice on the other end of the line says, clearly a bit panicked. "But there's been an accident at the resort, and they're starting to worry the employees." My heart drops.

"A fire?" I ask when Annette picks up thirty minutes later. It's long past her bedtime, I'm sure, but I used my own emergency line to call her, and considering it sounds like she's been keeping things from me, I'm not in the mood for niceties. "And an allergic reaction?" I expect some stuttering or lies or, at the very least, an apology keeping this vital information from me, but I don't get that at all.

Instead, the CEO of Daydream Resorts and my mentor, Annette Rhodes, sighs. "Let me guess: Chris called you."

Chris, the Manager of the East Coast locations, did, in fact, call me.

"Well, you sure as fuck weren't going to," I say, driving far too fast to my place. I closed my tab quickly upon leaving the office, knowing I needed to get home and pack.

"I've got it covered, Rowan." There's exhaustion in her voice, confirming that she was in fact asleep or close to it when I called, but

I really don't care. I held off on calling her until I got the full picture, texting or calling everyone at the impacted location I had contacts for, only to find the situation is way worse than I thought.

"Do you? Because from what I'm hearing, there have been no less than four incidents in the last three weeks, and the most recent was an allergic reaction at the spa that required hospitalization two days ago." A small gasp comes from the other end of the line.

"What?"

"Oh, I guess you haven't heard that one," I say with a laugh lacking humor. "I called Jonas, and he told me all about it. I'm glad *someone* decided I should be in on this." Jonas, the head of security, is the only person I personally vetted and hired. When I got in contact with him, he told me there have been multiple issues at the Keys location, not just this fire. "He also told me when he called to tell you he was worried something nefarious was happening that you told him not to worry you with it, and you'd handle it."

That was the most infuriating part of the call—that whatever was happening had been a known issue, and Annette had intentionally excluded me from it. She lets out a deep sigh before responding to my accusation.

"You're working on the opening for Malibu. This wasn't vital. I've got it covered." I groan, knowing that's not the case. I love Annette, but she constantly works with a *best-case-scenario* mindset, rather than a realistic one.

"How? How do you have this covered?"

"I've hired an outside investigation party to do some digging. I have full confidence that in the next two weeks, we'll find the source of this and resolve it."

She must be referring to Wilde Security, the company that established our security and safety procedures for each resort, ensuring that our elite and celebrity clientele receive the most confidential experience, if that's what they desire.

Her solution does appease me. A bit.

"In the meantime, Daniel has been instructed to talk to each department about any oddities that may have been occurring, so we can get a better idea of the span of this." Daniel is the General Manager of the Keys location and although he isn't my biggest fan, I can't say he isn't good at this job.

"I'm still headed there," I say, putting my car into park and swinging the door open before heading to the elevator that will take me to my penthouse overlooking Hudson City.

"It's not necessary, Rowan."

"You're the one who taught me there is no better way to keep track of things than by having boots on the ground. I'm going, even if it's just to oversee things for a bit. I'll work from the office there."

"You're supposed to be on vacation next week," she says. I almost forgot that she had forced me to agree to taking the week off next week, stating that she was worried I would burn myself out if I didn't slow down. That won't be happening any longer.

"Vacations can wait."

There's a long pause and another sigh before she speaks, and before she even does, I know what she's going to say.

"Rowan, we need to talk about your incessant working."

I roll my eyes as I watch the numbers on the elevator rise, impatiently waiting for it to ding at the top floor.

"Yeah, maybe after we figure out who is sabotaging my resort."

"Rowan—"

"How the fuck am I supposed to take a relaxing vacation knowing all of this is happening?" Silence fills the line, and I know I've won.

"I worry," she says. "You're going to burn yourself out. You're the future of this place, but not if you don't pace yourself." I started working at Daydream Resorts as Annette's intern twelve years ago, and she's told me more than a few times that she sees me taking over as CEO when she retires one day. It's part of the reason why I've worked myself to the bone, becoming the company's youngest VP of Operations as of six months ago.

"I promise that after the next opening and after this shitstorm is settled, I'll take a vacation. A full week," I say in concession.

"Three," she says instantly, making me feel like she's been waiting to pounce on this.

"You're insane." I laugh at the absurd idea.

"Two, and I remove you from all servers for that time so you can't work even if you try."

I contemplate that, knowing that I could still get my assistant to be my go-between to get things done. She doesn't have to know I'm thinking that, so instead of arguing when I have much more important things to do, I nod, then verbally agree.

"Yeah. Sure."

"Why do I feel like you already have some loophole planned?" Annette asks with a groan.

"Because you trained me well. I'll call you when I get to Florida." I hang up before she can argue. As I step off the elevator and into my home, I make my next call, knowing that my assistant is well paid to answer at nearly any time of day.

"Hey asshole," she says upon answering my call. I've threatened to fire Sutton Donovan more times than I can count, but we both know I couldn't function without her, snarkiness aside.

Middle child syndrome, she told me once, when I asked her why she was such a brat to me and sweet as pie to others. *I have an older brother and an older sister, both of whom are control freaks, and a younger sister who is utter chaos. I'm somewhere in the middle.*

For a completely unhinged moment, I think how she and Josie would get along well, before I shake the thought away, needing to focus. I can think about the gorgeous brunette once this mess is fixed.

Normally, I'd reply with something just as rude because that's what my assistant and I do, but instead, I get right to my point. "I need to get on the next flight to Florida." Sutton sobers up quickly, reading the seriousness in my words.

"The Keys resort? What happened?" A keyboard clacks in the background, and I know she's already on it.

"Allergic reaction," I say, throwing another pair of pants into my suitcase.

"Allergic reaction? I don't know if that sounds like an urgent issue or even the resort's fault. I mean—"

"Someone poured almond oil into the mud bath." Silence fills the line. "And three hours ago, someone lit the rental shack on fire, burned it to the ground. They've got it out now, but the cameras conveniently went down five minutes before and after, so we're shit out of luck on leads."

"Oh my god," she whispers. "Is everyone okay?"

"No injuries from the fire, and the allergic reaction was sent to the hospital, but they should be fine. However, there have been missed deliveries and lost stock over the last few weeks, as well as double bookings and cancellations for services at the spa that were attributed to miscommunications or oversights. Now I'm wondering if it was something else."

"So you think someone is doing this on purpose?"

"I don't know. But I do know that Gene Michaels is at the resort right now with his new girlfriend after that messy divorce and—"

"And if information about another one of his clients at a Daydream Resort is leaked without his permission, Leo is going to lose his mind," Sutton fills in correctly. I sigh and nod, even though she can't see it.

Sutton knows precisely how that could go, since a good chunk of our celebrity clientele are clients of Leo Sinclair. Sometimes he asks us to leak information intentionally, but the celebrity publicist usually trusts us with his top-tier celebrity's privacy. And up until last year, we've had a great record of ensuring just that. Unfortunately, nine months ago, the first of four leaks to tabloids occurred, each at a different resort, and we have been unable to determine the source.

All I need right now is *another* fucking leak on top of the mess we already have.

"Exactly. With everything else going on, I need to be on the ground. I need to get to the bottom of whatever's happening. Can you find me a flight there as soon as possible?

"Oooh, under cover mission. I like it," she says, continuing to click and type.

"I wouldn't call it that," I grumble as I start tossing things haphazardly into a suitcase. "Everyone knows who I am, so I can't exactly go under cover at my own resort."

"Boring," Sutton grumbles, then my phone against my ear pings with a new message. "Okay, got it. You gotta be at Newark in two and a half hours. That doable?"

"Perfect. Thanks, Sutton," I say, pulling three shirts from my closet and putting them into my suitcase followed by a dozen ties. I'm not sure how long I'll be there, so I might as well pack a good amount.

"You couldn't function without me, I know, I know. I'll add it to my file for my next performance review."

"You've never had a performance review, Sutton. You always fill out the form for me and file a raise for yourself."

"Exactly. I need to keep my notes up to date."

For the first time since my phone rang, I let out a laugh.

Sutton hums. "When you get a second, send me the details on what exactly you've got on this leak, and I'll try to see if I can find any overlap."

"You're a godsend," I say, then hang up and finish packing.

FIVE

JOSIE

My phone beeps the next morning, long after I've woken, worked out, eaten breakfast, and cleaned my apartment. The morning of a new assignment is like Christmas to me, and even though I'm already a bit of a morning person, I'm even more so one those days, my pulse excited with the prospect of some new havoc to wreak, some new puzzle to solve.

The last three weeks have consisted of small jobs, like last night, involving finding evidence of cheating, lying, and the like. Last week, my partner Rory and I spent three nights tailing a man whose wife was *convinced* he'd been cheating, only to find those secretive calls had been him setting up some grand anniversary surprise for her.

I give him a year before *he* reaches out to us, asking for information on his wife this time.

That being said, a tried-and-true destination undercover job has been a long time coming, and it's my favorite kind of assignment to get. Upon hearing the beep, I rush to my phone to check if our assignment has dropped and when I see Rory's name instead of Gabriel's, I deflate.

R: Let me up

Just then, the buzzer to my apartment goes off, and without even checking to see who it is, I hit accept. Two minutes later, Rory is walking into my place and locking the door behind her.

"You don't even check to see if it's me? Have you learned nothing in the years you've been working here?" I roll my eyes, then reach over to my counter, grab my pink, bedazzled taser, and buzz it.

"I've got good ol' Betty here."

She rolls her eyes. "You've never even *used* that thing."

"Isn't that a good thing? Never being in a situation where I have to use a taser?" I set down my trusty weapon before moving over to my couch and flopping back with a sigh. "Why are you here so early?"

"Assignment day. Gabriel told me to head here, and when we were together, he'd call and give us our assignment."

"How did you know I'd be up?" She rolls her eyes, as if I'm being purposely obtuse and she's annoyed by it.

"Because no one gets more excited on assignment day than you, Josie. *Everyone* knew you'd be up."

Fair enough.

As if he can hear our conversation—which, knowing Gabriel, isn't such a far off concept—both of our phones ping with a new email before my laptop, already open on my coffee table, starts to ring with an incoming call. We sit closer together without a word before I hit accept, a blank screen popping up and a deep voice coming through the speakers.

"Morning, Mavens."

"Good morning, Gabriel," Rory says, all business.

"Whatcha got for us?" I ask.

"Eager as always, Josephine," he says with a chuckle. All of the Mavens have talked a million times about what we think Gabriel looks like, because his voice is undeniably sexy, but we've never met the mysterious man we work for.

I'm on Team Old, Sophisticated Dude.

"I love a good overnight," Rory says.

"Well, this one will probably be more than a night."

I perk up, even more excited now.

"What do you know about Daydream Resorts?"

I rack my brain, trying to pinpoint the name, but Rory answers first.

"Luxury, all-inclusive resorts. Super exclusive, where stars go when they want to disappear and not be in the limelight, though there have been a few carefully planned PR leaks while there. I believe there are a dozen locations across the world?"

"Thirteen, now, as of last year. The newest location in the Florida Keys opened almost a year ago." The screen blinks from black to a slide show of images of the new resort, all white sand beaches, bright blue oceans, and a fully loaded spa. I sit forward, giving the computer my rapt attention. "Despite some push back from some of the board members, Daydream Resorts went forward with opening the Keys location, and things have been going phenomenally. It's one of the most profitable locations already, and has been attended by dozens of celebrities and even more high roller clients."

"But..." I say, because if there wasn't a *but*, we wouldn't be on this call.

"But there have been numerous instances occurring over the last few weeks, most recently one at the recreation building," Gabriel says, and the screen changes before us to show a photo of a burned-down building on the beach. Rory gasps and I try to take note of the structure, unable to even identify much besides the sand it butts up to. "Inside was over fifty thousand dollars' worth of equipment that guests could use. This is where the resort was keeping all of its outdoor equipment: canoes and stand-up paddle boards, that kind of thing. It was burned to the ground yesterday, and this morning, reports came back citing arson. When combined with the other issues—"

"Other issues?" Rory asks like an attentive student.

"Small things. All of the towels went missing for a day, only for them to be discovered locked in a storage room. Deliveries of food were cancelled without a word. Double booking or changing services at the spa. Small things that hindered guest experience, but weren't a big deal. Then a few days ago, someone added almond oil to the mud bath and caused an allergic reaction."

I cringe at the image.

"So it's escalating. Cameras?" I ask.

"We think whoever is doing it has access to the security footage, because they either know which cameras to avoid, or the cameras are down for maintenance."

I nod. "Security is in-house?"

"Yes."

"Do we have access?" Rory asks.

"Unfortunately, with this assignment, you aren't going in with any kind of real assistance. The owner isn't telling a soul, just in case intel gets into the wrong hands, and the culprit backs off. You'll either have to find a way to get access to security footage yourself or hack your way in. From what I've been told, it's state-of-the-art."

"Sure it is," Rory says with a smile. Where I can get intel from a suspect with a smile and chatting with people, Rory's expertise is computers and security: there are few systems she can't find a way into. "Do we have any suspects?"

"No," Gabriel says, and I nearly bounce in my seat at the idea of such a challenge.

I fucking *love* a challenge.

"No suspects?" Rory asks, confused because, typically we get some kind of idea of where to focus, even if it's incredibly vague.

"We've been hired by a CEO who wants to minimize any rash judgments. She wants you to go in as blind as you can, so her own biases or the biases of the other employees don't impact your review."

Basically, this is a dream assignment. *A blank slate.*

"But we think it's an employee?" I ask.

"The owner does, yes. The sabotage is confined to this location and spans around a three week period. No guests have stayed the entire duration." We nod silently in understanding. "That's all I've got for you. I'll be sending over a file after our call for you both to go over, including flights and your stay details. Anything else you need, just let me know."

"Assignments?" Rory asks. With each mission a Maven undertakes, we have assignments to make it easier. Often, we're some kind of employee since that is the easiest to blend in, but I'm kind of hoping for....

"Vacationers. You have two weeks, which is typical for high-end resort stays." I nod. The idea of being on vacation for *work* is absolutely thrilling.

"Good luck, Mavens," he says, then the screen cuts out. My inbox beeps with a new email as if on cue, and Rory's does the same. I don't bother opening mine yet; instead, I shift closer to Rory as she opens the email and the attached file with all the information about our assignment.

This is how every assignment goes. Gabriel gives us the rundown of what the client expects before he ends the call, and we get our file of everything we might need: players, employees, suspects, and their jobs. It also helps us determine how and what to pack which we do next.

After we read over the file, Rory heads to her place to pack while I do the same, and then we're off to paradise.

SIX

Suspect list for Daydream Resorts based on current intel:
everyone.

SEVEN

JOSIE

Rory and I are on the next flight to Fort Lauderdale, where we take a bus to one of the lower Keys, as the resort is located on a small island and is inaccessible by car. From what we've learned, employees take a ferry to work every day, which in theory narrows our pool. While there are a few other businesses and homes on the island that Daydream Resorts doesn't own, the majority of the land is Daydream property.

This also means we're to be in character from the moment we get on the ferry, playing the part of eager vacationers. We both know from the second we step foot on the property, game faces must be on, because in a situation like this, *everyone* is a suspect or a source. The only time that facade can fall is when we're closed in our room, with not an eye on us.

From what our research has shown, the Daydream resort is the epitome of luxury: a boat ride to the resort, then a five-minute drive on a winding road once you're on the property through a beautiful, wooded area.

As we arrive at the resort, I take it in in awe. It has a Mediterranean feel with lots of white and splashes of bright blue and orange, giving it a fun but clean and peaceful vibe. The front desk attendant is kind and smiling and tells us some of the excursions are out of commission, but, as expected, doesn't go into details as to why before a bellhop takes us and our bags up to our room.

Once closed into the two-bedroom suite Rory and I will share, I set my coffee from the lobby on the coffee table, flop onto the large couch, and groan aloud, my body sinking into the soft cushions. My mind rolls through days and weeks and months, and I try to think of the last time I slept in, much less the last time I went on a vacation.

It's been...a while.

Maybe after this assignment, I'll take a few weeks off. Sleep in every day, book a trip at one of these resorts, and rest for a while. If we manage to find the issue, which I'm confident we will, I bet I could get a pretty solid discount. Perhaps—

"No resting, my friend," Rory says after she finishes her sweep of the room for any bugs and cameras, poking my leg. "We've got work to do." I groan. The only flight we could get was not only a layover, but a red eye, on which I slept maybe an hour or two. It's officially noon the day after we got our assignment, and I am so exhausted I could fall asleep right here.

"Five minutes," I grumble.

"Nope." No one has a better work ethic than Rory, so much so that, sometimes, I think she might be an actual robot.

Slowly, knowing she's right, I sit up and reach for my coffee. I take a deep sip, hoping the caffeine hits my bloodstream quickly.

"Okay. What do we have?" I ask once I finish my internal battle with wanting to flop over again, shifting to the edge of the couch to give her my full attention.

Rory smiles wide, shoulders moving back as she pulls out the file she's created. Without looking, I already know it's color-coded and tabbed, with notes in the margins and ideas scribbled everywhere. I also know if I scan through it, the light purple ones will be the thoughts and ideas she's assigning to me, tasks I'll be expected to conquer personally. Which people I need to schmooze, what secrets I need to extract.

"We're looking at a string of events, the earliest of which were just brushed away as growing pains and or coincidences."

I nod. "Until the fire?"

"Until the fire. We've gotten more intel on other things that were originally dismissed, like finding three chest freezers unplugged last week. We've got cancelled food deliveries...lost towels. One morning, all the beach furniture was folded up and hidden in the pool house. Six days ago, a guest slipped and required first aid care after a puddle of oil appeared in the spa, the bottle of which was found in a nearby trash can and not a brand used internally. No one could explain any of these circumstances, but also, no one considered they could all be connected."

I nod. "Okay, so the most extreme sabotage was obviously the rental stand. Unfortunately, it's pretty well locked down, and the cameras were down." I reach into my bag and pull out my own folder with papers I've doodled on to begin to get my own thoughts in place. It's much less organized than Rory's. Some of the photos in the stack are from the remains of the building, as well as the "before" shots. "We do have these photos, though."

I spread them out onto the bed, and we both look over them once more with a closer eye, despite the fact that we've both done so a dozen times already.

"I wish we could see this corner better. I'd like to see where the fire was started." She points to a section of the burned-down rental shack. I flip through my photos to find what she needs but while one has a slightly better angle, I know it's not exactly what Rory wants.

"We could go look at it," I suggest.

"It's a crime scene, Josie," she says with an exaggerated eye roll.

I shrug as if that doesn't matter to me. That's because it doesn't, not really. Part of this job is going where you're not "supposed" to be. You'd be surprised how little you're actually stopped, so long as you act like you're allowed to be there. In general, the world relies on humans respecting implied boundaries and the inherent risk of getting in trouble.

"The main pool is not far from where the rental shack used to be —why don't we go there, hang out, and do some surveillance, then we can go over to the shack when we see an opening?" I ask, pointing to the pool on the map, then trailing my finger across it to where the fire was.

"What if someone finds us over there? Won't it blow our cover?"

Rory typically provides background on operations, but on one like this, it's all hands one deck. I'll definitely be the one handling the most person-to-person interaction with guests and employees, while Rory focuses on getting into the cameras and backend of things, but she'll also be on the ground to help validate my cover. I shrug, then tell her the truth.

"They might catch us, but people are stupid. They want the easiest answer to most questions. We won't blow our cover, not if we play stupid tourist, nosey guests who wants to see something interesting, or dumb girl."

"Dumb girl?" Rory asks with a disapproving grimace, and I smile.

"My specialty. It works best if a man is the one to catch us." I stand, putting my shoulders back a bit more, my full chest popping out, and make my eyes wide and my lips pouty. Then I cock my hip out while I twirl a lock of hair around my finger. "Oh, my goodness, I am *so* sorry. I had no idea I wasn't supposed to be in this taped-off crime scene. I thought it was just pretty decorations! Please, please forgive me." Rory lets out a loud bark of a laugh, and I return the smile. "Works like a charm every time."

"You're out of your mind, you know that?"

"All part of the job, my friend." Energized by the idea of a little snooping and trespassing, I move to my bag, digging through it. "Okay, come on. Bikinis it is. We've got some sunbathing to do."

.   .   .

BREAK

When we get to the pool, we begin my all-time favorite pastime: people watching. I'm convinced I was made for this job since I've always been the one to take note of people everywhere I go, listen to conversations I'm not a part of, and put together different tidbits to build a perfect profile for those around me.

Fortunately, the people watching is stellar here, with everyone sitting around in their bathing suits, more worried about how they look and what people might think of them than they are about enjoying their time in the sun. It's also because the people here are the richest of the rich, celebrities, and people who think they have enough money and ego to *be* celebrities.

To our left is a B-list television star whose attempt to break into film never quite materialized, so now her entire persona is defined by that one show from years ago. The irony of her reading a trashy tabloid is not lost on me, and I wonder for a single, catty moment if she's scanning to try and find the whisper of a mention of herself.

There's also a tech bro I vaguely remember from a video I stumbled upon recently, trying to explain the stock market and somehow making the concept even *more* confusing. Funny how his hair looks so much thinner in real life.

On the right side of the pool is a well-known eighties rock band member who, if I recall, was recently divorced in a messy case that stated infidelity as the main cause. It would make sense, considering he's here with a woman who looks barely twenty.

I also take note of the employees: which ones are attentive, who's on their phone, who whispers with coworkers, and who seems like an outcast. This is the key part of any early assignment: observing. We take in our surroundings, read people, and decide who we should target first. You can learn so much about people just by watching them, by decoding how they move when they think no one is watching them, and how that differs when they think someone *is* watching them.

"That one," I say, tilting my eyes to where a middle-aged blonde lays on a beach chair. She's in a cover-up, a thick book in her hands, seemingly reading. But moments before, she had a small, nondescript notebook hidden behind it where she jotted something down before sliding it back into her bag. The entire move was smooth, I'll admit, because if I hadn't been looking for the smallest thing, I would have missed it. But unfortunately for her, my job is exactly that. "She's taking notes of something. She's pretending to read, but her gaze hasn't left the couple at your two o'clock." Rory pretends to shift to dig in her bag while inconspicuously looking at where I tipped my chin.

"The leak?" she asks.

I shrug.

Among the corporation's list of things that have gone wrong in the past year are a series of unauthorized celebrity leaks from various locations. My gut and the owner's instinct tell me it's not related to the issues this location has been facing, but it's something of note as they haven't been able to find the source.

"Could be. It's not her writing a to-do list, that's for sure. She looked around right before and after, making sure that no one was watching her." Some people are just *not* good at being stealthy.

Rory nods in agreement and picks up her book to look less obvious, and I slide my sunglasses back up my nose, grabbing a book of my own. A minute or two later, a tall man with short-cropped hair and a wide, panty-dropping smile comes over to us, his shadow blocking my sun.

"Hey ladies, how are you enjoying your stay?" From the corner of my eye, Rory lowers her magazine and fights a sneer that would send him scampering off at the very last minute. There is nothing Rory hates more than pretty meat heads.

He's good-looking, of course, but the problem is, he knows it.

My least favorite kind of man. Of course, it doesn't help that my mind is still twisted up, thinking about Rowan and wondering if he's going to try and find me after the other night. I swear I can still feel the aftershocks of that orgasm, though it's probably just because it had been so damn long since I'd had one that wasn't self-induced. I swipe that thought away and get my head on the assignment at hand.

"Hello," I say, sitting up, leaning forward, and smiling at him with my most coy look. "It's been lovely so far."

"Glad to hear it. I just wanted to come over and introduce myself, since I haven't seen you lovely ladies here. I'm Daniel, the General Manager of this resort. We're so honored to have you here."

I give him a conspiratorial smile. "You know we're not celebrities, right?" His smile goes even wider, and god, from that look alone, I'm sure he gets whoever he wants, whenever he wants them. This is my favorite kind of target, because they never see my brand of coercion coming. The kind where I use all of their own weaknesses against them to get what *I* want.

"All of our guests are priority," he says smoothly. "Especially when they're as gorgeous as you two are."

"You're too kind," Rory says, fluttering her lashes. She's not the Maven who is known for conning men out of their deepest darkest secrets with a smile and a head tilt, but all Mavens are experts at flirting, and Rory is no exception.

"Did you two just get in? I think I would have noticed you by now if you had been here for a while."

I nod. "Sure did. Just arrived today and we have two luxurious weeks ahead of us."

He nods approvingly.

"Anything fun we should keep an eye out for?" Rory asks. "Excursions, nightlife?"

He seems to think on it for a moment before answering. "There's a mingling dinner and drinks tomorrow night in the main restaurant, and on Monday, there's a cocktail party. Dress up, meet some people, that kind of thing," he says with a shrug, giving us the same spiel that we heard at the front desk.

"What if we don't want the guest experience? What if we want to have some *real* fun?" I ask with a wink, and his smile goes a bit devilish.

"Real fun?"

I lift a shoulder. "You know. Employee parties, nights out. A local bar that's a lot of fun?" I ask conspiratorially.

"Oh, I don't know, there's a lot to do around here for guests on the resort grounds."

"Come on, I know you know where the fun stuff is," Rory says. "Just look at you." He thinks for a moment before looking left and right as if someone higher up than him is about to out him, despite him being the General Manager.

"You want a party?"

Rory claps and nods

"Yes! The guests here seem nice, but a bit too...stuffy, you know?"

He nods. "Trust me, I know. Everyone here is rich assholes." I raise an eyebrow because even if in real life I am anything but, I would have to be at least *one* of those things in order to be a guest at this resort. "No, no, not you guys, of course."

"Of course," I say with a teasing smile.

He looks around again before leaning in. "There's an employee party on Wednesday at eight. We have them once a month or so, to keep up morale. Dancing, drinks, that kind of thing."

"Oh, fun!" Rory croons.

"Guests normally aren't allowed, but I can pull some strings."

I lean forward, touch his forearm, and let out a small giggle.

"Oh, we would *love* that," I say with my most seductive smile that insinuates so much more than he'll ever get.

"Give me your room number and I'll make sure you get all the information."

I look at Rory, trying to judge if that's a good idea, then determine we need it and give it to him. He writes it in a notepad before slipping it back in his pocket. He smiles again and opens his mouth to speak, but before he can, he's stopped.

"Hey, Daniel!" A voice calls out from the other side of the pool, and he looks over his shoulder and sighs as if he knows he's in for it. "Daniel, can you come talk for a second?" a redhead asks, smiling deceptively sweetly. He stands then and nods at us.

"I gotta go. It was great meeting you two."

"You too, Daniel. See you on Wednesday." He smiles again before he looks over his shoulder and sighs. He looks tired, but professional, which is something I think would be expected if the resort where he works is experiencing incessant issues.

Daniel is currently on our very long list, though we don't have any true motivation for him. He holds the top position in the resort, and the application process for securing this role was lengthy. It doesn't seem like a logical move for him, unless there's something happening we can't yet fathom.

After he's gone, we continue sunbathing, Rory keeping an eye out for the best time to dart off to the taped-off crime scene while I look around, keeping my ears open for any kind of useful information or anything that feels out of place.

And that's when I feel eyes on me. Slowly, I turn my head to the sky and shift around the pool, trying to find the source without revealing what I'm doing. Finally, I catch the source of the gaze beneath my dark sunglasses: a woman. I pass right over her and her burning stare as if it doesn't exist, then turn to Rory, putting my back to the source of the killing glare.

"Seven o'clock, red hair, white uniform. Works here, I think." Rory reaches for her drink as she sits up, taking a long sip as she covertly looks to the side.

"My god, why does she look like she wants to rip out your intestines and use them to strangle you?"

My face skews up at the mental image.

"Rory, that is so weirdly specific." She shrugs as she lies back down.

"I listen to a lot of true crime."

"In this line of work? Where you get to not just hear about it, but witness how dangerous and deranged people can be?"

She shrugs. "It quiets my mind."

"Oh, you're a serial killer," I whisper, then sit back, fussing with my glasses as I do, taking one last look at the woman. Her arms are crossed on her chest, and Rory is right, she does look like she wants to kill me. I look at the pretty landscaping a few feet from her but keep her in my peripheral vision as she talks to Daniel, her jaw tight. He reaches a hand out to her, but she takes a step back before speaking to him, clearly annoyed. Her head tips towards us, and from here I can see him roll his eyes and throw his hands up exasperatedly.

"I think you were flirting with her man," Rory says under her breath. "No wonder she was giving you the evil eye. Do you think I should tell her that unless he's some hottie from your past, you're so totally uninterested?" I let out a loud laugh, louder than intended, but it helps to prove our point when Daniel's head moves our way. Almost instantly, the woman's hand moves to his jaw, shifting his head to face her.

"Oof," Rory says.

"Something to take note of. She's in an employee uniform. I wonder what she does?"

Rory shrugs but picks up her phone. A moment later, a ping comes to my phone, Rory having updated the shared note we use to keep track of things while out in the field, probably adding a description and photo for reference. I continue to watch the unhappy couple before she shakes her head and stalks off to the other side of the large pool area, clearly frustrated. Daniel sighs and walks off into the resort out of sight.

"I got photos of both of them for the files," she says, and I nod, but I'm still subtly watching the woman, who looks like she's about to throw a full-on temper tantrum, foot stomping included. I'm glad I am because in an instant, her face changes, eyes catching on something in the distance.

Then she starts moving with a purpose towards a man. He's not in a uniform like she is, and as soon as he notices her, her smile goes sweet. Not just sweet, but *flirty*. His back is to us, so I can only note he's maybe a foot taller than her, with dark hair. I watch her hand move out, touching his shoulder, and he dips it a bit as if to shift away from her. I laugh quietly at the entertaining show of rejection before Rory nudges me.

"Hey," she says, tipping her head towards where our first target is. I note that the area is free of anyone now. "Leave your stuff, let's go."

And then we're off.

EIGHT

ROWAN

"I feel like I'm being set up, but it's not me, Rowan. I need you to know that. I moved my whole family out here, changed everything so I could work this job, and you know I'm grateful."

I nod, knowing this to be true. Not to mention, Jonas just ended his family vacation two days early to come in after hearing about the issues that have been arising.

My gut tells me the source of the issue isn't the head of security at the Keys location. He was the one employee I handpicked for this location. When we opened this one, he was working as an assistant at one of our other resorts, and I knew he would be perfect for the job. I offered him a solid raise and covered his moving costs as an incentive to take the position. His wife was excited about the weather, but his kids, who are both in middle school, were upset. I can't think of a reason he'd try to fuck this up, knowing he'd get fired and most likely be blacklisted in the industry.

But then again, I can't think of a single reason someone would want to fuck with my hotel in the first place.

I arrived at the resort early yesterday morning, checked into a room, and instantly got to work talking to Daniel, the General

Manager, to find out everything that's been happening in the last month. He didn't give me much information I didn't already know, though I did find out a few more unreported incidents, such as double bookings of suites with no source attributed as well as numerous double billings to guests that resulted in rightfully angry calls and even threats. These events could seem innocuous and like some bad luck, but when combined, they start to paint an increasingly obvious and worrisome picture.

"You have to know, personally, that I think you're in the clear. But it doesn't look great," I tell him, and he nods. The security system going down right before the fire is a huge red flag, and since our suspect seems to know the exact steps to take to avoid being caught on camera, we have to assume they know not only the precise angles each is set to, but also where the hidden cameras are. "Is there anything at all you can give me? A direction, somewhere to investigate?"

Jonas sighs, a deep, broken sound, and I know the answer before he speaks.

"I've been trying to figure it out, to understand what the source is, but I can't pin it. It's different aspects of the business each time, varied enough that I can't focus it on a single department."

I nod, knowing this to be true as I've come to the same conclusion. I'm starting to think I'm just going to have to wait for the next issue to arise before we can narrow things down.

Just then, my phone rings, and I groan, hoping I didn't just summon one. When I look at the screen and see Sutton's name, my nerves increase. She only calls if it's something that needs to be addressed quickly, typically sending text messages or emails with updates throughout the day. I turn back to Jonas.

"Look, just keep an eye out, okay? Let me know if you find anything at all. I've gotta take this," I say, and he nods, turning back to the monitors as I hit accept and bring the phone to my ear.

"Please have good news for me," I beg my assistant, eyes closed and voice weary as I step into the hallway and move back towards my office. Silence fills the line, and my stomach drops to the ground. "Sutton..."

"Someone has leaked that Gene Michaels is there."

My steps falter, and my stomach drops.

"What do you *mean* leaked?" I ask, trying to keep my voice steady as irritation fills my body.

"I don't know," Sutton says. "Johnson over at *Fan Magazine* just called to give me an update. They can't stop it from running—"

"Why the fuck not?" I rage into my phone, ignoring the eyes that are moving in my direction. I give a tight smile to the couple actively glaring at me before I lower my voice. "Give them whatever they want, Sutton. Buy the story. They can't run it, not with everything we already have going on."

"You and I both know if they don't run it, it will get sold somewhere else, and they won't make even the smallest effort to ease the blow to us. We don't have contacts like this everywhere, and he didn't *have* to give me a heads up. He's doing us a solid by giving us that, Rowan." My pulse thrums in my head, the migraine that's been brewing for the last twenty-four hours making itself known once again. Tightening my jaw, I step into a small alcove and take a deep breath, attempting to think rationally.

She's right, of course. We need this contact at *Fan* to ensure we stay ahead of issues like this and to assist us in instances when we want paparazzi to leak information about our guests.

The first unintentional leak was at our Bora Bora resort almost a year ago. We chalked it up to a one-time incident, though we never confirmed the source, something I regretted when three months later, it happened again. This would be the fifth leak in a year, each at a different location, and we're no closer to understanding where the source is.

And it's *just* what I need right now, with everything else happening. But again, this is why I'm the youngest VP Daydream has ever had: because shit happens, and I know how to keep a calm head and fix things.

"Okay." I run my hand over my face as I try to settle my mind and think of next steps. "Okay. Call up Leo; give him a heads up. Tell him we're attempting to locate the leak now and we're locking the place down as we speak, so no paparazzi will come in, no matter what. We'll..." I run scenarios through my mind as I try and think of a good solution. "We'll limit phone access in public spaces and try to keep photos from spreading."

"I can draft up a notice for staff right now," Sutton says, voice going into business mode as well, and for the first time since she called while I was at the bar, a modicum of relief runs through me. *We can do this. We can manage this.* "I'll inform them to phrase it as an opportunity to unplug."

"Perfect. And in the meantime, we need to find out who keeps fucking with my resort." I start walking again, moving towards the pool area where, at this time of day, Daniel should be mingling with guests.

"Do you think it could be the same person?" Sutton asks, and my steps slow. "I mean, if someone has it out for the resort, wouldn't that be a good one to do?" I sigh and shake my head; then speak when I remember she can't see me.

"I don't think so. Those leaks started months ago, and never at this location."

In fact, they started two weeks after Wes and Harper Holden stayed at the Punta Cana resort. That leak was intentional, but the next one, revealing that a famous baseball player was fighting with his long-time girlfriend on the beach, was not. I had hoped it was a one-time occurrence and had legal update all of our staff's NDAs, but then it happened again at the Aruba resort a month and a half later.

It's an issue that's been plaguing me, but one that, all in all, is seemingly unavoidable. But now that it's tied with the Keys resort...

"I'll find what I can," she says, reading my mind as always.

"Thanks, Sutton. I—"

"I know, I know, you couldn't function without me and are going to give me a raise. Oh, gosh, no, I couldn't accept. Okay, fine," she says in an imagined conversation with herself. I let out a small laugh even though I'm not feeling jovial in the least.

"Just let me know if you hear anything," I say.

"Got it, boss."

The line clicks off as I make my way to the main pool in search of my fucking GM to try and find out what the fuck is happening here. Unfortunately, I'm stopped on my mission on the pool deck.

"Hey, Rowan, so happy you're here," Tanya, the spa manager, says, walking over to me, her long red hair swaying in a ponytail. The first thing I notice is that, while she's technically in uniform, it's about two sizes too small, making the white polo fit tightly against her chest and showing far too much cleavage than is acceptable for a workplace. I make a mental note to have Sutton confirm the uniform rules in the handbook and possibly have HR step in.

"Hey, Tanya. How are you?"

"Fine, except for you, know... everything going on." She says it far too loud to be around guests, but it's clear she's got full dramatics on now: eyes wide with fake panic and concern, pouty lips, her hand moving to rest on my arm. "It was so scary, that woman having an allergic reaction. I couldn't believe it."

"Have we figured out how that happened?" I ask. She shakes her head.

"No. The last time the mud was changed out was a week ago, and we used the same protocol as always." She swallows like she's nervous the finger is about to be pointed at her. "I was there when it was changed. I swear, we didn't do anything different or out of the ordinary. We've even cut out the most common allergens from the spa: almond and other nuts, soy, and gluten. We only do milk on request and have a detailed protocol for cleaning it up. We've even significantly reduced the use of fragranced items. I have no idea how it got in." I nod, knowing all of this already. I was the one who put most of these things in place.

"Do you have the logs for when people have gone in and out of the supply rooms? Have we cleared out the room to make sure there are no other items that could cause an issue?" All security went down the night of the fire, something we've been investigating with little to no result. Currently, my biggest concern is identifying who is responsible for this before something worse happens. Since we've found no evidence of who could have tampered with the mud bath, I'm wondering if we have even more issues with the security cameras than we are aware of.

"Yeah, we've made sure it's all gone. You know, I'd really love to talk about all of this. I'm just..." A deep, exaggerated sigh leaves her lips, making her breasts in her far too low shirt rise dramatically. "I'm so stressed about it, you know?"

"We have a great insurance plan," I tell her bluntly. "You should talk to someone." Annoyance fights with irritation on her face before that smile returns.

"I know, but I'd so rather talk to someone who understands the intricate details of this workplace, you know?"

I don't, but I can't say that because it seems like grounds for her to file a complaint against me.

"Well—"

"Hey, Mr. Fisher?" a voice calls, and relief that I'm being interrupted from talking to this woman floods me.

"Yeah?" I ask, turning to see the pool manager, Carol, looking at me nervously. This job was not the best choice for her since she can't stand confrontation, and I can guarantee that's what she's about to inform me of.

"Um, a couple of guests just walked that way, towards the rental shack. There's nothing really over there, but it's still dangerous, you know? I don't know what to do." She bites her lip nervously.

"Do we still have everything roped off?" I ask.

"Yeah, but you know how guests are. They see a 'do not enter' sign and they think it means everyone but them."

I groan, looking around. It's busy on the pool deck this afternoon and Carol seems to be the only one on shift right now.

"I'll handle it," I say, and she nods before a guest waves her down.

I nod, telling her to go assist them, and give Tanya a small, polite nod before heading off. Annoyed, I make my way around the pool, taking a shortcut through the pool house until I reach the edge of the beach. Two figures far off duck under the caution tape, and I curse low before continuing towards them.

It's not until I'm about twenty feet away that I catch a brief, familiar glance of one of the women's faces and freeze before shifting around the corner in case she turns again.

Because for some insane reason, I'm pretty sure I'm looking at Josie.

Josie, the woman who has intrigued and confused me for months. Years, even. Josie, whose dates I can't seem to stop myself from interrupting just to watch her jaw get tight with irritation. Josie who I bumped into at Dante's bar, who got my dick hard just by arguing with me, who willfully followed me into the office belonging to my friend, who let me push her against a wall and kiss her, who moaned when I slid my fingers into her, who called out my name when she came and, who most importantly, refused to give me her number.

Unfortunately, it wasn't the first time.

The first time I met Josephine Montgomery, she was an undergrad, and I was finishing the final year of my MBA. I'd been convinced by my friends to go out for once instead of obsessing about grades and work. There, I met Josie, who had been out celebrating her friend's birthday, and danced nearly the entire night with her. When her friends tugged her away to go home, I asked for her number. She gave me a coy smile, shook her head, and said she doesn't date.

I told myself it was fine, that I didn't have time for some party girl barely over twenty-one. Especially not when I was on the fast track finishing my MBA, a degree that Daydream was paying for since even at twenty-six, Annette saw some kind of promise in me I couldn't quite grasp at the time.

That is, until I saw her out a week later with some asshole whom I'd met in a statistics class the previous semester.

Doesn't date, my ass.

I avoided her that night and did my best to brush her out of my mind, but two weeks later, she was out to dinner with some other trust fund kid who had more money than sense, and I understood it then: she turned me down because I didn't have whatever pull she looked for in order for someone to be worthy of her time.

Unfortunately, for whatever idiots fell for her charm and met her rigorous standards, it seemed like none of them proved worthy of her for more than one date. For the next six months, until graduation, I saw her out multiple times, each with a different man, some other poor schmuck who fell for her act and was quickly tossed aside.

After graduation, I forgot about the brunette bombshell, instead focusing solely on work and climbing the ladder as quickly as possible to prove to Annette that her belief and investment in sending me to get my MBA were sound. Last year, at thirty-two, that hard work paid off, and I was promoted to VP of Operations for the entire Daydream Resorts: the youngest VP in the one hundre--year history of the company, and I moved to Hudson City, where Daydream's headquarters are located.

That was when I started spotting her out again. She was once more going on dates with powerful and wealthy men, except this time, I knew them personally. Many were clients, investors, or vendors for Daydream. The first time I bumped into her on one, there was a flash of utter irritation in her eyes before a wall fell over her face and she reverted to some kind of airhead sex kitten, all tits and doe eyes and silly giggles. All of it was hot; all of it was alluring.

But what I really wanted to see again was that irritation.

That was the look that made my cock hard.

So, every time I happened upon her out with someone I knew, which has been at least once a month for the last year, I stopped by, made some small talk with her date, and handed out a stealthy barb that succeeded in drawing her fire.

When I saw her at Opal, I was ready for more of the same: a quick flare of her irritation and then moving on with my evening, but this time, she wasn't actually *with* someone. This time, I took the seat next to her, flirted with her, chatted with her, and realized I fucking *wanted* her. Since the only woman I had been able to think about for the past year since she fell back into my life was her, I decided fucking her out of my system would be the solution. That is, until we were interrupted.

It was for the best, I told myself. A reminder of what's *really* important: work. A sign from some higher power that I couldn't veer from my path, and if I did, disaster was bound to strike.

But if that was the case, then what was the universe trying to tell me by putting her *here* and doing it *now*?

Peeking around the corner once more, I catch her side profile better, see the curves of her lush body, and realize it was not some trick of my mind: Josie is here.

Both dread and thrill rush through me at the realization, not that once again we're at the same place at the same time, but that she's here at my job during the biggest mess of my career.

Instantly, my mind starts reeling.

Why does the fucking universe hate me so goddamn much as to put this woman in my path, interrupt us in such an untimely manner, and then put her here *this week*? As if I don't have enough on my plate, the world drops this utter distraction of a woman into my lap.

Just my fucking luck.

NINE

JOSIE

When Rory says it's clear, we stand casually, making our way around the pool towards the beach, chatting as if we're just on our way to a spa appointment or reservation. Despite our cool exteriors, our attention is piqued, taking note of any eyes that might be following us or questioning us. Thankfully, we make it out of the pool area without an issue. Moving to the beach, I sigh with unmasked bliss when my toes meet the sand, another reminder that I desperately need a vacation. In the distance, there's a wall made of bamboo with a small *'Pardon our appearance'* sign to help mitigate the eyesore, with yellow tape lining the right side. With a quick scan of the beach, we note that it's empty before slowly meandering towards our target.

Finally, the charred building is in sight after we duck under the caution tape, and I fight a gasp when I catch the destroyed area in person for the first time. Rory is quiet as we take in the structure, and I begin taking photos on my phone of anything that might be of use to us to look at later.

A hot spot where I assume the fire started.

The charred remains of a few rental items.

A mostly melted stand-up paddleboard.

"Josie, over here," Rory says quietly, and I make my way to where she's staring at the ceiling. "Did they say there was a camera in the stand?"

I nod, trying to recall the information. "Yeah, but it went offline. They couldn't see anything, and then it was too far gone to check the camera, and I can see why."

Her eyes are focused on a spot on the metal framing of the building.

"I don't think so," she says, eyes fixed in place. "I think someone took it." She tips her head to the ceiling. "The camera should be there. It would still be there if it were burned in the fire."

And it's not. In fact, the spot where she's looking has slightly less smoke damage, less charring, almost as if... "Someone took it."

"And Gabriel didn't tell us?"

"There's enough here to look at; there's a good shot they missed it. Or it was so charred they didn't notice, and then someone came after to grab it. I'd have to double-check the photos we have to confirm one way or another."

"But why take the camera?"

Rory stares at it for long moments, coming over the area with a thorough glance. "I'd love to know the make and model. I bet their interior cameras and exterior ones are different styles, so they're more durable to the elements. Maybe this one kept the footage internally, like a secondary recording? If it caught our culprit, they'd want to take it just in case the footage was salvageable."

I nod at her rationale. "But someone would have to know that, right? That's not knowledge some random person would have."

She nods. "They'd have to know cameras pretty well if they were making assessments just by looking at them." She stares at the space once more, but I know we only have so much more time here, and there's a lot of area to take in.

"Let's check the outside," I say, and she nods as we make our way out of the other external structure. It's slightly less charred, though clearly destroyed, and I turn to ask Rory if she remembers any mention of there being a door before the fire when we're interrupted.

"You're not allowed in there," a familiar voice calls, and I freeze, my eyes going wide. I look at Rory, who is on the other side of the structure and now in my line of sight. Her body is frozen the same way mine is, our eyes wide and locked. Barely a beat passes before I give the smallest nod to her and put on my fakest smile, moving to where the voice came from.

Finally, I put a hand up to shade my eyes to get a good look at who I'm talking to against the blinding sun behind him. It hits me why the voice sounded so familiar. His hazel eyes lock on mine, showing the barest hint of shock before hiding once more beneath his annoyed mask.

"You," he says, low and assessing, and I feel the single word coast along every inch of my body like cool flames licking over my skin.

"You," I reply, my voice breathier than I mean for it to be, but that usually works in my favor. Unfortunately, it simply seems to annoy Rowan further.

"What are you doing here?" A moment passes, and I catch Rory moving closer out of the corner of my eye, but I refuse to break eye contact with this man. Just two days ago, he had me pinned to the wall in a bar, fingering me. And now, he's at the same location as my current mission.

"I work here." He pauses, and I try to run through the names and faces of the resort employees because I would have recognized his name before he adds, "Well, I work for Daydream Resorts. I'm here because..." Another hesitation, and then he shakes his head, but my mind is reeling. We have a file with all the resort's employees, from landscaping to housekeeping to restaurant staff to the General Manager, and I know he was *not* on that list. "It doesn't matter. Are you... Are you staying here?"

I nod.

A work emergency. I suddenly remember his words, a chill of understanding running through me.

You have got to be fucking kidding me. How much do you want to bet he's here because of the incidents that we are actively investigating?

This would be my luck: finally finding a man in Hudson City that I'm actually attracted to, and he ends up being...a suspect? He'd be a suspect, right? Our motto is that everyone is a suspect until proven otherwise, after all. And everyone who works for the resort and has access to cameras, maps, and security information would be a suspect from here on out.

"Yeah. I'm here with my friend," I say, throwing a bit of a flirt in my voice and tipping my head towards Rory. My long brown hair tied in a ponytail swipes along my shoulders as it does, and I don't miss Rowan tracking the movement. Maybe there's hope of saving this.

"Hey," Rory says, stepping out from around the corner. "I'm Rory."

He looks at her as she smiles and waves before meeting my eyes, part confused, part very much amused. I'm a little bit of both myself.

"Rowan," he says, and because the only thing I've talked to Rory about in the last forty-eight hours is the night in the bar and our current mission, she instantly knows who he is. His gaze moves back to me, heating me. "What are you doing here?"

I shrug.

"I told you, we're guests here. We got in this morning." I step forward and brush sand from my hand on my hip, along where the high-rise bottoms lay across my full hips. I'm grateful for the revealing bikini I'm in, but for once in my life, I don't know if it's going to work.

Rowan has always been immune to my charm.

"You're not allowed in this area. It's a crime site." I smile wide and flip my hair over my shoulder, pushing my chest out a smidge, but his eyes don't avert at all, locking on my face with indifference.

"Oh, is it really?" I ask, looking over my shoulder at the charred structure as if it weren't obvious. "I didn't realize."

"There's crime scene tape around it," he adds, like I'm an idiot, and in his defense, I am playing the part right now. It's not my favorite mask to put on, but I'd rather be perceived as an idiot than suspicious. It's why the Mavens work so well, specifically when it comes to men: they'd rather see a gorgeous woman with nothing between her ears than a woman on a mission.

It's also something I quickly learned after my glow-up in high school: we live in a society where someone sees a pretty face and a killer body and decides she's an airhead. I simply decided to use their assumptions against them. They want to think I'm some kind of idiot with a nice rack and let their guard down because of it?

Let them.

It works in my favor, after all.

"Oops. I thought it was just construction tape," I say with a giggle and a shrug. He blinks at me a few times before shaking his head as if he's decided arguing with me on this topic wasn't worth his time, just as I hoped he would.

"What are you doing over there? Construction site or crime site, it's obviously not a safe, appealing place to be." Thankfully, despite this man throwing me for a loop, I always have an excuse for being where I'm not supposed to be at the ready at any given moment.

"We saw a baby! We chased it over here to try and see if we could take a picture of it," I lie excitedly. Rory nods beside me, mimicking my excitement. Being undercover with someone is a lot like improv: you just say *yes*. That's why having a partner you click with is so important. If you don't get along well, there's a good shot someone will slip up. They have to be able to trust that you either have a plan or know how to talk yourself out of things, or else things will start to fall apart.

"A baby?" His eyes go wide with panic and shock, and I nod, playing into it.

"Yeah, it was super cute."

"I'm sorry, you saw a baby walking or, possibly, crawling over here, and you guys decided to chase it? And were you too slow to catch it? A *baby*?"

My brow furrows for a moment as if I don't understand. Of

course, I do, but confusing him like this and getting his emotions all jumbled makes it more likely he'll forget why he was so annoyed that he caught us back here sneaking in the first place.

"Oh, it was a turtle," I say with a wave of my hands and a laugh as if that were a common mistake. "A baby *turtle*." His shoulders loosen, and for a split second, I feel a trickle of guilt for making him worried. The man is clearly stressed out, and I just nearly gave him a heart attack.

I bet I could help with that stress problem, the little voice in my head that runs on lust and lust alone and has been thirsty since our unfinished moment in the bar says. I lock her back in her box.

"Well, you can't go there. The entire beach is blocked off." I look around with wide eyes and put a hand to my chest.

"Oh my goodness, we're so stupid," I look over at Rory, who has a similar, dopey, embarrassed look on her face. "I'm so sorry. I got excited."

"Well, now that you know, let's get out." Rory gives me a silent, subtle nod, telling me we already have what we need, which is good since I can almost guarantee security on this spot will be increased as soon as we head out.

"Lead the way, my man," I say, and then we follow Rowan in the direction we came. "It's so wild you're here. Rory, this is Rowan. Remember I told you about him. He works here."

"Oh, wow, small world," Rory says as if she hadn't already put that together, and I nod in agreement.

Rowan holds up the caution tape for us, and he glares at me as I duck under his arm. I give him a guilty smile as we step off the beach and onto a patio.

"You know, I have a spa appointment in," Rory says, turning to Rowan and looking at her watch. "Thirty minutes. Maybe since you already know each other, you could show Josie around the resort? We just got here, and she's absolutely terrible with directions."

"I don't know—" I start, but Rory's look and accompanying firm words stops me.

"You totally should. It's good to have a friend here. Someone who knows the place well." It clicks then: Rowan could be our first in and possibly the most valuable one, especially if he works in the corporate side of things, which is what my gut is telling me.

"You know, that's actually a really good idea," I say, turning to Rowan and smiling. "I can't read a map to save my life, and you seem to know this place well. What do you do here again?" I ask, despite knowing he never told me.

"No," he says, quick and easy, without even bothering to answer my question. I fight the urge to flinch, not because I'm hurt or disappointed, but because that doesn't happen.

I don't get turned down.

"I'm sorry?"

"I'm not showing you around," he says, and my eyes narrow on him, and I put my hands to my hips, suddenly annoyed.

"Why not?"

"Because I have better things to do." Then, I blink at him and tip my head to the side.

"You're kind of an ass," I say without meaning to, but it seems to be the right thing to say regardless because, for the first time since he caught us, a smile spreads on his lips.

"Yeah, I get that a lot."

Oh, there is no world where that should be hot. Not even the tiniest bit.

But with the smile and the way he said it, all low and sexy and accompanied by the knowledge of what his fingers can do to my body...it is. It is so hot.

Unfortunately, assholes totally do it for me. It's why I'm still single, of course. For some crazy reason, I want a man who is an asshole to everyone but treats me like a princess. Unfortunately, it seems that man only exists in my imagination.

"You were so nice at the bar," I say, my voice going soft. It's a lie, but I tell it anyway. As if without meaning to, his eyes move over my face, down my body, and back up again before smiling wider, like a predator sensing prey.

"I think that was an extenuating circumstance."

I roll my eyes because it seems he is also a liar. Unfortunately, unlike me, he's not very good at it. I step forward, closing the gap between us and putting a hand on his arm. It's covered in a thin, white button-down, too dressy for a casual beach resort, but I can still feel his warmth beneath my hand and his strong muscles flexing as I rest there. A rush runs through me.

I am a sucker for arms. It actually would be beneficial for my work ethic if he kept the business casual attire the entire time he's staying here because if he bared them, I might actually have a problem.

"Well," I start, smiling coyly up at him. "Maybe we can recreate those circumstances."

He stares down at me with a look of impatience, and it's then that I realize *it's not working*. Sure, he's a bit distracted by my every curve being on display in this bathing suit, but beyond that, he's either holding tight to some rope of restraint and professionalism, or he's just not falling for it.

And in that same moment, I decide to make it my new personal mission to get Rowan to look at me with the same heat he showed me in that bar, to make him want me, even if I won't cross that line now that things are different and this is for work.

It's a point of pride, being able to have a man falling at my feet. And I won't let Rowan Fisher ruin my perfect score.

"I don't think that's going to happen," he says, and it almost feels like he's saying it to my new plan, the side quest I'm about to take, and it just strengthens my resolve. I love a challenge, and he just presented me with the perfect one: crack Rowan Fisher once and for all.

And, of course, get whatever information I need from him along the way.

I sigh as if I'm put off before smiling. "Fine. Can you at least take me back to my room? Like Rory said, I'm shit at directions, and I wouldn't want to stumble on a crime scene."

"Again," he adds.

"Exactly," I smile. "If there's trouble, I'm sure to find it. Been that way since I was a kid. Probably best you make sure I get back to my room safe and sound, so I don't create chaos."

He looks like it's the biggest burden he could imagine before finally, he lets out another deep sigh and nods. Not completely immune to my charm, after all, I think, with a satisfied inward grin.

"Fine."

"Don't sound too excited, now," I say.

"Trust me, I'm not."

I roll my eyes, then shift my attention to Rory.

"Okay, well, I am pretty good with directions, so I think I can get myself to the spa with no problem. See you later, Josie. Nice meeting you, Rowan," she says with a smile, and then she walks off.

"What's your room number?" Rowan asks brusquely once she's gone.

"4819."

He nods before he starts moving towards the hotel without a word. I take a few quick steps to catch up, then have to almost jog to keep up with his speed and his long legs. "So, a work emergency, huh? Was that the emergency?" I ask as we walk into the lobby of the hotel. "Having to come to paradise?" The silence continues to hang between us as he takes a left turn.

"What do you do here?" I try a new question, trying to play it casual. Usually, whenever I hook up with someone, I conduct a thorough investigation into their life story, but for the first time, I didn't with Rowan. Not with my knowing him as long as I have, and then the morning after receiving our assignment. I'm deeply regretting it now.

"VP of Operations," he says succinctly, and I can't decide if that's amazing news or absolutely horrific. It's good because he's probably not our guy, considering he was in New Jersey just two days ago and only came to this location because of the sabotages. Bad because, well, he works for the company.

In fact, he doesn't just work for the company; he's high up the ladder.

"Do you like it?"

"Yes," he remarks simply, continuing to give me nothing.

"God, you're so talkative," I say with a laugh. He just glares at me, and I let out another giggle. It's not even part of my mask, part of the act I'm playing to lure him in, either. I just find his frustration hilarious. "You were much more amenable in the bar." I reach over and barely graze his pinky with my own. It's the barest brush, chaste, even, but it still sends a bolt of heat through me.

Well, *that* might be a problem.

"Like I said, different circumstances," he says.

"So you're back to thinking I'm some pretty little gold digger?" I expect him to brush it off, but to my surprise, he looks over at me with a fierce look.

"Now I think you're trouble, and I don't have the time for trouble."

I smile then because I'm considering it progress before he rolls his eyes and averts his gaze again. I take in our surroundings as he walks quickly to the other side of the resort where my room is located, making note of people and places and things to explore later with Rory before eventually catching sight of a sunny area through a set of French doors, flanked by tons of foliage.

"What is that?" I ask, looking to the right through large glass windows. I can see the glittering ocean far off and a few chairs, and my steps stop. The area looks like a dream, and suddenly, I want nothing more than to check it out.

"A lookout," he says, blunt as ever, continuing to walk but a bit slower as the gap between us grows.

"Can we look at it?" I ask. He stops moving then, turning to look at me with a glare.

"I thought I was taking you to your room."

"Would a detour kill you?" He stares at me, but before he can tell me that a detour would, in fact, kill him, as I'm pretty sure he wants to, I take off in that direction, my intrigue piqued as I push open a door. The area is empty, just a couple of chairs on the far side of the large area that lines the side of the building, taking in the sun. The entire area is gorgeous, with a glass wall that overlooks the beach and the ocean straight ahead, a sharp drop off of the cliff the actual hotel is built on. To the right is the wooded forest, a few hiking trails I saw on the brochures visible through the leaves. The area is absolutely breathtaking, with pots and planters filled with flowers and greenery everywhere alongside the most spectacular view.

"Oh my god," I whisper, looking around and deciding that tomorrow, Rory and I will spend at least an hour here, even if we get zero intel while doing it.

"This is why we picked this location," Rowan says, seemingly reluctantly, coming up behind me, waving an arm in the direction of the sparkling ocean with bright, crystal-clear water. I look over my shoulder at him and see his face cast in confusion like even he can't discern why he's sharing this with me.

"There's no one out here," I say, looking around. He shrugs.

"It's small and doesn't have the amenities the pools or other sounding areas have. Staff aren't assigned to monitor this area heavily, but that's part of why I like it. It's smaller but more impactful."

"Hmm," I say, taking in him and then the ocean. "Didn't peg you as the type."

It's not a line: I didn't peg this for him, and each time I find myself wrong regarding him, I get a bit more concerned. I'm never wrong. I can often discern someone's thoughts, desires, and likes within just a few minutes of conversation.

But Rowan seems to be a complete and total anomaly.

"What?"

I shrug and give him a playful smile, burying my own concern behind my charm. "You're the kind of man who thinks bigger is better. This is not bigger."

He's staring at me now, taking in my face without shame or trying to hide it before he answers, voice low.

"But it's better."

A long moment passes as I take him in. Fuck, he's handsome. So much more so than I gave him credit for the dozen or so times we've bumped into each other. Like this, smiling and at ease for the smallest moment in time, he looks completely different.

His eyes drift down to where I know the mark he left on my neck the other night is just barely visible, and his eyes flare with satisfaction. I didn't cover it up this morning, since I knew I'd be getting on a plane, and I forgot before we left for the pool, but now I'm wondering if, like so much of this trip, it was meant to be. That I met up with Rowan a few days ago was exactly for this reason: for him to be my source of information.

Without even meaning to, I take a step closer.

"This feels like kismet, you know?" I ask with a smile, pushing my hair over my shoulder and subtly leaning in towards him. "Both of us at that bar, then both of us showing up here? Right place, right time." He looks down at me, and a rush runs through me, pleasure and satisfaction rushing through my veins. He isn't nearly as unaffected as he's making himself out to be.

"I'm starting to think nothing is the right place, right time when it comes to you."

My heart pounds at his admission, and I force myself to take the deepest breath I can, inconspicuously, before I attempt to play it off.

"Maybe we should go somewhere and talk about it," I say with my sexiest voice. "We could get dinner together tonight."

I tell myself it's because I want to have more time to ask him questions, to crack through that exterior and convince him to let me in, but I know the truth: despite the fact that he seems utterly annoyed with me, I want to spend more time with him. I tell myself it's because I love a challenge that I took my need to make people like me and shifted and molded it into a career. But deep down, I don't know if I'm buying it.

I watch Rowan's face carefully as a dozen different thoughts cross his mind, holding my breath for his answer, but then the unthinkable happens.

He steps away.

"That won't be happening." My body stills with his emotionless words. "I'm here for work." He takes another step back, and to his credit, or maybe mine, he looks a bit pained. It's a small consolation, I suppose.

"What does that have to do with anything?" I ask.

"I don't fraternize with guests."

"Is it against company policy? You don't technically work at this resort, right?" I'd understand his hesitancy if it were, but he shakes his head.

"No, just my personal policy."

I tip my head to the side and give him a small smile.

"Well then, I bet you could make an exception for me," I say in my softest, most convincing voice. "We have history, after all." There's a moment, a slight, short moment in time, where his face shows hesitation, but then it's gone.

"You're going to have to try harder than that, Josie," he whispers, just as tempting as my own tone, but his is low and gravely and hits me in straight my belly, sending warmth through my body.

"What?" I'm dazed by him, lost in his eyes with their unfairly long, dark lashes.

"All those other men, they fall for your act, hook, line, and sinker. Not me." For the first time that I can think of, I'm speechless, a feat considering I love to talk, but there's no time to add anything when he tips his head back towards where we came. "Come on. I've got things to do. Let's get you to your room."

I shake my head, both in response to his attitude and in an attempt to clear my mind as I start to move in his direction. "God, you're such an—" Unfortunately, there's a small puddle on the ground that I don't notice, and I slip in my sandals, almost falling to my ass.

But I don't.

That's because a strong arm is around my waist, catching me and turning me into him as I trip. My hand reaches for Rowan's shoulder to steady myself. His skin is warm and firm under my hands, and my heart races, not from the fear of almost falling but something else altogether. His eyes take in my face, dipping from my eyes to my lips and back up before speaking.

"Are you okay?"

"Thanks to you," I say, and the words are breathy, though this time it's not intentional. He shifts me, that arm bandaged around my lower back tightening and pulling me in closer before his eyes dip to my lips once more, and I think for a moment, he's going to kiss me.

I'd let him.

It goes against every rule I've made for myself in the years since I've been a Maven, but I'd let Rowan Fisher kiss me right now.

"Are you two okay?" a voice calls, breaking the moment. Rowan steps back, his hand sliding to the bare skin of my waist and burning there until he's sure I'm on even footing. Then, he steps a full two feet away from me. If I wanted, I could reach out and touch him, but the distance feels like an ocean after being in his arms.

"Yeah," I say to my new enemy, the kind older woman who's simply worried about me. "I'm okay. I just slipped." But my eyes never leave Rowan's.

"Come on. Let's get you to your room before you get into too much trouble," he says, a reluctant measure of warmth in his words.

I smile then, a soft, self-indulgent smile.

"Good luck with that. I'm very good at finding trouble."

The hint of a smile plays on his lips, but it's gone almost as fast as it came as he guides me out of the area and back into the hotel. We walk through the resort in silence; my mind stuck on the way my lower back is still burning from the heat of his arm while Rowan is lost in his own thoughts.

"I'll see you around?" I ask when we stop at my door. He looks at me and opens his mouth to speak, but I can't let this door close on this easy target of information. I smile at him, knowing that while the answer is probably yes, since the resort is big, it's not limitless. "Hopefully."

"Hopefully not."

I roll my eyes and shake my head before stepping back. "See you around, babe."

He looks at me over his shoulder, his eyes burning, and I know I got under his skin. "Later, troublemaker."

A win is absolutely a win.

TEN

JOSIE

I'm pacing when the door finally opens, almost an hour after I get back to the room. "Where have you been?" I ask like a worried mother, moving towards Rory as soon as she walks in, looking relaxed.

"At my massage...?" she asks, clearly confused. "I told you that's what I was doing. Why do you look like you're in the middle of a full-blown panic attack?"

I throw my hands up in frustration.

"How could you get a massage at a time like this?"

"Because we have to look like real guests here? And it gave me a chance to talk to the people there? Isn't that the point of day one?"

She's right, of course: day one on an assignment like this is all about meeting people, finding leads, and assimilating as best as we can.

"Yes, but... Ugh!" I say, covering my face with my hands. "I'm panicking! And you deserted me!"

"Okay, cool the dramatics. I did not desert you. You had things covered, and I didn't think you were going to get anywhere with both of us there."

"Okay, well, I really could have used the backup, Rory."

Suddenly, her face goes from amused confusion to concern.

"What happened? Did something go wrong? Did he say something? Does he know about us? Gabriel said no one at the company knows about our being hired, but—"

I shake my head to ease her concern. "No, no. It's not that. It's just...I know him, Rory."

"Well, yeah, I figured that out. I already talked to Gabriel—he doesn't care. As long as you don't let it mar your thoughts, he's fine with using whatever connections you have to make this happen quicker."

I pause for a moment on the fact that she called our boss but decide to glaze over it, knowing we have bigger issues to worry about.I would have done the same if I were on assignment with someone who knew one of our targets.

"It's not just that some guy from my past is here, Rory. He works for the company. He's the VP of Operations!"

Her head tips as she takes in that information. "The VP of Operations?" I nod, and she continues after letting that information sink in. "I guess that explains why he wasn't on our list of resort employees we should consider. Why is he here?"

I know she's asking because the list we received from Annette, which included all employees we may encounter, was quite thorough but didn't include corporate management since they weren't expected to be here, and Annette believes this is a localized issue.

But here he is.

"I don't know!" I say, throwing my hands into the air. "He said he had a work emergency when his phone rang at the bar, so I'm assuming the same reason as we are."

She nods as if that makes sense before posing her next question. "Is he a suspect?"

"I..." I think about that for a long moment before shaking my head. "My gut says no. But..." There is really only one rule in the first few days of an assignment.

"Everyone is a suspect until they aren't," she confirms.

"Exactly." My logical partner nods once more, then begins thinking.

"Okay, so you use your knowledge of him to get close to him. Hell, you already hooked up with him, so it shouldn't be hard to spend some time with him. Sounds like a slam dunk." My face scrunches up with my next admission.

"He doesn't..." I sigh, looking at my hands in what feels akin to embarrassment. "He isn't interested," I murmur.

Rory releases a loud laugh at my words before finally responding with a shake of her head. "That's bullshit."

"I'm serious! I offered! He said he doesn't fraternize with guests." I groan, putting my hands to my head.

She pauses, then, understanding clearly washing over her. "So, wait, what's his issue with you? I don't really get it."

"Me neither!" I say, shoving my hands up in the air. "He was getting his master's when I was in college, and I was at a lot of the same parties and whatnot as him because I was running my side business."

In college, I began using my talent for flirting to coax the truth out of just about any man to help my friends. Sometimes, it was to find out if their boyfriends would cheat when tempted. Others wanted to determine if someone had stolen something from their room or just to get us into the most exclusive parties.

But quickly, friends of friends started coming to me, asking for these favors and actually paying me for it. I was about to graduate and head to the FBI academy, figuring I would use my skills for good there when Gabriel approached me with an offer I couldn't refuse.

And now, six years later, I'm a Maven.

"I didn't see him for years after he graduated, but then last year, he started showing up at the same places as me while I was on assignments."

"Okay. Okay," Rory says, pacing the way I was but in a much less frantic and frazzled way as she understands how things are a bit more complicated than she thought. "First things first, did you tell him what you do at any point while you were at the bar? Or in previous conversations?" I shake my head quickly.

"No. You know that. I never tell anyone what I do." In the nearly impossible case something like this happens, none of the Mavens talk about who or what they're assigned to with anyone the moment they've been given an assignment. Some of us, including myself, don't even tell people exactly what we do until it becomes absolutely necessary. "We didn't really get into getting to know you kind of things. He was an ass, and I was, well, me, and then the flirting started, and then..." My mind goes back to him grabbing hold of my hand and pulling me into the office.

"This is fine. Actually, this is good. We can work with this," Rory says, her mind clearly working on some new plan. Where I'm the one who executes and gets what we need from our targets, Rory is the planner and organizer, constantly tying up loose ends and figuring out the next steps. We're a good team, and it's why we're often paired together for assignments.

"Can we?"

"Yes. First, we need to figure out what exactly he does here," she says, opening her computer. "Name?"

"Rowan Fisher." She nods, then goes quiet as she spends a few moments doing god knows what before a wide smile splits her face, and she turns the screen to me. On the screen is a professional headshot.

"That's him!" I say excitedly, always impressed when she can do something like that.

"Don't look at me like I'm some kind of savant; I literally just googled Daydream Resorts and Rowan," she says with an eye roll, and I shrug, impressed, nonetheless. "Vice President of Operations," she confirms under her breath. "Thirty-three. Youngest one they've ever had."

"Is he single?" I ask, and her gaze snaps to me with a glare. "What? I'm just curious."

"Josephine." That's when I know Rory means business; the full name comes out.

"Aurora," I mock in return. Her glare continues, and I roll my eyes once more before explaining. "Just so I don't feel guilty about flirting. That's it." She gives me a disbelieving look, and I can't blame her.

"Sure it is." I ignore her as she does her work, clicking a few more times before shaking her head. "Yes. From what I can see, he's single. Doesn't even bring dates to the company events." A slight warmth runs through me, and I tell myself it's simply because I'm happy I didn't potentially fuck with a relationship. It's the only real time I feel guilt about this job: when my target is someone who is happily in a relationship, and I have to prove, once again, that men are pieces of shit.

While I'm lost in my thoughts, Rory continues typing, her near-platinum blonde hair spilling over her shoulder as her face scrunches with confusion before clearing.

"He was the main advocate for this location. An article that was published around the grand opening has an interview with him." She spins the computer my way, and a photo of Rowan standing in front of the resort's main attraction, the miles of pristine beach, is on the screen. I begin reading the article below.

Rowan Fisher tells us he was the leading champion for Daydream Resorts, choosing this location. "They wanted somewhere further from home, more of a destination. But I knew we'd have some great luck in this place. I knew it down to my soul. And now look at it—it's gorgeous. Perfect, even."

"I think your gut is right. I can't imagine he'd be behind sabotaging a location he was rooting for. It would put his entire career on the line."

I refuse to give in to the confusing relief running through me.

"Everyone is a suspect until they aren't," I say, more of a reminder for myself than anything else. If you knock anyone out too early, you lose context. Sometimes, people do things that make no sense until you dig deeper. "But at the very least, he wouldn't have been able to actually set the fire himself since he wasn't here. He would have to have had an accomplice."

Rory nods, continuing to click and type, probably making notes in the file she creates for every assignment we're on. "Maybe someone is trying to pin things on him? Or ruin it to prove a point?" she asks after a moment or two.

"I mean, it wouldn't be a bad idea if they didn't like this location." We sit in silence, both of us mulling over the thought, before finally, Rory breaks it.

"Okay, well, regardless, he's obviously into you. Maybe that's a good place to start. Butter him up, see what you can get from him." I sigh and shake my head.

"I told you: I don't think he's going to be into that."

"I saw the way he was looking at you, Josie." A rush of warmth slides through me since Rory doesn't say anything just to blow smoke or to make someone feel good about themselves. If she says he was looking at me in any kind of way, she means it. Regardless, I shrug, not wanting to cloud my mind in the least.

"Yeah, and I felt the way he was into me when he was fingering me in a bar office, but now, when I asked if we could get dinner, he said no. He doesn't hook up with guests."

"There's a first time for everything," Rory says with a smile, and I laugh.

"True, but I don't want to put my efforts where they won't be useful. We only have two weeks here." She looks at me like she's not buying it. I'm not really either, but I can fake it with the best of them.

"If anyone could crack him, it would be you."

I stare at her before I take a deep breath.

"Maybe. But can we focus on what we have control over right now? Who do we have on our shortlist?" She stares at me assessingly and must-see my desperate need for a subject change, because she nods and reaches to grab our list.

"The GM is an obvious suspect just because of his broad access to things. His job would be on the line, but maybe there's something more happening there?" she says, and I start to pace the room. I work best when I'm moving.

"And that redhead who got jealous. I want to figure out who she is and what her connection is to the resort."

Rory nods, then types. "That article said an investment firm was trying to purchase this location, but Daydream Resorts bought it out from under them in a preempt. The island never went to auction. We should add them to the list of potential suspects. Do we know who was heading that project?"

More clicks and a grimace that means she's not getting the info she wants before she continues her search. Finally, she gives me a satisfied smile. "A Horace Greenfeld."

"God, that's a shit name," I grumble, and she lets out a laugh. Still, I add the name to my mental list, hating how long it's getting. At the beginning of an assignment like this, the list always looks so daunting because just about everyone is a suspect.

"We need to check out the other incidents and see if he was here for those," I say. "And if not, where was he?"

"We need to do that for all of the employees of the resort," Rory says. "Find out who was on the clock, who was off." I nod, and she continues. "The cameras were clearly tampered with around the time of the fire since they all went down for about ten minutes. I want to know who has access to those. Annette won't give us access to them since that would raise alarms, but she said if I can find access myself, that would be fine." Rory smiles, and I return it, knowing how much she loves hacking into camera and computer feeds. "A great time to also test their cybersecurity, I suppose."

Not being given access to computers and cameras isn't unusual when we enter a corporate setting. Employees talk and whisper, so in order for our job to be done as seamlessly and as secretive as possible, it often makes more sense for no one to know why we're really here. Giving two random women that kind of access would set off alarm bells.

"While you do that, I'm going to look at the calendar of events and see what we want to focus on first. We already checked out the rental building—you grabbed your own pictures of that to look at later, right?" I ask, and she nods. We like to have our own evidence file whenever possible because, again, you never know who is a suspect or friend of a suspect. Once, we had a fire chief who was friends with an arsonist and doctored photos to hide evidence. You'd be shocked at how deep deception can go.

I pick up the pamphlet we were given at check-in, and remembering what the GM told us at the pool, I start scanning for times and opportunities.

"There's a meet and greet dinner tonight. We should definitely go to that. There were a few mishaps with food deliveries that might be related to the issue at hand. Maybe we can try and talk to some of the staff there, do our thing."

Rory nods and jots it down on our schedule before continuing to look through the pamphlet with me and making our plan.

ELEVEN

Suspect list for Daydream resorts based on current intel:

- Daniel, the General Manager
- Jonas, head of security
- Tanya, the spa manager
- Jealous redhead
- Horace Greenfeld

TWELVE

JOSIE

Once we collected ourselves, Rory and I venture out to explore some more, grabbing a late lunch at one of the more casual restaurants that had been facing delivery issues in the past few weeks. We don't notice any issues with food or service, but we do note a hostess who nearly starts crying when the GM goes over to ask her something and the chef on staff, who can be heard grumbling from the kitchen.

After that, we decide to head up to get ready for the meet-and-greet dinner and cocktails, putting on our best Mavens uniform—i.e., hot dress, big hair, sexy makeup, and sky-high heels. A hostess greets us and then leads us through the large room filled with about a dozen large, round tables meant for family-style serving and getting to know strangers, though since it's relatively early in the night, only about half of them are filled.

An older man sits alone at the table we're approaching, and Rory's hand moves to tap my fingers before she leans just a bit.

"I'm pretty sure that's Horace Greenfeld," she whispers, and my eyes widen.

"From the investment company?" She nods. "What the hell is he doing here?" My pulse quickens with excitement, wondering if this case might really be that simple. Rory shrugs but then explains.

"His social media shows him at a few of the Daydream resorts, so it seems there's no ill will from him for getting beaten out. He's the head of an aviation conglomerate, and this is one of the most luxurious chains." I scrunch up my nose, trying to fit that piece of information into what I already know of him as a potential suspect, but I'm unable to, especially not when the hostess sits us at the same table as him on the opposite side. He's preoccupied with his phone, giving me a good opportunity to take him in. The man is in his sixties but clearly takes care of himself and enjoys expensive things, as evidenced by his outfit, jewelry, and watch. He's alone, but the seat next to him is pulled out like someone recently got up. I look at Rory, who nods before I put on a shy smile, turning the man-eater on.

"I'm so sorry to bother you," I say, leaning forward across the table. His head lifts from his phone. "But is that a Patek Philippe Nautilus?" I tip my chin towards his wrist where the one hundred thousand dollar watch sits. He smiles wide, his eyes moving straight to my breasts, which are high and full in a pushup bra and low-cut dress, his body turning towards Rory and me. From the corner of my eye, she wiggles her fingers coyly at him and smiles, though I don't avert my gaze from the man in front of me.

A key part of winning over men with large egos is to make them feel like the only person in the room, rarely diverting your attention from them. For men who have more money than God, undivided attention is a currency in and of itself.

"It is. You've got a great eye."

"I'm a collector myself," I say, twisting my wrist towards him to show the vintage Cartier I'm so grateful I packed, a Christmas gift from Gabriel last year.

"Oh, it's gorgeous. Do you mind?" he asks, putting a hand out. He doesn't know the watch has an audio recorder in it that's taking note of this entire conversation. His cold fingers gently touch the delicate skin on the underside of my wrist as I show it to him. "This is a limited run; barely any exist. How did you get it?"

He sits back, but his fingers don't leave my skin. I fight the urge to pull my hand back, the flirty version of myself on duty instead of the introvert.

"A pawn shop back in my hometown. The find of a lifetime."

"You don't say. Are you two ladies alone?" I nod, and he smiles wider. "Why don't you sit with me? Move closer! No need for us to take up so much space, and you can tell me all about your collection." I look at Rory, who smiles sweetly and nods before we shift around the table closer to our new 'friend.' "Horace."

I grip his offered hand and give it a dainty shake. "Josephine. You can call me Josie, though. And this is my friend Aurora."

I'm pretty sure Rory corrects me and tells him her nickname, but I'm unable to pay much attention because I just watched Rowan Fisher walk into the room and greet a woman one table over from us before sitting down with a wide, gracious smile.

Dinner with a guest.

Interesting how he said he couldn't have dinner with me because it would be fraternizing, something he doesn't do.

I force my body to remain relaxed, to not let the brewing jealousy I'm attempting to ignore show on my face. Jealousy I certainly have no right to feel. He is not anything close to *mine*, and I am currently working on winning another man over. I don't think Horace would notice, if we're being honest, since he's rambling on about his watch collection, grabbing his phone to show each one. Still, I need to stay focused on why I'm here and what my mission is: getting to the bottom of who is sabotaging this resort.

With that reminder, I manage to push the distraction of Rowan down, and thirty minutes later, I've nearly forgotten about him. Horace has shown us dozens of photos of all the many luxuries he has while Rory and I oohed and ahhed at each one, fluffing up his ego.

"Is this your first time here?" he asks, finally shifting the conversation back to us, and Rory nods.

"Yes. We're excited to experience everything this place has to offer. You?"

Horace shakes his head. "No, no. I've been to many of the Daydream resorts, though this is my favorite."

"Oh yeah? That's so cool," Rory says. "What line of work do you do to allow for that?" She twirls a lock of her blonde hair around her finger and makes doe eyes at the man. He falls for it, of course.

"I work in aviation," he says, then thinks on it before giving us a condescending smile. "That's airplanes."

Rory's fingers dig into my thigh with irritation, and I bite back a groan of pain. Rory is not great at this part of the game: playing stupid for arrogant men who can't quite see past your tits, the ones who think you have barely two brain cells to rub together, so they have to spell things out for you like a toddler. It's not for her, with her Master's in cybersecurity and a brain as powerful as a super-computer.

But me? I'm used to it. In fact, I thrive on it: using people's short-sightedness against them and manipulating people to get whatever I need from them. It brings me a unique kind of joy.

"Wow, that's so amazing! I'd love to hear about the other locations you've been to," I say. He rattles off a list, and I try to take note of them, though I know Rory and her computer brain have probably already memorized each one.

"I've been kicking around opening my own resort, so it's impor-tant to know how the good ones are run."

I look at my partner, who gives me a look.

"I actually was interested in this location before it was bought out from under me."

My eyes go wide with shock, and my lips form a pitying pout. "Oh no! What a bummer!"

"Yes, I thought it would be perfect for a resort. Had a golf course in mind, instead of those ridiculous hiking trails. Who wants to go out into the woods when they're on vacation?" He sighs and rolls his eyes, shaking his head. "A beautiful resort, don't get me wrong, but it could have been magnificent if I'd had my way."

"I'm sure it would have been amazing," I say sympathetically, despite the fact that I hate golf and enjoy hiking.

"So, what are your thoughts on all of the chaos happening around here? We've heard some whispers about a fire?" Rory asks, tipping her head to the side and twirling a lock of hair on her finger. She leans in, arms pressing her cleavage together, and Horace's eyes slide right there before he speaks to her tits.

"Well, I think it wouldn't be happening if I ran the place, that's for sure." I let out a small laugh, and he shrugs. "Who knows? Maybe it'll get worse, and they'll sell the place to me for cheap just to get it off their hands."

My leg shifts, brushing Rory's in a silent conversation. Horace Greenfeld is most definitely a suspect, with means, motivation, and opportunity all in his favor.

But my mind can only hold onto that for a moment when he looks over my shoulder, his face splitting with a grin before raising his voice a bit. "Actually, let me introduce you to the man who outbid me. Rowan!" he calls, and my back stiffens. Rory's foot knocks mine under the table, though I can't tell if it's in an annoyed or panicked way. "Rowan Fisher, my man. How are you?"

I refuse to look over my shoulder to check if he's approaching, though I don't have to: I can *feel* him.

In moments, Rowan's presence is at my back, and then his hand rests on the back of my chair, reminiscent of so many other investigations he's crashed, reminiscent of just a few nights ago. If I concentrate really, really hard, I can imagine them against the curve of my shoulder, grazing the skin there like a taunt.

"Horace. A pleasure to see you at one of our resorts, as always," his deep voice says.

Rory's fingers tighten on my leg. I'm grateful for it, for her keeping me grounded. I don't look behind me, not even when I actually *do* feel his fingers grazing the skin at the back of my neck. It's probably an accident, but it jolts through me all the same in an incredibly concerning way.

"I was just telling these beautiful women that this is my favorite Daydream resort I've been to. Come, come, sit for just a minute." He pulls out a chair, and I feel more than see Rowan step away and walk around the table, not sitting but instead resting his hands on the back of the chair directly across from me. I can't decide which I hate more: feeling him behind me or having his heated gaze burn into me.

"And you've been to many," he says with a hint of sarcasm. His eyes lock with mine, and as seems to be the case with him, I can't seem to read what he's thinking. It's unsettling, considering I can *always* tell what a man is thinking.

Except for Rowan.

I try to decode it, to figure out if the heat is annoyance or attraction or a mix of both, and as I stare at him, I realize it's *jealousy* simmering there. A jealousy he is *very* unhappy about feeling.

In fact, looking back on numerous nights in dimly lit restaurants and bars, it's the same look I've seen time and time again, some brand of irrational jealousy mixed with irritation. I've never seen it so clearly, but now that I recognize it, I know I can work with it.

I smile wide, confidence flowing through me at this subtle sign I'm winning this battle.

"Exactly! Helps that the women at this one seem to be on another level," Horace says, giving me the perfect in to taunt the man across from me.

"Do you agree, Rowan? In your experience with all of the Daydream resort locations, are the guests prettier at this one?"

Long moments pass as I look across the table at him. It feels like an eternity as his eyes graze over my face, my hair, and what he can see of my body above the table, but he never looks around the room, never shifts his attention to Rory or any of the other gorgeous women nearby. My breath hitches, and my heart stops, but I force my body to remain relaxed and loose.

"There's a lot of beauty to see here," he finally says. If anyone else said it, I'd think it was a brush-off, a way not to hurt my feelings, but I'm looking Rowan in the eye right now, his attention burning on me, and I know. I *know* it's a quiet admission.

"Do you two know each other?" Horace asks, looking between Rowan and me. I smile gently and nod.

"We run in the same circles in Hudson City." A small smile plays on Rowan's full lips at that. "Are you here having dinner with a guest?" I ask.

His gaze shifts from me to Horace and back again before sliding into a sly smile. "I am. Seems you've made a new friend as well." Again, it's so subtle, almost invisible, but the tiniest flash of jealousy ignites. Fire blooms within me as well, settling in my belly in an unavoidable way.

"We just stumbled upon Horace, and he was so generous to keep us company while we ate," I say, gesturing to the half-eaten plate before me. "He's been showing us his watch collection and teaching us about how airplanes work."

"Well, knowing Horace pretty well, I'd say he's your type." He means it as a dig, and despite my best efforts, it works, sending irritation flooding through me. I open my mouth to argue, but before he can say anything, a perfectly manicured hand comes to rest on Rowan's arm, and his attention is diverted to the middle-aged blonde woman he was having dinner with.

"Rowan, darling, I hate to do this, but I have an appointment in ten I need to get to the spa for."

"Of course," Rowan says, turning towards her, finally breaking from my gaze. "Would you like me to escort you?"

My own brand of ugly jealousy blooms in me, something I've never had the misfortune of having to battle, much less while on assignment. It eases when the woman shakes her head in the negative.

"Oh, no, I know how busy you are. Thank you for having dinner with me." Her smile is sickly sweet, but my irritation simmers when instead of watching her walk off, Rowan's eyes shoot right back to me as if to assess. A flash of victory moves over his face.

"Well, I'm going to get back to my office," he says, nodding at our table. "It was nice to see you again, Rory, Horace." I don't miss how he doesn't say goodbye to me, and it grates on me. Rory kicks me under the table before looking at me with a *do your fucking job* kind of look because, despite it all, we both know if I can crack Rowan, he's pretty much the perfect source of intel.

"Actually, I need to use the ladies' room, and you know how bad I am at directions. Can you show me the way?" I ask, standing. Rowan looks from me to his high-roller client, whom he clearly needs to keep happy, before begrudgingly nodding.

"Of course. After you," he says, then puts an arm out to gesture me forward, though it's said through gritted teeth. We're out of earshot when, almost like he can't help himself, his hand going to my lower back in the faintest touch that I can feel all over.

"So you can have dinner with her but not me? From what I could tell, she's also a guest," I say low, for only him to hear, and when I look over at him, I regret it. There's a cocky grin on his lips as he looks down at me.

"Is that jealousy I'm sensing, Ms. Montgomery?" I wonder how he knows my last name. Did he find it out when I checked in, or did he ask an acquaintance at some other time we bumped into each other? We never had any real conversations in college, so I can't imagine he's known that long.

"If it is, what are you going to do about it?"

His steps slow with my teasing words as we step out of the restaurant into a much quieter, empty hallway before he turns to face me fully.

For a split second, I think he's going to kiss me.

For a split second, I hope and pray he's going to kiss me. To pull me into him, to press his body to mine.

But then he blinks and shakes his head like he's shaking the thought from it. "It wasn't planned. My boss asked me to stop by and say hello, and when I did, she asked me to stay for dinner. I didn't decline because her husband is on the board." It's a simple explanation, really, but it also feels like an appeasement. Like something he's sharing so I won't have my feelings hurt. There's also the basic point that he doesn't *owe* me any kind of explanation at all. My mind is churning on that fact as we stand, staring at each other before he speaks again. "And you?"

"Me?" I ask, genuinely confused.

"You and Horace. Seemed cozy."

I shrug, fighting a smile. "He's an interesting person. He also seems to know a lot about a lot of things."

Rowan steps closer then, and I take one back until my back is to the wall, his body towering over mine in a way I remember from the bar, in a way I *like*, even if I think I should probably be nervous. Though he doesn't touch me at all, I can feel the heat of him coming off in waves.

"There's something about you," he whispers, breath playing along my lips.

"That I am frustratingly gorgeous?" I ask, my own words so faint I almost don't hear them, but clearly, he does.

"Yes. And distracting, but that's not what I meant." I like the idea of him finding me distracting and gorgeous, but I don't have time for some flirty retort before he speaks again. "You have a secret, Josie Montgomery. And I'm going to find out what it is."

My heart pounds, trying to quickly work through thoughts and ideas of excuses and explanations, but as always, the simple answer is the best one.

"What kind of secret could I possibly be keeping?" I whisper.

"I have no idea, but it's driving me out of my mind. You're gorgeous, you're funny. You're smart, and you don't take shit from anyone. And yet, you seemingly choose to spend your time with assholes. Every time I see you, you're at the nicest restaurants in Hudson City with rich men you have no interest in. You—"

My pulse is pounding with a sense of thrill and danger, both because he's asking far too many questions and because he's taking this many notes about me. I cut him off to stop him and his train of thought.

"Who said I have no interest in the men I go on dates with?" With my question, his smile goes cocky, his eyes traveling down my body in a way that burns.

"Your body tells me everything I need to know." He shifts an inch closer, so my breasts are just barely grazing his chest, and I fight the urge to arch into him. "Your face? Your face is always on: you look so invested in every word he's saying, but your body couldn't care less. Your body looks like you're at a board meeting, taking notes." He shifts his head, leaning back just a bit and taking me in as if to prove a point before smiling down at me. "Unlike now. Your body now? Interested. Hanging on every word I say. Invested."

I fight the urge to shift away from him to counter what he's saying, but it would just prove his point further, and he would clearly catch the small move because he's *good* at this. An expert at reading me. I've never met anyone able to dissect tiny changes in movements and body language as well I can, and at this moment, I can't tell if it's annoying or the biggest turn-on of my life. No one has *ever* been able to see past the intricate walls I've put up; no one has ever been able to see beyond what I *allow* them to see.

Until Rowan.

"That's why I'm always so perplexed when I see you out. You're on, flirting and pushing your tits up, distracting whoever you're out with. But that's all it is: you're *on*. You're not there for your own pleasure."

"What do you know about my pleasure, Rowan?" I ask in a flirty whisper that I don't even mean to put into my voice.

He smiles then, all wide and devious like he was hoping that's what I would say next.

"I think we both know how in tune I am to your pleasure, baby."

I lick my lips, suddenly parched under his hot gaze.

"What are you going to do about it?" I whisper. "With your

unique knowledge of my wants and needs?" I don't know what my intention is for my question, but I ask it, nonetheless.

My heart drops when his demeanor changes as if a bucket of cold water is dumped over him before he steps back, cold air filling the space he just was. He shakes his head, running a hand through his carefully groomed, thick, dark hair and making a small clump fall to his forehead before he answers.

"Nothing."

I fight the disappointment from showing on my face, reminding myself I am here for a *job*. I am here to solve a problem, not to flirt with the VP of Operations.

"Then I guess you'll just keep bumping into me and getting that jealous little frown on your face," I say, stepping back toward the entrance of the restaurant, forgetting I came out here under the guise of using the ladies' room. Rowan's eyebrows furrow with my words.

"I don't have a jealous little frown."

I give him a pitying smile. "Cute that you think that," I say with a shrug before taking two more steps backward toward the door, a smile on my lips. "See you around, Rowan."

"Not if I have anything to do with it," he grumbles.

I laugh as I turn around fully and head into the restaurant without a second look. I make my way back to the table, a bit irritated and flustered despite my nonchalant act. Rory gives me a look when I sit, my jaw tight but my fake smile wide.

"No Rowan?" Horace asks; I shake my head.

"No, he had to go be a big party pooper and *work*," I pout.

"That kid. All work, no play." He sits back with a wide smile. "Now me? I'm the opposite. All play, minimal work. I already put in my work."

I flutter my eyelashes and open my mouth to say something, but an annoyed voice interrupts us.

"Are you done playing with the young things, Horace?" a middle-aged woman with blonde hair asks, looking down her nose at Rory and me. Horace clearly misses the rude move.

"Oh, Regina! You took long enough to get here. Ladies, have you two met my new friend, Regina?" The woman looks from Rory to me and deems us uninteresting. "I met her when I arrived here."

"Great to meet you," I say with as genuine a smile as I can give someone who clearly doesn't like me without even *knowing* me.

"She's a writer," Horace says, and despite his flirting with Rory and me tonight, it's clear he likes this woman. The exchange is almost endearing.

"Oh, that's so interesting. Where can we read you?" Rory asks with a soft smile that Regina returns, though hers is uncomfortable and tight.

"Oh, you know. A little here, a little there." I shift my eyes to Rory, who is already looking at me, our minds on the same page. As people who diligently avoid talking about our work, it's easy to narrow in on when someone else is doing the same thing. "Anyway, Horace, let's go. I'm getting very...tired." There's a purr in her voice that almost makes me gag, and when I look at Rory, she's fighting off a grimace of her own. "Would you mind showing me to my room?"

Horace, on the other hand, looks absolutely smitten with her and stands quickly.

"Of course. It was great to meet you, girls. I'm sure I'll see you around," he says. We agree and exchange goodbyes before we watch them head out together.

"Suspect," Rory says low, and I nod as she types both Horace's and Regina's names into her phone. "Okay, let's go. We have some research to do." We both stand and head out of the restaurant, and even though I feel good about the intel we gathered, I have a knot in my stomach.

"You going to tell me what happened with Rowan?" she asks as we step into the empty elevator.

I give her a quick look before digging into my small bag, pretending to look for something.

"Nothing."

"Bullshit. He looked like he wanted to simultaneously run away from you and tear your clothes off when you left."

"Well, he didn't tear my clothes off."

"So he ran away from you?"

I shrug then, still avoiding her eyes. "I told you, Rory. He's not into me."

She lets out a small huff of disbelief before shaking her head. "Sure, he isn't."

And I don't even have it in me to argue with her. Because, despite the back and forth, Rowan clearly is into me. But I'm starting to wonder if that interest could come at a cost.

THIRTEEN

Suspect list for Daydream resorts based on current intel:

- Daniel, the General Manager
- Jonas, head of security
- Tanya, the spa manager
- Horace Greenfeld
- Jealous redhead
- Regina (a writer?? SURE)

FOURTEEN

JOSIE

The following morning, I wake to an alert from the resort that the main pool is closed for the morning. After a bit of back and forth with Gabriel, I determine someone swapped a clear dish soap container with the chlorine, creating a soapy mess. An allegedly unsuspecting employee dumped it into the main pool like usual without checking the labels, and now the pool has to be drained, rinsed, and rebalanced, which means I know exactly where we will be today.

"Rory, you gotta get up," I say in my kindest voice once the sun fully rises. It's eight, and while I tried to let my friend sleep in, knowing she's not a morning person, we've got work to do.

"Oh my god, it's too early," Rory groans, taking a pillow from her bed and putting it over her face as if she would like to smother herself.

I laugh at her dramatics and draw the curtains open. "It's eight."

"Exactly. Too early. Can't they give us *one morning* in paradise before we have to work?" Despite her words, she sits up and stretches before looking at me with an entertained smile.

"Better than what Lana and Demi are dealing with," I say of our fellow Mavens, who are on a different case. "Did you hear they're assigned to some Monster Truck rally circuit?"

She nods, laughing. "Honestly, I can totally picture it. Lana is absolutely unhinged sometimes." Rory yawns before reaching over to the bedside table and picking up her glasses.

"We've got a new update."

That seems to perk her up.

"We do?"

I nod. "Someone swapped the bottle of chlorine for the pool with a bottle of foaming soap. The employee who dumped it wasn't paying attention to what the bottle said, poured in his normal amount, and then the jets and filters kicked on, making for a huge mess."

"Oh my god," Rory says with wide eyes.

"Apparently, it looked like one of those crazy bubble parties."

She lets out a laugh at the mental image before thinking about this new development.

"Do you think the pool guy is our guy?" I shrug.

"I mean, everyone's a suspect, but from what I understand, the guy is beside himself, upset that he made a mistake like that."

"Could it have been an honest mistake? Are they kept in the same room?"

"My research shows that the pool equipment and maintenance supplies are kept in a pool house that only stocks those things. The soap for bathrooms would be in a supply closet inside the resort, so someone would have had to bring it outside. I looked up a couple of commercial brands resorts like this typically order, and honestly, the bottles are shockingly similar-looking. It wouldn't be hard not to notice until it's too late, especially if it was dark and you were moving on muscle memory. But the person who restocked the room with the wrong thing would have noticed, more likely than not."

Rory nods before sliding off the bed, moving to the bathroom and starting to brush her teeth.

"Is that something trackable? Do they have to scan to get into the supply rooms or anything like that?"

I shake my head. "No, though, according to Annette, there is a paper log-in, log-out system, and the managers do a bi-weekly inventory on the computer to make sure everything is stocked up. But for small needs, they just jot down names and items to save time. I wouldn't be surprised if most people ignored those, though. It's too much work when you can just grab what you need and bolt."

Rory nods. "Cameras?"

I shake my head. "They didn't notice, but the camera pointing to the pool house has been on a 24-hour repetitive loop for about four days. It could have happened at any time, and no one would have noticed."

"So someone is hacking the cameras?" Rory asks, and there's a hint of irritation in the words since she herself has been unable to do that yet. As of last night, she's close but needs some more time to infiltrate their surprisingly strong system.

I shrug, not wanting to rub it in. "It seems so. Which means they have to have skill at infiltrating systems." She sighs heavily before spitting, rinsing her toothbrush, and turning to me.

"So, sounds like we're going to the pool today? I'd love to get in there somehow, see if we can see anything, and maybe even bug that pool house. We should also bug the other supply closets since this isn't the first time we've had an issue with the supply. Clearly, whoever our guy is, they have some skills with the security cameras, so we need some of our own." I smile, grabbing my red bikini and nodding.

"My thoughts also. That pool is closed today, obviously, but that means there will probably be more staff and guests at the other one. I wanted to get there early to grab a chair. Let's go."

An hour later, we're lying out by the pool, taking note of the people around us. A few guests are grumbling about their complaints, and the extra staff are trying everything they can to accommodate them, but today, we're more focused on the interactions between staff members. We both are holding books, but neither of us is reading them. Instead we're keeping an eye on which employees we might want to look into further. Which ones are grumbling to one another, which look stressed out, and which, if any, are basking in the chaos.

"They're definitely fucking," I say, low, my eyes not leaving the group to the right of us. It's four employees, one being the redhead we saw on our first day and another being Daniel, the GM.

"What?"

"The redhead and Daniel." I continue to watch. "And I don't think he's happy about it," I say of the third in the group, who keeps shifting his eyes toward the redhead and Daniel. He's younger, smaller, and wearing what I believe is the landscaping uniform.

"Is the redhead the same one who looked mad when he was flirting with you?"

I nod, not mentioning that she's also the one who was a bit too friendly with the man I now realize was Rowan.

It doesn't matter, I tell myself. *He doesn't matter.* We have a job to do here.

"Interesting," Rory says, and even though I don't look, I can feel my partner's burning gaze on me, and I wonder for a moment if that *interesting* was about our suspects or my own reaction.

"Looks like our target is cleared," I say low, trying to change the subject when I realize the fourth person in the group is the woman who was standing near the pool house. Rory nods and sets her book aside, leaving it on top of her towel-covered chair when she stands, and grabs her pool bag, slinging it over her shoulder as I follow suit, but leaving my own bag. To anyone else, it looks like two friends heading to a bathroom break, but I know that tote holds Rory's equipment to set up a listening device in the pool house.

Our plan is simple: I'm going to the poolside bar for a drink, the bar that conveniently has a perfect line of vision of the pool house. There, I'll be close enough that, if needed, I can create a distraction while Rory slips inside or finishes her job. I've been watching the room for over an hour, so I know that there is currently no one inside.

We walk slowly, keeping an eye on the pool house and chatting casually as we go so as not to seem suspicious before I tell Rory I'm going to get a drink while she 'uses the bathroom.' Instead of going right to the bathrooms, she takes a left and slips into the pool house. I slide onto a barstool, and I take my phone out, pretending to fiddle with it before the bartender comes over.

"Hey, there," he says, a wide smile on his lips. "What can I get you?" When I look up, it's one of the employees we've noticed at the resort a few times. He's cute, though young, and always stares at my boobs when we walk past him. Instantly, I put my mask on, a wide, goofy smile taking over my face as I shake my head.

"I'm not sure. I'm waiting for my friend and figured I'd get a drink while I was here," I say, a white lie of sorts. "She's always the last to get ready." He nods again, his eyes drifting to my boobs before going back my face. While I'm here, I might as well see if I can find anything out from him. I tip my head to the side, my silky hair falling in a curtain around my shoulders, and give him a wide, knowing smile. He blushes before looking around.

"What are you thinking? Give me some guidelines, and I can make something just for you."

"I'm thinking..." I say, a finger grazing along my lip, a move he tracks. "Something fruity. Fancy and tropical."

"Frozen?'

"Sure," I say with a smile. He's moving behind the bar, dumping things into the blender.

"So, how long are you here?"

"Two weeks," I say with a wistful stare. "I wish it were longer."

He looks up as he throws some strawberries in before popping the top on the blender and turning it on.

"Have you done any activities yet? An excursion?"

I shrug.

"Nothing crazy, just the cocktail mixer and laying out. We just got here a couple of days ago, and we were checking out our options. What's your favorite excursion? You seem like the kind of guy who likes to have fun."

"I, uh," he stutters, a blush burning over his cheeks. "I really liked the standup paddle boards, but they're not available right now."

"Oh, right," I say with wide, innocent eyes and a small frown. "The fire." He nods, and I add, "What was that about?" He pours my drink, a pink frozen thing with a heavy hand of rum, before topping it with whipped cream and sliding it to me. I give him a small smile, reaching out and touching his forearm. "I'm dying for some gossip!"

He looks side to side like he's worried someone might be listening, and for a moment, that familiar guilt of toeing the morality line hits me before I forget it as he starts talking. Then he leans his forearms on the bar. I lean in, too, keeping the pool house in my line of vision as I do, genuinely eager for his response.

"Honestly, no one's really sure, but they're pretty sure it was arson." His voice goes lower. "Someone turned off all of the cameras on the resort five minutes before it happened."

My eyes go wide as if this is new information to me.

"No way!" I say excitedly. "Does that happen often? Cameras turning off?" He shakes his head.

"No, this place is pretty well locked down, from what I understand. They see everything. We think it was someone who works here."

"Here? My goodness." I make my eyes wide and innocent like this is the first time I've heard of this, and he falls for it, nodding fervently. "What do *you* think?"

He shrugs, but the way his eyes shift again has me leaning in farther, this time genuinely interested.

"I heard that Jeff, who used to run the rental shack, was begging for them to move him to excursions. And now that the shack is down guess what he's reassigned to."

I gasp and let out a little shocked giggle. "No way!"

"Yeah. Crazy, right? I can't imagine doing something like that, risking this job. We all have it pretty good here. I can't imagine fucking up a gig like this."

I take a long sip of my drink, which tastes delicious.

"So you like your job?" I ask, genuinely intrigued. Employee morale can be a huge factor in an issue like this, though I haven't seen the employees seeming to be miserable here.

"Oh, yeah. Great benefits...get to be outside all the time...good tips if you're working directly with the guests. Gorgeous women..." he says, a cocky smile on his lips as he gets more comfortable. "Who would complain?"

I give him a flirty smile and try to think how long it's been since Rory entered. There's a back door that, according to the blueprints Rory got her hands on, is the exit she's planning to head out of, but she's supposed to come out and meet me here when she's done. It usually takes five or ten minutes to get her stuff set up correctly. I should still have a few more minutes before she's done.

I open my mouth to continue my conversation when I hear a familiar voice.

"Are you on the clock?" it asks. The kid in front of me doesn't hide his shock or panic, standing straight and paling. The panic is mine, too, because Rory is still in the pool house, and now Rowan Fisher is here once again while I try to do my job.

"Oh, Mr. Fisher. I'm so sorry, sir, she was—"

"Oh, Rowan, so good to see you," I say far too loud to be normal, but I hope to fuck Rory hears me through the walkie-talkie on my wrist. "I was just bugging him. He did nothing wrong. In fact, he was very tight-lipped. I was trying to get juicy secrets from him, and he didn't say a word."

Rowan's head tips, his jaw going tight in a way that shouldn't be hot. "Why are you looking for secrets?"

I roll my eyes like it's a silly question. "Why *wouldn't* I look for secrets? I'm a girl. I love to find out secrets." I lean in, my voice going low and conspiratorial. "Do *you* have any juicy secrets to share with me, Rowan?"

He shifts to stand beside me, and I resist the urge to look directly at the pool house, having to rely on my peripheral vision to keep track. Rowan notices everything, and I can't raise suspicions right now.

"I don't share my secrets with anyone," he says low, a challenge if I've ever heard one. I lean in a bit, turning my body on my stool towards his, my head tipped up to look at him as he glares down at me.

Without my mind's approval, my body heats. There's something about the way he's looking down at me, the way I'm looking up, the way he's standing while I sit... it sends my mind into inappropriate places it cannot be in, not while Rory is on a mission. Like he can read my mind, he sits on the stool, but it doesn't help with my dirty mind, not when he spreads his legs, putting his feet on the foot rail, the material of his slacks stretching on his thick thighs.

"I bet I could convince you to spill a few," I whisper, my words almost throaty. His throat bobs with the promise, and for a moment, I see it: a look of desire.

"Go back to work," Rowan says to the bartender, low and gravelly and not even averting his eyes from mine as he does. He's so close, I can feel his breath coasting along my skin, and I have to fight the full shiver that runs through me at it.

"Nice to meet you," I say, also holding Rowan's gaze. He mumbles something, but I don't dare move as my heartbeat thrums with anticipation.

"Isn't he a little young for you?" Rowan asks.

I raise my eyebrow and tip my head. "Excuse me?"

"That kid. A little young. And definitely not in the income bracket you normally go for."

"You really do seem to pay quite a lot of attention to me and the people I spend time with, don't you?"

His tongue runs over his teeth, and his eyes flare with irritation.

"Does it drive you crazy?" I ask, reaching over and touching the collar of his shirt, pretending to lay it flat. "That it's never you?"

My voice is low and sexy even to my own ears, and for the first time, I see it happen in real-time: my impact on him. Some guard he normally keeps slammed down is up for a moment, and I can see everything.

I've burrowed so far under his skin, and he absolutely hates it.

"Not in the least."

"Keep telling yourself that, but we both know you're into me, Rowan, and you don't know what to do about it." His jaw tightens, and I read every tiny shift of his body language that confirms my words. "It's probably better you try and keep your distance, though." I lean back into my stool, a playful, teasing smile on my lips. "You couldn't handle a girl like me," I say low, and even though I still have my mask on, keeping my *sultry spy* facade in place, it suddenly doesn't feel like a mask. It feels like me, a playful, sexy woman flirting with a man, except there's no hidden agenda for once.

I just want to watch him squirm and feel the thrill of the back and forth with him. That thrill tightens when a wolfish smile crosses his lips.

"Oh, I could handle you just fine, Josie."

"Is that a threat?" I ask with a laugh.

"It's a promise." My body comes alive with his words, with the images they create, with the memories of a dim office and the feel of his hands on me.

Just then, my phone pings with the sound that can only be Rory forcing me to break eye contact and check it.

Rory: Hey, girly! We need to reapply sunscreen!

It's code, just in case someone else gets a glimpse of my screen, but I know it means her task is done. I'm to meet her back at the pool so we can casually pack up and then head to the room to confirm the transmission is successful. Still, I don't rush off, instead staying a few more moments, basking in the heady pull of Rowan's gravity. I take a long sip of my drink, savoring the sweetness and the light burn of the rum before setting it down.

He stares at me for another moment before, as if against his own free will, he says, "You've got something..."

He reaches up and brushes a thumb along my upper lip, sending chills through my body, chills that pool between my legs. "...right there." When he pulls back, there's a small smudge of whipped cream on the tip of his thumb.

I hesitate for the barest of moments before deciding *fuck it*. I reach up, wrapping my fingers around his wrist. Holding eye contact with him, I pull his hand towards me.

Then I put that thumb into my mouth and swipe my tongue over the sweet cream with much more diligence than is required. Fuck, even *I* am turned on by the show I'm putting on for him.

At least, that's what I tell myself. It's all a show, all some master plan to win him over, to win this game that we've got going on. To get what I need from him, ever the man-eater. When I release his wrist, his hand drops into his lap like he's been burned, though his eyes are molten on me. Slowly, because my legs feel like jelly, I grab my drink and stand.

"Well, I gotta head out. My friend is waiting for me," I say, and my voice is almost inaudible now. A long beat passes as he stares at me before he speaks.

"Then I guess you should go," he says. Without another word, I start to walk away, moving towards where Rory is waiting for me, but I feel his eyes burning on me with each step. This time, I lose the fight at not looking at him in the last moment.

But I'm glad because when I look over my shoulder at him and confirm he was, in fact, staring at my ass the whole time, I give him a wide smile and get the privilege of watching that blush burn on his cheeks one last time.

FIFTEEN

When I return to my office, I don't check my emails.

I don't check my missed calls.

No.

Instead, I log into the security system and locate Josie at the pool. And then I watch her. I watch her chat and laugh with her friend in that tiny fucking bathing suit I wanted to rip off her body, and I resist the all-consuming urge to go down there and drag her up to my room.

When she leaves the pool deck for her room, I go into the bathroom and jack off, thinking about her plush pink lips wrapped around my cock.

That's when I admit to myself that this week just got a whole fuck of a lot worse.

SIXTEEN

JOSIE

When I get back to Rory, we hang out for a bit at the pool before heading to the room to debrief. There, I tell her about what the bartender told me, adding a new suspect and notes to our files, and she confirms that the transmission of the bug she planted is working correctly. I also fill her in on seeing Rowan again and the way he seems to keep showing up every time I'm trying to do any kind of investigation, though neither of us knows what it means or if we could work it in our favor, just that we need to keep an eye on it. We stay in for the rest of the night, Rory continuing to try and hack into the systems and succeeding on some smaller things, like the reservation systems.

I'm rinsing my face after scrubbing it clean that night when there's a knock at the front door. I give my partner a semi-confused look in the mirror before drying my face and walking to the door, opening it a crack. A young man in a hotel uniform, maybe nineteen or twenty, is standing there with a bored expression, a box in his hand.

"Hi, I have a delivery for Ms. Montgomery?" the employee says, and I tip my head just a hair.

"That's me." He shoves the box in my direction without another word. "Uh, thank you," I say, reaching for the box and accepting it gently. The employee nods and gives a half-hearted smile before walking away down the hall before I can even think to tip him.

I step back into the room, letting the door close behind me with a loud slam. Rory grabs the card from the top of the box and sits on the couch before I can say anything. I sit beside her as she reads it, the heavy box in my hands.

"Looks like I found you," Rory reads aloud, her tone filled with confusion.

I grab the card from her hands and skim it over with my eyes before letting the warmth of the words wash over me.

J-

Looks like I found you after all.

-R

It seems Rowan's not nearly as immune to my charms as I thought.

"What does that mean?" Rory asks, breaking into my thoughts. I stare at the card for a few moments longer before answering.

"At the bar, he asked for my number before he left. I said no. I said he was a powerful man; if he wanted me bad enough, he could find me."

Rory's lips twitch with a smile. "That's such a Josie move."

I return the grin before shifting my gaze to the box in my lap. I lift the lid from the box and see the bottle of whisky he drank at the bar, and I do my best to ignore the flutter of butterfly wings in my belly at the sight. Once again, Rory spots another small card inside before I do, grabbing it and reading it aloud.

"Since you seemed to like the taste last time." She looks up at me, confused again, though my body is reacting with need at those few words. "Were you playing him? You hate this stuff."

I remember the way he tasted when we kissed and my pussy clenches.

Oh, I am so fucked. The realization is even clearer when I feel a warm blush burn over my cheeks.

"He drank it at the bar. I told him I wasn't a fan, but when he kissed me..." I pause and swallow. "When he kissed me, he asked if I liked the taste of it then. On his lips."

She lets out a low whistle, clearly impressed, before using the box lid to fan herself.

I grab the card from where she placed it on the coffee table, reading the words scrawled on the heavy cream cardstock. I know instinctively that it wasn't written by some gift shop attendant or an assistant. Rowan took the time to write it himself.

"Is this him not interested in you?" Rory asks with a laugh.

I smile, unable to fight it.

"He said he couldn't have dinner with me because he would be fraternizing with a guest. But he was clearly jealous at dinner. And at the bar. And now this." A beat passes in silence as I try to reconcile this new information with what we already know about him before Rory breaks the silence.

"Is it weird that I'm suddenly finding a bottle of alcohol hot?" Rory asks.

"From him? No." I sigh, setting the box aside and flopping back on the couch, my mind reeling.

"That's it. He's our in," Rory says a minute into my spiral. My mind is still lost on the way Rowan's eyes ate up every curve of my body, the way his voice got low—half threat, half promise—and the way my body responded to it in a heartbeat. The heat that flared in his eyes as I surprised him by putting his thumb in my mouth. The way my pulse pounds a bit when he's around, the way I *want* him to *like* me.

That last part is the most worrisome.

Men don't impact me, not that way. I am always in control of whatever lust I feel. I'm the one being lusted after. I'm not the one lusting *for* someone. Not to say that I don't have my own moments of desire and need: I do, obviously. They're just on *my* terms.

"What?" I ask, still in a haze and trying to rationalize with myself.

"He's VP of Operations, Josie. He knows everything about everyone. He could be useful to us. He's our in. *He's* your target." My heart skips a beat with panic.

"I don't know—" I start, uneasy at the thought.

"Look, either we focus on him, and it is him, and then we solve this problem right off the cuff—" I open my mouth to argue, to tell my friend that we both know it isn't him, but she smiles and shakes her head, speaking over me. "*Or* you can use him for intel, *and* you can hook up with him and finally get laid." My eyes widen with her words.

"Excuse me—"

"When was the last time you got laid?"

"What does that—"

"Josephine."

I scrunch up my nose at my full name. For her benefit, I try to think back, but unfortunately, I can't.

"He made me come, like, three days ago," I say, avoiding the question obviously. She gives me a *don't be obtuse* kind of look that she has perfected.

"We both know that's not enough for you. You need insertion every few months to be happy, and it's been a while for you."

"Excuse me?!" I ask, sitting up.

"Tell me I'm wrong." I glare, but unfortunately, she's not wrong. I do enjoy sex, and it *has* been a while. Because she's not wrong, I change my angle.

"And you don't?" She instantly shakes her head.

"No. I DIY it on the regular. Men annoy me. You thrive off the blood of men." I let out a loud laugh and flop back once more on the couch. "But Rowan would be the ultimate catch for you," she insists.

"You're out of your mind." Still, the idea is enticing, and I should probably be a bit more concerned by how my mind doesn't immediately balk at it.

But why would I? He's attractive, and he's an expert on the case

I'm currently working on. Getting close to him is exactly what I would do on any other assignment. I need to remind myself of that.

"But won't that be an issue? If I'm flirting with everyone and trying to start something with him?"

"Never has in the past." She stares at me before her tone softens. "In any other circumstance, a man like him was into you; you'd be playing the game to get closer to him, find out more," Rory says, echoing my thoughts, and hearing it in her voice makes it more reasonable somehow.

"Okay..." I say slowly, then nod. "Okay. Yeah. That makes sense."

"You have to get close to him. Or *closer*."

"Easier said than done. He's already skeptical of me. If I start showing up in places, he's going to get suspicious. I need an excuse to get him alone, an excuse to talk to him without him questioning it."

"Didn't you say the hiking excursions were his idea? The article said he picked this location partially because of that, and Horace said he was disappointed it wasn't turned into a golfing range." I nod. "I wonder if he goes to them, the excursion fitness classes. Guests aren't allowed to go out on their own, and while he doesn't seem like the type to follow the rules, maybe he also thinks he isn't above the safety rules."

"Couldn't hurt," I say, thinking that, regardless, a hike might be a good idea both to clear my mind and get some information on the different excursions, especially with what the bartender told me about Jeff. Rory goes to her computer, probably accessing the reservation processing system, hacking away in a way I find almost mythical before she looks up at me and smiles.

"Fish, fish, we go our wish. It's like the spy gods smiled down on us: there's one more spot on tomorrow morning's hike, and wouldn't you know it, Rowan Fisher is on the list."

"Looks like I'm going hiking tomorrow," I say with a smile, pushing down the nervous energy that sits in my stomach. If I just ignore it, it will go away.

Right?

SEVENTEEN

Suspect list for Daydream resorts based on current intel:

- Daniel, the General Manager
- Jonas, head of security
- Tanya, the spa manager
- Jeff, rentals and excursions
- Horace Greenfeld
- Jealous redhead
- Regina (a writer?? SURE)

EIGHTEEN

ROWAN

I was already in a bad mood this morning, but I held a semblance of hope that it would be helped by a nice hike. I picked this location with the sole vision of having hiking excursions, and each time I'm here, I try to book at least one. This seemed like a great opportunity not only to get into the open air, but to keep an eye on the various activities. Except, when I arrive at the meeting spot, I see familiar curves wrapped in a light blue sports set I'd like to peel off her despite my better sense, thick dark hair in a high ponytail, and a wide smile on her lips as she chats with other guests.

I would like a single fucking day without Josie stirring my mind up, much less my cock, distracting me from the issue at hand. But these days, I think that would be asking for far too much. She's also chatting with *Horace*, who, I just found out, I'm going to have to deal with a whole lot more, now that he's agreed to stop his ridiculous decision to start his own rival resort and instead invest in Daydream.

For a split second, I contemplate turning around and get started working early, but then Sheila spots me and calls my name, so I have no choice but to join.

"Rowan, my boy," Horace says with a wide smile and I fight

everything in me not to grimace at this man calling me a *boy*. The woman he's been toting around all week is standing to the side of their circle, clearly pretending not to be fangirling over Gene Michaels.

Gene is a reminder of the call I received late last night from Leo, the one where he told me that yet another tip had been leaked, though thankfully, there were no photos to accompany it. While he understands that there's only so much we can do, he made it clear that this was something he would like solved sooner rather than later, as if I didn't have enough on my fucking plate.

"Good morning, Horace. Didn't expect to see you here," I say, putting a hand out to the man and shaking.

"Well, a little birdie over here told me she was most excited for these hikes of yours, so I figured I'd give them a go."

"You're going to love it, Horace, trust me. It's perfect weather for it," Josie says with a smile, and she's not wrong. It's a bit overcast, making the air a bit cooler than normal, especially with the sun not quite up yet. Before I can say anything else, Jeff who is running the excursion, starts to speak, telling us the rules and guidelines before we take off. As much as I want to settle into the back of the group and pretend I'm alone, I find myself walking between Horace and Josie.

"I still think this would have been a better golf course. Don't you, Josie?" Horace says a few minutes into the hike. I've been regretting coming with every step I take, any hopes of a peaceful, quiet hike long gone with Josie and Horace chatting non-stop. Josie looks around the woods with a content smile before shaking her head.

"Have to disagree, Horace. I love the woods. Love a hike. Plus, it attracts a different crowd. You can find a golf course anywhere, and, no offense, but golf is mostly for rich men who want to network. A place like this is meant to enjoy the outdoors with someone special, not try and get new clients." She shrugs and smiles once more, and I can tell that she has him wrapped in her web. Horace is watching her like she's some genius explaining the ways of the world. "Plus, hot girls like hiking. Golf is kind of stuffy and boring, and the outfits are much more limiting with country club rules."

I almost say that I don't think Horace would argue about short skirts or low cut tops the way some golf clubs do, but stop myself when a loud booming laugh leaves him, his hand clapping down on my shoulder.

"And this is why Rowan gets the big bucks, I suppose. He understands the market better than I ever could." His eyes graze over Josie in a way that makes my fingers clench into themselves before he smiles. "And you are definitely the market we'd want here."

"Well, I will absolutely be telling all of my friends about this place, that's for sure," she says, somehow knowing the right thing to say. When her eyes shift to me and light with a conspiratorial smile, I wonder if maybe she's doing it to *help* me.

But why the fuck would she be doing that?

"Hopefully they're all as young and gorgeous as you are," he says, and for some reason, I have the all-consuming desire to push the older man off the trail.

"Horace," Regina says from ten or so feet ahead, before I have to get a hold on myself. Horace shakes his head with a small smile and nods at the woman.

"Gotta go to my lady friend," he says. "She's getting a little jealous of the attention I'm giving our girl Josie. You've got her from here, don't you, Rowan?"

I nod. "Yeah, I got her," I tell him before he moves, grateful to be free of him as I watch him speed up a bit to catch up to Regina, who is still glaring at Josie.

"Thank you," I say low after a few minutes of silence as we move up an incline, my eyes locked to my feet, both to avoid Josie's eye and to watch my steps. "You didn't have to stick up for me."

"I wasn't," she says. "I just think a golf course would be stupid. Look how gorgeous it is out here. Knock all of this down for a stupid putting green? Gross. And selfishly, I like to hike."

A beat passes, and I speak before I have the chance to think better of it.

"I wouldn't have expected that."

She looks at me, her head tipping to the side in an assessing manner. "Why not?"

I shrug but answer anyway.

"Doesn't seem like your thing." I don't know why I'm so invested in what her *thing* might be, but I'm finding more and more I'm just that: invested in Josie, in what she likes, what she doesn't, in what she's doing, and who she's with. Lately, she's all I can think about, despite the fact that I have more than enough to think and worry about. "You seem to be full of surprises."

"That's kind of the point." She smiles, her breathing a bit heavy from the steep incline. "I like keeping people on their toes, getting them to underestimate me. Makes things much more entertaining."

"Well, you're succeeding with me. I never know what to expect when it comes to you." It's more truth than I intend to spill, but it feels like the right answer when she gives me a satisfied smile. "So you hike. You go on luxury vacations. You get free drinks from assholes who don't deserve you giving them the time of day." She raises an eyebrow at me with a small smile.

"You mean assholes like you?"

I can't help it: she got me, since I was one of the assholes she conned into buying her free drinks. I return the smile.

"Yeah. Assholes like me. So, what else do you do? What do you do for work?"

"I'm a micro influencer on social media. I take pictures and make videos about my life and post them. I get paid from brand deals and whatnot."

It's the truth, something I've known since I searched her when I found her social media channels with pictures of her around Hudson City and at different luxury locations, but despite that, it doesn't quite fit. Despite the shit I give her about being a gold digger, looking for some rich powerful man to fund her expensive lifestyle, the more I get to know her, the less I believe it.

It doesn't fit her, somehow. I believe she likes nice things, but something in my gut tells me she likes earning them herself, not being given them.

"Do you like it?" I ask, trying to make sense of it, and she smiles.

"Yeah, it's a blast. I get to keep my own schedule, get dolled up and take pictures of myself, and make money doing it. Brands send me free stuff. I get to go on trips like this and write it off because I'm making content." Well, I guess that explains how she can afford to come to a place like this.

"And you make a living doing that?" I can't quite wrap my head around it.

She nods. "I do well for myself."

"That's...that's impressive," I say, and she shrugs. It's then that I realize she isn't comfortable talking about herself, another red flag I should be taking note of, but I can't seem to hold any of them against her despite my best efforts.

"I mean, it's nothing like you," she says, distracting me.

"Me?"

"The youngest VP of Operations that Daydream has ever had. That's much more impressive." My brow furrows with confusion because while I told her my job, I didn't tell her anything else.

"How did you know that?" And for a short moment, I see it: a flash of panic. Not embarrassment or nerves because I caught her Googling me, but panic that she's been...what? Caught?

As quickly as it came, it's gone, hiding beneath that pretty, ditzy mask she wears, the one that is so fake, it actually makes me angry when she puts it on. It's the one she wears when she's on those dates, the one that I've watched melt away a handful of times when she goes toe to toe with me, the one that she set aside that night in the bar.

I shouldn't be so aware of Josie and her different expressions, but the truth of the matter is, while I've been intrigued by this woman since she turned me down six years ago, I've been obsessed with

Josephine Montgomery since Stephen Jones invited me to crash her date with him, since he walked off and she showed me her true self, since I realized this woman is the first I've met who can hold her own and never backs down.

It only got worse each time I've bumped into her since, but my obsession came to a head when I heard her moan my name. She's so unlike any other woman I've met, the ones who will do anything to impress me, to get a date with me and try to lock me down, that I can't help but be infatuated with her.

Except none of it adds up.

"Oh, Horace was going on and on about how amazing you were last night."

When she lies, her dimple doesn't come out.

I noticed it the third time I saw her out in Hudson City, that time with Jerry Callahan, a former investor at Daydream before he was charged with embezzling from his firm, when she told me she was happy to meet me, making Jerry believe it was our first introduction.

When she's taunting me, tempting me, fucking with me, that dimple is deep in her left cheek. Ever since the first time I saw it, I've wanted to swipe a thumb over it, ideally when I'm buried deep inside of her.

"I'm assuming with all that ladder climbing, you haven't had much time for dating.

"I don't date," I confirm.

"That explains the attitude. Not getting some will make a man bitter."

I turn my head to look at her and smile. She doesn't look my way, meaning I catch her profile and the small play of a grin on her lips instead.

"I didn't say I never get laid, Josephine. Just that I don't date." When I answer, I continue to watch her face to track the changes, and I'm not disappointed in what I see: the slightest tightening of her jaw, a shift of her shoulders back, a centering breath—the tiniest flare of *jealousy*.

"Well, maybe you should try. A couple of dates here and there might help with your shitty attitude."

"I've got bigger priorities. Dating doesn't mesh well with my lifestyle."

She lets out a huffed laugh like she finds that ridiculous. "Priorities? What kind of priorities could you have? You're doing better than every other man your age, I think it would be okay to put yourself first just a bit."

I look ahead of us to where Horace is talking loudly to Jeff at the front of the pack, to Gene and his girlfriend talking in hushed, cozy tones, and for some reason, I explain.

"I owe a lot to my boss. I was an intern for her during my undergrad, and she saw something in me. She took me under her wing when I was just starting there. She saw something in me that no one else, not even myself, did. Trained me, let me shadow her. Fuck, she's the reason I even went back to school to get my MBA. She petitioned the board to cover the cost, saying it was an investment in *their* future."

"That you were the future?" she asks, clarifying, and I nod, lost in the memories.

"So, I don't like to waste my time on distractions that don't matter. I don't have time for Friday night dinner dates and regular weekends away. My schedule is chaotic and even if I have a low-key week planned, things come up and I have to be ready to go visit a resort on a moment's notice. Unfortunately, although a lot of women like the idea of hitching themselves to a wealthy, powerful man, they don't like the reality."

I tried dating over the past few years, but it never went well. It always ended in an argument and a 'this isn't working for me' text. At the end of the day, despite my expressing it explicitly at the beginning of the very first date, choosing my job over a woman never seems to be what they're looking for.

"That's insane," Josie says low after a long beat, and I look at her, confused. "They have to know that your passion and hard work are what make you what you are. That's the attractive part: not the money. Not the power. The drive." She's not looking at me, instead looking somewhere far off, but I can't stop staring at her. "That's the sexiest part about a successful man: not what they have, but how they *got* it. Hard work, determination." She shakes her head, a small knowing smile on her lips now. "The ones with power and wealth, but also time on their hands? They were either born into it or thought they deserved it without putting in the effort. *That's* not sexy. I don't get how some people can't see that, can be attracted to the career but not the drive."

I'm silent as I watch her obvious confusion mixed with a hint of irritation, and once again, I'm at a loss.

Who the fuck is this woman?

And why is she so fucking perfect?

And how is she *single* still?

"You know, I just don't get it," I say with a disbelieving laugh.

"Get what?"

Without meaning to, I confess everything rumbling around in my head, thoughts I've had for a while, but now that I've spent time with her, feel more prevalent.

"You're perfect. You're beautiful and funny, you're insanely smart, even though you hide it, playing the idiot woman. You could have any man you want. You clearly make enough to afford two weeks at a place like this, and yet you're always out there dating these assholes who, you and I both know, you are so out of their league it's not even funny. It doesn't add up."

Finally, she turns to me, taking me in for moments as we walk before she speaks.

"What's your theory?" she asks, further confusing me.

"My theory?"

"You seem convinced that I'm something other than what I say. What's your theory?"

I don't miss how she doesn't deny that she's hiding something. Still, I shake my head, giving her my honest answer.

"I don't know. I don't know, and honestly, Josie? It's driving me insane."

Her smile goes wide. "So, you're admitting you can't stop thinking about me?"

It always comes back to this with her, trying to get me to admit I'm into her, something that, at this point, we're both well aware of.

"Absolutely not," I lie.

Her smile goes wider, like she expects that. "That's fine; the gift you sent me last night did it for you just fine. Thank you for it, by the way. It's my new favorite drink."

I almost forgot about the stupid decision I made to send her up a bottle of the whiskey I drank at the bar, the one that was on my lips when we kissed, with a note reminding her that I found her after all.

"Maybe we should enjoy it together tonight."

A wave of heat that has nothing to do with the weather rushes through me at the ways I could enjoy Josie.

But that's a terrible idea.

"I told you: I'm not here to fraternize with guests," I say with a sigh that sounds disappointed even to my own ears.

She tips my head to the side and aims a smile at me. "Is that so?"

I nod, though when her smile widens, I know it was the wrong choice, that somehow I set myself up for her sass.

"Then what are you doing up here, chatting with me?"

"What?"

"There's a big group here. You don't have to stand with me." My jaw goes tight with her point, realizing that once again, she's proving her point, winning this battle of ours.

"Your denial is so cute, though, Rowan. Keep telling yourself that."

It's a reminder I should keep an eye on Gene and his girlfriend, making sure they're having a great time despite the leaks, and try to track if anyone is showing him too much interest. I could be schmoozing Horace, who is apparently going to have some sway over my paycheck in the future, or even talking to Jeff, who was the last person on shift before the fire.

Instead, I'm back here chatting with Josie about my job and my dating life and letting her twist my mind once more. For a split second, I see a hint of resigned accomplishment on her face, like diverting my attention was her goal even if it's not what she wants, but it's gone as fast as it appeared, and I don't have time to play games with her.

"You're right," I say bluntly. And then I quicken my pace and move towards the front of the pack where the aging rock star is. And even though I chat with Gene and later, Horace, I can't deny that I'm grateful when she moves to the front of the pack where I can watch her ass move with each and every step.

Thirty minutes later, we take a break, Jeff distributing snacks that the hotel packs for the guests before sitting on a tree stump in the clearing right next to Josie. I spent most of that time talking with Gene, who, thankfully, seemed incredibly impressed by the resort and understanding about the issues we've been facing. I also spent those thirty minutes watching Josie, who moved almost effortlessly through the group, chatting and laughing with nearly every person, making friends everywhere she went.

I hated it.

I hated that I couldn't let myself have that part of her, couldn't let myself be distracted by her when for some fucked up reason, that's all I want right now: to let myself be distracted by Josie.

And now she's flirting with my employee while I listen from five feet away.

"So do you like doing these excursions?" she asks him. He smiles at her, not in a way an employee smiles at a guest, but in a way a man smiles at a woman whose pants he'd like to get into, and I force myself to eat my dry as fuck granola bar instead of interrupting.

"Oh, yeah. They're my favorite part of the job."

"What else do you do around here?"

His hand reaches up, and he scratches the back of his neck. "I used to do the rental shack a few times a week, but..."

She gives him a small grimace. "Oh, I heard about that. What happened there?"

My mind goes back to when I first found her at the resort, behind the caution tape, and exploring the remnants of the rental shack.

"No one really knows. The cameras went out, and then the rental shack was," his hands making a poofing motion. "Gone."

"That's just crazy. Do you think it was an accident?"

He shrugs. "Who knows?"

"But what are *your thoughts?*" she says with a pretty smile, leaning over and gently touching his arm. Without meaning to, I let out a quiet grunt, but she hears it, her head moving in my direction. She tips her head a bit like she's trying to figure something out—figure me out— but I'm tired of Josie decoding me.

"I think it's time we continue our hike," I say, standing then walking over to where they're sitting, my eyes firm on Jeff and avoiding the glare Josie is giving me.

"Oh, yeah, of course," Jeff says, looking at his watch, where the ten-minute timers he set clearly still reads two more minutes. "All right, everybody, let's get going."

BREAK

She's at the front of the group with Jeff, chatting with him, and he's smiling down at her like she is sunshine personified, and my hands are starting to cramp from the fists I've curled them into.

What was supposed to be a way to clear my head has only muddled it more, and I need this hike to be over so I can head back to my office, figure out who is sabotaging my hotel, and get the fuck off this island.

It's while I'm mentally plotting out the rest of my day that it happens. I watch as Josie steps over a patch of the trail that looks a bit more leaf-covered than the rest of it and instantly loses her balance. She stumbles, her shoe looking like it's rolling smoothly over something and making it impossible to catch her footing before she falls off the trail, a chorus of shocked gasps following her as she does. Jeff falls as well, a pained cry coming from him as he hits the ground with a sickening thud.

But I barely take note of that as I watch Josie collapse into the dirt, her eyes going dazed. In a heartbeat I'm pushing past guests quickly, rushing to get to her side, to check on her.

"Josie!" I shout as people move to the side, letting me through. *I need to get to her.* It's all that's moving through my mind as she slowly moves, shifting to her elbows. I avoid the mess she fell on before getting to my knees next to her. Tucking an arm beneath her shoulder, I help her sit up slowly.

"Shit, Josie. Are you okay?" My heart is pounding with panic and concern as I look into her slightly dazed eyes.

"I...Yeah. I think so," she says, her voice unsteady. I don't think she hit her head, but everything happened so quickly, I'm not sure. I look into her eyes to check for a concussion, though I have no actual idea how you check for that. I'm a fucking businessman, not a doctor, though in this moment, I'm regretting every life choice that led to me not being able to properly help her right now.

"Are you sure? How many fingers am I holding up?" I ask. The group has moved to surround Jeff, who is continuing to cry, whispers of *it's broken* coming to my ears, but I only have eyes on Josie as I lift two fingers.

"Seven," she says confidently, and my heart sinks to the ground.

"Fuck," I whisper, reaching for my phone in my pocket. "You must have hit your head, I—"

She lets out a laugh and shakes her head, sitting up fully without my help and bending her wrist, which I think caught her fall. She winces a bit, and I grab it, fingers grazing over skin to check for swelling that I don't find. But still, I don't let go of her warm hand, instead wrapping it in my own.

"I'm joking," she says. "You had two fingers up."

I groan and close my eyes, my head dropping as a mix of irritation and relief rushes through me.

She's okay.

She's okay and I know that because she's fucking with me still.

"Don't be cute," I mumble, a hand moving to the stray lock of hair that's escaped from her ponytail and tucking it behind her ear.

"You think I'm cute?"

I smile because I can't help it. It's probably the adrenaline, the relief that she's okay making me soft. Even in this state, she can't fight the urge to taunt and tease me.

And I think it's about time I admit I really fucking like it.

"I think *you* think you're cute," I say, because it wouldn't be *us* if I let her get away with her shit. She sits up a bit more, continuing to flex her wrist and ankles as if checking if she's okay.

"That's because I *am* cute. I'm more worried about what *you* think of me." I release her wrist when I'm satisfied that there isn't anything broken before moving a hand to her chin and tipping her face up to look at me, checking for dilated pupils.

Or so I attempt to convince myself of.

"Yeah, Josie. I think you're cute, but you already knew that." She smiles, the radiance of it easing something in my chest that tightened when I saw her fall. Without meaning to, my thumb grazes her cheekbone gently and she leans into my touch.

"I didn't hit my head. I'm...I think I'm okay. Jeff, though..." She tries look over at him, but I hold on to her jaw, forcing her to look at me.

"I don't give a fuck about Jeff right now. I care if you're okay." Her eyes go soft, a matching smile pulling at her lips as her hand lifts to rest on my cheek.

"I promise, I'm completely fine. Just a little winded," she says with a weak laugh. "I should have been looking where I was going."

My jaw tightens because we both know that falling on that slick patch was most likely not due to her not paying attention. Even more so when I finally let her go and move over to where she tripped. Using a hand to shift the leaves and dirt aside, I get a glimpse at what the true culprit was.

There are two dozen or so glass marbles in a shallow metal pan dug into the ground. There was no way she could have seen it coming, not unless the leaves were moved, which, considering this trail is pretty well littered with leaves all the time, seems impossible.

And then I belatedly realize I'm witnessing yet another sabotage of this place, this one in real time.

BREAK

"Have you checked her out?" I ask the medics once more as they load Jeff up into a gurney. He clearly has something broken and has to be brought to the main island to get proper care, but despite him being my employee, I don't even care. All I can find it in me to care about is Josie. Josie, who, much to her chagrin, allowed me to carry her down to the entrance of the hike, who has sat on the chair I placed her in the whole time, and who has humored me each and every time I came over to check on her in between talking to guests, employees, and medical professionals.

"Rowan, I'm fine. Short of an MRI, there is nothing else they can do," Josie says with a laugh, standing and walking over to me. I contemplate the logistics of getting her an MRI, and she must see it because she shakes her head, laughing once more.

"No. I don't need any kind of medical intervention, Rowan. I'm fine. Really." I sigh, taking her in and fighting the all-consuming desire to pull her into me, to feel her against me in order to reassure myself she's okay. "Really, I'm fine. It was just a fall."

Closing my eyes, I take in a deep breath and let it out to try and bring myself back down to reality.

"I'd love to at least give you some kind of complimentary service at the spa as an apology."

She shakes her head. "That's not necessary."

I groan. "Please, let me make it up to you."

The words are sincere, but they confirm that Josie is feeling just fine when her lips tip and her eyes light up with mischief. Suddenly, my mind is full of all of the ways I could *make something up to her*.

"Breakfast," she whispers.

"What?" I ask, confused, my mind still on rumpled sheets and soft skin.

"Have breakfast with me. It's almost ten."

It took some time to get out of the woods and to handle all of the guests, but I didn't realize it was that late. I told myself I was going to keep my distance, not when there's something about her that I don't understand, something that in my gut I know ties to everything going around here. But then she fell, and that panic lodged in my chest, knocking common sense out of the way.

What could one meal with her hurt?

"Come on. Take me to breakfast, and I'll completely forgive you for the egregious misstep of allowing me to get so terribly injured," she says with a playful smile.

"Fine," I say with a sigh, and then I'm pulling out my phone to make a call.

NINETEEN

ROWAN

Because I'm a complete and total idiot, I don't take Josie to one of the six restaurants that are probably full of guests having brunch. Instead, I call Sutton and ask her to arrange a private meal at one of the beach cabanas. I tell myself it's what she deserves, considering she got injured on my watch and if I wasn't being such a judgmental ass, she probably would have continued to talk my ear off instead of moving up front with Jeff.

Deep down, though, I know that's not the truth. Otherwise, why would I endure what I know is sure to be a near painful interrogation from my assistant the next chance she gets? Between a private break-fast and the expensive bottle of whiskey I had Sutton help me send to her room, I know she has questions.

To be honest, I don't think I have the answers.

Whether I like it or not, I'm intrigued by Josie. Not just because she's gorgeous and funny and confusing in a way no woman has ever been, but because she's hiding something, and I'm not the kind of man to let that kind of thing go. Not when she showed up at my resort right after a catastrophe and seems to be finding herself in the vicinity of every single sabotage since.

"Do you do this a lot?" Josie asks after we're served, giant platters of fresh fruit, waffles, and bacon laid out on the table before us. She holds an iced coffee in her hand, using the straw to stir it to her liking before taking a long sip

"Do what?" I ask, pretending like I don't know as well as that I haven't been watching her mouth the entire time.

"Fancy private breakfasts? Taking advantage of the benefits of this place? You don't seem the type." I shrug, then give her a half lie.

"I don't know. Not a ton, but not never." Because the only time I've done something even close to this was to wine and dine a high-profile client or a potential investor. Not as an apology to a woman I can't stop thinking about, despite my best efforts.

She lets out a little hum, tipping her head back and closing her eyes as a warm breeze licks over our skin. "I haven't been out on the beach yet, but it's nice. I also love how you have to leave your phones behind when entering shared spaces. Makes for more mindfulness."

"That's the hope," I say. I don't tell her that that's a relatively new policy, that the 'no phones in shared spaces' rule was added to prevent unapproved leaks, or how my own phone right beside me, the ringer on loud just in case yet another emergency arises.

Suddenly, though, I'm wondering—when was the last time I turned it off?

Even more, when was the last time I intentionally didn't work?

The revelation that I can't actually identify it hits me in full force, and for the first time, I wonder if Annette's constant musing that I need to take some time for myself actually is founded in some truth.

"You seem stressed," she says with a laugh, and I realize I was lost in my own thoughts, staring out at the blue ocean rolling in while contemplating my life. I shake my head and sigh, trying to focus. My focus doesn't improve when my eyes shift to the gorgeous brunette next to me, grabbing a strawberry by the stem and biting into it.

"Sorry. I'm a shit companion. I've got a lot going on, with the mess that's going on at the resort. Even here, I can't help but let it weigh on me." On its own track, my mind moves to things that could be done in this private cabana that would relieve stress adequately before I force myself to wipe it clean. A boner in a cabana with a guest would absolutely not help any of my current issues.

There's a beat of silence before she speaks. "Why?" I turn to face her, not understanding the question, only to see she's not even looking at me.

"Why?"

"Why are you under a lot of pressure?" She sits back in the chair, as if she doesn't have a single care in the world, and stares out at the ocean. Her dark hair is out of its hair tie and draped over one shoulder, her long throat beckoning my lips, that workout set still hugging every lush curve.

This is probably the most off her flirting game I've ever seen her, but somehow, it's also the most gorgeous, the most tempting. I shake my head to knock the thoughts out of my mind because I have enough going on without adding a woman, much less *this* woman.

Before I can think of a way to answer, her head turns to me, those wide green eyes opening to lock on me before she speaks again, this time softly and filled with empathy. "What pressure are you under, Rowan?" And then she does something so strange, so soft, it throws me aback.

Her hand lifts, reaching over and grabbing mine, squeezing it tight.

I don't know if it's the Florida heat or the fact that I didn't sleep much at all last night, or the chaotic morning, or way she's touching me so gently, or maybe it's just Josie, getting to me the way she always seems to, but I answer all the same. A deep sigh leaves my chest, and I close my eyes.

"Something's going on with this place." The words are quiet, but her hand tightens around my mine, so I know she heard me. "Small things, stupid things, but they're getting worse. First the fire, now this injury on the hiking trail." I wait a moment and then the words keep spilling out, each one easing something in me as I share it, like giving a piece of this burden to Josie is actually easing it.

"It's my ass on the line if I don't figure it out. Some people in the Daydream hierarchy opposed this location. It's not fancy enough, not elite enough, but I saw the appeal and I pushed for it. And now..." I take a deep breath that doesn't seem to get deep enough into my lungs before I let it out. "The fire report said it was arson. Someone started it intentionally. And things are going missing and tips keep getting leaked, which is a huge fucking privacy concern, of course." I'm rambling now but it feels good to finally lay this at someone's feet, to share all of the shit weighing me down.

"Tips?"

"Celebrities. The fact that they're here, and who they're with. This place is supposed to be a place of solitude. Somewhere they can come and hide away from the cameras, and someone is spilling that intel to the press." I sigh, remembering the call I got late last night from Leo, checking in on what we're doing to ensure the privacy for his clients. This sabotage shit won't even matter if Leo decides our resort is untrustworthy. He could destroy a business with the quietest whisper if he wanted to.

"So who's the leak?" she asks, looking at me.

I smile, and it feels genuine, something I'm noticing more and more around her. "If I knew, it wouldn't be an issue, would it?"

She returns the smile before tipping her head to the side. A gentle wind blows, and a few pieces of hair shift in front of her face. She reaches for a clip on her bag, then raises her hands and twists the hair up until it's a dark mess on the top of her head.

I force myself not to look at her breasts, at the way they perk up with her arms lifted like that, or the mouth-watering way right below that, her waist dips in before flaring to her full hips, a perfect hourglass.

If I had a type, it would be Josie.

But I don't because having a type leads to relationships, which I have negative time for—not these days.

"It is just this location?" she asks, and I furrow my brow, confused, mentally stuck on her curves and my own desires.

"What?"

A dark lock slips from its hold, and she tucks it behind her ear. I'm mesmerized by her, watching each movement intensely.

"Is it just this location that the leaks are coming from?" I hesitate for a moment, then shake my head because *Fan Magazine* has gotten at least four exclusive stories about events at resorts across our portfolio. I'm never this open about things, but it seems Josie has some kind of innate skill at pulling information from me.

"No. Four others as well."

She nods like that makes sense.

"So it's unrelated to whatever is going on around here?"

"Why are you so curious?"

She shrugs nonchalantly, then a playful smile appears across her lips.

"I love good gossip. I love eavesdropping. I love tea and mysteries and a good, juicy story."

For a moment, my mind freezes on her words, words that ring true in my knowledge of her.

It's something a reporter would say.

Could I be sitting across from my leak? I try to run through our conversations, remember if she told me she's been to other locations, but I can't quite remember, though I make note to look into it once I'm back at my desk. "I'm sure you do," I say with a laugh, trying to play it off.

"What's that supposed to mean?"

She doesn't ask it as if she's offended, just a simple question.

"Every time I bump into you, you're talking with someone, trying to get them to spill some kind of secret." That seems like a safe answer, and when she doesn't look alarmed, I think I'm right. Instead, she shrugs, then puts her elbows to the table, looking at me with a sly smile.

"I don't know what you're talking about," she says with a shrug and a devious little smile. A beat passes of silence before she speaks once more. "Are you going to the party tomorrow night?"

I shake my head. "That's for guests."

"Oh, I'm sure the VP of Operations could come. I know I'd love to see you there." She shifts closer to me, her arm brushing along mine. She lifts her arms, unpinning her hair and letting it fall over her shoulders. My eyes can't help but follow the move, the way it lands across her tanned skin, then follow to where some of the strands fall between her breasts. She takes a deep breath in, making them rise and fall, and once again, my eyes follow.

It's intentional.

Somewhere in my common sense, I know it's intentional, some act she's putting on to distract me, but I can't find it in me to care.

"I brought a really pretty dress," she says, her voice a flirty whisper.

I'm under her spell, and she knows it.

"Did you now?" I ask, and my eyes shift from her hair and her breasts to her lips. Her pink tongue darts out, wetting the bottom one before biting it and nodding. All I can think about is the way that tongue felt on my thumb the other day and how it could feel in other places.

I reach over on instinct, hand moving toward the lock of hair between her breasts, pausing right before I do, realizing the line I'm most definitely crossing. Our eyes lock, and the teasing look is gone from Josie's eyes, replaced by full parted lips and wide eyes and undeniable need that is echoed in my own body.

"You can touch me, Rowan," she whispers, and the words go right to my dick.

I shouldn't.

There is enough complicating everything in my mind, enough shit on my plate right now. I don't need to add a beautiful woman—a guest—who seems hellbent on getting under my skin to that pile.

But I want my fingers on her skin.

I want to feel her warmth, her softness, to hear her breath hitch. It's becoming an all-consuming desire, a distraction, and I know she's the only one who will ease it.

My hand moves once more before I touch the strands of her hair, and her breathing stops, suffocated by the promise we can both feel in the air between us. When my fingers graze her skin as I push the hair behind her shoulders, my cock stirs. *From my fucking fingers grazing her skin.*

When my hand moves back to her neck, grazing the skin there, my thumb presses along her thrumming pulse. My mind blanks on all the reasons I don't blur lines. I can't think of a single reason I shouldn't press my lips to hers.

"You can kiss me," she whispers, those wide green eyes nearly begging me to do as she offers. I let out a shaky laugh, my thumb starting to swipe along her neck.

"I think that's the worst idea I could have, kissing you," I whisper back.

"Now, why is that?" I should stop, but as seems to be the case when Josie is around, I can't seem to find my filter.

"Because everything in my life is already a mess, and you seem like the kind of woman who thrives off of chaos." With that, she smiles. Some people might be offended by my words, but not Josie. No, she seems to take it as a compliment. A challenge, even.

"But that's the best kind of way to live. Spontaneous. Chaotic. Life is too short for neat and orderly."

It's a reminder that my life is just that and has been for some time: neat and orderly and...utterly boring. Empty. That night in the bar with her, I felt a void I hadn't realized existed begin to fill, and having her close once more, I'm desperate to repeat it.

But before anything more can happen, my phone rings, and for the second time in just a few days, I'm pissed about it. I don't know where this was going to go, and any of the dozen images I've created in my mind are terrible ideas, but I can't seem to convince myself that I wouldn't have thoroughly enjoyed each and every one of them.

"I thought we weren't supposed to bring those in here?" Josie asks as I pull away, standing and. As seems to be the way when Josie is near, I smile wide.

"I'm the boss. I get to make and break the rules."

"I wonder just how many you'd actually break, Rowan," she whispers before reaching for her own bag and standing.

"I've got a meeting in fifteen. That was an alarm."

"Well, work calls, I suppose. Thanks for breakfast, Rowan." And before I can even prepare myself, she's leaning forward, moving to her tiptoes, and pressing a kiss to my cheek. I stand there dumbfounded as she smiles wickedly at me before walking away, hips swaying, that ass a target for my eyes. And when she turns to look back at me over her shoulder a few years away, she smiles again, confirming that she once again caught me staring at her ass.

I am so completely screwed.

TWENTY

JOSIE

The next day and a half are uneventful, and after our chaotic morning and intimate breakfast, Rowan does everything in his power to avoid me. In fact, I don't see him for the rest of the day after our breakfast, nor do I see him the following day. We also seem to be hitting wall after wall while trying to get further in the narrowing of our suspect list.

This is why tonight's cocktail party is important: it's a great opportunity to mingle and watch employees work. We're both in full Mavens' attire, and I'm finishing up my dramatic smoky eye makeup for the evening while Rory sits at the small desk and continues to jot down thoughts and ideas, trying to find connections.

"There was another leak," Rory says, a pen behind her ear, scrolling on her phone. "Mentions of Gene rubbing sunscreen on his new girlfriend. No photos, fortunately, but they seem to be from the same day we arrived here."

"The same day we saw Regina Reynolds jotting something in her notebook." I think about that contemplatively. I have my own gut instinct on it, but I pose the question to Rory all the same. "Do you think she could be our guy?"

She thinks on it for a moment before shaking her head, confirming my own thoughts.

"Regina? No."

We'd already determined that Regina is probably the leak, though, from Rory's hacking, she hasn't been to other resorts, so we can't be completely sure just yet. But she's not responsible for the sabotage.

"Look at the data. The leaks span too long and over multiple resorts. Whatever is happening here is a centralized issue. The leak is a problem, don't get me wrong. But it's not our issue for this assignment. The problem just happens to be here at the same time."

I tip my head, thinking. "Okay, that makes sense. The leaks started, what? A year ago?"

She nods again. "According to Annette and my research, September of last year. Four resorts since, no rhyme or reason to where, though I'm assuming there's someone higher up giving her intel on who is going to be where." She gives me a look, a question I can interpret without words, and I shake my head in answer.

"No, no. I don't think it could be Rowan."

She gives me a look, not disbelieving but asking for more information for me to explain. We never judge one another's gut feelings, but we expect each other to explain them.

"I told you, I got him to open up at breakfast. He's stressed about the leaks and not in a tell-me-to-make-me-feel-bad-for-him kind of way. He seemed shocked that he let the leaked info slip at all." My gut tells me that slip of his is why I haven't seen him since breakfast. Not because he's exceptionally busy, but because he realized he was far too comfortable around me.

"I agree," she says, surprising me a bit. "I just need to make sure we're always on the same page."

I nod, understanding, before changing the subject, not wanting to talk about Rowan.

"Okay, so what next? Jeff is off the list for the foreseeable future," I say of the excursion employee with a broken leg. If he were our guy,

I doubt he would have purposely injured himself in a way that, from what I've heard, he will need surgery.

"Next, I want to try to get some information from employees. I think our guy works for the resort. Horace would be the easiest, most obvious suspect, but my gut says it's not him." We both know that having an innate connection to your gut is half the battle in this career. "He doesn't seem the type to want to put that much work into something. But I'd also like to confidently cross him out, so engaging with him more would be good."

I nod, agreeing. "Knocking him out for good early would clear our list up. He's going to be at the cocktail party tonight."

"How do you know that?"

"I may or may not have bumped into him at breakfast yesterday. He was very disappointed to see you weren't with me, but I told him we'd try to make an appearance tonight."

I smile and nod.

"Well, I wouldn't want to disappoint him," I say, spraying a healthy dose of perfume into the air and walking through the cloud before sliding into my shoes to head down to the party.

BREAK

"I'm going to get a drink, talk to the bartender," Rory says as we move into the ballroom where the cocktail hour is being held, and I nod. Bartenders see all, so if you can get one on your side, it's always a good thing. I look around, trying to find a target, and my eyes narrow on the incoming hallway as I spot Horace and Regina.

I turn back to Rory, who is in a gorgeous short, light green dress that flares at her hips and stops at mid-thigh, her blonde hair moving down her back in a straight curtain. My dress is strapless, tight all over, and a pretty burnt-orange color that looks amazing with my hair, which is blown out into loose waves, my makeup all smoky eyes and a red lip. Essentially, I'm in full-blown maneater mode.

"I'm going to stick around up here, I think. Then wander around, see if I can catch anything." She gives me a perplexed look for a moment before nodding, never questioning my methods the way I never question hers, and we part ways.

I mingle a bit at the entryway, smiling and nodding to a few other guests I've seen around before.

That's when I catch Regina waving for Horace to go ahead of her into the party, putting up a one-minute finger and tipping her head towards the ladies' room. He nods, then moves towards the main room.

Regina doesn't head into the bathroom as implied. Instead, she steps back and moves through her bag in a way I've done myself a million times. She's not looking for anything, not really. As she digs, her head moves up, observing, looking down the hall and into the party, then towards the lobby. It's a move I've done a million times, discreetly trying to take in your surroundings and find something worth noting without drawing attention to yourself.

I smile at Horace as he walks past, who nods before getting pulled away by Daniel, who clearly wants to show the high roller around. Regina's eyes look like they could be locked on her date, but I know better. From where I'm standing, I can see her eyes are locked on Gene and his new girl, Jenny, as they approach the party, and I realize there's a good chance Regina knew they were coming in behind her and she wanted an excuse to catch an extra glance at them. Jenny gives the attendant a wide smile and thanks him, rejecting a drink before she walks into the cocktail party.

My stomach churns as Regina reaches into her bright blue clutch purse that matches her dress, pulling out a phone and tapping the screen a bit before slipping it back into the bag and making her way to the entrance of the party, shoulders back and smile wide. Not the fake kind of wide like she needs to put her carefully curated face back on, but the kind that says job well done. Mission accomplished.

I don't like it.

Not at all. And, unfortunately, it has nothing to do with her invading someone else's privacy or breaking the rules of this establishment.

To my absolute horror and utter denial, it has everything to do with the conversation yesterday with Rowan and the look of concern on his face when he confessed it was weighing on him. Everything to do with how exhaustion clung to him almost visibly, how his shoulders slumped when he told me about the press leaks, and how, despite his best efforts, he couldn't solve the problem. And most of all, I'm horrified at my sudden urge to try and alleviate it.

Maybe I could help in this small way. It wouldn't help our mission, and it wouldn't stop whoever is causing trouble around the resort, but I've begun to convince myself that it will help clear the air, one less thing muddying the waters of our investigations.

I watch as Regina moves casually, grabbing a drink off a tray that's being graciously walked around in the lobby. Finally, she reaches the entrance to the main room.

"I'm sorry, ma'am, but there are no bags at the cocktail mixer," the employee at the door says, tipping her head towards a gilded sign that reads, "No phones or bags, please!"

"Excuse me?" Regina asks scathingly. The attendant gives her a soft, apologetic smile, clearly used to this reaction and totally unfazed.

"To create a better experience, we insist that no one bring any personal items into the ballroom."

"But... But..." She's floundering, trying to find an excuse to be the exception before she says, "But this has my medication in it." Regina lifts her clutch to her chest, and I roll my eyes at the obvious lie. God, some people are just not good at bending the truth.

"If there are any life-saving medications that you need to have on you at all times, they should have been on your file," the attendant says with concern, then taps at a tablet that was sitting next to her a few times. "Let me look—"

"No, no," she murmurs. "It's not..." Another sigh before she looks around the space and into the room where Gene and Jenny disappeared. "It's not life-saving. Just gas pills." The attendant gives her another far too soft and understanding look.

"Well, if you need anything in that bag at any time, you can either request that we get it for you or leave the party and grab it from the room over there." She points to where people have been leaving their belongings all night.

"How do I know no one is going to steal anything?" she asks, further piquing my interest. Now, what could she be hiding in there that she doesn't want anyone to find?

"It has video recording from all angles. Is there something highly valuable in there? We can take it and secure it for you in a safe where no guest can access it."

"No, no," she says a bit too quickly to be casual. "I'll..." She looks like she's contemplating leaving before a loud laugh comes from the room, and she sighs. "I'll put my things in the room." Then she storms off to the coat room. I stay standing at the very entrance of the party, seeming to be enjoying the view of the ocean from one of the many windows, but I'm really watching the reflection behind me in the glass to track when she leaves. Finally, she does, looking a bit begrudged, but smiling at Horace, who meets her not far into the room. He takes her arm and leads her into the party.

Rory is inside, and I know she'll keep an eye out once she sees Regina enter, so instead of following her into the party, I make my way to the bag room.

Once they're out of sight, I make a gesture like I forgot something in case there are any eyes on me, then make my way towards the bag room. I'm semi-surprised when I'm allowed to enter without any fanfare or proof that I've left something inside. Then I look around the room like I'm looking for my bag, but really I'm looking for Regina's bag, and also to see if anyone is in the room or entering soon.

The only other person in here is a woman, who is finding a far back corner of the room to leave her bag. She looks around the room, and I avert my gaze as I scan the room for the blue bag. Moments later, she walks out, and I let out a relieved sigh as I spot the blue clutch. As I approach it, I attempt to look as casual as possible for the benefit of any security cameras and discreetly try to reach for my phone, which is tucked into my bra strap.

Then I'm moving through Regina's bag. Her phone is right on top, and I quickly grab it, praying she's one of those people who uses a common password. 123456 doesn't work to my dismay, but I smile when 111111 does, opening to her most recent screen, her notes app. Instantly, I start taking photos. The most recent note says, "J not drinking, pregnant?" which makes me nauseous. This asshole is not only invading people's privacy, but speculating about the poor woman in this way. Any mission featuring celebrities always brings a mixed feeling of ickiness, partly because while I am thoroughly entertained by celebrity drama, I also can't imagine my private life being so on display, with every move being dissected in such a way.

As I move through her notes, I see that a few days ago, she wrote the couple was at the pool, enjoying the sun, and he was rubbing sunscreen into her.

Bingo. She's our leak: for this location, at least.

I look around the room and listen for an incoming guest before I slip out her wallet. There is her ID, which states her name is Regina Sands. It's not the name she gave us and the hotel, but not too far out of the realm. I wonder if we expand our search to simply guests named Regina around the time of the leaks, what we would find. Quickly, I snap a picture before slipping it back in and continuing my hunt.

That's when I hit the jackpot: a business card tucked carefully between the folds of her wallet with the contact information for an editor at *Fan Magazine*.

I take one last photo before sliding my phone back in my bra, before I close everything up and hang the purse back up, straightening my back as I stand and smile at my own job well done. I may not have pinpointed the culprit of the sabotage, but I have found the source of the celebrity intel leak. It feels good to be able to give something to the client.

I'm just about to try on my heel and head to the party to schmooze a bit, when I hear a familiar deep voice fill the room.

TWENTY-ONE

ROWAN

I wasn't planning to come to the cocktail party tonight. In fact, I've been trying to avoid Josie to the best of my ability, but somehow, I find myself walking towards the side of the resort with the ballroom. The cocktail party is a weekly event at the resort, where guests are encouraged to dress up and mingle, meet fellow guests upon arrival, or have some fun before heading out.

But I know that it really means that Josie will be in a gorgeous dress meant to draw attention, and all eyes will be on her. Although I'm well past the point of admitting I'm headed there with the sole intent of seeing Josie, I'm telling myself it's because she was hurt not long ago, that I want to make sure she's okay. I mean, it's my duty as the highest-ranking employee at this resort right now to ensure a valued customer is well-treated.

She could sue, for all I know. Right?

Right.

The truth is, everything Josie Montgomery does is a complete and total mind fuck. Every time I bump into her, although I leave annoyed or frustrated, I also leave a bit lighter, as if the bantering we do relieves some kind of pressure that has been building up within me long since before the issues at the resort began.

I know I should be more focused on these fucking sabotages, trying to figure out who is setting them up and why, but no matter how hard I dig, I keep hitting wall after wall. None of it makes sense, and none of it adds up. The only thing I could reasonably think is that the culprit is someone who wants this resort to fail. Horace Greenfield could be a good option, considering he checked in nearly two weeks ago, around the time the first issue occurred, and was the closest to securing this location for himself before I outbid him. Unfortunately, I can't find any real proof to tie the issue to him, other than the fact that he's been on the site during all sabotages.

But instead of trying to figure out where he would get the opportunity or who would be his accomplice on site to do this, I'm walking towards the cocktail party, eyes locked on a woman in a burnt orange dress. Dark hair spills down her back, and her hips sway as she moves towards the room where we have guests leave their bags so they can have a better time at the cocktail party. I get stopped by an employee who has a question about hors d'oeuvres, but I keep an eye on the room for her. Once I'm free, I finally move towards the room to find it empty of everyone but Josie.

She's in a nearly sinful orange dress that, from this distance, I can see hugs every curve to perfection, closing the top of a blue clutch before hanging it on one of the dozen or so hooks lining the wall.

"Dress looks good," I say, and her body jolts. When she turns and sees me, her green eyes are wide and panicked, and in a rare moment of her dropping her guard, I can see past the bombshell mask she puts on all the time and see the *real* Josie. A bit silly, definitely still flirty, but now, there's a hint of nervousness. Maybe even *shyness*. The ego in me wants to think it's because I'm here, but in my gut, I know it's not that. It's something different altogether that I still can't quite pinpoint.

"Oh hey, Rowan. Funny seeing you here," she says.

Josie thinks she has a killer poker face, but the truth of the matter is, I can read her every emotion as if it were my own.

"I work here," I say, leaning into the doorway, continuing to watch her. She smiles and shrugs before I watch her mask snap into place, the sultry version back.

"What are *you* doing here?" I ask, taking a few steps into the room and closer to her. The party is in full swing, so guests have stopped visiting the room frequently, something I'm grateful for. I enjoy having Josie to myself, especially when she least expects it.

"I, uh," She lifts the strap for a bag that looks nothing like something she'd carry around, not that I've been taking notes. It's also bright blue when she's in an orange dress. I don't know all that much about women's fashion, but it doesn't exactly match. "I was told we can't bring our bags into the party. Dropped mine in here." I stare at her for long moments before taking a few steps in her direction until there are just a few feet between us.

"Is that right?" She nods, licking her pink-painted lips, and my eyes linger there for long, long moments before I push off from he doorway and take a few steps into the room. "What were you looking for?"

"Oh, you know. I just wanted to make sure I had a clear idea of where all my belongings were, in case something goes missing.

"The room is pretty well guarded. Don't think you have to worry about that." She takes a step closer to me with a heated smile, and even though I know she's playing some game, even though I'm pretty sure she's intending to create a distraction, I can't seem to think clearly around her.

"Yeah, well, you can never be too careful. Does this mean you're done avoiding me?" She says, reaching up and moving to touch the collar of my shirt. Like this, there's barely any space between us and I have to slightly look down at her.

I like it far more than I should.

"I haven't been avoiding you," I say, a half lie. I did see her at the casual restaurant this afternoon and decided that room service to my office was the better option than dealing with the distraction that is Josie. But that was just good time management, not avoidance.

I'm not even buying my own lies at this point.

"So you don't find me completely off-putting?" she asks, her voice a sexy whisper that I feel in my cock.

I should step away.

I should keep things professional.

But I can't stop hearing her words from the cabana playing in my mind: *You can touch me, Rowan. You can kiss me.* I lick my suddenly dry lips, and she tracks the movement with clear fascination.

"I think I made it explicitly clear in that office that I found you anything but off-putting." My voice is low even to my own ears, and it sends a shiver through her, something I watch with utter satisfaction.

"But now..." She tips her head with the unspoken question.

"But now you're a guest, and I have enough on my plate with everything going on around here."

She smiles then. "And yet here you are. With me." Her words come out in a whisper, and I don't know if she moves or I do, but the gap between us lessens, although we still don't touch.

"It's starting to feel like the universe is throwing you in my way," I say.

A little laugh leaves her lips, and it sends warm puffs of her breath coasting over the skin at my neck.

"You make it sound like it's a punishment," she says. I shake my head, finally admitting, at least to myself, that it's not. It's anything but.

"I've been around the world, and I've never met anyone like you," I whisper, the words lower and more gravelly than I intend.

"I'll take that as a compliment," she says with a husky laugh.

Without my mind's permission, I reach for her hand and tug her close. She stumbles but catches herself on me. Her hands fall against my chest as her entire body molds to mine. She's short even in those heels, and I have to look down at her. Her chin tips up to look at me. Without hesitation, her hands slide up my chest, leaving a burning trail as they move to my neck, fingers moving into my hair, her nails scraping along my scalp.

This woman is dangerous, and she knows it.

I just can't seem to find it in me to care.

"Good. It was one."

Then, I don't think—I just move. I wrap an arm around her waist, molding her body against mine. My other hand moves up her back, touching the bare skin there before tangling in her long, soft hair to position her head where I want her. Then I tip my head down, my lips melting into hers.

There's no hesitation, no moment of pause or uncertainty; instead, her hands find their way around my neck as she tugs me closer, her lips parting with a gasp. I take the chance to slide my tongue between them, and she lets me in eagerly, fingers tightening on my neck. A soft, sigh of a moan leaves her as my tongue touches hers, tasting her.

It's even better than I remember.

All sweet sugar and spice, exactly like the woman herself, and it's all I can do not to throw her over my shoulder and take her upstairs to my room. Instead, I shift our bodies, pressing her against the wall and grinding into her as I devour her mouth. I'm already hard at her mere touch, and when she feels it, another sexy sound leaves her, her hips shifting closer into mine. In response, I groan, a hand moving to her hip to adjust her, sliding a thigh between her legs, her silky dress hiking up a bit as I continue to kiss her deep, our tongues twining.

She doesn't take a moment to overthink anything. Instead, her hips start shifting, grinding against me, and the groan that comes from me this time comes deep from my chest. My lips move down her neck, and I use my hand on her hip to move her against me, guide her, to encourage her to take what she needs. I'm out of my fucking mind with need and want, fueled by the quiet moans leaving her lips, by the throbbing in my cock. I remember what she sounded like when she came, and I want to hear it again.

Right before the moment I break, before I take this much further than either of us would be comfortable in a public place, quiet giggles fill the room, and my body tenses against hers, as I realize someone else is in here. The reality of what I just did—what *we* just did— comes crashing over me. I just pressed a guest against a wall in a room, ground my dick into her and made her moan while I kissed her. It's a major lapse in judgment and probably breaks *something* in the lengthy contract I signed when I became a Daydream employee, but I also can't find it in me to care.

When I finally get the guts to look down at her, her eyes are wide and knowing, a small smirk playing on her lips.

Not a hint of shame or embarrassment present.

This fucking woman.

"I really have to get to the party," she whispers, her voice husky. I take a moment to avert my eyes from her and check my watch, real- izing I have a meeting in twenty minutes myself that I should already be in my office preparing for. I nod before moving, making sure she has sure footing before stepping back. "We should do this again, though. Soon."

"No," I say firmly.

"Excuse me?" She asks with a laugh.

"This was a lapse in judgment, I told you, I don't have time or space to deal with whatever you're looking for."

"Wild of you to assume I'm looking for anything."

I stare at her and decide I need to nip this. Once and for all. Because I can't have Josie Montgomery blurring my mind for the next week and a half. I'm here for one reason, and that is to figure out what the *fuck* is going on at this resort. Instead, I'm taking her to private breakfasts and rushing to her when an employee breaks a leg and following her into coat checks.

"I don't think—" I go to argue, but she ignores me, talking over me with her voice low, only for my ears, with a smile that is dangerous and beautiful and completely biting.

"You know, you play uptight asshole businessman who doesn't give a shit really well, but I like the other side of you better.'

"Other side?" I ask, even though I know I shouldn't.

"The bossy side of you. Quiet, demanding." She licks her lips, then hums like she likes the way they taste. "The making me feel good side." I fight the urge to grab myself and readjust my cock because that would be far too obvious, but her eyes and her teasing grin shift there anyway, knowing. She takes a step to the door, her eyes still on me, a playful smile on her lips. "See you around, Rowan," she says, coy and knowing in that playful voice I so desperately want to hate but can't find it in me to do so.

"Later, troublemaker," I say without thinking, saying the name I've assigned her in my mind. Her eyes light with pleasure before she winks, then turns and heads out the door.

I stand there for long moments, staring at the door she left, completely dazed, the way she always seems to leave me, only popping out of my reverie when someone else walks in. That's when I turn to the bag she was moving through. A blue bag with an orange dress doesn't quite match up, so before I can think twice, I'm opening the bag she was digging through and slide out the wallet to find who owns it.

I won't lie: I expect to see Jenny, Gene Michaels' new girlfriend's name on the license, but I don't. Instead, I see the woman who is with Horace. I stare at it for a beat, trying to understand what interest Josie would have with her before sliding it back into the bag, not wanting anyone to catch the VP of Operations digging through guests' bags.

I could confront her, go right into that party and ask what the fuck she's doing here, because in my gut, I know it's not to enjoy the sun and sand.

But I don't. I know myself too well, know if I do, I might make a stupid, rash decision, like throwing her over my shoulder and taking her to my room, the potential of her being the journalist leaking information to *Fan Magazine* be damned. Instead, I return to my office and resume work.

But later that night, after two more meetings with resorts on the other side of the world, my mind is still reeling, and there's just one dark-haired beauty to blame.

TWENTY-TWO

JOSIE

I don't tell Rory about the kiss right away, unsure of how to approach it. It helped that while I was showering, Rory caught a break and finally found an entry point into the resort's cameras, which means we've been messing with the different live feeds to see what we have access to. She hasn't been able to hack into the cloud for previously recorded videos, but it's definitely a step in the right direction.

We're in our comfy sleep clothes, sitting on my bed, while Rory types up our daily report on what we've found, who we talked to, and current suspects. Gabriel will review it at some point tomorrow morning, edit, and send a censored version to the client, primarily focusing on our current suspects and the reasons and methods we've used to narrow them down.

While she does that, I'm trying to figure out how to tell Rory what happened in the coat room as well as what I found out.

"Oh, it looks like we have an update from Gabriel," Rory says, reading over her email before reading a line out loud. "Intel Annette wanted to send your way after seeing your most recent suspect list was that Horace Greenfeld recently purchased a very large share of

Daydream resorts. It seems his loss is their gain, as he decided not to pursue his own chain, but instead invest in theirs."

I look at Rory, intrigued. "So is he no longer a suspect?" I ask.

She shrugs. "It would seem that way. I can't imagine that he would want to devalue his purchase after he's already done. Before, yeah, so it would be cheaper, but not after."

"We can probably back-burner him at the very least. If anything happens where he's obviously lied, then bring him back, but for now, we have enough to worry about."

I nod in agreement, then take a deep breath, knowing this is a perfect segue. Before I can find the courage, though, Rory turns her body away from her computer, looking at me fully with a motherly expression on her face.

"Hey, Josie?" she says in a gentle tone.

"Yeah?" I ask.

"Are you going to tell me what happened?"

I decide my best bet is playing stupid. "What?"

"You disappeared, then came back twenty minutes later, nearly *whistling* to yourself, lipstick a mess."

My jaw drops open. "You didn't tell me my lipstick was a mess!" I nearly shout, and she smiles.

"It's not that the lipstick was all over; it's just that it was nearly gone."

I groan and put my head in my hands. I should have brought my lip *stain*; it's totally kiss-proof. But I didn't think to, because I don't do this.

I don't kiss my marks.

I'll flirt, I'll tease, I'll imply, I'll touch an arm and show cleavage, but I never cross that line. I never blur things because, in this job, your focus needs to be absolutely precise.

When I lift my head, she's staring at me still, raising a knowing eyebrow as if I'm a petulant teenager caught with a hickey.

"Okay. So..." I start, taking a deep breath and remembering the super hot moment in the coatroom. I haven't given myself much space to think about it since I had been at at the cocktail party and then we had the huge break with the camera feeds, but now that I have the space to... Still, I owe an explanation to my partner, so I continue. "I saw Horace and Regina coming our way, and also Gene and Jenny. Regina waved Horace into the party and said she was going to the bathroom, which was clearly bullshit because she stopped in a corner to watch Gene and Jenny then wrote something in that notebook of hers. She tried to get into the party right after, but—"

"Bags weren't allowed in," Rory says, picking up the thread.

"Exactly. So she put her bag in the bag room and I went to...investigate." Her eyes go wide, and I hurry to explain. "There was no one in the room, I swear. But I did find this," I say, reaching for and scrolling on my phone to show her the photos I took.

"Fuck. So the leak *is* her." I nod. "Have you sent these to Gabriel yet?" I shake my head and watch as she sends them to herself. "I'll add them to the daily report," she says, moving across the room to her computer to do just that. "Continue," she orders.

I sigh. "And then Rowan came in."

Her body stills, and she looks up at me. "Did you distract him?"

"I tried," I say, then drop my face in my hands when she raises an eyebrow. "I tried flirting, but he's immune to my charm, Rory."

She lets out a snort of a laugh. "No, he is not."

"Yes, he is!" I say, throwing my hands into the air. "That's why I had to kiss him. To distract him from asking too many questions about my being in the room!"

"You *kissed him*?" she asks, finally stopping her typing and looking up at me. It's not so much *shock* on her face, but more like awe. She knows this isn't what I do: I don't kiss my marks. I don't kiss suspects. I don't kiss leads. I'm all talk and no follow-through, only ever flirting and nothing more.

"He walked in on me investigating! Kissing him was my diversion."

"Jesus, Josie!" she says, more laugh than reprimand. "So he caught you going through her bag?" I shrug.

"I don't think so. I told him it was my bag. It was bright blue, but he's a man. He's not going to realize it wasn't mine." I look away, remembering it all once again before shrugging. "It doesn't matter. He's not really *into* me. He's...immune."

She stares for a long moment before shaking her head and turning to her computer and continuing to type out the email before hitting send. My phone pings with a new message. I know I was CCd on it, but I can't even double-check because then she's turning to me fully and looking at me with intention.

"I'm saying this with so much love, Jose," she starts, and my gut clenches because she only starts a sentence like this if she thinks I'm going to completely deny whatever fact she's trying to share. "But the man is so deeply into you, and from what I'm seeing, has been for *some time*. Like since-you-were-in-college, some time."

I roll my eyes and shake my head, laughing her off. "He likes the man-eater. He doesn't like Josie." I laugh, but Rory doesn't, instead looking at me with a soft, sad tilt of her lips.

"God, I'm so tired of you doing this to yourself."

"What?"

She stands then, moving to the couch and sitting next to me with a face I don't really want to see, before taking a sigh and reaching for my hand.

"I love you more than anything. My best friend, my partner, I trust you with my life, literally. You know that. So when I say this, I need you to know I'm saying it with all the love in the world." I grimace at her out-of-character, mushy statement.

"I feel like I'm not going to like whatever it is you're about to say."

"You might not at first, but eventually, like always, you'll see that I'm a genius and always know best.

"You are your own worst enemy, Josie," she says softly.

"They're all the same, Rory. Men like the appeal of me: they like the flirting, they like the body, they like the package. They don't like the reality. They surely don't like that my job is flirting with other people, typically men. They don't like that I work non-stop. They don't like that I'm unreachable sometimes." I could go on for days, but this is not the first time she's heard this rant.

"The right one will."

"Oh, and the right one is Rowan, I suppose?" I ask with a laugh, ignoring the flutter in my belly.

"I don't know," she says honestly, with a shrug. "What I do know is you're into him. What I do know is, despite yourself and despite seeing the worst in people, you want a relationship. What I do know is that in the four years of working with you, you've never dated someone."

I roll my eyes, eager to shift the focus. "Is this *not* the pot calling the kettle black?"

She confidently shakes her head. "No." I raise an eyebrow at her reply, and she continues. "I don't *want* a man. I am incredibly happy with my vibrators and my hand, and my work. You are a people person. You want a person, Josie."

I twist my lips, not liking the way emotion is bubbling in my chest with her words.

My best friend, though nerdy and introverted and with her thick wall keeping out anyone she doesn't want to see in, has a soft soul. She continues to stare at me before she sighs and smiles softly at me.

"But you'll get there eventually. When the right one proves himself worthy," she says. "In the meantime, let's figure out who is screwing with this place." I smile then and nod in appreciation at her change in subject before we get to work.

An hour later, Rory is still trying to sneak into the backend of the security system, while I'm moving from live feed to live feed, trying to find something of note and trying not to get unbearably bored.

"I've got it," Rory whispers, and my body lights up with excitement.

"Really?" She nods, continuing to stare at her screen.

"Yeah. I think I can get into the cloud, but I need to get into the security room." My excitement builds while also tempering.

"The security room?" I ask.

She nods, then gives me a wide smile. "Want to play lookout tomorrow?"

TWENTY-THREE

ROWAN

"You look like shit," Annette says early the next morning on our weekly call, which I have been struggling to pay attention to. I've only been able to think about two things since I left that coat room last night: Josie's lips and the purse she was rifling through.

"What?"

"You look like shit," she repeats.

"Well, we're currently dealing with someone who is becoming increasingly dangerous and loud with their sabotage, and I can't figure out who it is or why it's happening. Not sure how I'm expected to sleep tight knowing that." She looks at me, then shakes her head.

"No, it's not that. You look... You look guilty."

"Guilty?" I ask, my pulse pounding because I *am* guilty. Last night in a public space, I pushed a guest against a wall and had her grinding her pussy against my leg. I would have made her come like that if we hadn't been interrupted.

"I actually," I start, then sigh, running a hand over my face. I didn't *want* to tell Annette about what happened, but I know I have to. "I actually have to talk to you about something."

"Oh?" Her eyes go wide with panic. "Rowan, do not tell me you're quitting. I'll do whatever I have to to keep you." That makes me smile a bit, relieving a bit of the pressure.

"No, but I'll keep that in mind next time I want a raise." She rolls her eyes but doesn't continue so I move forward. "I know that..." I hesitate, trying to pick the best words as I always do, but ever since Josie came back into my life, that skill seems to have disappeared. "I know that in the handbook for resort employees, fraternizing with guests is against the code of conduct."

A small smile flitters over Annette's face before melting away as she crosses her arms over her chest and leans back. "Okay."

"I'm not fully clear about how that impacts upper management and resort guests," I say low, since I read multiple handbooks and couldn't quite figure out if I fall under that umbrella. "But if it does, I need to disclose to you that a guest currently at the resort is an old acquaintance of mine and we've....well, we've reconnected."

"An acquaintance?"

I nod, then explain. "Yes. We went to the same university when I went back for my MBA, and she lives in Hudson City. We bumped into each other at a bar the day before I came here, and she came out to stay at the resort the following day."

"So you're...what? Dating her?"

"I mean, I haven't really had time to..." I decide this is not the path to go down and shift gears. "We keep bumping into each other, so I've spent some time with her since coming to the resort. Last night we, um." I can feel the blush burning on my cheeks and avoid the small screen in the corner that shows my own face, knowing I'm red. "We kissed last night."

Annette nods.

"What's her name?"

My brow furrows because I'm not sure what that has to do with anything, but I give it to her anyway.

"Josie. Josephine Montgomery."

"Josie. Pretty name."

"Yeah. Um...am I in trouble?"

"What?"

"Am I going to be fired? I know she's a guest, but—" I stop my rambling when her laugh fills the room.

"You're not fired. In fact, I'm relieved, if we're being honest."

"What?"

"My god, Rowan. All you do is work. When was the last time you took some time for yourself?"

"I—" I start, but she shakes her head and cuts me off.

"I'm proud of you for growing this business as quickly as you have. Your determination has clearly paid off. I've always valued and admired your hard work, but I also want you to be here a long time. If you burn yourself out by having no life, you're going to quit and pull a Don Draper, join some kind of meditation commune, and we'll never hear from you again."

"I think that's a little—"

"You work too hard, Rowan. You're going to send yourself into an early grave. You should go enjoy your success a bit."

"I'm the youngest VP of Operations this company has ever had. I didn't get that by sitting back and doing nothing."

"But what is it all for?"

It stops me; my body jolts with the words. "Excuse me?"

"What's it all for? What are you working yourself to the bone for?"

"I—" I hesitate when I realize I...I can't answer.

"Just something to consider, you know? If you're doing it all just for the ego of it all, then I hope you're getting what you want out of it, but that's not very you. You like the accomplishment, but you don't like the bragging rights. So what's it all for?"

"I..." I say, confused. "I want to make sure you know that your investment in me is worthwhile. I owe it to you. I would never have gotten where I am if you hadn't championed me."

There's silence before she speaks. "Is that why you have no social life? You want to prove yourself to me?"

"I have a social life," I say, but don't deny the other part.

"Dinners with clients do not count, and you know it. Rowan. I..." She sighs like this is now weighing heavy on her. "I think when you get back, we need to talk about this concept in your head that you owe me anything other than doing your best and living your life." Silence fills the line before she continues. "So no, Rowan, I will not fire you for having a previous connection with a guest and acting on it. In fact, I insist you take some time during her stay to do something with her. A hike, a dinner, a spa treatment, I don't care. But do something for *you*."

I open my mouth to argue, but she shakes her head.

"I don't want to hear it. I insist." I roll my eyes are her tone. "I have to get to another meeting, but one last thing before I go."

"Yeah?" I ask.

"The celebrity leak was found."

My pulse skips a beat.

"The leak was found? You couldn't have started with this?" I ask, and she laughs.

"We had other things to cover. But yes, late last night I was brought a name and we've since been able to confirm it was them," Annette confirms. "They've been escorted off the premises and blacklisted across all resorts and those of a few competitors with whom I'm friendly. We all agreed that we need to set a precedent for this kind of behavior."

My mind is reeling, though I can't deny the rush of relief moving through me.

"Who was it?" I ask, curious.

"An..." There's clicking on the other end before she responds. "A Regina Sands, though she was staying at the resort under Regina Reynolds. Her first name matches with the stays surrounding every other leak." The name tugs on my mind, but I set it aside for a moment to ask the more important questions.

"Is she responsible for the issues at the resort?"

A sigh fills my ears, and I know the answer before she even says it.

"Unfortunately, I don't believe she is related to the issues we're facing. I can't see a reason why she would want these resorts to suffer if she's making a pretty penny on revealing the secrets of our clients. From what I can tell, she received her intel from a popular celebrity travel planner."

"Hmm," I hum, my mind working overtime. "Wait, she's been spending a ton of time with Horace—"

Again, Annette sighs.

"I know. Trust me, I know. It seems just to be a coincidence, Horace giving attention to anyone who gave him the time of day."

"Oh, come on, Annette, he—"

"If he hadn't invested in the company three days before he left for his stay, I would agree. Or even if the news that we were struggling with this issue got out, impacted our stock, and *then* he bought it, I'd get it. But when I spoke with him this morning, he said he was happy to be on board, and I quote, despite the out-of-our-control issues we were facing, he believes in the company and, more importantly, he believes in you."

I fight the urge to feel pride, especially since I can't fucking stand Horace Greenfeld as of late, something I tell myself has *nothing* to do with his flirting with Josie.

With her name on my mind, that niggling fact that I set aside comes back to the surface.

Regina Reynolds. Regina Sands. I saw that name recently.

At the cocktail party last night.

Where I found Josie going through someone's purse—*Regina's* purse. When I caught her, she distracted me successfully with her charm and her lips.

What if...my mind reels, trying to put two and two together and unable to make four. Lately, I've been thinking about the past year that I bumped into her, and noticing a pattern that brought alarm to my veins: of the eight men I can remember she's been on dates within the last year with, six of them faced some kind of exposé. Embezzlement, cheating, a messy divorce. If I looked into it, how close would those exposés be to when she was out with them?

I had thought for a moment Josie might be some kind of journalist, that maybe *she* was our leak. She said she was a micro influencer, which I was able to confirm through my own research. However, it would be the perfect cover to gain access to exclusive spaces, places where celebrities might be.

But now...

Now I'm even more confused.

A phone rings on the other end of the call, and Annette sighs. "I have to go, Rowan. Let me know if you need anything at all. And make sure to rest and take care of yourself. You sound like shit."

I laugh at her constant refrain and shake my head, trying to knock Josie out of it.

"Will do," I say absentmindedly, turning back to the lobby as Annette hangs up. Sliding my phone into my pocket, I step out onto the balcony of my office to get some fresh air and attempt to clear my mind. Unfortunately, I find myself even more distracted as I peer down to the patio before the pool deck. The sun catches on gleaming dark hair, my eyes narrowing in on it instantly as if it was singing to me and me alone, and when the owner of the thick ponytail turns, that theory is confirmed when I see Josie and Rory. They're whispering to one another, heads moving from side to side like they're looking for something before Rory nods and they move left, out of my line of sight.

Without thinking, I close the balcony door and head out to my office towards the lobby.

When I get there, I look for dark hair and devilish curves. When I don't see her, I turn towards the direction I saw her and Rory head and almost miss her as she slowly moves down a side hall. It's an employee hall, mostly, just a stock room, control room, and a side entrance to a break room, so there's no reason for her to be here, but

I'm so stuck on the thrill of finding her, I don't let my mind wander too much.

"What are you doing?" I ask her back, my voice the only noise in the quiet hallway. Her body jolts with panic before she whirls around to me, wide-eyed and nervous.

"Oh hey, hi, Rowan," she says, that mask falling across her face as she gives me a soft smile.

"What are you doing, Josie?"

"Me?" she asks, putting a hand to her chest.

"Yes, you. There's no one else in the hallway." She looks around to confirm that, and her body eases a bit.

"I...uh...I was looking for more towels. I spilled some water, and now mine are all wet."

"You could have called the front desk," I suggest, closing the gap until there's just two feet between us.

"Oh, I didn't want to bother anyone."

"So you're just...snooping around my hotel looking for towels?"

Her head tips to the side and I know a snarky response is coming.

"Your hotel? I didn't realize you owned the place. Very fancy. What are you doing over on this side of the resort? Don't you have work to do or whatever?"

"Don't change the subject, Josie." I take a step closer, and even though I tell myself it's because I'm ready to play her at her own game, I can't deny that my body feels like a magnet drawn to hers, desperate for contact.

"But there are so many better subjects I could change to." I feel her tease in my cock and force myself to ignore it.

"Your room is in another tower. Why are you looking for towels over here?" A flash of nerves comes over her face before it's gone, and she smiles.

"Aww, you remember where I'm staying?" She flutters her lashes at me, and something in me snaps. I take another step forward, and she takes one back, the pattern continuing until her back is against the wall, my hands planting against the wall on either side of her face, not touching her but caging her all the same.

She's an expert at fogging my mind and making me question everything, but now I'm thinking it's intentional. She's intentionally confusing and distracting me, and I'm dying to know why.

"Is this what you do?" I ask, stepping closer and pinning her in place. "Use your charm to get out of trouble? Flirt and flip your hair and bat your eyelashes until whatever poor schmuck you've got your sights set on forgets what they're really doing?"

She smiles wide and somehow, in my heart of hearts, I know that's the truth.

I don't know what Josephine Montgomery is doing here, but I somehow know in my gut it's not because she wanted to take in the sights of the Keys.

I told her we wouldn't be kissing again, and I think part of me knew even as I said it, I was lying. I need to kiss Josie more than I need to breathe.

"My charm doesn't work on you," she whispers. "It never has."

"I didn't realize you were so blind," I reply just as softly. A small gasp leaves her lips, and I lean down, pressing mine to the pulse in her neck, feeling it pound against my lips. "I've been charmed by you since you turned me down six years ago."

Her body stiffens at my words, but I don't let myself get too caught up in her, get distracted, not when it's my turn to distract her until she confesses something. *Anything.*

"You know, this morning, my boss informed me that our leak was found." Her body stills, and my adrenaline increases at some innate knowledge that I was right; she has some kind of link to it.

"Why are you telling me this?" she whispers, attempting to show disinterest and failing. Without hesitation, I reveal my hand.

"Because I think you know something, Josie."

"I don't know anything," she says too quickly. I smile then, brushing my thumb over the spot in her cheek where that fucking dimple usually lies.

"You're a good liar; I'll give you that. Most people wouldn't see it. But I've been watching for a year, obsessing over every moment. Watching you flip your hair, dissecting what's real and what is bullshit. I don't know what you know, but you know something. I just can't figure out what. I know you're not here just to take in the sun and sights."

I shift a hand and cup her cheek, a thumb brushing over her full bottom lip, and my eyes focus there as her tongue darts out, tasting me. I bite back a groan, determined to hide how she impacts me just as well as she does. When I shift my gaze back to her eyes, hers are shifting back to me at the same time.

"Kiss me, Rowan," she whispers, a plea in her words. My brows furrow in confusion at the stark change of subject, but then her hands are lifting, one cupping me behind the neck, the other holding my cheek.

"What?"

"Kiss me. God, it's all I've been able to think about. Please. Kiss me." A long moment passes as I take in her words, the need and desire in them, as I pick through them to determine is she's being truthful. She is, I decide, truthful in her assertion that it's all she's been able to think of.

But something tells me this is also another distraction, another move in the game she's playing, so I shake my head gently.

"I'm not kissing you again until I figure out what you're doing here, Josie."

I expect her to tell me she doesn't know a thing.

I expect her to tell me that I'm insane, making things up.

I expect her, in her own way, to use her power of distraction and change the subject once more.

But she doesn't.

Instead, she smiles.

"Well, then I guess we'll just have to continue this dance next time we run into each other," she says.

I shake my head, disagreeing. "I think not."

Her phone beeps, and she smiles; for some reason, she looks satisfied. Then she ducks under my arm and steps away from me before walking down the hall. When she's a few feet away, she looks over her shoulder at me and smiles.

"Next time you pin me against a wall, I really hope you're ready to make good on your promises, Rowan. I'm tired of the teasing."

And then she's gone.

TWENTY-FOUR

Suspect list for Daydream resorts based on current intel:

- Daniel, the General Manager
- Jonas, head of security
- Tanya, the spa manager
- Jealous redhead

TWENTY-FIVE

ROWAN

After I tell Josie I won't kiss her until she tells me what she's doing here, I make a vow to stay away from her to avoid her further messing with my head. I didn't go to the beach cabanas when I saw her and her friend there yesterday, after I found her in that hallway, and I didn't interrupt when I saw her flirting with a guest at lunch today. I didn't find an excuse to bump into her when she was wearing yet another tiny dress to an early dinner at one of the more formal restaurants, nor when she stopped for a drink on her way back to her room.

I've been able to sate my need for her through the resort's CCTV footage. For better or worse, watching her has become a habit of mine. Some might call it a sickness. It's been almost three full days since I felt Josie's whimpers while she tried to ride my leg, and I have to say, it may have been hotter than hearing her moan my name in Dante's office as she came.

It's been a day and a half since she begged me to kiss her in the hall, and I turned her down. I thought it was a testament to my restraint and a turning point in my obsession and distraction, but now, as I flick through the live cameras to see if she ventured back out this evening, I realize I've just funneled it into a different format.

At least this one doesn't reveal to her how deeply I'm entangled in her web.

That justification itself is just another example of just how fucked I am. But until I can figure out what's happening in this resort, I can't allow myself to give in to the distraction she poses.

I'm on a call now, listening to someone blather on about numbers and margins and reservations, shit that normally I would already have memorized, but I can't find it in me to care.

No, instead, I'm flicking through feeds to try and find where she might be.

"And in Q4 we anticipate—"

That's when I see it: Josie at the employee party.

Josie's hand on the arm of one of the guys who manages the landscaping, her head tipped back, and, despite the feed being silent, I can hear her laugh. He says something else, and she takes a step closer, flirting in that way she does. A part of me recognizes the sexy look on her face is different than the one she uses when she's talking to me, but I still can't focus enough to seem to care.

I wish I could say the fury running through me is because there is a guest at an employee get-together, but I can't. Not in the least.

"I'm sorry, I have to go. Can you just send me an email with the notes and let me know if there's anything you need from me?" I say, interrupting his spiel. I know all eyes in the meeting are on me and confused since this is so out of character, but I just don't care. My eyes are on the feed where Josie's body is swaying to music I can't hear, and I know every man in that room is watching her.

"Yeah, of course. I—" But I can't hear, because I'm closing my computer and standing, making my way out of my room and down the hall to the elevator where I know the employee party is being held tonight. We try to do these once every month or so to encourage employee morale.

When I step into the room, it's loud and chaotic, laughter and chatter filling the room, music playing loudly, and no one notices me enter quietly.

No one except for Josie. It's as if she's pulled towards me subconsciously, like she feels the same unexplainable magnetism I feel towards her, like I could find her in any room, any time. Her ass is tipped into someone from the kitchen staff's crotch as she grinds, his hands hovering over her hips but not touching, thank fuck. I feel my jaw get tight as I note the tiny tank top she's wearing, clearly without a bra.

That's when she smiles at me. Smiles like she gets some kind of satisfaction at knowing I'm here, watching her, exuding jealousy. I wonder if she somehow knows how hard I fought finding her.

The song ends and she stands up, turning to her dance partner and thanking him before walking off the makeshift dance floor, a pep in her step as she approaches me.

"My, my, didn't expect to see you here, Rowan."

"What are you doing here, Josie?"

"What do you mean?"

"This is a staff party. You're not staff."

She shrugs as if that doesn't matter at all. "I was invited."

"So what you're saying is you flirted your way into an invite?"

She smiles sweetly. "What does it matter to you?"

I tighten my jaw because it shouldn't matter to me. Not at all, but every fucking time I even think about her moving her attentions to some other man, I feel absolutely violent. It's been like that for years, but now that she's at my resort and I have no way of ignoring it, it's only gotten worse.

"You know, you keep getting all flustered and jealous when you see me getting any sort of attention. Seems like fan behavior," she says before I can answer, her eyelashes fluttering as she takes a step closer to me. It wouldn't take much to close the gap between us, to press her body against mine, to press my lips to hers, to tell everyone in this fucking room that she's mine.

But there's something about this game we're playing that I like too much to end now. The flirting, the teasing, the tempting and taunting, the push and pull. I like it far too much.

"Trust me, troublemaker, I am not jealous," I say with a small shake of my head, and her own smile spreads, her voice going low and sultry.

"Oh, but you are. We both know it. You've been jealous for months that it's never been you, haven't you? That's why you're in such utter denial of how badly you want me."

One more tiny step to me, not touching but close enough to feel her body heat.

"Whatever you want to believe, Josie."

"Hmm. I guess we'll see, won't we?" she says. Just then, the music starts, and a noise of approval goes through the room, a dozen or so people moving to the center to start dancing. That's when Rory comes over, grabbing Josie and tugging her to the center. But when she looks over her shoulder, her smile has gone wicked, and I know I just started a war.

Ten minutes later, I'm still at the employee get-together even though I should probably be in my office getting something done. But I can't seem to find the will, so instead I'm leaning against a wall, watching her. The makeshift dance floor is full, bodies pressed against each other, and Josie and Rory have spent the entire time with their bodies pressed to each other, laughing and having a good time. I can handle that.

I can handle watching Josie have a good time with her friend, her eyes occasionally shifting around the room to find me and smiling when she does.

Something tells me that even if someone was lucky enough to lock down Josie, they'd have to be okay with that flirty side of her, and in that moment I realize I could handle this. I could handle the wild version of her, the flirt, the chaos, so long as at the end of the day, it's my eyes she searches for in a room.

That is, until a pair of hands move to her hips, tugging her back away from Rory and into a man's chest. I recognize him as Dax from food service, and I also note the quick flash of panic in Josie's eyes. I almost move to interrupt, but the nerves melt when she looks through the room again, finding me. That jealousy she accused me of having flares, and she smiles before looking over her shoulder to the man behind her. She keeps moving against him, and he returns the look.

Then her eyes return to me as they start to move together, her hips swaying to the beat of the music, their bodies moving in time. That smile on her lips goes knowing, like she understands what she's doing, and I fight the urge to tighten my jaw, to give anything away to her. Instead, I settle in against the wall, watching her with a challenging raise of my eyebrow. She shakes her head and that smile grows before one hand moves to cover his on her hip and the other moves up and back, cupping the back of his neck. Her hips moving against his seductively, and I'd think she was being genuine, actually enjoying this dance with that ass, but her eyes tell me the truth.

It's tease. A taunt. A test.

A challenge.

Come get me. Win me over. Prove you want me. Take what you want.

My mind is screaming at me to do just that, despite my better judgement, despite knowing that I've got enough on my plate to add the whirlwind that is Josie. I'm here for work, not fun, after all.

But you can do both at the same time, can't you? My mind reminds me. It goes over the conversation with Annette yesterday, her telling me she worries about me, about my not having a life, not having balance.

And most importantly, how in the last week I've had more fun arguing with Josie, despite the train wreck that is this resort, than I can remember.

I'm lost in thought, battling over my decision when I watch Dax press his lips to her neck. It's not excessive, just a gentle brush of lips on skin, but it sets off something in me, snapping that final tether on my restraint.

Fuck it.

Fuck this game we're playing.

Fuck keeping my distance.

Fuck whatever secret she's hiding away.

God, right now? Fuck this job if it means I lose the first woman who has made me feel this wild and untamed.

I push off the wall, stalking towards Josie in the middle of the dance floor. Her hips continue to shift against Dax, grinding and moving as I approach, but a smile pulls at her lips like she knows she's won.

"Hey, Dax, do you mind if I talk to Ms. Montgomery for a moment?" He stops moving altogether, stepping away and lifting his hands in the air.

"Oh, of course not, Mr. Fisher. I'm sorry, I know she's a guest, but —" I shake my head, not in the mood to argue about the fact that we have many times over insisted that the employee events should be employees only, no guests allowed.

"It's fine. Come on, Josie." I stand there waiting for her to move towards me, but she doesn't. Instead, she stands next to Dax, arms crossed over her chest like a petulant child who is mad that their parent ruined their fun.

It makes me want to drag her into another room, put her over my knee, and spank her.

"Josephine," I say, jaw tight. She continues to glare before finally sighing and moving towards me. When she's close enough to touch, she looks over her shoulder, and her smile beams.

"Two minutes, Dax. Then you owe me a dance." Dax fights a smile, but nods before I finally take Josie's hand.

"Let's go," I say, the words a deep growl as I fight back the suddenly consuming urge to toss her over my shoulder.

"Rowan—" she starts, but stops as I tug her away from the dance floor, my mind moving through options on what rooms are nearby and empty. She stumbles a few times in her tall heels before I tuck an arm around her waist and pull her into my side. The feel of her warmth against me is almost worth the dozen or so eyes following us.

"Rowan," she tries again once we're in a quiet hallway, but I'm holding on by a thread of sanity. There's an empty office right down this hall, and I just need to make it there.

"Not yet," I say through gritted teeth as my hand reaches into my pocket for the universal keycard that will open the door. The lock gives a satisfying whir and click when I scan the card, and then I'm whipping the door open and pulling Josie inside before closing us in.

Then I'm pressing her against the wall with my body, no longer having any reason not to. Something in me calms at the feel, at having her alone, at her being mine, if only for this moment. That's when her smile goes wide and cunning, like she knows she just won it all.

"Not jealous, huh?"

I shake my head, unable to fight a smile of my own. "Not even a little."

"You're such a fucking liar," she says with a laugh.

I stare down at her, at her soft, full pink lips, at her wide doe eyes, at the way her chin is tipped up just a hint, waiting for what's to come.

But I want her to cross the line. I want to get my own tiny win in this game of ours.

"Kiss me," I order.

"Excuse me?"

"Kiss me." Then I give her more, a confession of sorts. "Because if I'm the one who breaks, I think I might never stop."

I feel her body shiver at the promise, and when she looks at me, I think she's going to do as I asked. Until she smiles.

"Were you jealous?" Her voice is whisper soft.

"What?"

"Were. You. Jealous? Watching me dance with that man?"

There's a moment of silence, and I know in my gut that this is the turning point between us. This is the moment where I can either confess the truth and win her, or I can lie and lose her.

And I don't want to lose Josie.

"I've never wanted to hit someone more than I did watching you flirt with him on the fucking CCTV. I'm so fucking lost for you that

I'm stalking you, scraping through soundless camera feeds for the smallest snippet of you." Her breathing halts, her eyes wide and panicked as she looks over my face, and I lift a hand from where it's braced on the door, moving a lock of her hair back behind her ear. It's gentle, a stark contrast to how I actually feel in this moment. "You were right," I confess. "Every time I saw you sitting across from some asshole we both know didn't deserve you, all dressed up and beautiful and way too fucking tempting for your own good, I'd be pissed it wasn't me. So yeah. I was jealous tonight. And I was jealous of Jeff on the hike and at the pool bar, and when you were flirting with Horace, and every single time I saw you out with someone who wasn't me. Is that what you want me to tell you? Is that—"

But suddenly, my rant is over, cut short. Because then she's kissing me.

Somehow, it's even sweeter than the time in the coat rack, hotter than the time in Dante's office, because she's the one taking the reins. Her fingers are in my hair, tightening her grip to pull me closer to her as I dip to devour her, to match her energy. We kiss like that for long, hot moments before her tongue slides against my lips, and I take over, a hand moving to her jaw to hold her where I want her. Her hips start to move, shifting and grinding against where I'm already hard for her, and I move my hand from her jaw to her hip, pulling her further into me.

Her lips move down my neck, tasting and licking and sucking, each kiss going straight to my cock.

"I thought you weren't going to kiss me again until I spilled some deep-seeded secret," she murmurs against my skin, and I laugh at how I completely forgot about that threat of mine.

"I don't fucking care if you're in the CIA right now, Josie, not when the promise of tasting you is fucking suffocating me." She moans at my words, and a satisfied smile pulls at my lips.

And in that moment, I know it's true: I don't care who she is or what she's doing here, because in my gut, I know she isn't here to mess with me or my hotel. I don't know why she's here but right now, I don't fucking care.

TWENTY-SIX

JOSIE

It started as me kissing Rowan, but now he is undeniably kissing *me*. "I knew you'd break," I moan as his lips move over mine, as his tongue tastes me, needy and frantic in a way that makes my mind fuzzy and common sense blur. There's just him and me and the feeling of his skin on mine. His hands are moving to my hips to hike my skirt up. I wonder if he's going to fuck me here, against this wall.

I'd let him. Right now? I would *absolutely* let him.

"You're such a fucking brat," he growls against my lips.

"What are you going to do about it?" I whisper, my pussy clenching, a dozen possibilities of what Rowan Fisher could *do to me* rushing through my mind. Finally, he pulls back from the kiss to look me in the eyes, a wide smile on his lips.

"Whatever I want."

My heart skips a beat.

Men like this don't usually do it for me. Men who are all ego and swagger. Men who think they can get any woman with a mere smirk. It's why I've been confused by my attraction to Rowan since I met him, but suddenly, I get it.

He doesn't think he can get *any* women.

He thinks he can get *me*.

And that makes all the difference.

Before I can give any kind of witty response, his hands are moving, his knees bending, and he's lifting me and moving through, from what I can tell, a relatively empty office, towards a desk in the center of the room. He sets me on the very edge then uses his hands to help situate me, hiking up my skirt.

"Does this...does this mean you're done avoiding me and pretending you're not wildly into me?" I ask as he peppers kisses down my neck, my skirt now bunched around my waist. He steps closer, so his body is against mine. The only things between us are his pants and my underwear. He lets out a laugh, the full, free one that I've only ever heard him use when he's talking to me.

"Yeah. I guess it does. There's no point in it, after all." His lips move down my neck as his hand slides up my thigh, his thumb brushing along the gusset of my wet panties. We groan in unison as he does. "I can't seem to resist you."

"You're stuck in my trap," I whisper, my hand moving to his neck to pull his face to mine.

"Gladly."

I want to say something, argue or gloat, but I can't because his hand is going up my thigh then down into my underwear, his hand cupping my pussy and sending all rational thoughts from my mind. My hips arch into him, desperate for something, anything, but he just holds me there.

"Because when I've got you like this," he whispers, hand tensing against me. "You're all mine." His finger slides through my center, pressing against my entrance but not going any further.

"Rowan," I whisper, but I can't say anything else when he slides two thick fingers into me. My eyes drift shut as I moan with pleasure.

"You're so fucking wet," he rasps, sliding them back out and using that wet to circle my clit. "Who are you wet for?"

"You, God, fuck. You."

He chuckles and I'm rewarded for my admission when he slides them back in, harder this time, then crooks those fingers against my g-spot. My head falls forward to his chest as I groan loudly. His free hand moves then, tugging my hair until I look up, pulling another mewl from me at the bite of pain.

"Keep it quiet, troublemaker," he growls low. "Or I'll have to stop."

I shake my head, my eyes wide, the look probably desperate. His fingers continue to move in me, now at a slow, leisurely pace, like he has all the time in the world, like I'm not needy and desperate for him. "There are a lot of people out there. I wouldn't want them to know I'm fingering a guest in here."

I tighten around him, and I know he notices when his lips tip up in a smile.

"I knew you'd be a dirty girl," he mumbles, bending his fingers, and my eyes drift shut as a small whimper leaves my throat. "You like that, don't you? The thought of everyone knowing just what I'm doing in here to you?"

I'm overcome with need as the pleasure builds. As his lips move along my neck like he can't help himself, as his thumb starts to slowly and gently graze over my already swollen clit.

"Rowan," I beg in a whisper.

"What do you need?"

I lick my lips, weighing my options, but land on the truth. "I need you," I whisper.

"How?" A shiver runs through me. "How do you need me, baby?"

"I need you to fuck me," I breathe, my hips moving against his fingers, his hand still in my underwear. A deep, pained groan falls from his lips, and my forehead falls to his shoulder.

"We don't have time for all I want to do to you the first time I slide inside you, Josephine."

I let out a noise close to a whimper, and in any other situation, I'd be embarrassed by it. But not right now. Not when Rowan's fingers are inside of me, not when he's talking so dirty to me.

"But," he says, and my body goes still at the promise that hangs in the single word. "But if you can be a good girl and agree to be quiet, I'll lick this pretty pussy for you." His thumb circles my clit.

"Yes," I whisper frantically, my hips lifting, his fingers going deeper. "Yes, yes, please. I'll be good."

He lets out a guttural noise at my words, and I tighten around his then nearly squeal when he moves to his knees without warning, his fingers leaving my pussy and my panties, gleaming with my wetness in the low light before he uses a thumb to pull the center of my thong to the side. Then he pauses there, kneeling before my cunt, taking me in. A smile stretches across his lips.

"Oh, I'm going to love when I can take my time with this," he whispers reverently to himself before running a finger from my pussy to my swollen bundle of nerves. I watch as he uses his pointer and middle fingers to part me, and when he sees me, he lets out the sexiest, most pleased sigh. His breath hits my center, and I clench, my body begging for something to fill me. "God, you're fucking pretty."

"I need you to—" I start, unafraid to beg, but he shakes his head before sliding a finger inside of me.

"I already know exactly what you like, what you need. I already know your body better than you know it, and I've never even been inside of you."

His thumb pulls my panties further over so his large hand can grip my thigh, and the sting from the fabric against my skin has the pleasure increasing somehow. But I can't focus on that new development, because this head is lower and he's flattening his tongue, running it over me from entrance to clit. He lets out a deep rumble when he tastes me, the vibrations shocking through me and making me buck. But his grip on my leg keeps me in place, his fingertips digging into my soft skin.

When his tongue slides into me and I whimper, my head falls back to my shoulders as I try and catch my breath. The pleasure hits in lightning bolts, but I still need more. I move again, looking down my body at my skirt hiked to my hips, my thong pulled to the side by his thumb, the rest of the hand holding my thigh open, his mouth working me as his fingers pump inside.

It's all-consuming, the pleasure. It's nothing I've ever felt before, so perfect and skilled, not like he's done this hundreds of times to hundreds of women, but like he was trained on exactly what *my body wants*. Like he knows what *I* need, what I crave, and just how to give it to me.

He smiles around my clit as if he knows what he's doing to me and then crooks his fingers. His tongue flicks quick and light over my clit and I know it's going to be huge, I can tell, the kind of orgasm you feel once in a blue moon, the one that washes your body with heat and cold at the same time, the kind that sends your body quaking.

And he knows it's going to give it to me. His eyes lock onto mine as he continues fucking me with his fingers, and I can almost *hear* the demand.

Fucking come, Josie. Come for me.

But he forgets that I like to win every game I play, especially the ones I play with him.

I lift one of the hands I'm using to hold myself up on the desk, moving it to the back of his head and holding him in place before I rock my hips, taking what I need. "Make me come, Rowan," I demand. And when he grunts into my cunt, the vibrations of it mixed with the stronger suck on my clit and the deeper thrust of his fingers, he does just that. I bite my lip as my head falls back, my hips moving in time with the hard thrusts of his fingers as I come, tumbling into the most intense orgasm I can remember, stars blooming behind my eyes as I make every effort not to scream his name.

Slowly, I come back to myself, the sharp pleasure shifting to soft waves as he continues to clean me with his tongue, as he slides his fingers out and looks up the length of my body with a satisfied smile on his lips.

He *knows* he just did well.

Slowly, he stands, moving between my legs and putting his wet fingers near my mouth. Holding his gaze, I lean forward, nearly deep throating the wet digits as I clean them for him. He lets out a rough breath, his hips moving to grind against me before he slides his fingers out. I smile wickedly.

"Your turn?"

He looks torn.

"We don't really have time for that. Someone is going to notice you're missing soon."

I shake my head, then slide off the desk, standing. "I can make it quick. I really should even the scales, after all." I smile then and he mirrors it.

My phone beeps, and I know it's Rory, but still, I ignore it. She's probably looking for me to relay some kind of intel or make sure I'm okay. Nothing that can't wait.

Instead of moving to my phone, I lower myself to my knees, looking up at him with wide eyes and a devilish smile. "You can make it quick, can't you?" I ask. His hand moves, cupping my cheek, thumb moving over my dimple reverently before tangling in my hair.

"With you looking like that? Yeah, I can make it quick." I smile then. My hand moves to his fly, but just as I do, an all-too-familiar ringtone fills the room.

"Fuck," he says.

"Tell me that's not something you have to answer." He reaches into his pocket and looks, closing his eyes in pained dismay. "*Fuck.*"

"What?" I ask, looking up at him, still on my knees. He looks down at me and closes his eyes.

"Never in my life have I regretted getting this fucking job more than in this moment."

"What's wrong, Rowan?" His hand moves to my elbow and he pulls me up to him, pinning me to him with a strong arm and kissing me deep. Despite my earlier orgasm, I feel that need bubbling in my belly once more.

"Work emergency. I gotta go," he says with a groan.

"Emergency?"

I wonder if that's why my own phone is buzzing...if that's why Rory is trying to get in touch with me.

"Knowing you, you'll find out sooner or later."

Now I don't like the sound of *that,* I think to myself. Does that mean he's on to me?

A hand tucks a lock of hair behind my ear. "The little trouble-maker, always finding herself in the middle of problems."

My body relaxes a bit with his explanation, and more so when he presses his lips to mine, this time soft and gentle.

"Next time," he says. "Next time, our phones are getting locked out of the room. No interruptions."

I let out a laugh and shake my head. "Deal."

His eyes flare with desire, and I wonder if he thought I would argue that. I guess with this game we've been playing, that's the tactic I should have taken, but I'm over it. I'm over the game, over pretending I don't want him, over running through hoops to find excuses not to give him to him.

It's complicated and it's messy, but I want to make whatever this is work.

"Tomorrow. Breakfast."

"Tomorrow?" I ask with a smile,

"Yeah. So long as this isn't world-ending." He lifts his phone, which starts ringing again, and he laughs. "Then I want to have breakfast with you." A wide smile spreads across my lips, and fuck, I don't know the last time I felt this light, despite the fact that I know another shit storm is waiting for me the second I leave this room.

"Okay," I whisper. He pulls me in tight, a puff of air leaving my lips with an *oof* before he kisses me, long and deep, but quick.

And when I slip out of the room by his side, the only thing bringing down my high is the guilt I feel over the stolen keycard in my pocket.

TWENTY-SEVEN

JOSIE

"What's going on?" I ask as I enter the room, noting my partner is already there on her computer. I spent a minute alone in the quiet office fixing my clothes and, admittedly, looking around for anything of use, but it seemed like an unused office that held nothing. Once I confirmed that, I walked out of the room and headed right back to our suite.

"A lot," Rory says with a smile. "There was a break-in in one of the rooms."

My eyes widen as I take in her words. "What? A *break-in?*"

"Not long after you disappeared, I did, too. I placed a bug in the staff room next to where the party was, since I figured I could pretend I was drunk and lost if someone caught me in there. Thank god for that, because some alert must have gone out, and the party broke up. A bunch of employees went to the room to gossip. From what I can tell, it was a high roller repeat client whose room was broken into." She pauses like whatever she's going to say next is important, and I brace. "And the cameras went out for five minutes."

"Like the fire," I whisper, sitting on the arm of the couch beside

Rory, whatever buzz of the night had been washing away. "So it was planned?"

She shakes her head. "The cameras being down wasn't scheduled this time."

My eyes widen once more. "So someone did it intentionally?"

She shrugs. "I'm just going by what I've heard in the break room and in the pool house. They say the feed looped previous footage for five minutes during the break-in, so the security didn't realize."

"The employees are talking about it in the pool house?"

"Yeah, the maintenance crew was doing their night tasks and gossiping."

Not for the first time, I'm grateful for Rory's decision to put a bug in there.

"We need to put more in the break rooms," I mumble, contemplatively. Rory nods, though we both know if it were that easy, we would just do it. When she broke into the security control room, we almost got our entire cover blown by Rowan showing up. I was able to distract him, but it's clear he knows something is going on, but hasn't figured it out yet. For now, I'd like to keep it that way.

"The police scanners say nothing was taken from the room, but I can't confirm or deny that."

'Nothing taken?" I ask, confused. "You said it was a high roller client?"

"Yeah. Some tech bro with a lot of zeros behind his net worth."

"There had to be at least *something* in there worth money. Why not take anything?"

She shrugs. "My guess is it's just sabotage. Not them trying to do anything more than in the grand scheme of things hurt the reputation, the safety, and the trust in the organization."

I nod because that makes sense, even if a part of me knows we're missing something important. I just can't see it yet.

"The cameras went out, and this time it wasn't scheduled. It's safe to assume, I would think, that it has to be someone in the security office who has something to do with this?"

"I'd say either someone in security is our guy, or he has an accomplice. Why else would that be happening? Someone with skills and experience is the only one who could feasibly short the cameras like that. I'm not sure *I* could do it just yet. It took me a full week to get into those feeds."

"I want to get to know them a bit, and anyone who has access to that. Can we see it, and who went into that room in the past, say, forty-eight hours?"

"You mean besides me?" Rory asks with a laugh, and I return it, but still she nods. "Yes, I'm already running a search for it, as well as any coding I might be able to find that would lead to how it was shut off and then turned back on. I'm not sure if it was real time or a scheduled loop."

I nod.

"Now, while I'm doing this, tell me what happened," she instructs. "After Mr. Tall, Dark, and Handsome dragged you off." I feel my cheeks flame. I suddenly feel shy, which is so wildly out of character for me. I tell myself it's because I've never done this before, gotten involved while on the job, but deep down, I know it's because it involves *Rowan*.

"What do you mean?"

Rory gives me a head-to-toe before smiling wide and shaking her head, her fingers still moving on her keyboard like some kind of robot.

"Did you get laid?"

"No," I say, my fingers moving to my necklace and playing with it, trying to distract myself. She stops typing finally and continues to look me over, assessing like a mother trying to test her daughter for lies.

"Yeah, you don't have the *I finally got dick* look about you. But you do have...a look." I continue to stare, knowing that avoiding her eyes will just make her more suspicious, and then, finally, she smiles. "He made you come. Ate you out?" A blush burns on my cheeks. "God, I'm good at this." She laughs before looking back at her computer screen. "Still nothing for him?"

I roll my eyes. "No, he also got the SOS call and had to leave before I could return the favor."

"Was it good?"

I nod. "So good, Rory. Like shouldn't be legal, good."

She smiles then, and my mind wanders over the last few hours and how it felt like Rowan and I had actually made...progress. He clearly still is suspicious of me, but I think he's moving past it. But it puts me in such a strange spot that makes my stomach tie in knots. Rory continues looking at me, reading my face before her brows furrow.

"What's wrong? I thought it was good?"

"I like him," I whisper, almost *ashamed* to say it.

"Glad you can finally admit it," Rory says with a laugh. I look at her, shocked, and she rolls her eyes. "Oh, come *on*. I'm not stupid. You've been in denial from the jump. The day you started complaining about some hot rich guy who crashed your dates, I knew there was something. The universe clearly got tired of you two taking your sweet time, throwing you two together on the same island."

It's strange to hear my very logical best friend discuss topics like the universe and fate.

"I just...I want to make things clean. Everything is very muddled right now, with work and him and...I don't know. Lying to him is really eating at me, but I'm not comfortable sharing who we are or why we're here with him, not yet, at least. Plus, Annette didn't tell him for a reason, and we have to respect that. But I can see...something with him, and I don't like starting it this way."

But I also know it's what has to be done, and honestly, if I want anything beyond the next week or so with Rowan, there will *always* be parts of my life that won't be accessible to him. I have to be okay with that. It's why I've stayed single for so long: men are not okay with this line of work, especially when it includes flirting with men and having to keep secrets. Early in my Mavens career, I tried to have a few boyfriends, but it always ended in heartbreak and disaster.

Since then, I've kept things easy: engaging the occasional fuck buddy to scratch the itch, but keeping them at arms distance. It's worked great, but suddenly, the idea of it makes a distinct loneliness that I've even hidden from my subconscious impossible to ignore.

I want *a person*, and I'm starting to understand I want that with Rowan.

"If he's the right one, he'll be fine with it," Rory says softly, and I nod, knowing she's right. I won't give up this career I love so much for a *man*. Another beat passes before she speaks again. "You know you have to tell Gabriel, right?"

I sigh and nod. "Yeah." I look out the window, at the blue waters crashing on the shore, and for not the first time, I wish I were on a real vacation. God, after this assignment, maybe that's what I'll do. "That can be a tomorrow task, you know? For tonight, can we just...change the subject? Talk about the case instead of my imploding love life, if you can even call it that? Actually," I say, remembering what I snagged. "I got you a gift," I say with a small smile, waving the keycard in the air, trying to ignore the niggling of guilt that runs through me once more at the idea of stealing from Rowan.

"No way," Rory says with a wide smile, reaching out for it. I shrug. "Where did you get that?"

I grimace at the reminder before answering.

"I stole it from Rowan. It fell out of his pocket during the...well, you know, and I slid it under my things then into my pocket without him noticing."

She stares at me, awestruck, before looking over the card. "Is it universal? Is it coded to him? Can you get into any room with this?"

I shrug. "Not sure. I couldn't ask specifics without seeming weird."

"It's fine, I can use this to find out." She digs through her luggage, which is filled with equipment, and finds what looks like a credit card swiper. She plugs it into her computer and grabs the keycard, then opens a new screen and starts typing before scanning the card in the device. I sit patiently as she works her magic, and a few minutes later, she squints at the screen and smiles wide.

"Josie, I don't think you realize how much you just gave us. This will let me hack into the entire system."

"Is that...good?" I ask, half joking because I never know with Rory.

She glares at me like I'm an idiot. "Yes, it's good. It means we can see all card entrances and exits for all employee keycards, past and present. Some are assigned to people or account numbers, but it seems like universal cards like this are generic and not linked to anyone in particular."

"Sounds a bit like a hole in their security," I grumble, and she nods.

"Trust me, I already have a file created for Annette on all of their weaknesses and how to fix them."

"Of course you do," I say with a smile. "You're nothing if not thorough." The heaviness from a few minutes starts to lift as I sit up straighter, grabbing a notebook and pen to start jotting things down. "Okay, so this has been a productive night. We need to officially add security personnel to our main list. What else do we have?"

"I got a few things at the party," Rory says. "One, Carter, the kid from landscaping, was absolutely plastered, and he had a lot to say to anyone who would listen."

"Let me guess, you were all ears?"

She smiles proudly. "Well, of course. It seems he got Tanya her job, and he feels like she's throwing everything away by hooking up with Daniel."

"So, we've confirmed they have a thing?"

She nods, and my mind moves over the jealous redhead at the pool. We need to fast track figuring out who she was, especially if Daniel is hooking up with some other staff member at the resort as well. "Why would he care about that? And why would that be her throwing her job away? I didn't see anything in the employee handbook about hooking up with coworkers, though I supposed the GM hooking up with employees wouldn't be great, but mostly for him, right?"

"I don't know. But he also told me that Daniel is the biggest player on the resort, always flirting and breaking hearts."

I shrug. "I could have called that," I say with a small laugh.

"Also, the reason the hostess was crying the other day is because she was dating the chef, and they broke things off. Unfortunately, Daniel wouldn't move her to another restaurant, so she's stuck working near him all day."

"Oof, rough," I grumble. "Though I don't think that makes either of them a suspect, really. Unless she's mad at Daniel and wants to make him look bad? But this seems like a lot of work to go through because you're stuck working near your ex."

"Agreed, but it's good to have on hand."

I nod again.

"Who wasn't at the party?" I ask, flipping the notebook and starting to jot down all the people we saw. We met so many people there; it was the perfect place to investigate the staff. Though, even we couldn't fully foresee another sabotage happening while we were there.

We each start rattling off names, and Rory begins to sort through the photos she took on her phone under the guise of taking selfies with new friends before cross-checking each person to see if we can find where they were before and after the party. Then we pull out our list of all of the resort employees who were on the clock and use our newer access to the cameras to track them all. There is a third list of employees who were neither working nor at the party, although none of them overlap with our primary suspect list. Still, we push them onto our secondary list just to keep track of them.

"I think we need to go to the spa," I say.

"Ah, what a sacrifice this job is," Rory says with a smile that I return.

"I want to see who we can talk to there. Maybe we can find something out about Tanya?"

She nods. "We should also try and find the break room there, see if we can bug it." She starts clicking and clacking before she smiles. "Done. Two spa appointments at three tomorrow."

"Perfect," I say with a smile, looking through the other activities over her shoulder. "I'm going to hit up the Pilates class at noon."

"Oh?"

"The guy I was dancing with runs it, and he was very chatty before I got dragged away." We exchange a smile. "I'd like to get a handle on him, see what he might know, how he acts on the job."

She nods. "Okay, perfect. I want to do a bit more digging on this," Rory said, lifting the keycard, "tonight, but if you want to go to bed early, that's totally fine with me."

"No, no," I say with a shake of my head, reaching for the file of papers and photos we've been accumulating. "I'm going to keep going through these, see if I can find anything."

Like I could sleep right now with the adrenaline running through my system, both from my time with Rowan and the pro.

"We're close," Rory whispers.

I smile, knowing she's right.

TWENTY-EIGHT

Suspect list for Daydream resorts based on current intel:

- Daniel, the General Manager
- Jonas, head of security
- Tanya, the spa manager
- Jealous redhead
- All security personnel

TWENTY-NINE

ROWAN

The next morning is packed with attempting to ensure Jacob Barlow doesn't leave us a horrible review, much less sue us after his suite was broken into, and talking to the local police to ensure the report is in place. I also wanted to confirm they have noted the previous issues we've experienced: once we find out who is doing the sabotage, I sure as fuck plan to press charges to the full extent.

This means that, unfortunately, I don't get to have breakfast with Josie as I requested; instead, I send a breakfast platter up to her room as an apology, along with a note explaining that I've realized I don't have her number yet. Normally, having to blow off plans for work wouldn't bother me, since my career has always taken priority. But as is happening more and more since Josie stumbled into my life, today I wish I had a normal job, or at the very least, a healthier work-life balance.

It also makes me realize that I am in much, much deeper than I had been telling myself—not just for the last week, but for the last year. Still, there's something about finally crossing that line in my head, of admitting that I don't care whatever her agenda is, I just want her, that makes me finally admit it to myself. That realization, mixed with the way rage simmered in my veins at the sight of her dancing with someone else, brought me to the conclusion there's no fucking hope in staying away from her. What's the point of pretending?

I've spent the last week and a half trying to avoid her, and last night, at seeing her in the arms of Colton, something snapped.

Fuck decency.

Fuck what is "right."

Fuck work and needing to focus on nothing but hitting some invisible milestone I'm starting to understand I'll never truly be happy with.

Last night, I felt more fulfilled having Josie in my arms than I ever have by any professional accomplishment in my life. Even more, knowing that at some point today I plan on making time to see her, dragging her into a corner and kissing her breathless, actually pushed me to be more productive than normal and finish what's necessary for the day early, meaning all I have to do for the day are a handful of phone meetings.

Like the seemingly obsessive man I am, I keep a tab open while I'm on one of those calls, tracking Josie and Rory's room number so I can see if and when they sign into one of the restaurants or order something from a bar with the intention of either pulling up the cameras to watch her until I can make time to meet up with her.

One of the marketing execs is droning on during what I think is a useless weekly board meeting that should really be an email when that tab pings: Rory and Josie just checked into one of the more casual restaurants on the property for lunch.

Lunch. I check the time and my schedule, realizing it's eleven, and my next call is at one.

I could take lunch off, right?

Everyone has to eat, after all. Additionally, I could use it as an opportunity to get a sense of the restaurant, mingle with the staff for a bit, and see how they're doing. With everything going on, it's almost impossible not to spend time at the various locations. Right?

"Hey, something came up, I actually have to head out," I say, interrupting the drawn-out play-by-play conversation of someone's most recent golf game. "I have last-minute lunch plans."

Annette gives me a soft smile, probably understanding my true intention, and nods slightly.

"But I was just getting to the best part!" Jeff Dower says with a faux disappointed groan that isn't as faux as he wants to make it out to be.

"He is finally getting a life, let the man live," Annette says. "Go, Rowan. I don't want to even see you online for two hours."

I don't ask how she knows I'm on my way to Josie; instead, I just accept that in the past week, nothing makes sense and maybe I should just take it as it comes.

Hell, maybe this is just what balance feels like. I wish everyone goodbye and close my computer before heading out, and a few minutes later, I'm entering the restaurant, not even bothering to check in with the hostess.

Upon scanning the room, I see her sitting at a table in a little yellow sundress, little bows tied at her shoulders, and a pair of sunglasses on top of her head. Rory sits across from her, with Daniel leaning on the table. He seems to have just told a joke because her head tips back, a hand going to her chest as a laugh leaves her lips.

But it's not real.

I don't know if last night made me an expert in all things Josephine Montgomery or if I've always had this specific knack, but something about the tone of it is fake. I watch for a moment longer as the scene plays out, and not for the first time, I see it: it's all off. Some kind of tactic, winning him over, playing into her beauty to get something...but what?

I still haven't figured out what game Josie is playing. For an ugly split second, I wonder if she's playing with me, as well, but I brush that off, unwilling to even contemplate it.

It's clear to me Josie has some kind of underlying mission or goal, but I know somewhere deep in my gut that I am a hitch in her plans, something fucking it up, just like she's messing with my ability to concentrate on work when I need to. I think in the last twenty-four hours, I've grown to like that, to like that we're on some kind of fucked up but even playing field.

I walk over and interrupt their conversation, putting a hand on the soft, warm skin of her back. Her body jolts, and she glances over her shoulder, alarm written over it before the look melts into something softer. Sweeter. A kind of happiness that I'm there washing over her face.

"Rowan. I didn't expect to see you here," she says with a smile, turning her body a bit more towards me.

"Hey, Daniel. Can you go up to Mr. and Mrs. Barlow's new room and check that they're completely happy with everything, no needs or concerns? Whatever they want, it's on us for their entire stay. And I want you to make sure you're checking in regularly. After last night, we need to ensure the rest of their stay is a dream." Daniel's jaw tightens before he looks down at Josie, or, more accurately, her breasts, before his gaze moves back to me and he nods.

"On it. See you ladies later." Josie wiggles her fingers at him as he turns and walks away, while I gesture towards the table.

"Do you mind if I sit?"

"Here?" Rory asks with skepticism in her voice, and I hesitate.

"I mean, I can just—"

She lets out a laugh before shaking her head. "No, I'm just surprised. You've been making an Olympic sport out of avoiding my girl," Rory says with a wide smile and a tip of her head towards Josie. "Except for last night, of course."

I know then they had some kind of girl talk. It's expected, of course, since they're clearly close, but I still feel an embarrassed blush bloom on my cheeks and my blood heat at the reminder of what happened last night.

She does this to me, Josie—makes me feel like some teenage kid with a crush and an incessant boner.

"Rory, stop! You're going to scare him off!" Josie moves a chair next to her, tugging it out, then patting the seat. "We'd love for you to eat with us."

"Sorry, sorry; he makes it too easy! Look at him! He's turning red," she says as I take a seat.

"Well, be nice." Then she turns to me. "So, what are you doing here?" Josie asks, and I smile, leaning back in my seat.

"I figured I'd take some time away from my desk. Get some fresh air. Saw you were out to lunch, and I figured I'd come by."

Josie smiles, then looks to Rory. "He watches me on the CCTV, apparently. Likes to see what I'm doing."

Rory lets out a boisterous laugh. "Oh, he'll fit right in with you and me."

Josie gives her wide eyes before turning back to me. "You're going to...take time off?" she asks, her brows furrowing. "Seems a little out of character for you."

"It is, but I think it's long overdue," I say with a smile, then sigh. "Plus, I uh, had a conversation with my boss yesterday, before the party. We talked about you." Her eyebrows lift, asking a question without saying anything, and for a moment, I think I see a flash of something—worry, maybe? But then I realize she is probably worried about my boss not approving of this, so I explain quickly.

"Upper management fraternizing with guests is a bit of a gray area. It's technically out of the question for the employee, but I'm not really a resort employee. I wanted to run it by her before..."

"And...?"

I give her a small, self-deprecating laugh.

"Honestly, I think she's relieved to find out I'm not a complete robot. She essentially kicked me off the team call we were on, insisting I don't come back until my meeting later today."

Josie lets out a loud laugh, her head tipping back and her dark hair tumbling in glossy waves.

"So she's cool with you fucking a guest?" Rory asks with a raised eyebrow.

"Rory!" Josie chides her friend, a pretty pink blush blooming over her cheeks and creeping down her neck and chest. I'd give a lot right now to be able to see just how far down it goes.

"What?" Rory asks with a shrug, like it's not a strange question to ask a relative stranger.

"For one, we haven't even fucked," Josie says, giving her a deadpan look.

"And whose fault is that?" Rory asks, and watching the two argue is kind of fun.

I sit back with a smile, crossing my arms on my chest and for a tiny, insane moment, I think I could really fucking like this. Spending time with Josie and her friend, watching them argue back and forth, seeing that her need to argue doesn't stop with just me. A sense of fitting in, of unpressured enjoyment, seeps through me, and it concerns me for a moment how unfamiliar it feels.

Is this what I've been avoiding by working nonstop? This light, unpressured feeling in my chest? Or is it a Josie-specific reaction?

"The fucking universe?" Josie says, waving her hands in the air. "Who knows? Personally, I'm beginning to think the world hates us and doesn't want us to fornicate."

"Fornicate?" I ask with a choked laugh.

"That's the proper term, Rowan," Rory says primly, like I'm an idiot.

I just shake my head and widen my eyes, while lifting my hands in the air, the universal sign for *I'm not touching that.*

"So? She's cool with it? Your boss?"

"I mean, I didn't tell her about the fornication plans, but she said there's no issue with you and me..." I try and think about how Annette worded it, and land on "spending time together."

"Yeah, probably for the best to keep that part to yourself," Josie says, patting my arm. I smile at her, then put one arm around her shoulders and use my other hand to tug her chair closer to mine before pressing a kiss into her hair before the server comes by to ask about what we'd like.

"So, Rowan, do you have any brothers?" Rory asks after we place our orders for lunch.

"No?" I ask more than answer.

"Dammit," Rory mumbles, and Josie lets out a laugh.

"Sisters?"

I shake my head. "Only child."

"Where did you grow up?" she asks next.

"South Jersey, a small town called Ashford."

Josie nods, and Rory looks like she's taking very good notes in her head.

"Why does this feel like an interrogation?" I ask with a laugh.

"I mean, it kind of is. She's my best friend, and I hold her well-being above all else. And men are..." She shakes her head like she's disappointed in the species as a whole, and knowing the men I work with, I can't fully blame her.

"That's fair. Okay, what next?"

"Are you close to your parents?"

I look from one woman to the other, suddenly nervous. "If I say no, is it going to be a check in the negative?"

They look at one another, a silent conversation going on between each other before Josie responds.

"Is there a reason?"

I tip my head to the right before confessing. "Yes and no. I'm an only child to two parents who had me later in life because it was what they were 'supposed' to do. They enjoy working and traveling, and although I'm grateful I'm here and all, they probably shouldn't have had a kid. Once I was out of the house, they sold the house and left to travel. We see each other a few times a year."

"Is that why you're so close to your boss?"

"Close to his boss?" Rory asks in a questioning way.

"She's more of a mentor to me," I correct before she gets the wrong idea. "But...yes? I guess? She's been pivotal in my career, and I share a lot with her. I wouldn't be where I am right now without her."

Josie and Rory look at one another, some silent conversation happening before Rory nods, and Josie smiles. I assume I passed the first round of interrogation when Rory seems to settle into her chair, grabbing her drink and taking a long sip. I turn to Josie then.

"So...you?"

"Me?" she asks.

"Close to your parents?"

Josie shrugs. "Close enough. Holidays and birthdays, a couple of dinners a year, but they live two states away, so it's not too often. I travel a lot, obviously, and they..." There's a moment of hesitation before she continues. "They don't understand my job."

"Influencing?"

She blinks for a moment, then nods, quicker than necessary.

"Yes. Exactly. It's not a real job to them."

Her answer is honest, but something about it is off, that same something that I can't quite put my finger on.

"Okay, enough third degree," Rory, who started the third degree, might I add, says. "What's your favorite Daydream resort, Rowan? Josie and I were saying we absolutely want to visit another one sometime soon." My mind rolls through ideas, most of them of Josie and me at a resort together, neither of us working, before I answer.

We spend the next hour chatting, and I continue to get to know the women, Rory more than happy to spill her friend's secrets, like how Josie is apparently amazing at darts and likes to con men out of money at bars playing it, or that once she snuck her way backstage at an Atlas Oaks concert and still keeps in touch with the lead singer's wife because of it.

"Where are you to going next?" I ask as our plates are taken away.

"Well, I am going to lay out by the pool, because my tan is greatly lacking," Rory says with a contented sigh. This one is crazy and wants to actually do things. Then we have an urgent appointment at three."

"Oh?" Josie rolls her eyes.

"I'm taking a yoga class on the beach. I'm not running a goddamn marathon."

"When's that?" I ask, trying to think of how much time I can steal with her before my next meeting.

"One," she says. I look at my watch, seeing it's 12:30.

"I can walk you," I say with a smile, thinking of what dark corners there are between here and the beach where the afternoon yoga classes take place.

"What a gentleman," she says.

Rory rolls her eyes, seeming to already know where my mind is. "Yeah, real gentleman when he drags you into a corner to feel you up." Rory laughs, and I wonder if I truly am that obvious.

"Rory," Josie says with wide eyes, and Rory laughs.

Josie might like picking at me, but Rory likes picking on Josie, and it's fun to watch. I realize then that her picking on me, poking and prodding and teasing, might have been her way of being into—or at least friendly with—me all along. It's just her own strange brand of affection.

"All right, all right," Rory says, standing and hefting her bag over her shoulder. "I'm out of here. Have fun, you two."

And then it's just Josie and me.

THIRTY

ROWAN

"Sorry about Rory, she's very protective of me," Josie says after we leave the restaurant.

"I don't mind." She looks up at me like she doesn't believe me, and I shrug. "I like it. Clearly, she cares about you. That's a good thing," I tell her, meaning it.

She smiles softly before explaining. "She doesn't usually get the opportunity to interrogate someone I'm into, so I think she saw the opportunity and ran with it."

'Because you avoid bringing them to her?" Silence hangs between us as we walk. As I take a left to go the quieter route to the beach, the one mostly employees take, I look at her. She's biting her lip, contemplating what to say. "Or...?"

"I haven't really had someone *to* bring to Rory. Not in a long time, at least." A light blush blooms on her cheeks as my brow furrows.

"You haven't?".

"I don't really..." She closes her eyes like she's about to make a confession, and I squeeze her hand, trying to reassure her. "I don't really date. I haven't found one yet that was worth my time enough that I wanted to introduce him to my friends."

"I see you on dates all the time," I say and regret it instantly when her face drops.

Fuck. I have to stop bringing that up, rubbing in her face the many times I've seen her out with other men. Not only does it not matter; it's really not any of my business. She wasn't mine then; we didn't have anything between us, and she's an adult, able to do whatever she wants. I open my mouth to argue, but she cuts me off.

"They're..." she says, looking off into the distance and taking a deep breath before continuing. "Those dates aren't what they seem."

A part of me wonders *what* they are, but I don't ask. It's not my business, I remind myself.

"It doesn't matter what you do with your life or who you date. Right now, you're here with me, and that's all I care about," I tell her. It's what I should have been telling her from the start, but we've already concluded that I'm both an idiot and an asshole. Relief washes over her face, and she smiles up at me. In that moment, I realize my words are the truth: I don't care what Josie is hiding, what secrets she's keeping, so long as she's by my side and smiling at me like she is right now. I return her smile and squeeze her hand as we continue to move.

"So you took time off work to come eat lunch with us," Josie says, breaking the silence. She sounds satisfied and a bit amused by that fact.

"Yeah." I take a moment to gather my thoughts and shift gears before adding, "I thought I'd feel guilty about it, but I don't. The world kept spinning, the business hasn't fallen apart just because I didn't supervise every single action," I say. "I'm starting to wonder if maybe there's more to life than working."

I'm starting to believe that *more to life* is holding my hand and smiling up at me right now.

"Why do you sound so confused by that?" she asks with a laugh.

"Because I am." I laugh as well, shrugging. "I don't think I've ever said that before. I love work."

"Except..."

"Except there's this brunette who I can't stop thinking about, and every time I'm at work, all I can think about is spending more time with her."

"She sounds pretty awesome."

"She is," I say. "I keep wanting to ask her out, except I've recently realized I don't even have her number." She turns her head, our steps slowing as we approach the entrance to the beach where I'm going to leave her.

"Maybe you should ask her for it," she says. "Have you tried that?"

I shake my head with a smile.

It's wild how light I feel when it's just Josie and me, how when she looks at me like that, I forget that my world is on fire and nothing makes sense. For a split second, the world revolves around Josie and her smile and the warmth that radiates from her.

I stop and use her hand in mine to tug her into my arms. She lets out a little *oof!* as she hits my chest, but her arms go to my neck instantly, warm fingers on bare skin sending a rush of need through me.

God, I'm so gone for this woman if that's what a single touch does to me.

"Can I have your number, Josephine?" Somehow, her smile widens, the dimple I fucking love going deep as she nods before reaching into my pocket for my phone. She lifts it, puts it to my face to unlock the screen, then raises an eyebrow at me.

It takes a moment before I realize why she's hesitating, why she isn't just inputting her number like I asked: she's making sure she's okay to use my phone. The arm on her waist tightens before I move us, tugging her over and back into an empty alcove that's hidden and spinning her until her back is to the wall. Her eyes are wide when I settle my gaze on her, wanting to make sure she not only hears but understands what I'm going to say next.

"You can go through my phone anytime you want, Josie. 102418."

"What?"

"The code to my phone. 1024198." Her lips part, and I have to fight the urge to kiss the look off her. "I trust you, troublemaker."

A flash moves through her eyes, maybe guilt at whatever secret I know she's holding onto before it's gone, before a wide, genuine smile spreads over her lips. She moves to her toes, pressing a soft, quick kiss to my lip before shifting her attention to my phone and sending a text to herself. Her phone dings with a new message before she slides the phone back into my pocket.

When she smiles up at me, what little bit of resolve I had left melts away, and I dip my head and press my lips to hers. Instantly, her hands shift up, tangling in the hair at the back of my neck and pulling my face closer, deepening the kiss.

I shouldn't do it. Really, I shouldn't. But as I kiss her, her body shifts, and mine does too, and somehow, my thigh ends up between her legs as I seem to find it doing more and more often lately, and I'm pressed against her heat, just a pair of tight spandex shorts separating her and my skin. A breathy sound leaves her lips, moving straight to my cock as I grind into her.

I'm so desperate to feel her wrapped around me, even though I have a call soon and she has a class to get to. I shift to move back, to ensure the head on my shoulders is calling the shots rather than the one in my shorts. We can't do anything. Not right now, I tell myself.

But then she's moving away from me, moving to her knees before me, and looking up at me.

This isn't the first time I've seen that visual. Not even the second. But I've never seen that look of determination in her eyes before. My cock is hard in my shorts, and she smiles as she palms it through the silky material. I let out a quiet noise of pleasure as she does.

"Your turn this time," she whispers.

"Josie," I groan, but my words are stopped when she unzips my shorts before she slides her fingers under the waistband of my underwear and tugs them down just until my cock is free. The elastic sits under my balls, adding additional pressure that has me biting back another moan. That is a wasted effort, though, when her hand wraps around me, pumping. My mouth is slack as I watch her wide eyes, her satisfied smile, her small hand gripping and twisting a bit as she moves towards the head, somehow knowing exactly what I like.

"What are you doing, Josie?" I ask, looking around. This alcove is dark and far out of the way—really, there's no reason for anyone to be over here, though she has proven time and time again, guests don't really care about that kind of thing. My back is to the entrance, so even if someone did happen upon us, I'd be blocking the view of her. Still, I can't find it in me to care, surely not when her hot wet tongue flattens on the tip of my cock. Surely not when her plush lips wrap around it and suck.

She releases with a pop before smiling up at me. "What do you think?"

"I don't—" I start, but then slowly, I watch inch by inch of my cock slides into her mouth. Air leaves my chest as it does, and the warmth of her mouth has my balls tightening. Her eyes are wide, locked on mine.

Then she starts to move, bobbing up and down, my cock sliding deep into her throat then back out as she sucks the tip. My hand moves to rest on the back of her head, to guide her the same way she did me. I don't press, even though I want to, not wanting to break the moment, especially not since this is the first time we've done this.

But as seems to be the way with Josie, she looks at me and knows what I want.

Her hand moves to mine, grabbing it and wrapping my fingers around her ponytail as she continues to move her mouth over my length. She wraps my fingers around her hair and makes me tug. "Fuck, Josie," I rasp through gritted teeth, my cock twitching in her mouth and as much as she feasibly can around me, she smiles. She likes getting to me, something only she has ever been able to do.

"Is that what you want, baby?" I rasp, low and gravelly. "You want me to fuck your face and pull your hair?"

She gives me a small nod and a moan of approval, something I feel more than hear. I grit out a choked sound before doing as she asks, wrapping the length of her hair around my fist and pulling, using the grip to guide her head how I want it, to show her how I like it. Her back arches, her full mouth muffling a moan as her eyes drift shut just a bit with pleasure.

I bet if I slipped my hand between her legs right now, I'd find her drenched. Her hand moves to my hip for balance as she continues to suck me, her head bobbing, her tits bouncing in her bra that has little support as she moves.

"Pull your top down," I say, desperate to see her for the first time. I'm not even slightly disappointed: full breasts, tight pink nipples I want to play with, to suck, to pinch. I'm a bit preoccupied at the moment, but she...

"Play with them while I fuck your face," I instruct, and she groans along my cock, before moving a hand to her breast, cupping it and squeezing the nipple hard, rolling it between her fingers. She moans when she does, her tongue moving along the underside of my cock with vigor now.

The sight is fucking magnificent.

"God, I want to see my cum on your tits," I growl low, almost to myself, the hand in her hair tightening and pulling yet another strangled noise from her. She's enjoying this just as much as I am, and I can see her hips shifting with need. My own need deepens, turned on by her clearly being turned on, the most vicious cycle known to man. Then she pulls back and sits on her heels, pushing her breasts together for me as if she'd do anything at all to give me what I want. Her eyes are wide and her pink lips are perfectly swollen from sucking me, and I know I'll have this memory tucked into my mind until the day I fucking die. My hand goes to my cock, wet with her spit, pumping it. She mewls then, pouting as if wanting it. She *wants* me to come all over her chest. I smile then and shake my head.

"No, no, not here. Not this time, not when there's no way for me to clean you up."

She *pouts*. The woman *pouts* then, and my orgasm creeps closer as I grit my teeth to hold it back. The thumb from my free hand moves to her mouth, pulling on her lower lip until she opens for me. "No, I'm just going to come in here, if that's okay with you. That'll be just as pretty."

She nods prettily, squirming as she kneels before me. She's desperate, a state I've seen her in before, but this time it's different. She's not desperate to come; she's desperate for *me* to come.

Without hesitation, I move my hand back to her hair, tugging her head to my cock and fucking her face once again. "When I come," I say through ragged breaths. "Hold it, you hear me? I want to see my come on your tongue, Josephine." Her eyes widen and she nods, and that's what does it, what has me gritting my teeth and biting back a loud grunt as I come in her mouth, the pleasure too much, too consuming, that all I can do is watch her wide eyes, her lips wrapped around me, and thank whatever universe continued to bring us together until we finally got the hint.

When I'm able to come back to myself, I pull out of her mouth. "Show me."

She opens her mouth and I see it there, my cum pooling on her tongue. I've never seen anything prettier. I let out a deep growl, and I watch as she fights back one of her own. I believe in my bones that this woman was made for me in every sense of the word, especially in this moment when she's getting off on my pleasure almost as much as I am.

"What a fucking good girl you are," I say, stroking a finger down her cheek then moving to wrap my hand around her throat. "Swallow now, baby. Let me feel it."

She does, and beneath my palm, I feel her throat muscles work, swallowing me down.

Finally, I tuck myself back into my pants, utterly pleased that she stays on her knees while I do, before I bend and help her up to her feet. I can't resist dipping a hand around her breast, feeling it's warm weight in my palm and tweaking the nipple before fixing her bra top. Next time, I'll have my lips there. Next time, I'll ensure we have all the time in the world, not a single distraction to divert us. In the meantime, I take a step, pinning her to the wall and lowering my lips to hers.

"You don't have to kiss me," she whispers quickly against my lips before I can actually kiss her.

"What?" I ask, confused.

"You came in my mouth, Rowan. I don't expect you to kiss me." There's an embarrassed laugh that tells me everything I need to know about the assholes she's been with before, and the need to erase it from her takes over. One last time, my hand moves to her ponytail, gripping it and positioning her face where I want her before I press my lips to hers. Not a peck, but a deep kiss that tells her everything I'm feeling, the gratitude for what she gave me, and the need for even more. I slide my tongue into her mouth, tasting the mix of us there, and I groan into the kiss, deepening it further. Her hands grip my neck, and we stay like that for a long moment before I finally pull back, resting my forehead on hers.

"It's an absolute honor to taste myself on your tongue, Josie. To know how it got there, that you trusted me enough to give me that? Means everything to me." Her eyes go soft, and I know it was the right thing to say.

After a moment, my hand moves to her hips, fingers playing at the edge of her shorts. I want to make her feel just as good as she made me feel.

"We don't have time for me," she whispers with a shake of her head and a small smile. I check the time on my watch and see there's just a few minutes before her class starts. Even though instructors aren't supposed to let guests join classes late, they can make an exception if I want her there.

"I'll make time," I say, but she shakes her head.

"No. No, I'll wait. It'll be better if I have to wait. Plus, the scales are still unbalanced between us. I can't have a three-to-one ratio." My lips find her neck, and a shiver rolls through her before I move up, nipping her ear and whispering there.

"If I have my way, that ratio will continue to be wildly uneven, Josie. Once I get you naked beneath me, you're going to come so many fucking times you'll lose count." Her breathing hitches, and I push my hips into hers, my cock starting to harden once more at the mere promise. "Only then," I say, my lips moving down her neck as I take in her uniquely Josie scent there. "Only after I've made you come a dozen times am I finally going to slide into your pretty pussy and drag another dozen out of you."

"Oh god," she whispers.

Suddenly, I'm seeing the value in making her wait, in dragging out the anticipation. Still, I don't plan to drag it out much longer.

"Even if I have to tie you to the bed so you can't run off on some secret mission and throw our phones into another room." Her body tightens just a bit, and I let out a low, rumbling laugh before running my tongue over the skin of her neck. "Why do I feel like you'd like that? Me tying you up and not letting you go until I've had my way with you."

"Because I would," she says. "Tonight?" My mind rolls through my schedule, and I let out a defeated sigh, remembering my meeting with the inspectors for the new resort tonight. As much as I'd like to skip every meeting today, this one is particularly important to stay on track for the opening.

"I'm busy tonight. A call I can't miss." I huff my disappointment into her neck before pulling away and looking her in the eye. "But tomorrow night. Me and you, all night. Mutual satisfaction. Many times over." Her head lifts, heavy eyes looking at me before she speaks.

"I feel like you need to at least wine and dine me first," she says with a taunt in her words.

I smile, loving that I never expect her not to argue with me on every little thing. Except, it turns out, when I'm fucking her face. Then she's pretty good at following instructions, it seems.

"Dinner? Dessert?"

She smiles again.

"Dessert is good enough for me," she whispers. "We can always order dinner in after round one."

I can't fight the strangled noise at her teasing, and she giggles.

"Dessert. Six o'clock tomorrow. Tell Rory you won't be coming back to your room."

"It's a date," she whispers, and I smile wide.

She mimics it before pushing on my chest. "But right now, I have a yoga class to get to, and you have a boring call." I sigh, knowing she's right, before stepping away and grabbing her hand and moving her out of the alcove I dragged her into, already counting down the minutes until tomorrow night.

THIRTY-ONE

JOSIE

"What was more relaxing, this treatment, or Rowan eating you out yesterday?" Rory asks as we walk out of the spa locker room after our salt scrub treatment, looking nice and shiny with our bags slung over our shoulders.

Bags that were necessary for our goal to bug the supply room for the spa.

This time, we had enough time not only to install an audio bug, but a video as well. With our culprit able to mess with the camera feeds seamlessly, we decided we needed to step up our own game.

"Oh my god, you're ridiculous," I say with an exaggerated eye roll and a light push of her shoulder.

"So you're not going to answer? I guess that means that he's not as good as—"

I'm preparing to defend Rowan's skills when we hear it.

Shouts.

"Help! Someone!"

Rory and I look at one another quickly before we bolt in the direction of the calls. It takes less than thirty seconds before we find the culprit, a middle-aged woman with a look of panic on her face as she points towards the sauna. "Someone is stuck in there! The keyboard is malfunctioning, and it won't let her out! It's too hot, I think."

We look at the sauna window, where a woman's hand bangs at the foggy glass.

Instantly, I run to the door, pulling and tugging and hoping maybe it's just stuck, though my gut tells me otherwise. Coincidences like this don't just happen, not while we're on a case like this. This is intentional, and it appears our guy is becoming increasingly dangerous.

"Call 911," I say to Rory, moving around the sauna to see if there's an emergency shutoff button. There is, but *fuck*—its wire has been clipped. I look at the plug and contemplate pulling it to disconnect the power, but I don't know if the door would remain locked or if it would trigger some unlocking mechanism. And if it remains locked, I don't know what the process is for the machine coming back on once it has power once more. There are far too many variables when time is of the essence.

"What's going on?" a woman in a Daydream Resorts polo asks, coming over and looking worried.

"Someone is stuck in there," the woman we found frantic informs her. "It's too hot, and I think she's going to get hurt."

"The emergency stop is clipped," I say to Rory, who still has her phone to her ear. She relays the information to the operator on the line.

"Is there any way to get in there?" I ask, noting that there's a scan for a keycard on the side fo the door. I try slipping mine in to see if it fits, and it does, but the machine makes a beeping noise to indicate I don't have the correct card type.

"There's an override," the employee says. "We need to find someone higher up; they have overrides on their keycards."

"You don't have it?" I ask, tipping my head towards the card on a badge reel at her hip. She shakes her head, looking genuinely sorry.

"I'm housekeeping, I was just grabbing the laundry. Someone

who works over here should have the right access, though." She looks around, and just like us, finds no one in the vicinity. But how? How would that be, considering there are normally a dozen or so people in this area. As if reading my mind, she responds. "It's Wednesday. They have their weekly meeting around this time, when it's not too busy. They're across the spa right now."

"Do you know where they are?" I ask, and she nods. "Go get someone. Now." I turn to Rory, who is pulling her phone from her ear.

"Paramedics and fire fighters are on their way, but they're coming from another island," she says, looking panicked.

"Call security for the resort. They should have their own cards that override everything," I say, and she nods, finding the number quickly and calling as I dig through my bag. We used the card twice this morning to place bugs in staff spaces in order to monitor if and when the cameras go out next, but right now, I'm grateful I snagged this from Rowan. As much as I don't want to use it because it will reveal I have it, I'm going to assume that it's a forgivable, or at the very least, explainable offense as I move towards the sauna's keypad and swipe the key card.

I hold my breath as I wait for a reaction from the computer before the screen lights up, the light turning green to indicate that it was a valid request. Options pop up on the screen, including raise temperature, lower temperature, and then I see unlock. I hit the button quickly, and relief floods through me when I hear the door unlock, a mechanical whirl happening as the woman opens the door. The guest is bright red and sweating, and when I feel the wave of hot air that releases, I feel bad for how horrible it must have felt in there, especially if she started to panic from being trapped. I hold on to her to steady her steps before moving her to a sofa in the corner.

"Someone get her some water. Small sips." I turn to the woman. "Someone is coming to help right now." Just then, a booming voice sounds, and my entire body stills.

"What is happening here?" The familiar voice calls.

Rowan's voice.

Of all the people to come to our aid first, it had to be him. Of course.

"Someone was locked in the sauna," the original woman says, pointing to where the door dinged a bit from where we tried to break in. "It locked and was far too hot, and no one could get her out."

"How was it locked?" Rowan asks, since I'm sure there are safety protocols within the equipment.

"A wire was snipped," I say, my breathing finally starting to even out from the endorphin run. The shakiness in my hands is back, though, and it has nothing to do with helping that woman. It has everything to do with the speculative glare on Rowan's face.

"Why are you here? Are you okay?" he asks. His face is a mix of confusion and worry, and the guilt is eating deeper into me. Rory is helping the woman cool down, making sure she doesn't pass out or drink too much, too fast, but she answers all the same.

"We had our scrub appointment—we mentioned it to you this afternoon. We were just leaving when we heard the ruckus and came to help."

His gaze shifts to Rory, but then the other woman, attempting to be helpful and probably experiencing an endorphin rush of her own, adds on. "And thank God for that—they know how to override it. They saved her."

Her words make my body go cold, and Rowan's head snaps back to me.

"Save her?" he asks, eyes boring into me.

The other woman answers before I can.

"She had a universal keycard and used it to open the door. Housekeeping didn't have one that could override it."

God, I wish this woman would just shut up.

"But you did?" Rowan asks, eyes boring into me. Again, that causes churning panic creeping into my veins.

This is the moment I was afraid of. The moment that Rowan starts to put things together, when he starts to realize that some things just aren't adding up. When does the previous entertainment of being in the 'right place at the right time' start to become far too suspicious? He's said he knows that I'm hiding something, suspects something, but in this moment, that cautious suspicion could easily teeter from being entertaining to being concerning. Right now, it looks like I could be his number one suspect. The moment that mixing work and play teeters into the territory of breaking my cover. Not just mine, but Rory's as well.

But still, I can't lie. Not now. Not about this.

Not to him.

Not when my mind is getting more and more consumed and guilt, when I want to remove all the little white lies that lie between us until there's nothing left. "I—" I take a deep breath and look at Rory, whose eyes are on me, as well. She gives me a subtle, barely noticeable nod, telling me she trusts me with whatever I'm about to say, that she believes that this is going to be just fine. While it doesn't appease me, not in the least, it does stem some of the panic in my veins, just enough for me to come up with a reasonable response. "I accidentally grabbed it yesterday. I must not have realized it at the time, but I tossed it in my bag this morning and forgot about it, forgot to tell you I grabbed it."

"So you just happened to have my keycard when you're at the spa when an issue happens?" His jaw is tight, and I see it then—he's not buying it. "Seems like interesting timing, no?"

My eyes widen then.

"I—" I start, but more voices enter the room as Daniel and the jealous redhead come stumbling in. It's then I notice her name tag: Tanya, spa manager. I also note that her shirt is skewed, and the zipper to Daniel's pants is undone.

My mind reels with this evidence. Does that knock them out as suspects? Clearly, they were...preoccupied during the sabotage. Or maybe it was the perfect cover, each of them a witness to one of their whereabouts.

I mentally slot that into my notes while trying not to panic at the way Rowan's eyes have never left me, the way he's staring at me with disbelief and...fuck. *Hurt.*

I need to get out of here. I need to get back to my room with Rory, to remember why I'm here and not let my fumbled emotions get in the way

"I.. um," she starts.

"I'll let you guys handle this. I'm going to go back to my—" I interrupt, but Rowan cuts me off.

"You're staying here. We have to talk."

I don't even look at him when I reply, too many conflicting emotions at play. "I don't think—"

"Stay. Here. Josephine." My body goes still with his words, and I feel the blood drain from my face. Is this it? Is this my cover being blown? That's never happened before. Maybe this is exactly why we're not supposed to get involved with someone on a mission.

Rowan turns to her then. "Rory, you can go." My veins turn to ice, but she smiles.

"Okay. Let me know if you need anything; I was here with them as well. If they need me to give a statement, I'm willing." Rowan's shoulders relax just a hair. It's almost indiscernible, but it happens all the same, and he nods.

"Thank you. I'll let you know if we need anything."

Break

Nearly an hour later, the woman is off to the hospital for some basic care and monitoring, though she seems okay, and I'm following a tight-jawed Rowan to his office. He hasn't talked to me since he asked me to stay except to ask me to follow him. I stood in a corner most of the time, panicking about what to say to him, how to talk myself out of this mess. Still, it wasn't time wasted: I took many mental notes, watching reactions and faces, tracking where eyes diverted. While

Daniel looked absolutely wrecked at the idea of another guest getting hurt, profusely apologizing not only to the guest but to Rowan as well, Tanya looked distraught in another way. Panicked, almost. With each passing moment and every added piece of evidence that this was not an accident, her face seemed to grow paler, and she kept checking her phone as if waiting for a reply.

Is she involved? Is she our guy? Maybe she went to Daniel to distract him, to make him hard to reach if and when an emergency occurred.

But what would the motivation be?

And why would she continue to use her own department? If she was trying to fuck with the resort as a whole, why would she continue to mess with the spa? I would assume she would have to recognize it would put a target on her head as the issue.

But I can't think of it any longer when we finally step into Rowan's office, a gorgeous room with a balcony and a beautiful view of the ocean behind him. Unfortunately, I can't take it in, not when he's staring at me like that, as if I am a child who has explaining to do.

"What were you doing there, Josie?" he asks, finally breaking the silence as he leans against his desk and crosses his arms on his chest. His jaw is tight, and the levity that I was starting to see on his face this afternoon is completely gone.

"I told you. I'd just gotten done getting my scrub. We were on our way out—"

"If I weren't completely entwined by you, I might have started to wonder if you were behind at least some of the issues plaguing the resort a long time ago." Every molecule of blood leaves my face. I knew this was coming. Rowan is smart and attentive. But still, there's something about hearing the accusation out loud that turns my stomach.

I had convinced myself, I think, that if we could just get past the last few days of this mission, if I could just close the case without any real questions, it would be fine. But that clearly was wishful thinking. It's a double-edged sword, after all: I'm into Rowan because of how attentive he is, how he notices things...but it's his attentiveness that is coming back to bite me.

"It wasn't me, you have to believe me, Rowan. Seriously," I whisper. He doesn't move. He doesn't breathe. He doesn't blink. And when he does move, it's to speak his next words, low and emotionless. Robotic, even.

"Why were you down there? Your appointment was at three, but when I came, it was nearly six. A scrub is not three hours long, Josie. Why are you at almost all of the locations when something goes wrong? Why do I keep finding you places you shouldn't be?"

"I—"

He shakes his head like he's dismayed and doesn't want to hear my excuses before cutting me off, leaning in a bit.

"You know something. I know it. I don't know what it is, or how you're involved, but you know something. You know something about what's going on here, and you're hiding it."

I shake my head, wanting to refute it but not able to, but he keeps speaking. "Was meeting you at the bar planned?"

That twists in my heart.

"No," I say, quickly and firmly. "No, Rowan. It wasn't. I just happened to be at the bar, and you were there, too."

He nods like he believes at least that, and relief rushes through me. It's gone just as quickly as it came.

"And here? What about you being here?"

I open and close my mouth a few times, trying to decide how to answer before I do.

"It had nothing to do with you. I didn't know what you did for work, much less where you worked. And even then, how would I have known that you were coming to this resort?" I don't deny that I'm here for a reason

"If you're working with someone here, you could have assumed I'd make my way here once the fire came to my attention."

I can see his line of thinking, really, I can, because if I were in his shoes, those are the connections I'd make. But I need him not to. I need him to stop digging, stop searching. My eyes are wide and pleading when I say my next sentence.

"I need you to trust me, Rowan. I can't tell you right now, but as soon as I can, I will. I promise."

It's more than I've ever given anyone, on a mission or not. I've never told anyone I was casually seeing or hooking up with someone about my job, but Rowan isn't either of those.

That's the conclusion I've been slowly coming to terms with over the past few days. I finally found a man who I want to give a chance to, who I want to prove to me that not all men are liars and cheats, and now, because of this job I love, I might have fucked it up before it even started.

He changes the subject then, and my pulse pours.

"Where did you get my keycard?" he asks, his voice low and deceptively calm. I am anything but calm in this moment.

"I... I... I...". I stutter, unsure of what to say, how to talk myself out of this. "I found it with my things yesterday. I must have grabbed it without thinking the other day, I don't know, Rowan. I swear, it was just a happy circumstance. I was here because I thought you might be here and—"

"A happy circumstance," he says with a humorless laugh, disbelief in the words. "So you were at the party the other night—was that also some plan to distract me? Using jealousy to get me distracted so you could break into the room? Or your accomplice, I suppose?" Guilt lashed through my stomach once more. "This afternoon, were you stealing something else? Giving Rory a free pass to set this up for the next sabotage, knowing I'd be distracted by your mouth?"

My eyes are wide as his words hit their target, slicing deep. That's exactly the conclusion I would come to if I were in his shoes, but hearing the accusations thrown at me hurts.

"Rowan, I can't believe you would even ask that. You really think I would do that?"

"What else am I supposed to think, Josie? You were at the scene of the crime holding my stolen keycard. Sometimes one plus one equals two."

"And sometimes things aren't what they seem," I say, my voice wavering, my hands out at my sides. "Rowan, it wasn't me. I know what it looks like, but it wasn't. You have to believe me."

"No, I don't." A sudden look of sadness crosses his face before it's once again smothered by anger. "I don't have to believe you."

It's the truth, of course. He doesn't have to believe me. And really, he shouldn't. But, god, I hoped he would.

"Rowan—" I start, my voice cracking, but he cuts me off with a shake of his head.

"Look, I have things to do," he says, tipping his head towards his desk. "Go back to your room. But don't go far, in case we have to ask you any questions." I stare at him for long, long moments where I wish things were different, where I wish I was allowed to tell him everything, but that's part of the job. If I spilled it all now without talking to Rory and Gabriel, I could lose my job. I could blow the case. I would lose the trust of people I care about.

So I nod, and I turn away, hoping to hear him call my name to try and work this out.

But I never do.

And as I'm walking back towards my room, I realize that while I may have kept the true nature of the mission safe, I may have ruined all we might have had.

THIRTY-TWO

JOSIE

I'm a mess when I get to our room, barely able to fight back the tears rimming my eyes until I open the door. When I do, Rory stands from where she was sitting at the desk, notes sprawled around her, and waits until the door slams behind me. I lean against it, my body unable to hold myself up any longer, and let the first tear finally fall.

"Oh, honey," Rory whispers in her sweet, soft voice that she doesn't use often, before moving to me and pulling me into her arms. "That bad?"

"He doesn't trust me," I cry into her shoulder. "And of course, he shouldn't, but I want him to. I want him just to trust me and let me solve this, and then I can tell him everything. But he's so fucking stubborn, and, of course, I get it because I wouldn't believe me either but...fuck!"

Slowly, she guides me to the bed, and I sit on the edge next to her, taking in a few deep breaths to calm myself before I spill everything about the rest of my afternoon and, most importantly, the look Rowan gave me before I walked away.

Ten minutes later, I've finished telling Rory everything: what I saw while the paramedics helped out the woman, what happened when the police came to file a report, how the employees reacted, the seeming confirmation of Daniel and Tanya hooking up, and most importantly, what happened with Rowan.

"You need to call Gabriel," Rory says, her face soft but serious. "I know we talked about this, about you starting something with him, but it's getting messy, and it could break our cover. He's beginning to get suspicious." I nod, knowing she's right. "I'm not saying you can't... whatever with him. But if it impacts the job..." She sighs. "People are getting hurt, Josie. It's one thing when it's silly stuff, bubbles in a pool, or deliveries missed, things that only hurt the guest experience or the bottom line. But now we're facing multiple cases where someone was going to be hurt."

I nod, knowing she's right.

"I don't know what to do," I whisper, my eyes watering. I don't know the last time I cried: it's not my thing, and being raised as a tomboy in a house of brothers and a single dad meant crying usually resulted in teasing.

But that ache in my throat isn't only because of that, and I know it.

"Call Gabriel," she says softly. "I'm going to go to the pool, sit out, and see if I can see anything. Meet me at dinner in," she looks at her watch. "An hour?"

I nod and stare at my phone and the name on the screen while she gathers her things and heads out the door. Finally, I take in a deep breath and hit call.

It rings twice before the mysterious man answers.

"Montgomery," the familiar deep voice says, and despite my nerves, I settle. Gabriel feels like an old friend, someone I can trust with my whole being, and I know it's because in this job, I have to. But it also feels like I can be honest with him, something I'm sure is a curated veil, since so much of this job relies on trusting the people we work with.

"Hey, Gabriel," I say with a low sigh.

"To what do I owe the pleasure?" Typically, on assignments,

Rory is the one to call Gabriel. I'm usually out playing my games and winning people over while Rory does her behind-the-scenes work, making it easier for her to be the first line of contact.

"Something happened," I admit quietly.

"Mhmm," he says. Gabriel is like a dad who is never mad, just disappointed, which makes it all the worse when you have to admit something shitty to him. I never want to let him down, and a mishap like this feels like just that. I've never even gotten close to breaking my cover on an assignment.

Until Rowan.

"We stumbled upon a sabotage while we were planting a bug and ran to fix it. It was a danger to guests, and we couldn't let it play out on its own, so Rory and I made the executive decision to step in."

"Okay," he says, clearly following but giving me the room needed to expand. I take a move before continuing.

"The reason we were able to stop it before someone got severely hurt is because I stole one of the universal keys." The silence hangs and I explain further. "I snagged it while..." A blush burns over me, head to toe, and I'm glad this isn't a video call. "Getting intimate with Rowan."

"The VP of Operations who you knew from your past," Gabriel says, a statement rather than a question.

I nod, though he can't see it, before speaking. "Yes. And I'm happy I had it because it kept the guest safe, but also..."

Once again, he fills in the blanks. "It created some questions."

"He asked me to stay while he handled things, and after everything was cleared up with the police, he brought me to his office to ask me some questions. He...he knows something is off. Knows we're not here for vacation. He has for a while, but he's let it slide because I think he thought it was just something silly or inconsequential, but then someone got hurt and I was holding the key, literally. He said he doesn't trust. I wouldn't tell him what he wanted to hear, and he said he doesn't trust me and told me to leave." The memory hurts just as bad as the reality, but the vision of his betrayed face is almost the most painful. "I just..." My voice cracks. "I just don't know what to do. I think..."

"You're getting too close," he guesses before I have to say it out loud, which I suppose is a relief.

"I didn't mean to," I whisper my confession. "It just happened. He's a good guy, and I like him, and it's just...it felt unavoidable. Something that was always going to happen, always inevitable."

"He's the one who has bumped into you on dates, correct? The one who sat with you while you were out with Stephen Jones?"

I nod, though he can't see me. We tell Gabriel everything that happens on a mission, both for safety and job security, so Rowan has made his way into a few of my final reports at this point.

"Maybe..." I start, thinking about the idea that's been sitting on my heart for a few days now as I continued to get myself more and more tied up on this mission. The more I blurred the lines and dipped my toes into gray areas, the more I wondered... "Maybe I'm not the right one for this job," I say low. "Maybe you should call in back up, see if—"

"He's really getting under your skin, isn't he?" Gabriel asks with a laugh that cuts me off, and I freeze.

"What? Rowan? No."

"He's far enough that you're questioning yourself. Far enough that you're pushing aside the steadfast values you typically hold, for better or worse." My stomach churns with his words that I know are true.

"There are two things I think you should know: one, your client has informed me that recently, Mr. Fisher also told her about your relationship—" Relationship feels like such a big, scary world in this context. —"He was concerned that she would be against it since you were, in theory, a guest. She was not and encouraged him to pursue the relationship." I knew this, at least, from what Rowan told me. "She did not tell him your role in the Mavens or why you were at the property." A mix of unease and relief washes through me.

"Two, with that intel, Annette and I both agreed it might be for

the best if you tell Mr. Fisher about your role. From what I understand, Aurora is still unable to access the internal communications
system for the resort, as well as some of the saved cloud data, which
could give her a significant advantage. Pooling resources could be the
best plan of action."

A mix of apprehension and relief wash through me. This would
have been great to have known, say, four hours ago. Still, that means
outing Rory, and I'm not the most comfortable with that.

"But—"

"I would like you to discuss the decision with Aurora first, of
course, since you'd be revealing her as well, but I believe she'll be
okay with it as well."

I sit on this for a moment before taking in a deep breath.
"Gabriel, I need you to know, this job is important to me. I would
never, ever get involved with someone while on assignment," I say,
feeling the need to defend myself. "This is..."

"It's different. I know. And the fact that you have kept me up to
date every step of the way is why we don't have a problem."

"But what if..." I hesitate, unsure of what to say or if I should even
say anything. "What if..."

"What if it becomes more?" He asks, answering my question. I
don't respond, but he knows my answer anyway. "Then it becomes
more, Josie."

"But...this job..." Is secret. Is important to me. Is a part of me.
"This job would get complicated if I'm with someone, wouldn't it?"

"This job is not supposed to be your life. It's supposed to be part
of your life."

"It's not my life."

"When was your last date?" he asks.

"That is incredibly personal," I say, aghast.

"I have sat on work calls where you and Aurora or Demetria or
Alanna tell me the ins and outs of your menstrual cycle."

I roll my eyes, partially at everyone's full, legal names being used.
"Because certain jobs are more effective at different times of the

month! My boobs are insane when I'm ovulating, and Demi becomes a demon when she's about to get her period. She can't win over a shark when she's PMSing, and we all know that. It's—"

"Yeah, yeah, yeah, basic biology. I'm just saying. I've also heard you and Aurora talking about whether you spit or swallow."

I try not to react, but the mere mention of swallowing reminds me of this afternoon with Rowan.

I really am fucked, aren't I?

"So, I think asking about your last date before this mission is valid," he continues. I sigh, then think, unable to remember the last time I was on a date that wasn't for work. Three years? Four?

"Well..." I start, brow furrowing both because I can't remember and because I don't know what it has to do with anything. "No? But that's because this job makes that complicated. I can't tell anyone—"

"That has never been a rule."

"Excuse me? We have very clear instructions—"

"Your contract says you cannot tell anyone without consulting me. But you can, in fact, tell people you care about, people you trust. I do require that they sign an NDA, which, for some people is a deal breaker, but I would never expect you women to be single forever." This throws me completely, but he keeps speaking. "But I would also assume that a man like Rowan Fisher would not only understand, but appreciate an NDA."

I let out a small laugh, acknowledging that fact.

"This job shows you a lot of the shittiest parts of people, men especially," I say, my true reason for avoiding relationships.

I can't see Gabriel, but I swear to god I can hear him shrug.

"That's kind of the risk of life, isn't it? Gotta find someone you like enough to commit to, then trust they won't fuck you over. With a gut like yours, I know you'll always make a good choice."

"So, what you're telling me is I should go find him and tell him everything and hope he's still into me after?"

Gabriel chuckles then.

"I'm telling you to trust your gut, Josephine. You have a great one;

it's why I hired you. You only trust it when you're on a job. Try trusting it off the job. If you didn't trust him, didn't think he would respect you and your career, you wouldn't have even gotten close to this far into something with him. You wouldn't be upset at the possibility he wouldn't believe that you're telling him the truth. You wouldn't be as tangled up as you are." I lift a lip in a.sneer that he can't see, but he laughs as if he can. "You know I'm right."

"What if he doesn't want to hear it?" I ask in a nervous whisper.

"That's the first step, right? Try?"

"Right now?" I ask, nervous, and Gabriel laughs. The man laughs.

"I mean, considering you just left him, maybe give it some time. Sleep on it, decide how you'll phrase things, and talk to Rory. But soon. Don't let it simmer."

I crunch my nose and then ask my next question, feeling now like I'm talking to a parent who is giving his teenage daughter advice rather than my boss. "What do I... What do I say?"

He lets out a soft, kind sigh. "That's all up to you, Maven. If you're comfortable with it, you can tell him whatever you'd like—at the end of the assignment, he'll be made aware of the company, anyway."

I sigh, then nod. "Okay. Thanks, Gabriel. So I'm not fired?"

"No, you're not fired, Maven."

"Okay. Thanks, Gabriel.

"Anytime, Josephine."

Then the phone clicks off. As I hang up, somehow both more conflicted and more confident, I wonder if Gabriel is secretly a romantic at heart.

THIRTY-THREE

ROWAN

She's lying.

She has a tell, and I don't think even she knows, but she has about a dozen tells that I see every time she tells a mistruth, and she is *lying*.

About what, I don't know, but I'm going to find out.

That's all I'm thinking as I let Josie walk away from me, the look of hurt and panic bright in her eyes. The look hurt but I also knew I needed her to leave, to give me space to get my thoughts together before I said something I couldn't take back.

That's why I'm in my office before the sun rises after what felt like the longest day of my life, one where I spoke to numerous reporters and police officers and investigators trying to figure out what the fuck happened. I spoke with the sauna manufacturer, who informed me that the issue was that the wires were cut in a way that allowed the sauna to still function, but the safety feature wouldn't activate. This is not common knowledge; someone would have to know exactly which wire to snip in order to manage it.

At this point, I don't trust a soul here. Everyone is a suspect in my mind, everyone worthy of further investigation, and no one can be fully trusted. It's why, when I should be getting ready for a full day of meetings, I'm sitting at my desk reviewing all the different security feeds from the past two weeks. Our guy seems to know the angles to avoid, and when they can't avoid, they have the ability to break into our system and mess with the feed. But I have to believe they aren't good enough to catch *everything*, so I've decided to spend the next however long period of time watching every single minute of footage I can to find something. Anything.

Starting with yesterday, in the spa.

According to the timestamps, it's an hour after their scheduled treatment ended, but Josie and Rory are still in the spa area. That's when they walk into the main lobby area, looking around as if checking for people before entering a supply room that I know is marked 'Employees Only.' Josie tries the door and fails, but then pulls something from her bag: a keycard. I bet if I check the recent scans, I'll see it's *my* keycard. The door opens, and she steps in before looking around. Similar to the night I caught her in the bag room, she takes out her phone, snapping photos of what I think is the sign-out sheet as well as the supplies in the room. Rory moves in quickly and does something further that the cameras don't catch while Josie stands out front, seeming to be on lookout.

It reminds me of the time I found her in the hallway, and she wouldn't tell me what she was doing.

What *is* she doing? If I went by what it looked like, I'd say she was plotting or planning some kind of sabotage, that she and Rory are the culprits we're looking for, but it just doesn't make sense. My gut can't accept that as the truth.

Especially not when she hears something and starts moving towards the sauna. I switch the cameras to watch her enter that room, watch the look of genuine panic as she investigates the problem before, as if it's her last resort, she pulls the keycard out of her bag and overrides the sauna.

She looks panicked and concerned, but the way she and Rory jump in, calm and cool-headed like they've encountered emergencies like this before, tells me this isn't a simple case of right place, right time.

That's when I start making a list of all the places I've caught her and how many of them align with incidents that've occurred at the resort, both before and after her arrival.

She arrived after the rental shack was destroyed, but that's where I found her on her first day at the resort, checking it out. Investigating? Looking for something? She told me she was there because she saw a turtle and walked to take a picture of it, but it doesn't add up.

Then she was with me near the pool house the day the main pool was flooded with dish soap.

And, of course, she slipped on the hiking excursion.

My mind starts moving, remembering small details, like telling her about the leaks just a day before the source was found, the source whose bag she was digging through at the bag check room. I told her I was stressed about it, and the next day she...solved it? But how? Who could she have told if not me?

Obviously, there's something I'm missing, and I am determined to find it, but my mind is swirling as pieces start to fall into place, a timeline that is starting to make sense, but also, no sense at all. Moving to the security footage from that night in the bag room, fast forwarding through before I finally see Josie walk in. She looks around, watching a woman leave before moving right to the blue bag and opening it. She sifts through, then grabs her phone from her bra before taking photos. She looks...smug, as if she discovered something to confirm her thoughts, and then she jumps in panic after she's slipped it all back in the bag.

Because I walked in, I know, but I can't help but watch it on camera; the entire interaction plays out, her sauntering to me, teasing me, then tempting me into kissing her. Saying she was playing me feels wrong, the wrong adjective for what happened, but she was definitely *distracting* me. And distracted I was. My head keeps moving through times we've bumped into each other and landing on the time I saw her at the bar waiting for Rory. I try and remember times and dates, then find her walking towards the bar. I click over to another camera to catch where she came from, and my heart stills.

As I watch Rory walking with Josie, then stepping away to the pool house, while Josie continues to move toward the bar, where she sits and watches the pool house intently.

My mind is buzzing.

Why was she digging through Regina's bag? Why was Rory in the pool house, and why do they wind up everywhere when something happens? What the fuck is happening? I don't think they're the root cause of the acts of sabotage, so what could it be?

Suddenly, a memory ignites in my mind.

I've got it covered, Annette had said when I offered to come and find the person responsible after the fire. *I hired an investigation firm.* I didn't ask who because I'd assumed it was Wilde Security, as they typically do this kind of work for us.

But...what if I was wrong? What if it wasn't them at all?

That's when I start digging.

Aurora Daniels arrived with Josephine Montgomery on Friday, and the trip was purchased and booked a day previously, not something we see too often, but not completely out of the blue. The credit card used is Aurora Daniels' business card. It takes me a bit of digging through channels I probably shouldn't know how to or be allowed to access because the original business is a shell company owned by a different company. It takes an hour of searching each shell company before I find what I believe to be the true company name.

Maven Investigations LLC.

There's no website and no social proof or information about the abstract business, but there are a few forum posts, and quickly, pieces start to fall into place.

Gorgeous women finding discreet answers for all of your most pressing needs.

Then I dig into the reviews.

I hired the Mavens to find proof that my husband was hiding away assets to avoid paying alimony.

I contracted the Mavens to find out if an employee was stealing money.

The Mavens helped me find out that my competitor was getting information from my staff.

The last one catches my attention: *Maven Investigations helped me find who was leaking information from my tech company, something that no one on my team had been able to catch. They're discreet, efficient, and professional. I highly recommend them.*

There are no names or any other information attached to the company, though I do find what seems to be a referral number that leads to a generic voicemail where you're instructed to leave your potential job, location, and budget, and they will contact you if it's a good fit.

That's when I follow my gut instinct and make a call.

"Who is she?" I say as soon as Annette answers the phone.

"Rowan, so pleasant as always. How can I help you on this fine morning?" Annette says with an exasperated sigh. I'm pacing my office as she goes through her greeting, fighting the urge to punch a fucking wall.

Because, somehow, I know that Josie was sent here to investigate my company.

"Who *is* she?"

"You're going to have to be more specific than that, Rowan."

I know she knows; I can tell by the way she's dancing around the question, but I don't have time for these games.

"Josie Montgomery. Who the fuck is she?" Silence fills the line, a first in my experience. Annette loves to chat, and is rarely at a loss for words, so I fill in. "I did some digging, found her stay was paid for not by her, but by some kind of company card. It took me a while to unravel the LLCs, but eventually I got there, and I'm not liking what I'm finding. Who is she? What is Maven Investigations? Because right now, I'm heavily hoping you're the one who hired them. If not, we have big fucking problems." My breathing is heavy even to my own ears, the adrenaline coursing through me.

A deep, annoyingly calm sigh comes through the other line. "Can you do a video call?" my boss asks.

"I don't want a video call, Annette; I want answers!"

"And you'll get them, but I want to watch your face to make sure I don't have to call security to make sure you're not going to go off your rocker when I tell you." My jaw goes tight, my stomach twisting at that, at the confirmation that something is amiss, and I was right to be wary.

"Annette..."

At that moment, a call rings through my laptop.

"Answer that," she says brusquely, then hangs up the phone. With a deep sigh and a look in the mirror in my attached bathroom to school, my features and fix my hair—a mess from running my hands through it—I sit in the desk chair and accept the call. Annette is sitting there, not in her office yet, but at what I believe is her kitchen table.

"I would like to start this by informing you that you were never a suspect of mine."

My gut drops. *Suspect*.

"Jesus Christ," I grumble.

"But as you know, someone has been meticulously messing with the Keys resort. Since you were, in fact, the main champion for this location, I was pretty sure it wouldn't have been you since it would have made *you* look bad and that's so far out of your character. Not to say that people who sabotage things make the most sense. But you do have enemies, people who want your job, people who want to make sure you don't get *their* jobs, so I didn't want to broadcast to *anyone* I was bringing in the Mavens."

I open my mouth to say something more, but I'm cut off again when she continues her explanation. "Josephine Montgomery is an investigator with the Mavens and is there to figure out who is to blame for the problems plaguing the location."

"So Josie is an investigator?" My mind is reeling, thinking of all the places I've seen her, all the places we've bumped into one another. Finding the info for the reporter, behind the crime scene, at the sauna...it all makes sense, now.

"Yes, and a good one, though I should have known you would unravel that fact. You aren't great at letting mysteries lie."

Was this all a sham? Our reconnecting, our hooking up, the flirting, the feelings... "Did you know I knew her? Before I told you?" There's a moment of hesitation that makes my nerves rise. "Annette."

My patience is running thin, and even though I know I can't, I want to storm out of the office and find Josie, demand answers, and find out if any of this was even real. Since that would be completely idiotic, I focus my interrogation on Annette.

"Yes, I was informed of your previous interactions and history with her early on, and was told it wouldn't be a problem, especially once I told the Mavens you weren't a suspect in my eyes. She's been very up front about...a lot of things with her boss regarding your connection."

Fuck. That might mean that Annette might know I've hooked up with her while she was here. That's so unprofessional. It would be grounds to fire me, and— "Calm down, Rowan, you're not in trouble. These are greatly extenuating circumstances, and we are all very aware of that." Silence takes over as I continue to go over these new facts, slotting them into what I already knew.

"Were you ever going to tell me?" I ask, suddenly, confused and hurt.

She sighs. "It wasn't mine to tell," Annette says with a sigh.

"Oh, come on, I—"

"My contract with the Mavens indicates I am to keep not only the work that they're doing for me, but their existence, to myself, unless it is for a referral, at which point I can only give their name and information. Telling anyone puts not just the company at risk, but the investigators as well. They find out sensitive information that has, in some cases, exposed crimes. It wasn't mine to tell, Rowan."

I sit there, contemplating.

It seems that Josie's job is an investigator of some sort and she does it very much under the radar. From what I've read, the company she works for is incredibly successful in what it does and with the results it achieves.

"She stole my keycard," I say, almost petulantly.

Annette shrugs. "I wouldn't give them access to anything in order to avoid suspicion, but I told them if they could access things on their own, I was fine with it. They've been able to hack into most of the systems, but they didn't have a universal keycard yet."

I want to be annoyed that she stole *mine*, especially during a moment of intimacy, but I'm starting to understand it.

And more so, I'm kind of grateful that by stealing the card, Josie was able to help the guest as soon as possible.

"What, so I just move on, pretending I don't know this?"

"They have a job to do, Rowan. You need to let them do that job, and I'm sure she would rather be the one to tell you about her job when she's ready." There's a pause before a smile spreads on Annette's face. "Though, I'm sure you can sweet-talk your way into getting her to spill her secrets to you." My brows furrow, trying to make sense of what she's saying.

"She uses her looks and her charm to get whatever information she wants out of people. In your case, I would hazard to guess that turnabout is fair play." There's a sneaky smile on her lips as she shrugs. "I happen to know that her boss has recently approved her telling you about what she does."

Turnabout is fair play.

Huh.

I hadn't thought about that.

Because the truth is, as I sit with this information, I understand why Josie couldn't tell me what was going on, especially when I realize it's part of her job *not* to share that. That being said, I don't want secrets between us anymore. If anything, I want to help her on her mission to figure things out. I bet with my increased access and her and Rory's training, we could quickly close this case.

And maybe then you could take an actual break, a real vacation with Josie.

Annette smiles at me then, clearly seeing some kind of resolve on my face, before she nods.

"All right, well, it seems like you have some work to do today. Let me know if you need anything from me. Otherwise, I'll see you at the board meeting next week." And then the screen goes black.

I sit back with a small smile and a shake of my head, sighing and also deeply relieved as I begin to formulate my plan.

THIRTY-FOUR

JOSIE

R: Dessert?

Reading the text for the fourth time doesn't ease the pounding of my heart. I've spent the entire day continuing our job, interacting with guests and employees alike, trying to find new angles to investigate while pretending as if my stomach hasn't been in knots all day.

I thought about making an effort to find Rowan somewhere in the resort, looking at the cameras to find out where he is and bumping into him, but couldn't stomach the idea of him either avoiding me or ignoring me. My mind has run through a million different ways he could respond to my finally telling him the truth, and because my mind is my own worst enemy, few of them were positive.

Last night, I told Rory all about my conversation with Gabriel, and she agreed that when I felt like the time was right, I should let Rowan in on what we're doing here, but I've been too much of a scaredy cat to do so. Except now, he's texting me for a little chat.

He's asking about *dessert*.

Remembering our conversation before everything imploded, I can't help but feel a thrill at the thought of it, since that could mean so many different things.

Food?

Sex?

Despite common sense, I find myself wondering if maybe I could put off the much-needed confession just for a bit, just in case he decides he wants nothing to do with me after. At least then I'd have one night of complete pleasure before I broke my own heart.

"Why do you have that face?" Rory asks, looking at me over her computer as she pulls details on all the employees. After an unfruitful day where we made no headway, she's back in her happy place. She's still unable to hack into the employee database where payroll and hours worked and clock-in and out times are, but she's making it her mission to crack that tonight.

"I just got a text from Rowan. He wants to grab dessert, I think." My stomach is a flutter of nerves and panic and, admittedly, excitement, something I'm strangely getting used to when it comes to Rowan. But right now, the nerves are almost outweighing everything else, excitement.

"Are you going to say yes?"

I flop on the couch with a heavy sigh before moving to my elbows and answering.

"I don't know. What do you think? Should I?"

She tips her head left, then right, before answering.

"I think it would be sketchier if you refused, but I also know that if you want to keep your distance, that would be fine. I support your decision either way."

"Why are you being so nice?" I ask with a sneer, not used to this gentler version of Rory. She shrugs.

"I don't know. Trying something new. Plus, if Gabriel trusts it, I have to trust it. This job doesn't work if we don't trust the big guy."

I nod, knowing that also to be true. I also know the truth of what she doesn't say: *the job doesn't work if we don't trust each other.* At the end of the day, Rory trusts me to make the decision I feel will be best, not just for myself, but for the case.

"What if he asks me about the card?"

"I think you know what to say if he asks about that," she says, a sympathetic look on her face.

"Or I could just avoid the subject altogether," I contemplate, always happy to avoid uncomfortable conversations whenever possible. Healthy? Probably not. Good for my anxiety? Questionable. My preference? Absolutely.

Rory sighs, then stands before moving toward where I lie on the couch. When she stretches out a hand to me, I take it begrudgingly before she pulls me up to her.

"Reply and say you'll be ready in twenty. Get hot. Then go have dessert, get laid, and tell him the truth."

"In that order?" I ask because I could possibly work with that. She gives me the look a mother gives her child who is trying to avoid eating vegetables.

"In whatever order makes the most sense." I grimace at her, and she lets out a laugh before reaching for my phone and offering it to me. "Go. Text the hot man and go get some. I don't think it's going to be as dire as you fear." I stare at the phone like it's a grenade before groaning and taking it, knowing she's right.

J: Yeah, I can be ready in twenty

I hit send on the text and leave my phone face down on the bathroom counter while I go pick out my hottest dress and underwear set I packed, going for *femme fatale, couldn't resist me if he tried* vibes. By the time I head back to the bathroom to fix my hair and makeup, I already have a simple reply from him telling me where to meet him.

When I arrive at the lobby in the hottest red dress I've ever owned and my highest heels, my hands are shaking. When I see Rowan leaning against the wall beside the restaurant he told me to meet him at, my heart nearly stops. He's too fucking handsome for his own good, and I wonder if he even knows it. In dark slacks and a white button-down, once more rolled to the elbows, his hair pushed back neatly, he's every woman's dream man.

He's *my* dream man, which makes the sudden reality that I might lose it all even more painful. The last time I saw him, he was rightfully mad at me or, at the very least, confused and frustrated, and we haven't addressed it in the least.

But when he sees me approach and pushes off the wall to take a few steps towards me, his face beaming, I almost forget it all. The lies, the assignment, the assumptions, the accusations.

He looks like a man excited to go on a date, nothing more.

And when he pulls me into him, one arm wrapping my waist and one going to my hair before he kisses me deeply, the rest of my nerves melt away. He pulls back, a heated smile on his lips

'You like dessert?"

"It's my favorite food group."

He smiles then, passing his lips to mine again.

"You look beautiful," he murmurs.

"It's a special night," I tell him, low and full of anticipation.

His look goes dark and wanting before he dips his head again like he can't help himself.

"Do you want to go get a dessert, or do you want to come up to my room with me?" he whispers against my lips. A shiver runs through me, but before I can tell him that I would *love* to go up to his room with him, a different response tumbles from my lips.

"Are you still mad at me?" I ask, desperate to know the answer. I realize that I need to know before I can even think about relaxing.

"I was never mad, Josie," he says, his lips brushing along my neck, sending a thrill through me. "I was confused. I was stressed."

"And now you're not?"

"Now I want you more than any of that matters."

I can work with this, I tell myself. I can handle that. I can deal with the rest of it...later.

Right now, I'm going to live in the present. And present me wants Rowan Fisher.

"Then upstairs," I whisper. "We can order up dessert later."

And when he smiles wide, I know it was the right answer.

THIRTY-FIVE

JOSIE

We walk up to Rowan's room in silence, Rowan walking so quickly I feel like I'm almost running behind him. When we get to his room, he pulls out his keycard and tugs me inside, slamming the door shut behind us and pinning me to it as he does.

"I need to get you out of this," he says, lips to my neck, and I moan at the idea of it.

"Zipper in the back," I say, my own fingers moving at the buttons on his shirt as his lip move over whatever skin he can find. It's frantic and frenzied, the need to expose and touch as much skin as possible once and for all. His fingers find the zipper and tug it down before using his teeth on the straps, tugging them off my shoulders until they fall down, my dress following suit. He steps back, looking me over.

"You're so fucking beautiful," he whispers, taking in me like he's never actually seen something so breathtaking in his life.

Now, I have a good ego and great self-confidence. Once I got out of my awkward phase in early high school, I always knew I looked good in a fifties bombshell kind of way, no matter what the current body trend says. Smooth skin, lush, wide hips, and a small waist all make even my mouth water when I look in the mirror.

But never in my life have I felt as gorgeous as I do right now, naked in front of Rowan Fisher, his fingers roving over every inch of my body. He's looking at me like I was carved out of the most precious material with him and him alone in mind. Like he wants to keep me, to preserve me. To make me his.

Finally, he shakes his head like he's knocking himself out of some daze, and steps closer to me, tugging my naked body into his clothed one.

"Do you remember when I said I was going to tie you to the bed and have my way with you, so there was no way we wouldn't finish what we started?" Heat runs through me, desire and need, and so much lust I think it might consume me coursing through my veins with his mete words. He holds up three silky ropes that I don't remember him grabbing, and my mind does not want to spend too long on the how of how he has them, just the why, until I take a closer look and see it isn't rope at all, but ties tied together.

"My god, how many ties do you have, Rowan?" I ask with a laugh. "I don't think I've seen you wear more than one or two while you're here."

He gives me a boyish smile that I fucking love before shrugging. "They're easy to throw in a suitcase, and I never know how many to bring or how long I'll be somewhere. I brought a bunch." He shakes the fistful with a smile before gently wrapping his hand around my arm.

He has me sit on the edge of the bed, then shifts my arms behind my back, stacking my wrists over each other before he ties them together with a gentle, assured movement. My breathing escalates at the touch of his fingers on my bare skin, my ability to touch him removed. "At any time, you say stop, and we're done. I let you out of these, and I fuck you nice and sweet. He presses a kiss to the inside of my wrist, where I'm sure he can feel my pulse thrumming.

"And if I don't?" I ask, my voice a mere whisper.

"Then we're going to play. And there will be no interruptions." There's a smile in his voice before he presses another kiss to my neck, and I shiver. He moves to the foot of the bed and continues his quick work, using his tie-rope to tie one leg and then the other to each bed post until my legs are spread wide on the bed. It's not uncomfortable, just enough that I feel stretched. On display. For his enjoyment.

It's absolutely thrilling.

"Look how fucking pretty you are," he groans when he stands back to survey his handiwork.

"You're still dressed," I note, taking in his body.

He smiles, a wicked one that goes straight to my core.

"I'll undress when I'm ready. I'm in control, Josephine."

Another shiver runs through me, both at the look in his eyes and the idea of him being in control.

With my job, I'm always in control. Always on, always aware. Otherwise, it could be dangerous. But here, with Rowan, I feel safe. Able to turn it off, to let him do with me what he will. A sense of ease runs through me at the realization, the understanding that I trust him so completely.

"You've been telling lies, Josie," he whispers, and a shiver rolls through me. I should feel nervous about his statement, but instead, my body is heating up.

"Lies? Me? Never."

He smiles wide, a hand moving up my inner thigh.

"Mmm, I think we both know you're not being completely truthful," he says, his hand grazing back down the same path and moving up my other leg. "What are you doing here at the resort?"

Oh my fucking god.

Is this what I think it is?

"I'm on vacation." The lie slips so smoothly off my tongue, an impulse from years of doing this that I almost convince even myself. That's half the battle in this job—in telling half-truths and complete lies, you have to do it so well, you sell even yourself on the story.

And I'm really good at my Job.

"You know, I kind of thought this was going to be more...touching instead of talking," I whisper.

"Oh, there will be plenty of touching, Josie. Once you tell me what I want to know." His fingers trail up my inner thigh, and my heart pounds with anticipation. I can feel it all over, but most intensely between my legs.

"Is this...is this an interrogation?" I ask, fighting back a shocked laugh. He raises an eyebrow at me.

"Is there something you should be interrogated for?" There's a smirk on his lips as a finger runs over the seam where my pussy and thighs meet, teasing but never touching where I need him most.

"I..." My goes blank when he takes that finger up and over my pubic bone and down the other side. "Rowan," I whisper. I'm unable to focus on anything but my need and the promise of him.

"Can I touch you here?" he asks, moving his hand to hover almost politely over my pussy.

"Oh my god, yes, please," I beg and again, he smiles before using his thumbs to part me, moving to his knees on the floor and staring at my center.

"God, you're pretty," he mumbles to himself, then runs a finger through my center. "All wet and needy, exactly how I think I'm going to like you best." A shaky breath leaves my lips. "Do you need me, Josie?"

I nod frantically. "Yes. I need you. Please."

That seems to appease him as he slides a finger inside. My body tightens around the digit instantly. We both groan in unison at the feeling of him sliding inside me. Quickly, he slides out and inserts another slowly, and when I try to buck my hips up to get more, I remember I can't. I can't do much of anything tied to the bed like this. "Oh, fuck."

He chuckles deviously before moving his fingers faster.

"At my mercy, at my whim," he says, fingers moving faster, crooking up as they slide in, brushing against my G-spot. I realize then I'm already close, faster than I've ever climbed there before. I don't know if it's just the long lead-up, the fact that I didn't come yesterday, or that I'm tied up and at his mercy, but I'm not questioning it.

"Rowan, please," I beg softly, and he smiles down on me.

"The first one will be a freebie, just for being my good girl," he says, and even though I'm confused and stuck on the first one, I nod, pleading. "Some goodwill to remind you that, regardless of everything, I trust you. I believe you. I'm going to take care of you."

I nod, looking down my body at him.

"Yes, yes. I'm good. I'll be good, Rowan." I need it more than I need air right now and he must see it because he puts his thumb to my clit and starts to pump a finger into me. My hips move as much as I can without bending my knees, without breaking the unspoken rules, and in just a few moments, I'm tipping over the edge, screaming his name as an orgasm washes over me.

Except he doesn't stop. His fingers keep moving, keep fucking me, though it's slower now, more torturous, and he's added a thumb to my clit. I don't get to bask in the relief of the orgasm he just gave me because my body is already moving back to that same state of need.

"I've never seen anything hotter than watching you come, Josie," he murmurs, eyes locked on where his fingers are working me. I tighten around him, and he groans. "So fucking pretty, watching you take me. I could do this all night, you know. Make you come."

I shake my head because, as delightful as that sounds, I want more. I want...I want everything.

"Please, Rowan. Just...." My mind doesn't work, not right now, not like this, when my body is already gearing up for another orgasm from his endless ministrations, his fingers that already seem to know my body so well. "Please just fuck me."

He smiles up at me, and a devious look is written across my face. "I will. Once you tell me what I want to hear."

His eyes roam over my body, tied up and at his mercy, and I understand completely. He's tied me to his bed not just to have fun and make me feel good, though I know that's part of the plan, but to convince me to tell him the truth of why I'm here. There's a glint in his eye, like he already knows the truth and wants to hear it from me, wants to pull it from me.

But despite it all, I've never felt safer than I do in this moment with him.

Right now, I feel completely cared for. I know in my gut if I told him to stop, really stop, he would drop whatever game he's playing. He would step away, untie me and, if I wanted, he would fuck me sweet and slow.

But I don't want him to stop.

In fact, I'm liking this new game, liking that he thinks he's going to win so easily. And even more, I like the idea of proving him wrong.

"Never," I say in a whisper, a seductive smile on my lips, the maneater in the word.

Somehow, in my heart of hearts, I know none of this matters. He's having fun, and this is just another game of ours. He's not actually trying to force anything out of me. Somehow, I know this is a competition for both of us to see who can hold out the longest.

And I love winning. Not to mention, I'm really the one winning right now. I hold onto that thought as a third thick finger slides into me, stretching me deliciously before slowly gliding in and out. My pussy tightens around him, already eager for what I know I'll be getting later. My head tips back, my eyes drifting shut as I let my body take what he's giving me. My hips move in tiny thrusts in time with his movements, and I moan loudly, really playing it up.

He lets out a low "fuck," and I know I'm doing well when I look and see him staring at me with heated eyes, clearly as turned on by the pleasure he's giving me as I am receiving it.

This isn't too bad. In fact, I bet I'll win in no time. When his thumb joins once again, rubbing intent circles over my clit, another orgasm hits, and I call out his name as I come around his fingers, my second of the night.

Once more, the pleasure comes quick and flows through me like a wave, but before I can completely ride it out, he's gone, removing his hand and leaving me feeling...unsated. My eyes snap open to look at him, and there's a broad grin on his lips.

He knows.

He knows exactly what he just did, what he's doing to me.

He's having fun.

"Rowan," I whine.

"What's wrong, troublemaker?"

"I need..." I shift my hips, dying to close my legs to get some kind of friction, only to be frustrated when I remember I can't.

"You thought I'd really just make it that easy for you, Josie?" I kind of did, if we're being honest. He sees that look on my face and smiles a devilish smile once more before moving to bend over the bed, his face just inches from my pussy. His fingers start playing again, soft, gentle caresses that slide through my wetness before he lets a slow breath out, the wisps of it coasting along me in a delicate torture.

"Can I kiss this?" he asks low.

"God, yes, please," I whisper, then watch as his head dips down. His tongue is hot and wide and wet as it takes one long swipe along me, the tip of his tongue dipping into my center just a bit before sliding up and over my clit. When his lips circle it, he sucks gently over the over-sensitive bud, and my back arches off the bed.

But other than these small shifts, I can't move, and suddenly, I'm feeling the full brunt of what that entails. I can't use a hand to press his head to me, can't wrap my legs around his back to get the angle I want. I'm open and at his mercy, unable to move. I never thought this would be something I would like, but right now, right here, with Rowan the one holding all of the power, I fucking love it.

"Oh, fuck, Rowan."

He pulls back to look up at me, that wide, taunting grin across his lips.

"Oh, I'm going to enjoy this a fuck of a lot," he says in a groan before moving his face back to my pussy. My hips try to roll as his tongue moves against me, as he slides a finger deep into me, making me scream as bolts of pleasure strike through me. It seems the few times we've been intimate, Rowan has learned a lot about my body and what I need, because somehow he avoids giving me exactly what I need to tip over the edge. He alternates between short, hard sucks at my clit and fluttering teases across it, to fucking my cunt hard with his fingers to simply pressing against the spot inside me that makes me scream. His head moves back, those fingers deep and still inside me, his face wet with me.

"Are you going to tell me?" he asks.

I smile despite it all.

"I have nothing to tell," I say in a whimper. He smiles then, dipping down to continue eating me with a fervor, this time giving me everything I need with such precision, I know it's intentional.

I can't take it. I'm falling over the edge with his name on my lips as the white-hot orgasm slices through me. I anticipate the relief it brings and the moment of sanity I'll feel when it passes with bated breath.

Except it doesn't come.

Rowan doesn't stop.

Instead, after my first orgasm rolls through me, his mouth latches on my clit, two fingers fucking me hard as he continues to suck and lave at my clit on a mission.

"Oh, fuck, Rowan," I groan, and when he moans against me, I come again, this time harder and faster, the heat washing over me for a moment but somehow leaving even less relief. "Rowan!" I cry as his relentless torture of my clit continues, extending the orgasm or maybe just adding a second on to the end of it. I'm losing track of reality as pleasure rolls through me, over and over.

Finally, when I think I might break, he relents, sitting back on his heels to gaze over my body. My chest is heaving, my mind is muddled, my body a mess. Meanwhile, he sits there completely dressed, though the hard bulge in his slacks at least tells me he's torturing himself as much as he is me.

"What are you doing here?" he asks as I try and catch my breath, and it takes a moment for my brain to come back to this orbit, to understand there was a question at all.

"Wha...?" I pant.

"What are you doing here? At the Daydream Resort?" My mind tumbles as I try to figure out what he means and what he's saying before I remember our game. Finally, my senses start to return, and my training kicks in, falling on the story we've told everyone.

"A girls' trip with Rory," I say. His big hand moves to the path of skin, using my knee and wraps there, his thumb swiping rhythmically over the soft skin of my inner thigh, a taunt as he shakes his head.

"That's not the real reason you're here."

My pulse pounds.

"Yes, it is," I insist.

He looks at me with a fake-sad smile and shakes his head before his mouth drops to my clit again, sucking hard, tongue moving against my swollen bud as two fingers fuck me. It builds so fast, I can't breathe and right as I almost fall, he stops.

"Rowan, please," I whine, and he looks up at me, assessing.

"Do you want me to stop?" he asks, all seduction and needling gone from his tone. His eyes meet mine, and I see it there: the desire, the intrigue, but also the caring.

He isn't just asking if I want to be untied, if I want to be released and have full control of my body once again. He's asking if I want him to stop his line of questioning, if I want him to drop it.

And something tells me that just as he told me, when he tied me to his bed, he would stop as soon as I asked, and he wouldn't question me again, not until I was ready to confess it all.

But I am ready.

Not only do I trust him implicitly and want to no longer have this lie between us, but both his boss and mine have given me the go-ahead to let him into my biggest secret.

"No," I whisper in answer, and his smile widens with understanding. Then he moves back to teasing me, pinching my clit before fingering me.

"Tell me you're not here just for a vacation, and I'll give you a prize," he promises, his eyes dark and fixed on mine, his hand moving to cup his cock and shift it. The pleasure is cresting, the need almost tangible as my body rocks and shifts to no avail. I want to touch him. I want him to fuck me. I want him to take me, finally, and I think if I give him this, I might just get it.

So I break, if only in a small way. "I'm not here for vacation!" I shout, and he smiles down at me.

"Good girl. Now for your reward." I wait for him to stand, to undress and fill me, but he doesn't. Instead, his head drops to watch as he fingers me hard and fast, focusing on my G-spot with vigor. But right before I come, he stops, moving to my clit, rubbing fast and hard. A new kind of pleasure builds, a pressure I can't explain or control. Soon I'm panting his name, my body shaking, but once again, as I tip on the edge, he changes it, moving back to fingering me.

"Rowan!" I shout in protest and anger, but the man laughs.

"Trust me, Josie I'm going to give you something so good," he says, a promise I can't deny in his words. His jaw is slackened as he watches my pussy with anticipation and a hand moves to my lower belly, pressing a bit as he fingers me.

"Oh my god, oh my god," I groan, almost animalistically as a wet sloshing sound comes from between my legs.

"There you go, baby, just like that," he says. That pressure builds and grows, and a panic comes with it.

"Rowan," I whine, almost in worry but he smiles wider.

"I know, troublemaker, let it happen. Let me take care of you," he whispers, right before moving his hand, straightening it and sliding the bottom of his finger over my swollen clit hard and fast until the pressure peaks and I come. As I do, a gush of liquid leaves me, and I scream at the sensation. Distantly, I hear Rowan groan in admiration, He keeps rubbing, slower and softer as I ride it out and come back down to earth.

"Now that wasn't too hard, was it?" He asks, rubbing my wetness into my skin. It feels like it's everywhere, the bed soaked with my orgasm, and I know that this man just made me squirt for the first time.

And I kind of want to beg him to do it again.

Rowan gently slides a finger inside of me, watching as my body greedily takes him once more. "God, you get even prettier every time you come, you know. And this," he says, then pulls his fingers out before rubbing the whole of his hands over my pussy, palm on my entrance, fingers grinding over me clit. I let out a ragged moan as need somehow creeps back into my veins slowly. "Gets pinker and pinker. Wetter and wetter. Are you going to be satisfied if I don't fuck you tonight?"

I shake my head and whine.

"Rowan." I breathe heavy, my pussy throbbing, aching. I've lost count already on how many times I've come, but he's right: it's not enough. I'm empty and needy. I won't feel satisfied until he slides inside of me, fills me.

"You know," he says conversationally, bending over my and pressing a kiss to my belly. "Someone is out to ruin this hotel." My heart pounds, not from his words but from his lips circling my nipple now, sucking before and the blowing on the wet peak. My back arches with pleasure. "And while I don't think it's you, I think you do have something to do with it."

My eyes narrow on him, and I raise an eyebrow, trying to maintain whatever higher ground I possibly could have.

"Why would someone be out to ruin your hotel?"

His finger moves deeper in me, and my head rolls back a bit with the pleasure of it.

"That's the question, isn't it?" he asks. He moves further up my body and kisses me then, finally, and I think that might be my biggest undoing after all. His lips on mine, the taste of my cunt on his tongue as it slides inside my mouth. "I think you're here to help me find out." It's a quiet whisper and I almost argue it, but then his fingers are gone from inside me, and I can't focus on anything but the emptiness. "Tell me why you're here," he whispers into my neck.

And then his hips are between mine, his hard cock grinding into my clit through his slacks, and I groan. It's somehow more pleasure than when he fingered me, when he ate me out, than when he made me squirt and I know it's the promise of what's to come that has me finally giving him my confession, one I think he already knows somehow.

"I'm here on an assignment," I whisper, and he pulls back to look at me, a wide smile spreading over his face.

"That's my good girl," he groans, rocking his hips into me, shifting the angle of his hips until I'm gasping his name. Like this, he's fully in charge, and it's a true testament to how well he already knows my body somehow. In just a few moments, I'm falling over the cliff again, coming from the pressure of his cock against me and his panted breaths and quiet groans against my neck and nothing else.

When he pulls back, I see the need in his own eyes, I decide the game can be over. I just want to experience the totality of this soul-consuming pleasure with him, finally.

"I'm here to figure out—" I start, but then he moves away from me, and I moan. "No! No, Rowan, I'm going to—" His smile is wide as he stands and his fingers move to the buttons on his shirt, undoing them quickly before moving to his pants. I watch him in fascinated silence as he undresses, all taut muscles and broad shoulders, a light dusting of hair on his chest that, if my hands were free, I'd ghost my fingers over. And most impressively, his long, thick cock, the tip red with need and desire, precum dripping.

I can't find words or taunts or confessions as he moves between my legs, hands moving to my hips and shifting my body down so my knees bend, so I can lift my hips a bit. Then he's rubbing his thumb over my clit, round and round and round.

"Are you on birth control?"

"What?" I ask, so dazed that this question feels out of place. He smiles like he finds this—me—entertaining.

"Are you on birth control? I was tested and everything came back clear recently." I suck in air as I finally grasp what he's saying, then I nod. "You are?" I nod again, and he smiles wider. "Kind of important you use your words for this part, Josie. Consent and all."

My tongue come out to wet my lips before I nod again and finally make words happen.

"I just had my annual. I'm all good. On the pill." He grips his cock, and I watch through my parted legs as he strokes himself, and I groan at the sight.

"So I'm good to fuck you bare?"

Again, I groan. "I'll beg if I have to," I say without thinking.

He lets out a loud laugh, so heavily contrasting the moment and the night, and I love that about him, about us.

"You don't have to beg, baby," he says, then rubs the head of his cock over my swollen cunt, starting at my clit and sliding down to my entrance before moving back up. "Not this time, at least."

"Really? Because it's starting to feel like I'll have to beg you to fuck me soon," I mumble, widening my legs as I watch him move over me, a hand on the bed beside me, the other around his cock.

"I know why you're here," he says, so low I almost don't hear it. At the same time, he slowly presses the head of his cock into me. "I know you're here to figure out what's going on. I know you're here to save my hotel."

My breathing is erratic, not just because of his words, but because of his actions, because of the way I'm stretching around him, the way he's so thick that despite the insane amount of foreplay I've had, I can feel that stretch at all.

"Rowan," I mewl, hips moving to try and get him deeper. Instead, he stops moving all together, the hand that was on his cock moving to my hip to hold me in place and keep just the head of his cock buried inside me.

"You're here to help me, aren't you?" His thumb moves against me from where his hand is on my hip, quick but not with enough pressure to make me come.

"I—" A sharp inhale as he swipes over my sensitive, swollen clit, and I tighten around him. At least he's now in the same seductive torture as I am, if the look of absolute torment that crossed his face is anything to go by. "Yes," I finally confess. "I'm here to help you."

His face goes soft then, his hand moving to cup my cheek.

"You're such a good girl," he groans, and then he slides into me all the way.

He's long. He's thick. He fills me in a way I've never felt, so completely and perfectly. I moan as he does it, something he mirrors. Once he's deep inside of me, he holds there, eyes locking with mine, and I see it all there. The trust. The adoration. The need. The desire. The connection we've had for longer than either of us has been able to admit.

It's all there, out on the table, my secrets and his, and finally, it's just us. His hips slide back slowly, and he slides back in, and I moan his name. The need suddenly fills my veins and I want nothing more than to hold him to me, to claw at his back as he fucks me.

"Please, Rowan," I whisper almost frantically. "Please. I want to touch you." He groans deep as his cock slides into me again, and I bite my lip, feeling yet another orgasm brushing at the edges of my consciousness before he reaches behind me, cupping my back and moving to my wrists with his other hand, making quick work of the binding before rubbing them. I shift, bringing them between us while he presses the sweetest, softest kiss to the skin. He does this all while he's still buried deep, and I can't help but tighten at the gentleness he's showing me.

"Ankles," I whisper, and he turns. It slides him a bit deeper into me. He groans as I tighten round him, but he continues to untie my ankle restraints as well. When he's done, I wrap all four limbs around him, his hands moving to my hips to hold me to him.

I've never felt so safe and complete in my life.

"So fucking pretty, so fucking perfect. So fucking mine," he murmurs, his lips dropping to mine as he slides out and then into me. I moan at the feeling of him moving against swollen, sensitive flesh, gripping him tighter with my arms as I pepper kisses along his shoulders, his neck, anywhere I can reach.

"Yes, I'm yours, Rowan," I moan.

"You've always been mine, haven't you?"

"Oh my god, yes," I agree, face in his neck as his thrusts become harder, deeper, more consuming. He's grunting now with each movement, and each time he bottoms out, I tighten.

"And I've always been yours," he says through gritted teeth, like he needs to get this out before he lets it take over him.

"Rowan," I scream. That's what makes me clamp down on him and give in to the pleasure. The confession that it's not one-sided, but I own him just as much as he owns me, is what sends me over the edge.

As I tighten around him, my face burying into his neck, I come and come and come around him. It's bigger and better than anything I've ever felt, and something in my soul knows it's because it's him. I'm screaming his name, chanting it even, a prayer on my lips as he fills me with his own orgasm. And when he lays me down, cleans me up, and climbs into bed with me, I settle into his chest knowing there is no longer anything between us.

THIRTY-SIX

Rowan

It's all out on the table and somehow, despite my going into this knowing for the most part what I was going to hear, I'm thrown a curve.

But that could just be because I finally came inside Josie and made her mine, whether she knows it or not. I'm not letting this woman go, assignment or not.

I found Josie Montgomery in a bar and then fate forced us back together over and over until finally, I got the hint.

"So you're a spy?"

She lets out a loud laugh at my question before rolling over and on top of me. It feels...strange, knowing I just fucked her within an inch of her life while trying to get her to confess who she was to me.

I could have just been a normal human and asked her point blank, and there's a good chance she would have told me, but this was much more fun—and somehow, much more *us*.

We're chest-to-chest when she speaks, and I can feel the vibration of each word against my body as she speaks.

"I mean... yeah," she says it like it feels weird to say, which it may be, considering how secretive she is. "But not in like a James Bond, super spy gadgets, save the world from impending doom kind of way."

My hand glides over her hair, so soft and silky, I can't find the will to stop sifting my fingers through it. She lets out a little sigh, her eyes drifting shut as she does.

"What is it, then?"

"It's more...investigations. Most of my assignments are smaller scale PI type shit. Find out if a husband is cheating, if someone is hiding money, or proof of fraud. We all have our own specialties: Rory is great at cybersecurity and hacking. Though, I will say, the Daydream Resorts systems are great. She's been able to get into a few things, but not all. It's driving her insane."

I smile at that with a bit of pride.

"I'm the one who hired that out and made sure it was perfect. A friend of my assistant runs a top-notch security firm and set it up."

"Well, she hates you for that. Another friend of ours is great at ingratiating herself into the craziest situations to gather information; she's a chameleon. Another can lie so efficiently, even I'm not convinced I know her well."

"And you?"

"I'm the maneater," she says with a wide smile.

I raise an eyebrow at her. "Excuse me?"

She lets out a happy laugh. "We all have titles. Specialties. I'm the maneater. A few smiles and flips of my hair, I have a man eating out of my hand and confessing all of his deepest darkest secrets." She moves her fingers along my chest.

"You don't say." I smile, and she returns it. "What else do you do besides flirting your way to get idiotic men to spill everything to you?"

That easy smile fades, and I worry I may have gone too far, asked things I shouldn't have. Her hand lifts, a thumb caressing over my cheek before she bites her lip.

"More often than not, I put on a skin-tight dress that leaves little to the imagination and a full face of makeup and work it. I go to a party or a bar or even a fucking dog park and I find whoever I think could give me the intel I need. Sometimes it's our actual target; sometimes it's their best friend, or their older brother, or a coworker. Anyone who might know something about what I need. I flirt, charm, and work my skills, seamlessly getting them to confess something I need, and then I disappear."

"The bar?"

She smiles then. "The bar was me brushing up on my skills. I'd just gotten off an assignment where we determined a man was hiding money from his soon-to-be ex-wife to avoid alimony."

Rowan makes a disgusted face, further endearing him to me, and I nod. "Yup. So I went to the bar, saw that guy, and knew he was married. I have already shared all our information and what I know with his wife. The bartender—she's a friend of mine—got pictures. The wife can now file her own divorce or hire the Mavens to do more of a deep dive and make her a winning case file."

"So that was pro bono?"

She shrugs.

"Sometimes I can't help it. It's too easy, too fun. I've been like this since college, stealing people's secrets from them."

"You said that once. That you wanted to get all of my secrets from me."

It was when I caught her flirting with the bartender the day the pool filled with suds. When, for a split, finite second, I thought about throwing her over my shoulder and locking her in my room for the day, trying to get her out of my system.

Except now that I've had her, I have a sneaking suspicion I won't be able to get her *out of my system*. Not for a long, long time.

"I..." She pauses and I wait patiently for her to answer. "It's not like that, not with you. I know...all of this is a lot. The spy stuff, the maneater stuff." Her face screws up adorably. "But it's not like that with you. I swear. You're not...a target." I raise an eyebrow in disbelief, but she shakes her head. "Not really. I tried, trust me. I wanted to compartmentalize, but I couldn't. Ask Rory. You have to believe me, Rowan. I swear, I—"

Her voice goes frantic with nerves and panic, and I run a hand over her hair, trying to soothe her.

"Hey, hey," I say, shifting to grab her chin and force her to look at me. She hesitates for a beat before her body relaxes, seeing something in my gaze that soothes her.

"I know," I murmur. "I know, troublemaker." Her lips tip up. "So I'm dating the maneater, huh?"

"We're dating?" she asks, a self-satisfied smile on her lips. "That's so weird. I don't remember having that conversation with you." I shake my head at her, already realizing that if this stands the test of time, the way I have a gut feeling it will, this is my future. Constantly being needled about everything, a contest, a competition at every turn.

God, I can't wait.

"I wasn't planning to ask you, I figured it was kind of a given. But if you want, I can tie you up again and pull an answer out of you if you'd like."

There's contemplation in her eyes, and I let out a laugh, pulling her closer to me and pressing my lips to hers. "You need recovery time. But if that's what I need to do to get you to agree we're dating..." I say, my words dialing off. She considers it for a moment longer before laughing and shaking her head.

"No, no, I think you've earned me."

My chest goes warm with her words. "Finally," I say, pressing my lips to her neck. "I feel like I've been trying to earn you for fucking years."

"Years?"

I shrug because who am I to deny it now?

She shifts then to get a better look at me and smiles. "Speaking of that, what was your deal with me?" she asks, a question I was hoping we could avoid, but I guess it's as good a time as ever to answer. If she puts her cards on the table, I need to do the same. "You hated me from the start, even before you moved to Hudson City. You'd see me out in college and glower at me. I didn't get it, because we'd only ever met in passing before that."

I sigh and take in a deep breath. "We spent a whole night together. Your twenty-first birthday," I say, starting slow. "You were at Park Seven, and I bumped into you. We danced pretty much the whole night."

"What?" she asks, eyes wide, confirming something I realized pretty recently: Josie doesn't remember that night. She was obviously drunk, but I guess I'd never realized just *how* drunk.

"Yeah," I confirm, then her brows furrow and she speaks low, almost to herself.

"102418. Your passcode." My lips tip in a smile. I should have known it wouldn't take long for my brilliant girl to understand.

"The day I met you," I say. "I didn't realize until recently, I swear. I think that day has always just stuck with me."

"Sure, Rowan," she says with a laugh and I can't be annoyed: I wouldn't believe me either. "So what happened next?"

"You were leaving, your friends saying it was time to head out. I tried to get your number, set up something so we could have a date."

"*I don't date,*" she whispers.

"Yeah, that's what you said then, too," I tell her with a smile. "And then a week later you were out with some frat asshole and...I took it personally."

I run an embarrassed hand through my hair. It was years ago, and I'd held on to it for years. I wonder what would have happened if I'd just been an adult at any point between then and now and talked to her about it? "He was some rich asshole I knew from class, and I thought you'd turned me down because he had what I didn't."

I let the words hang between us before she shakes her head vehemently.

"Oh my god, no. Rowan... If anything, not coming from money is what keeps you *in* the running," she says, and I can't help but let out a laugh.

"Thank you?" I question.

"I just mean...with my job and, even back then, I met a lot of assholes with more money than common sense. They're all the same, and they're all assholes."

"Back then? Were you a Maven then?" She shakes her head.

"In college, I had a bit of a... side hustle. I'd tempt girls' boyfriends. A loyalty test, so to speak. See if they'd fall for it before they got in too deep with him and got their hearts broken. You'd be shocked how many did," she says, and I shake my head.

"No, I wouldn't. I've seen you work."

She smiles like it's a compliment, which I meant it as. Now that I have the full picture of what she's been doing on all those dates, I see it for the game it is, the trap it is, and she *is* amazing at it.

"But once they fell for it, I still had to follow through on the dates or else they'd start to add things up, you know?"

Slowly, I nod, understanding.

"So you weren't on dates? They were just so you could keep your cover?" She nods. "Good practice, I suppose. How'd you go from that to the Mavens?"

She shrugs. "No one really knows how Gabriel finds us. I was about to try and enter the FBI academy after graduation, but he offered me a job first. It was the perfect opportunity to use my unique skills."

"Flirting?"

"Conning men out of whatever I want them to give me."

"Mm, well, it's worked on me," I say, rolling to my back and pulling her on top of me. "What do you want?"

"What have you got?" she asks with a smile.

"I think it's better I show you," I say low, rolling once more until

I'm hovering over her. Her own smile widens, and as I start to kiss a trail down her body, she puts her hands behind her head.

"I think that's a great idea."

THIRTY-SEVEN

JOSIE

Josie

"I need to tell Rory, you know," I say, long after a second round and once again, more orgasms than I can keep track of. I thought it was some kind of trick, his own spy-level method of interrogation: orgasms until I cracked. But I think the truth of the matter is that making me come is Rowan's own personal kink.

I am so totally okay with that.

But now we've cleaned up and I can see a new text or seven blinking on my phone on the bedside table. Knowing it's my partner makes dread pool in my stomach.

It's not that I'm worried about whether Rory is going to be mad at me: she's made it clear that she's fine with my getting involved with Rowan, and Gabriel has confirmed that. She was also more than okay with my telling him everything.

It's more that I know there is no way Rowan is going to be okay with watching from the sidelines while Rory and I solve this mission, and she is not going to be okay with adding on someone from outside the organization.

"Is she your boss?" he asks. I shake my head before explaining.

"My partner. We do assignments together a lot."

"So you go around the country and what...? Solve crimes?"

"I mean, kind of. We do a lot of smaller assignments in the tri-state area—that's where we are most of the time. But occasionally we get something big, and we'll be shipped out somewhere. I live in Windale, right outside Hudson City." He nods like he's digesting this new information.

"Good. That's great news." My brows furrow, not understanding before he expands. "I'm in Hudson City," he says low, brushing his lips along my temple, and I smile wide, understanding what he's saying without actually saying it: it's good because once this is all done and over with, we'll still be close to one another.

Just like me, he isn't looking for this to end as soon as this case is solved.

"And your boss—"

I shrug. "I don't know him, but I get my checks on time every other week, so I can't complain much."

He lets out a laugh and shakes his head like that sounds insane to him, which, I suppose, for regular people, it would be.

"I've never even seen him. He calls us or does faceless video calls. Kind of weird, but you get used to it."

"I couldn't do it, not knowing who I work for, not knowing where I'll be next, not knowing what I'll be doing next..." He shakes his head, like the idea alone is sending him into a tizzy, and I smile.

"That's because you're a boring paper pusher."

"Boring, huh?" he asks, with a wide smile, and my god, I don't think I've ever seen him look so loose, so relaxed and unbothered. I like the idea that I brought him that peace, no matter how short-lived it may be.

"Oh yeah. Super boring," I say, stepping over to him. For a moment, I think we can delay the inevitable with one more roll in his bed. He must see my intention poorly hidden on my face because he grins, shakes his head, and shifts until he's sitting on the edge of the bed.

"Why do you seem so stressed about telling Rory?"

"Because I am." He chuckles, and despite my roiling nerves, I can't help but smile as well. I'm all smiles, a giant weight lifted now that there's nothing between us.

Okay, and probably that I've finally gotten some.

"Why?"

"Are you going to let Rory and I do our job without your input?"

He looks at me with a bit of a shy look. "I was kind of thinking that I could help," he says.

I let out a deep sigh.

"Yeah, that's what I thought. And while I'm fine with that, Rory is going to see it as a bump in her carefully crafted plan. Where I am Type Q and essentially a human tornado, she is Type A plus. She will not be fond of a random man coming into our mission."

"But I have access to—" he starts, but I shake my head, sitting up and pulling the blankets up with me.

"That won't matter to Rory, not at first. What will matter to Rory is that we had a plan and then you and I fucked and—"

"Does she know that?" he asks, staring at me, not annoyed but... intrigued.

"We're girls, we talk, just another thing you'll have to get used to, my man." I expect a glare, but instead, his arm wraps around my waist, tightening and pulling me close before pressing his lips to my hair like he likes my calling him my man. "She's happy I found you again, happy that I seem to be happy with you, but she also knows that this," I wave my hand between us, "is a distraction. We have a job to do here, and technically, we only have five more days to do it."

"Five days?" he asks, and if I'm not mistaken, his tone is one of disappointment.

I smile.

"Our stay is two weeks. We could extend, but eventually, it

would look sketchy, so ideally, we have to figure this out before our stay is over."

He nods in understanding. "Are you close?"

I tip my head back and forth before sighing. "Close, but not close enough."

A beat passes before he nods, then stands. "Well, then, let's get it over with."

He moves across the room to the dress, pulling out a pair of underwear and tugging them up his legs with ease.

"What?"

"Let's go to Rory and tell her we're together."

I fight a smile because I like that, tackling a task I'm not looking forward to with him.

"Together, huh?" I ask, standing and moving across the room to him, sliding my hands up and pushing my fingers through his hair. It's all mussed and messy, and despite my loving his put-together corporate look, I love this version even more because I know not many people get to see it.

"Oh, yeah. You think I'm letting a maneater like you slip through my fingers?" I roll my eyes and push on his chest, but his fingers wrap around my wrist, tugging me in close once more. "I'm joking, Josie." His whisper in my ear sends a chill down my spine. "About you being a maneater, but definitely not about not letting you go. The universe can only give you so many signs before it stops caring if you take the hint or not. And I'm telling you right now, I'm taking the hint."

I look up at him with wide eyes and realize he's right: it's crazy to be stuck here with him just days after we finally hooked up, but if there's one thing I believe in, it's that the universe sends signs.

"Maybe we should honor that sign one more time before we head to Rory. Cement it, you know?"

His smile goes wide and he dips his head, pressing his lips almost chastely to mine before stepping back and shaking his head. He moves back to the dresser for a pair of loose shorts and pulls them on as well before tossing an oversized tee to me.

"No putting it off. It won't get easier. Come on."

BREAK

I send Rory a text as I walk towards our room in Rowan's giant Daydream Resorts tee and my thong from earlier, telling her I have some exciting news. It's a bit unfair, but what else am I supposed to do, you know?

C: Excellent, get back here ASAP. We have a call with Annette soon to update her.

Well, I suppose that's good timing.

We make our way down the hall, and I'll admit: it feels like a death march. Rory is the smart one. All logic, no games, no emotion. Just right and wrong and nothing in between. I know that some of that is because of something that happened with an ex of hers, but she's never given me more than the basics on it, and I've never picked.

Finally, we're across the resort and standing in front of our door, and I stare at it like I'm walking into my death.

"God, you're dramatic," Rowan says with an eye roll, then reaches into his pants pocket for his universal key, the one I returned to him yesterday. Before I can stop him, he's sliding it into the door and turning the knob.

"Rowan, no—" I start, but it's too late—the door is pushing open, and I can't put it off anymore as Rory's head pops up from where she's sitting behind her computer, eyes locked on my...boyfriend? as he tugs me into the room. The door slams shut behind us with an ominous thump.

"Hey, Rory," he says, all smooth and sweet. I wonder if maybe he was lying—he could be great at this job, at convincing people to do what he wants. Rory stands then, taking a few steps towards us before crossing her arms on her chest and staring at me like I'm a teenager sneaking her boyfriend in past curfew.

"Hey, Rory? I've got someone who can help us," I say with a hesitant smile before lifting up Rowan's arm. I didn't run this angle past Rowan, but I also feel like it's the best shot at getting what I want. Because despite it, I want Rory to let Rowan help us, because the truth is, we're at a standstill with this investigation.

"No," she says instantly with a shake of her head.

"What?" Rowan asks, but I let out a bone-deep sigh.

"No way. No boys allowed. Sorry, Rowan."

"But," he starts, but she shakes her head once more.

"I know that you two must have cracked the seal on the sexual tension that has been leaking out all week, and I already gave you the go ahead on telling him everything, so that's cool, but no. This is Mavens' business, and that means no boys allowed. You can fuck him again after we have our debrief," Rory says, looking at me with her hands on her hips.

Well, this is going exactly how I expected.

"Rory—"

"Don't Rory me. He's a boy, Josie. We have a mission and not much time to solve it."

I soften my eyes, the way that always works on any unwitting person, but Rory has seen it so many times, I'm pretty sure she's immune.

"Just this once, Rory. I promise," I say, my hands going into a begging motion.

"No! He is not a Maven! I feel like I've been really cool with this whole thing," she says, waving her hand in our direction to indicate us being said whole thing. "But this is too far."

"Rory—" I start, but Rowan cuts me off.

"What would you need for me to prove I can be an asset?" he asks, and I turn to him with a glare. This will only make it worse. He can promise her the world, and the more he argues, the more Rory is going to get annoyed with him.

"What?" Rory asks.

"I have access to everything. What do you need? My logins? My work phone? My computer? Email? I'll give you whatever you want."

"We don't think you're a suspect," I say low, because while access to cameras would be nice, his personal phone isn't necessary, but Rory ignores me, tipping her head to contemplate his offer.

"You'd give me your logins to things?" Rory asks.

"I want this person caught just as much as Annette does."

"What do you have access to?" she asks, and Rowan smiles then, wide and panty-dropping. That's when I realize this is his own version of being a maneater, some kind of Corporate Ken version I'm strangely very attracted to.

"What do you want access to?" he asks.

"Everything," Rory says with a sweet smile.

"Then it's yours. I just need to grab my laptop from my room." My partner nods, and I sit in awe of the two of them...collaborating? I guess I should have seen it coming, what with them being cut from the same cloth and all.

"Perfect. That will give us a few minutes to talk about you fucking the common sense out of my best friend and partner while you're gone."

"Rory!" I say, mouth agape, but Rowan just laughs, bending down to press a kiss to my forehead.

"Got it. Chat away, girls. I'll be back in ten."

Rory smiles then, finally. "Better make it fifteen, with the way she's walking a bit bowlegged."

Even after the door slams behind him, I can hear Rowan's laugh booming through the hallway.

THIRTY-EIGHT

Rowan

"We believe that the culprit is an employee," Rory says the next morning as we sit around a pile of half-eaten room service breakfast and multiple computers. Files and notes are sprawled around, and new annotations have been added to the margins to add in the new input I brought to the table, both with my own knowledge and the access to the systems I gave them.

During the night, Rory and Josie moved from staff room to staff room with me playing lookout to plant as many listening devices as possible, along with a few cameras going in the more trafficked areas. That way, if and when the cameras go out next, they'd have their own to view. I also managed to get Rory a housekeeping dress to make going into other spaces during busier times easier. It was good feeling useful while they did their job.

"So do I," I agree. "It might even be two people, since the deletion of the camera intel is too close to the acts being carried out. It would be pretty difficult for it to be the same person."

"We're looking at someone in the security room," Josie says. "Like Jonas." I shake my head, somehow knowing that he isn't to blame.

"My gut says it's not him. Too obvious and too messy. He moved his entire family down here for this job, and the first day I was here after the incidents, he told me he was worried someone was setting him up."

Rory glares at me. "That sounds like the perfect lie from someone who is sabotaging your hotel. Or covering it up."

I shrug. She has a point, one I can't reasonably refute. "I'm just giving my insight. I think someone lower in that department than him might be a better option, or even someone who just has a history with computers." I lift my hands up when Rory glares daggers. "But you guys are the experts." She continues to glare at me before rolling her eyes and returning to her computer.

"Good. Because he's staying on our list."

I nod in understanding. I don't care who is on their list, really, so long as we catch this asshole and soon.

"So, who else is on your list?" I ask. This is after Rory dug through all of my electronic devices, my room, and my office, sweeping for bugs and burner phones and hidden messages and things I never even considered before determining that I was, in fact, not the culprit, nor that the culprit was watching me for any reason.

She still looks at me with the barest hint of irritation, but I think we're past the point of *he's a boy who can't sit with us*.

Maybe.

Who knows, really.

Josie is clearly nervous that I'm not going to like her coworker or vice versa, but in contrast, I really freaking like her. She's fact driven and doesn't take bullshit, something I very much appreciate. I like how decisive she is, how black and white and critical she is, and most of all, how much she cares for my girl.

And Josie is just that—my girl. Some invisible string that tied us together has brought us here, and I refuse to look this opportunity in the face.

"You first," she says with a raised eyebrow, crossing her arms on her chest. I let out a deep laugh and shake my head.

"Rory, stop being a pain," Josie says with an eye roll, but I reach over and grab her hand, squeezing it reassuringly to let her know I really don't mind.

"It's fine; I get it. Trust is earned, not given." That sentence alone may have accomplished more than half of what I've said to Rory because a small smile I've never seen is at her lips, and she nods in acceptance. "Right now, my biggest contender is Daniel Cooper."

"The general manager?" Josie asks. "Why?"

It's not in a disbelieving way but in a *why do you think that* way. I sigh before explaining.

"He isn't my biggest fan, so it would make sense that he would want me to look bad, making the location I lobbied for fail. He applied to work for corporate six months ago. He almost had the job, but when he interviewed with me, I cut it."

"How come?" Rory asks, tipping her head to the side.

I shrug because it's not one specific thing I could point out exactly, just a gut feeling. Still, I try.

"He's just not there yet, not ready for corporate. He enjoys the day-to-day grind of working at the hotel and being the head of the team. Which is great for a GM, but if he were to go to corporate, he wouldn't be at the top of the food chain. I don't think he would be the right fit. Not yet, at least."

"And he knew it was you who turned him down?"

"I mean, I don't think anyone told him that specifically, but he had an interview with me and then was told he was out of the running. Afterward, we hired for the position externally."

Rory cringes, but it doesn't faze me. It's business, and I don't take people's feelings into account when it comes to business.

"Well, you should know he's on our list, too. This is good intel to add," Rory says. "We couldn't find a motive previously, since the hotel not doing well makes him look bad as well."

"We're also pretty sure he's fucking the spa manager," Josie says, and my head snaps back.

"What?" I ask with what I'm sure are comically wide eyes. Rory nods.

"Oh, for sure. When they came into the sauna after the last incident, his buckle was undone, and her lipstick was smeared."

"That could be a coincidence—"

Josie gives me a soft smile in a you sweet, sweet, naive boy kind of way.

"That lipstick was also on his collar," she explains.

"Okay then, probably not a coincidence," I mutter.

"We're really good at this, Rowan," Rory says, a hint of earned irritation in her voice. "We don't put anyone on our short list just because."

I lift my hands in concession.

"You're right, you're right. I know the company, but I don't know the employees as well as I should. You guys have been doing all the heavy lifting."

Rory looks at me for a long minute, taking me in before a small, almost imperceptible smile spreads on her lips, and she nods, as if she finds me acceptable, as if she's approving.

"I could ask my assistant, Sloane, if she knows anything about the employees. She's much more personable and chats more."

"I think the bar for that is on the floor," Rory says under her breath, and Josie, while fighting back a laugh, hits her friend gently in the arm.

"No, no, she's right. A valid criticism," I say, looping an arm around her waist and tugging her in close. It's been too long without her right by me. Now that she's mine, I somehow know it's going to be a while before I feel sated by her touch.

"Okay, well," Rory says. "Since we both have Daniel on our list, let's start there: what can we do or find to either pin this all on him or cancel him out?"

"With my accounts, can you get into the email server, see if there's anything obvious or incriminating there?"

Rory nods, lighting up, but deflates just as quickly.

"Yes, but I believe Annette already had someone do all of that, and it came up empty."

I nod, expecting that. If Annette was worried enough to hire the Mavens under everyone's nose, she would have had Wilde Security look into the easy stuff first.

"Is there a way to monitor his personal devices without having them in our possession?" Josie asks.

Rory tips her head to the side, like she's contemplating the idea before nodding again.

"Yes," she says slowly, like she's still trying to figure it out in her mind. "We could track his incoming and outgoing messages that were going to any device via a tracking device and a mobile network interceptor. We'd have to plant it in his office, and I'd bug it at the same time. I'd need about an hour uninterrupted, though."

I look to Josie in part awe and part panic.

"She's scary, isn't she?" she asks with a laugh. Rory narrows her eyes. "In a hot way!"

"I'm not going to touch that one at all," I mumble.

"Good call. It was a setup," Rory confirms, and Josie laughs.

"You passed," Josie says, not bothering to argue her friend's accusation.

"I thought being together meant all of that fucking with me shit would end."

Her smile goes devious, and I suddenly know that will never be over. Josie will never stop teasing and taunting me.

"Good luck, bud," Rory says, reaching over to pat my arm in consolation.

"Okay, so what's the plan?" I ask. "How do we distract him for over an hour without causing alarm?"

"And that, my sweet boy, is where I come in," Josie says with a smile.

THIRTY-NINE

JOSIE

Josie

"I'll be in meetings most of the day, but keep me updated, okay?" Rowan asks after our morning planning session. I nod before he leans in, giving me a deep, hot kiss that is far too short for my liking before stepping back with a smile.

"God, you two are sickening," Rory grumbles from behind me.

"It's great, isn't it?" I say with a laugh. Rowan shakes his head then heads off down the hall to his room to change before going to his office. After that, I get all dolled up in my Mavens gear before we make our way to the little cafe, where we plan to set up and keep an eye out for our target.

It's about noon when our plan goes into action, as I grab a cup of water and move quickly towards the pool deck, noting the exact spot Daniel is. I shift at the last second, slamming into his chest and in turn, spilling water all down my front, drenching my top.

"Oh, god, I'm so sorry," he says as soon as I step back, looking at the spill rather than my face.

It was planned, of course, as was the fact that I wore the light pink lacy bra I put on under this very thin white tank. Both are so thin that when the ice-cold liquid hits, my nipples peak instantly. If you look hard enough, as Daniel does, you can probably see the entire outline of my nipple.

When his eyes go right there, I know in my gut my mission is already accomplished.

"Gosh, I'm such a klutz," I say with a bit of a giggle and a self-deprecating smile that works every time. "I wasn't looking where I was going."

"No, no, it's all me. I can't believe I didn't see a pretty thing like you." His hand reaches up and wipes some water off my shoulder, and I fight making a face at the contact. Why do strangers think it's okay to touch someone? "God, I'm so sorry. You're absolutely covered in water." I look down and give another small giggle before flipping my thankfully dry hair back over my shoulder.

"Oh, it's no big deal. It'll dry. Like I said, I'm a klutz. This kind of thing happens all the time."

"Please, let me make it up to you," he says, and I flutter my lashes, leaning in just a bit into his space, fully playing the part of an enamored, flirty woman who is super into him.

"Yeah?" I asked, touching the collar of his shirt and pretending to brush off something that doesn't exist.

"Oh yeah. I insist, actually."

"How would you do that?" I bite my lip and make my eyes go wide. His eyes move to my lips.

"Let me cover a dinner at Aces for you. Are you here with anyone?" He hesitates like he just realized he may have made a crucial mistake, then looks to my ring finger, finding it empty. "A boyfriend, maybe?" I shake my head and let out a laugh, the one I reserve for stupid men who always fall for it and shake my head. My body shifts with the over-exaggerated move, and I know my breasts also sway in the minimal support bra, something his eyes track.

Honestly, it's almost a letdown when they fall for it this easily.

Where's the fun in it? "No, no. I'm here with my best friend, Rory." His smile returns then.

"Good to hear. Come to dinner tonight, I'll make sure you get the best table, the best service, I promise."

"Will you be there?" I ask, twirling a lock of my hair around my finger and making my face pouty and hopeful. He looks around, like he's afraid someone will see. Rowan, maybe? When the coast is seemingly clear, he lowers his voice.

"I can't actually have dinner with you since I'll technically be on the clock. But I can sit with you, get to know you a bit. But only if you promise not to tell." He gives me a wink that looks more like he has something in his eye than a hot come on, but I pretend it hit its mark.

"Oh, I would love that. I feel like we would have so much in common."

"Tonight," he says. "Six?"

"That would be amazing. I don't have any plans."

He gives me a smile the big bad wolf would be jealous of before he gets my info for the reservation. Then I'm off, looking over my shoulder as I do to give him a little wink and a wiggle of my fingers before I turn the corner. As I do, my phone buzzes in my pocket. I grab it, expecting to see Rory's name, but instead it's Rowan's.

R: Get to my office. Now.

I smile as I slide the phone back into my pocket, turn left instead of right, and head towards the office that is currently Rowan's, conveniently located in a dead-end hallway that is currently empty.

I don't have to knock as I approach the closed door, as it opens before my fist even hits the wood. His arm reaches out, hand wrapping around my wrist and tugging me inside and into him before he closes the door behind us.

"God, watching you work your magic was the hottest thing I've ever seen," Rowan growls as his body presses me against the door, something he seems to really love doing.

"You were watching?"

"I've been watching you on the cameras every fucking chance I could since you arrived at this place."

A thrill runs through me at the thought. He mentioned it once before, but I didn't realize how often he'd been doing it.

"Too bad there weren't any cameras in my room," I whisper as he presses his lips to the skin of my neck. His body goes still before he pulls back, taking my face in.

"Why? What would I have seen?"

I smile wider then and lean forward, pressing my lips to his.

"Oh, I don't know. Let's just say anytime I was in the room alone, I really had to let out some... pent-up feelings."

The groan that leaves him moves through my body, making my pussy clench.

"Fuck, Josephine."

I like it when he says my full name, even more than when he calls me his troublemaker. It feels intimate, like I'm some sultry version of myself only he gets to see. "I want to watch that."

"I wouldn't be opposed to it," I whisper into the quiet room. He growls into my neck, his fingers moving to the hem of my wet shirt when his phone rings.

"That's my two o'clock," he says with a pained groan.

"Cancel it," I whisper, moving my hips up.

"I can't. It's the call with the inspector that was cancelled the other night after the sauna. I don't have to say much, since it's mostly the building team ironing out issues, but I have to be present."

I pout before I step back and smile.

"Party pooper. Well, do you mind if I hang in here while you're on your call? I have some stuff I could do in here."

He looks at me skeptically before shrugging.

"I don't mind." His hand cups my center, a finger sliding up my skirt and against my pussy, pushing my panties inside of me before he steps back, an obnoxious smirk on his lips. "You're soaking wet," he says when he moves to his desk.

"Yeah, I really wish you would take care of that," I grumble, and he smiles, shaking his head.

"I meant your shirt." I look down at the wet tank, my nipples even tighter in the cold air conditioning of his office.

"Oh, yeah. That, too."

"In that closet, I have some shirts if you want to change. Let your stuff dry on the balcony." I nod, then move to the closet, happy to find an oversized T-shirt that says *Daydream Resorts* on it. I will be stealing that, thank you very much. Shucking off my wet tank and bra, I slide the shirt over my head, then shimmy my skirt down, leaving just my underwear. When I look over at him, his eyes are taking me in, and I smile before moving to the balcony at the back of his office and laying my skirt, tank, and bra on the ground. It should dry quick, with the sun high and beating down hard. When I enter again, I move to where he's sitting and press a kiss to his cheek. He grabs my waist to hold me in place, then turns to get my lips on his before speaking.

"I'll be muted most of the time, but my camera will be on," he says. "So if you don't want anyone to see you, stay over there." My gut sinks as I nod, then I move to sit in the comfy chair and pull out my phone.

"You...don't want anyone to see me?" I ask, trying to sound casual but feeling unsure. He shakes his head and smiles, like he senses my concern.

"I figured you'd want that to stay between us for a bit longer, and maybe you'd like to be in something other than my tee and your panties. Not that I'm complaining."

"I guess it makes sense, we haven't, you know, had that conversation—"

He looks at his watch, then groans. "Fuck it," he says low before quickly moving to me, tugging me up until we're chest to chest. "I want everyone to know you're mine, Josie. That's what you are, conversation or not. You're mine. If you'd like me to take this call with you on my lap, I'll be happy to. It'll cause a stir, but if that's what you need, what you want, then we'll do just that. I'll show everyone you're mine."

His hand moves to my hips and tucks me in closer. I can feel he's still hard from teasing me before. "Is that what you want, troublemaker?"

I bite my lip because in a way, I do. The idea of sitting on his lip in his shirt while big, bad Rowan Fisher does his big boy job is incredibly attractive.

But also, so is *watching* him do his big boy job. So I shake my head.

"No. I'll sit here and wait for you to be done," I say in a whisper.

"When I'm done with my call, do you want me to take care of you?" he murmurs against my neck, his hand moving up under his shirt and then under my underwear to cup my ass. The tip of his middle finger moves, drifting until it just barely grazes my entrance, and my breathing goes ragged.

I've had Rowan Fisher more times than I can count, and yet I still want more. I'm unsatisfied and needy anytime I go more than a few hours without him inside of me.

"Next gala or black-tie event, you're on my arm. Preferably in that orange dress or something similar."

"You liked that one?"

"I've jacked off thinking about peeling you out of it more times than I should admit." The visual pulls a mewl from my lips, and his tip up in a satisfied grin.

"I have a lot of others," I whisper, moving to my tip toes and grazing my lips against his. "All of them are very pretty. All of them are very tight."

"I can't wait to see you in and out of every single one." I smile then, and he returns it, squeezing my ass and pressing his lips to mine one last time before stepping away.

"Now sit there and be a good girl while I do my job." He has such high expectations for my behavior. Poor man. I smile, then do as he asks, getting comfy while he moves back to his desk. He takes me in, sitting there, and smiles like he likes the view.

"Hey, team, sorry I'm late," he says, and a chorus of hellos fill the room. A few more remarks are shared before he nods and sits back while the meeting begins, something about a new location and blah blah blah. His eyes shift from the screen to me, and even though he doesn't smile, I see his eyes go soft, like he likes the sight of me in his office with him. We sit like that for a few minutes, Rowan working while I make my plan.

When he's when I stand, slide my panties down to my feet, and stepping out of them. His eyes track my every move, and a wide smile spreads on my lips. He may have thought he won, that his tease was more than enough to get me to submit to him, but I don't think he's ever had a woman like me.

Might as well show him what he's in for.

Then I sit back down on the comfy armchair in the corner of the office, relieved he closed all the blinds before I arrived, and prop one foot up on the armrest of the chair, spreading myself wide for him to see, the oversized tee pooling around my waist.

Rowan blinks a few times before leaning out of view of the camera before he speaks. "Josephine, what are you doing?"

"Taking care of myself," I say, the words breathy as I slide a hand down my body, hips bucking as a finger trails over my clit with feather light strokes. "Oh, god." The words are a whisper, and my hips rise to get more—and, of course, give Rowan more of a show.

"Josie," he says low, but when I look at him, his eyes are locked on the spot between my legs. I take a finger and slide it inside of me.

"Fuck, I'm already so wet," I whisper. My lips part, and a soft moan leaves my lips. "I'm so wet for you, Rowan."

"Josie," he warns again, but I ignore it, sliding a second finger in and rocking my hips to simulate what I really want. His eyes are locked on my pussy and it heightens my pleasure, taking me higher faster than ever before. My fingers slide out, circling my clit and my head tips back as I cup my full breast over his shirt. "Fuck," I hear muttered and when I look back to him, his eyes are dark as he watches me play with my clit.

"I'm already so close," I whisper, but I know he hears it when he lets out a slow, shaky breath. That's when something changes in his eyes. His shoulders go straight, he sits back in his chair and crosses his arms over his chest, and smiles. The man *smiles*.

"Do not come until my meeting is over," he instructs,

"Rowan—" I start, a bit frantic because I'm already sitting on the edge, his eyes on me, and my fingers know exactly what I need to do the job quickly. But I'm cut off when he clicks his mouse and speaks.

"That sounds like a great idea, Jim. What do we think the time frame for that would be?"

He's unmuted.

His hand doesn't move back to the mouse as I hold my breath. Jim seems to answer, though I can't even attempt to understand what words he's saying, not with the self-satisfied look Rowan is giving me. He presented a challenge for me not to come, and he knows me well enough that I refuse to back down.

My fingers slow their movements, because with the heated look he's giving me and the need coursing through my body, there is *no way* I could avoid coming and doing it loud when I did. His eyes go confused when he notices, before a dark smile spreads on his lips.

He leans forward, clicking his mouse once more and then looking back at me. "Don't you fucking stop, Josephine. You wanted to play this game, now play. And don't you dare come until I'm deep inside of you." Then he clicks again and nods at the screen. "Great idea, Joe." My mouth drops open, and I stare at him wide-eyed. He raises an eyebrow in challenge and *fuck* if he doesn't know that will always get to me.

So I fight back.

I bite my lip and slide two fingers inside of me, fucking hard and fast as I climb the hill, biting back a moan as pleasure floods me. Then I remove them when I get too close, making wide circles around my throbbing clit as I come back down from the edge. His smile is devious as he watches while I continue the torture I've brought upon myself.

But I get the power back when I take those two wet fingers from my pussy and move them up to my lips, sliding them slowing into my mouth, my tongue moving over them to clean my wetness off. His eyes flare with approval. at the show, and I decide to make it into just that: a show. I slide the fingers back, making a crude intimidation of sucking him off, going far enough to make myself gag. He shifts in his seat then, and I know I'm getting to him.

For a moment, I contemplate moving to my knees and crawling under his desk to suck his cock, but I'm not totally sure what angles his camera catches.

Maybe next time

Instead, I lift my shirt more until my breasts are revealed and I circle my nipple with my wet fingers, pinching and twisting, trying not to make a sound as the pleasure builds, as my other hand moves back between my legs, circling my clit. My mind goes scrambled, my only focus being to stay silent and not come, but eventually, somewhere in the distance, I register the conversation dwindling.

"All right, thanks, everyone. I'll talk to you soon." The group says its goodbyes, and then Rowan is clicking, and standing, and moving my way.

"Rowan," I moan, finally able to speak as he prowls towards me. "Rowan, please." Now that his meeting is over and he's moving my way with a look of determination, I need him. I need him to fill me, to let me come, to *make* me come, to do *something*.

His look is absolutely devilish.

"I should make you wait," he says, undoing his belt as he watches my fingers continue to work myself, avoiding the most sensitive part for fear I'll come before I'm allowed. "But that would be a punishment for myself as well. He kneels before me, tugging on his thick cock that is at the perfect height to slide into me now. "Hold yourself open for me," he says, and I do as he asks, fingers moving under my knees and pulling myself wide. He smiles and takes his whole hand, grinding down on my wet center.

"Fuck," I groan.

"Such a fucking tease, you are, my little troublemaker," he says. And then he shocks me by pulling his hand back and slapping my sensitive pussy. It reverberates through me, and I bite back a loud moan, my head moving back with the pleasure of it and my eyes shutting as he finally slides into me.

That's all it takes.

I think it's okay, since I followed his rules, but as soon as he slides into me, I come on his cock. His arms move, wrapping me tight against his chest as he fucks into me, holding my head to his neck as her groans into my ear, the sound of it taking me even higher.

"God, such a fucking good girl, holding out or me. A bad girl, making me want you when I have to work. Fuck. That's it, baby. Squeeze around me; God, you feel so good." He continues to ramble on, my body shaking as he fucks me before the orgasm finally leaves me. I'm not sated though, not when his cock is still sliding into me hard and fast, not when his filthy words are being whispered into my neck. And surely not when he slides out, leaving me empty, and stands. His cock is soaked in my wet, and when he grips my hair, I moan, knowing what's coming.

"Suck it, Josie," he says, then pushes my head as his hips move forward, my mouth greedily wrapping around him. The mix of my taste and his nearly does me in. My thighs try to clench, to relieve some of the pressure, but they stop on his legs as he's standing between them.

"Finger your pussy, keep it nice and wet for me."

I moan gratefully, then circle my clit as his cock hits the back of my throat. I keep my eyes trained on him as he fucks my face, feeling a single tear fall as I slide a finger into myself. "So fucking pretty," he whispers, a thumb moving to swipe it away almost reverently. I moan around him and start to fuck myself with my fingers, empty and needy once more as his cock throbs in my mouth. He smiles down at me before sliding out. I mewl in protest at the loss, and he lets out a little laugh before shaking his head. Then he bends, putting hands beneath my arms and shifting and moving me until I'm bent over the arm of the chair, spreading my legs wide for him as he lines his cock up with my entrance.

His hand wraps around my hair, and he tugs, my head moving back as he slides into me.

"Oh, fuck," I groan as he pulls out and slides in again, slow and torturous. His free hand moves up the loose shirt, pinching my nipple hard.

"Josie." His hand goes to my shoulder, pulling me back as he fucks into me, my back arching and my mouth dropping open. "Gotta stay quiet, troublemaker, or else everyone knows I'm fucking you in here," he warns, and I hesitate. Not because I don't want anyone to hear me, but because there is something that is so fucking hot about everyone hearing me, I almost come right here.

Because a part of me does *want* everyone in this fucking hotel to know that Rowan is mine, that he's fucking me and *only* me.

He might be a jealous, possessive idiot, but so am I, it turns out. He groans through clenched teeth as I tighten around him. "Fuck, Josie. You can't do this to me. I have so much shit to do, and instead I'm bending you over my chair and fucking you." I let out a laugh that is cut off by a moan when he slams in particularly deep, tugging my hair as he does.

"Then make me come, and you can go back to going your boring big boy job," I demand.

"You're such a fucking little brat, aren't you?" he says through gritted teeth. His hips start moving harder and faster, and I moan loud without meaning to. That's when his hand leaves my hair and wraps around my mouth as he pounds into me, the couch shifting beneath him. My clit bushes into the arm of the love seat as he presses me deeper over the air before his voice takes me over the edge I'm teetering on.

"I need you to fucking come around me, Josie," he says, a low grown. "I—"

But he doesn't have to say more because I'm bucking my hips back, taking him that much deeper and tightening as I come harder than ever before, biting into his hand as I do. Moments later, he bites back a groan into my neck and fills me. After he comes, he lets go of my mouth, then uses a hand to brush my hair over my shoulder, the gentleness of it such a stark contrast to moments prior.

"I'm absolutely wild for you, Josephine Montgomery," he whispers, almost to himself, but it fills me with warmth all the same.

"Good," I reply. "Because I feel the same way."

We're still catching our breath, his cock still deep inside of me when I ask, "Do you think my clothes are dry yet?"

His laugher fills the room, a sound I vow to make it my mission to hear regularly.

FORTY

JOSIE

Josie

"Do you need a safe word or something?" Rowan asks as I sit at the vanity in his bathroom, getting ready for my 'date' with Daniel tonight. The dark purple dress I plan to wear is draped over his bed, and I'm finishing up the final touches on my makeup. I look over at him blankly.

"A safe word?"

"Yeah, you know, if something goes terribly wrong and you need me to storm in and save you?" I try to school my features for a moment but fail when I let out a loud laugh. He glares at me as I recover before reaching for a blush brush and adding a bit more to my cheeks.

"Oh, you sweet, sweet boy, thinking I need saving."

"I'm just saying whoever the person is, is clearly not opposed to hurting someone."

I turn to him and give him a sympathetic smile, knowing this is all new to him.

"Rowan, I've been doing this a long time. I will be fine."

He sighs before nodding. "So remind me of the plan?"

"I will go on my date, and I'll be wearing an earpiece to record the conversation if needed. Rory will be able to communicate with me to let me know if I need to buy more time or if she's done. It should take anywhere from one hour to ninety minutes."

"It's not just drop and go?" I shake my head.

"No, it's tracking incoming and outgoing messages for all devices within that vicinity. With it, she should be able to hack them off-site so we can double-check for any burners, etc."

"That's possible?" he asks, his face a mask of shock and concern that makes me laugh just a bit. I nod.

"You'd be absolutely horrified at all Rory can do with this equipment," I say with a shrug. "I tend to purposely forget her skills because if I don't, I might go into a spiral." He looks like he's starting to do just that, something that does make me giggle, but I pat his shoulder. "Nothing to worry about, unless you fuck me over. Then she might try a little bit of retribution."

He lets out a breath. "Noted. So she needs two hours, and you're going to buy her that time?"

"That's my plan. Flirt, taunt, show some cleavage, whatever it takes to keep him at that table until I get the all-clear from Rory." His face changes, almost infinitesimally, and my gut drops, knowing that it's time to address this. "I guess we should have the talk," I say. His brow furrows before he stands up straighter, his hands sliding into his pockets.

"The talk?" My stomach churns, but I turn to him in the vanity seat and lock my gaze on him.

"My job is flirting. It's talking to all kinds of people, often men, and making them think they have my full attention, respect, and interest in order to convince them to spill their secrets. I'm good at my job. I *love* my job. I will not be stopping my job any time soon." I close my eyes and take in a deep breath, before opening them again, softening my expression. "I like you, Rowan, but I love my job. If you make me pick, I will choose my job over you." Despite my bravado, I'm nervous. I know this is a lot to ask of someone, much less in a very new relationship, but I want to have the best of both worlds. Desperately.

Silence fills the space for long, long moments, and that nervousness churns hard, turning to panic before, finally, he moves. He leans forward, reaching for me on the chair and pulling me to my feet, then into his chest, before finally speaking.

"I know what I signed up for," he says against my lips.

"What?" I ask, my heart stuttering.

"I know what I signed up for when I agreed to start this with you, Josie. You told me your job."

"You fucked it out of me," I grumble, and he smiles, probably sensing my body responding to the memory. *Not the time, body.*

"Hmm, that was a good time, wasn't it?" I glare at him, but honestly, I don't think it's very convincing. He keeps going. "But what I'm saying is I did not walk into this relationship blind. I know who you are, what your job is, and what that looks like. If you're worried I'll have some kind of issue with it, you can stop worrying. I know in my gut this will work, because I understand your job. I think you also get that mine can be long hours and random calls I can't ignore when we're eating dinner or when I'm trying to make you come for the tenth time." I smile at that, but he keeps talking. "I want this to work, and I think you do, too. So I think we're both willing to accept all of that if that means we get each other."

He steps closer to me, a hand resting on my lower back.

"I'm going to have to go on dates with other men," I whisper, remembering the handful of times I tried to date in college while running my side business, before I decided it wasn't worth the strife. The men I dated could never get past my job, so I stopped trying.

"Am I happy that you're going to flirt with another man, do what you can to get his dick hard and get him nice and pliant so that you can wring him for all of his secrets? Not particularly. But is that your problem? No. So long as, at the end of the day, it's me you fall asleep next to, I'm good. I'm confident enough in myself and in us."

He pauses, staring at me, before continuing. "The truth is, you can flirt and flaunt and you can make every man in the room wonder what it would be like to have you as their own, but I'm the only one who gets to know that. I'm the only one who knows what you're like when that mask is pulled off, who knows what you sound like when I fill you."

A shallow breath leaves my lips, and a small smile paints his. "I'm the only one who knows the places to kiss to make you moan. That alone is enough for me. You think I'm not okay with that? Having all of you when everyone else only gets hints and scraps, when they get teased but never given more? Hell no. It's a gift you're choosing to give me, Josie, and I'm honored to have it."

I stare at him for long, long moments, trying to ascertain his truth, but see nothing but. My face breaks into a wide smile, and I put a hand to each side of his jaw and pull him in for a deep, grateful kiss.

"God, you're perfect, aren't you?" I whisper, and he smiles.

"Perfect for you, I hope."

I press my lips to his once more in answer before his face goes a bit clouded. He adds, "I would prefer if you don't kiss anyone, but I also understand that's not something I can expect, nor my place to ask."

I lean back a bit to take him in before my head tips to the side. Then I smile and shake my head.

"You don't know, do you?"

"Know what?"

"Rowan, honey. I've never kissed a target before."

"What?"

"I've never kissed a target or a suspect. Never. You were the one exception. It was why this was so complicated for me." My thumb grazes along the hard lines of his cheekbone, stubble scraping along my skin as I smile softly. "I'd already kissed you, knew how much I liked it. I thought if I did it again, it would muddy my mind even more than you already had."

A beat passes before a grin of his own breaks out along his lips. "Oh, you had it bad from the beginning," he mumbles against my lips.

"Real bad," I admit in a whisper. Then he kisses me long and deep, showing and sharing each crumb of the joy and gratitude we each feel, before finally, he pulls back.

"Okay, it's time for you to finish getting all dolled up for your date." Without meaning to, I grimace at the reminder but sit down all the same.

"Why do you look like that?" He asks with a laugh

"Like what?" I ask, reaching for the lipstick to apply it.

"Like you're annoyed as fuck." I meet his eyes behind me in the mirror as I glide the lipstick over my lips, painting them a pretty pink. He's once again watching me while resting on the bathroom wall, and I like this: him keeping me company while I get ready, talking about our jobs and expectations openly and honestly like adults. Just *being* with him.

"Because I realized that I'm going on a date with someone else before I go on a real date with you," I admit. His face goes soft at that, like he really likes my words, and even though I'm annoyed, it brings me joy, knowing I brought him joy. "It's annoying."

"I wouldn't call it a date," he says. I let out a small laugh at the irritation now on *his* face.

"I bet he would. And, again, it's *annoying* that he gets to have a dinner date with me before you do." The irritation melts away, and he gives me a soft smile.

"Is my little troublemaker sad we're not going on a date?" He stands behind me and I watch in the mirror as his hand moves to my cheek, thumb moving over my cheekbone.

"Yes," I pout like a petulant child instead of a full-grown woman. He dips down and presses a kiss to the top of my head.

"Well, as soon as we can, I promise to take you out. Show you off. The whole nine."

"The whole nine, huh?" I ask with an eyebrow raised and a smile.

"Oh yeah. Wine and dine, baby." I can't help but laugh as I look at him in the mirror.

"And what all does wine and dine include, Mr. Fisher?"

"Well, first, we have wine. And then I dine." He wiggles his eyebrows at me.

I can't help it: I let out a loud laugh at his terrible innuendo. "Dine, huh?" I ask.

He nods, dipping his head down and pressing his lips to the spot right below my ear on my neck that makes me shiver, his tongue dipping out to taste me there. My pulse pounds in response.

Because I'm a brave girl, though, I swat him away.

It would only take another press like that to completely mangle my mind, to have me forget that I have a job to do and thirty minutes to finish getting ready.

"We don't have time for that right now, unfortunately," I say with a sigh filled with genuine regret. Then I look over my shoulder. "But hold that thought." A deep laugh fills the room as I take out the clips holding my hair back and pick up my curling iron to touch up a few things.

"You don't have to do that, you know," he says. "You look gorgeous with your natural hair." I smile as I release the perfect curl.

"I know."

He lets out a loud laugh, shaking his head.

"I'm just saying, you don't have to go all out. You'd win him over regardless."

With that, I set my iron down.

"I guess we should have this talk, too," I say with a sigh.

"Oh?" he asks, clearly entertained.

"I don't do this," I say, moving my hand down my body and over my hair, "For other people. Yes, there are certain styles that consistently perform better for my job. However, I spend an hour styling my hair because I want to, and because I like the way it looks. If you want this to be a thing, you've gotta accept that sometimes, I'm going to take two hours to do my hair just to go to the grocery store. Sometimes, I'll throw my hair in a ponytail and not wash it for a week, but that's because *I* want to. I like doing my make up, so if you tell me I'm prettier without it, I'm actually going to get pissed, no matter how well-intentioned you are. And sometimes, I'll wear a tiny dress or a low-cut top: again, for my job—it can be a requirement because men are often distracted—but I still do it for myself. I've had men in the past not like that, not be into it, and I've ended things quick because of it. You will not be the exception to that rule."

Silence hangs in the air between us, and even though I stare at him with a bit of anticipation, I know this is a hill I'm willing to lay it all out on. I am me, and no one and nothing will change that.

But he doesn't leave me hanging for long, instead standing and taking two steps to me before his hands move under my arms, tugging me in close. My hands go to his chest to catch myself before sliding up and around his neck.

"Let me get one thing exceedingly clear: you look gorgeous no matter what. A bikini or sweats or nothing, though I can't lie, when it's just the two of us, I highly prefer nothing." I can't help but smile, and any unease I felt washes away. "I don't care what your hair looks like, as long as you like it. You could wear a three-inch-thick layer of makeup or none at all and the mere thought of you would get my dick hard." A shiver runs through me, and he smiles when he feels it. "You do whatever you have to do to make yourself feel pretty, but you'd better be doing it for you, not me. Surely not for any of those assholes. I don't care what you're wearing or how your hair looks, so long as you're happy and you're mine. Got it?"

He looks so firm in his words, so insistent that I not only hear them, but understand, that I have no other choice but to smile.

"I think so," I whisper. Then he smiles wide and dips his head, his mouth moving over mine, and I know I could so fall for Rowan Fisher.

And the craziest part is that it doesn't scare me at all.

FORTY-ONE

JOSIE

Josie

Dinner is painfully long, partly because it's an upscale, multi-course dinner, and partly because despite his insistence that he couldn't have dinner with me, Daniel never leaves the table, sharing each dish with me off one plate—*my* plate. I fight a cringe each time he reaches across the table to take a bite of my food, smiling wide at me like this is normal.

I was right.

To Daniel, this *is* a date.

Still, it's my job, so I tough it out, knowing the more time Rory has in there, the better, ensuring she won't be interrupted. Finally, though, things start to get interesting when a familiar redhead comes over, a tight smile on her face. She doesn't even look in my direction, just stands beside Daniel with a tight grimace before tipping her head to the door.

"Daniel," she says. "I need to talk to you."

He sits up a bit straighter, and his face goes a bit pale.

"Tanya, I'm with a guest."

Her jaw goes tight, and she gives him a forced smile.

"It will just take a minute," she says, again not looking in my direction.

Daniel looks from Tanya to me, and I smile and nod.

"No worries," I say. "Work comes first."

He gives me a grateful smile before he reluctantly stands and follows Tanya, who doesn't even look back at him.

"Daniel is leaving with Tanya," I say low as I lift my glass, pretending to take a sip. "He is leaving the restaurant through the main entrance."

"Tracking it," Rowan's voice says in my earpiece. He's probably in his office watching the feeds. "They're going..." There's a pause before he speaks. "Into a supply closet."

"Ooh, interesting. One we bugged?"

"Yes," he says. I put my glass down and look around the room, putting a hand to my mouth and pretending to rest there.

"Rory, how are you doing?"

"Almost done with the office," she says. "Going as fast as I can."

"Please. I'm dying of boredom."

"He doesn't seem to have much personality," Rowan agrees, and I smile behind my hand

"Unlike you?"

"I think you know damn well how much personality I have," Rowan says low. Heat runs through me in response.

"Ugh, gross, you two," Rory says. "I'm on the line."

"If you finish faster, she could leave and—" Rowan starts, and I have to roll my lips between my teeth to hide my laugh.

"Rowan, I could absolutely ruin you if I wanted. Don't push me," Rory threatens, and Rowan laughs. He *laughs*. It warms me through, just the sound of it.

"I'm joking, I'm joking," he says.

"A fucking comedian," Rory grumbles.

"He's heading back in, Rowan says, all humor out of his tone. Tanya is...headed to the lobby."

"Got it," I say, straightening as Daniel comes back in with an apologetic smile on his lips.

And a very pink cheek. Almost like he was slapped.

"Everything okay?" I ask as he sits, then shrugs.

"Oh, yeah. She just..." He looks around like he's looking for someone who will tell on him before he lowers her voice. "She gets jealous."

I tip my head. "Of what? Me?"

He smiles then, wide and confident. "I mean, anyone would be jealous of you," he says. "But anyone I give a lick of attention to."

"Why? You're just coworkers, right?"

A blush creeps over his cheeks. "Well... We hooked up once," he says. I call bullshit internally as he continues. "But I think she's more into me than I am into her. She had just gotten out of a pretty serious relationship, and I don't think I should have taken her up on her offer."

"I totally understand that," I say with sympathy, though Tanya just shot to the top of my list. If she's jealous of Daniel, who seems to flirt with everything that moves, she would have motivation to make his job a misery.

Daniel changes the subject quickly and my—*our*—main entree comes out and we fall back into the same pattern of boring conversation. I'm trying to drag every moment out of dessert and praying I won't have to convince Daniel to have an after-dinner drink with me when I get confirmation.

"Rory's done," a voice in my ear says, gravelly and hot. A thrill runs through my body, both at his tone and the fact that we've completed another step in our plan. It's why I love this job: the excited thrill that runs through me when we accomplish something, the insane endorphins that rush through me. I normally hop on a treadmill or do a workout when I feel it, but the idea that I have a more than willing companion here to burn off this excess excited energy with send that feeling buzzing higher. "Get out of there as soon as you can. Meet me in my room."

My pulse skyrockets at his tone, filled with promise and need and desire.

Oh I am *so* getting it good tonight.

"That was phenomenal," Daniel says, knocking me out of my haze as he sits back with his hand patting his stomach.

"It really was," I agree, despite the fact that I had one bite of the chocolate cake. I don't even care: after Rowan *takes care* of me, I know he'll take care of me in another way, ordering a dozen different room service meals for us to pick at. "Thank you for a wonderful night."

"It doesn't have to end here," he says, leaning forward with a suddenly smarmy smile on his lips. "We could continue it, head to the bar, get a few drinks, see where the night takes us." I fight the curl of my lip, and I'm grateful my hands are in my lap because it makes it easier for me to grab my napkin and place it on the table. "I'm off in," he looks at his watch. "Twenty minutes."

I check my watch and give him a faux sad look. "Unfortunately, I have an early bedtime. Thanks for the offer though. Maybe next time?"

He looks disappointed, but I'm already standing, and making a scene wouldn't be a great look, especially not when he's supposed to be *working*.

"Oh, uh. Yeah. That would be...that would be great."

He stands as well, moving around the table towards me. "I'll be at the pool early tomorrow morning. Maybe I'll see you there?"

"Wonderful. I'd love to," I say. He puts out two arms to give me a hug, and I awkwardly reach up to shake his hand. Before he can take it, there's a shout from the kitchen, then more shouts echoing throughout the restaurant we're in. My head snaps around, looking for what's causing the disturbance before I hear it.

"A mouse!"

Except it's not just a single mouse skittering through the restaurant and, presumably, the kitchen. It's at least a dozen tiny, furry little things, squeaking as they run along the floor of the restaurant. Guests scream, dishes falling as people panic, moving towards exits quickly. A woman even gets on a table like some kind of cartoon, though my gaze moves right to Daniel, assessing.

That's when I see he is sitting on the chair, feet up, arms around his knees in fear like he's afraid one of the surprisingly cute mice will climb up his pants leg.

Sighing, I mentally cross out Daniel.

BREAK

"Oh my god, they were *everywhere*," I say, walking into our room a few hours later. Rowan is stuck downstairs, once again having to appease guests, deal with the police, add to his previous report, and deal with an exterminator. This time, however, he's on our team, so we know anything he sees or hears will come back to us.

Right now, I just want a shower to wash away the tired night.

"Oh, good, you're here," Rory says. "We have a *lot* to talk about."

"Find anything?" I ask.

Rory tips her head, neither confirming nor denying.

"No pings or emails to Tanya or Daniel leading up to or during the sabotage."

"You bugged Tanya as well?"

She waves her hand over the housekeeping uniform she's wearing. "Her work devices, yeah. With this outfit and Rowan in my back pocket I can pretty much bug any room." She looks away from her computer to me before adding, "Don't worry, I didn't bug either of your rooms. Gross."

And for that, I am grateful because I want to be able to look my partner in the eye again.

She clicks a few more times before turning the computer towards me where a screen displaying a storage room appears.

"Should I be nervous?" I ask, a brow lifted at her ominous tone, and she shakes her head.

"No, no. It's just..." She hits play and I can hear low sounds outside of the room.

"Is that one of our cameras?" I ask and she nods in confirmation.

"Right outside the restaurant. Time stamp is 6:41." I open my mouth to say something, but close it when Daniel and Tanya walk in, Tanya's jaw tight and angry, Daniel looking clearly annoyed.

"What the fuck is that?" on-screen Tanya says, throwing an arm towards the door once Daniel closes it behind him.

"What?"

"That *guest*," she says. "The one whose tits you can't stop looking at."

Oh. So they're fighting about *me*.

"Tanya, baby—" he starts with exasperation in his voice.

"Don't you, Tanya, *baby,* me, Daniel. I can't believe this."

He steps closer to her and sighs, but she steps away.

"It's part of the job! I spilled water on her, I offered to comp her dinner make up for it. She's flirty—I didn't want to insult her and get a negative review!"

I smile to myself at my successful flirting, but a small part of me feels bad because I *hate* when I seem to get in the middle of a relationship.

"You think I'm really that stupid, Daniel? I know you, remember. I know how you work."

"If you're going to be such an uptight—" He doesn't get to finish what is clearly going to be a rude insult, because a ringing slap on his cheek cuts him off.

Honestly, he deserved it.

"You're out of your fucking mind," he says with a shocked shake of his head. "This is over." And then he leaves to go back into the restaurant. I remember him touching his cheek a bit when he returned, seeing the pink mark, putting the pieces together.

For a moment, I thought he and Tanya had left to set up the mice, but considering he was only gone for a few minutes during dinner and we have footage to show his every step, I don't believe he could be the one who actually let the mice go, which lowers him on our suspect list, if not removing him completely.

But Tanya moves a bit higher on the list when she sniffles in the staff room and then takes in a deep breath and puts her shoulders back, as if gathering herself.

"He's going to regret this, fucking with me," is all we can catch before she's out the door. We sit in silence after Rory pauses the video, indicating there's no more to this stream.

"It seems like they're dating, or at least she believed they were," I say, remembering Daniel saying they hooked up and she thought it was more. "He's a flirt. We've seen him flirt with half a dozen guests by now, not including Rory and me. If Tanya gets jealous every time she catches him, and she throws a tantrum, maybe that's it. You heard her say he's going to regret fucking with her. She could easily have left that room and released the mice."

"Agreed," Rory says. "Plus, it's definitely not Daniel. When I went in there, I was able to bug his transmission and copy his hard drive. He was the one who referred us to Annette."

My eyes widen.

"What?"

"It seems he used our services for his ex-wife two years ago. When he realized no one could explain the issues at the resort or pinpoint the source, he suggested the Mavens to Annette."

"No fucking way," I whisper. "How did you find that?"

"With Rowan's help, I have access to the email server for the company. He sent the email on the night of the fire."

I sit down next to Rory and let out a heavy sigh. "If it were him and he knew we were efficient, he wouldn't have suggested we come to investigate. Does he know it's *us*?" I ask, waving a hand between myself and Rory.

She shakes her head. "No, I don't even know if he is aware that Annette took his suggestion."

"Do you think he suspects Tanya?" I ask, thinking out loud.

Rory's face looks contemplative for a moment before shaking her head.

On the bright side, we can reliably knock out Daniel as, at the very least, the person executing the sabotages, since he sat with me the entire time except for a few minutes near the beginning of the dinner.

"I also found this once I got back to the room and started digging," Rory says, pulling up another screen. "I haven't been able to get much from the cameras that have been altered, but I did manage to find this hidden on some back of a backup of a backup in the cloud." She hits play and I see a clip of a man in a dark hoodie, head down, leaving a room with a bag, something large sticking out of it.

"Is that...?" I ask, my heart pounding excitedly.

"The room that was broken into? Yes," Rory says with a smile.

"Oh my god," I whisper, leaning closely. "Who is it?"

"I can't determine that, but I do think..." she says, moving screens and showing me a screen grab. "I had Demi clear this up."

"That's a camera," I say excitedly.

"I think it's why they went into that room. Someone had stashed it in there. The Barlows had checked in early the previous day, so they needed to get in and get the camera before it was found."

"That's why nothing was taken," I say in awe. "We need that camera."

Rory gives me an apologetic look. "Unfortunately, I can't find any other clips with hoodie man in them."

I groan. It feels like we are *so close* but nothing is giving us what we need to close this case, or at least take the final steps to do so.

"We're close, Josie," Rory says sympathetically.

I smile at her and the way she knows exactly what I'm thinking.

"I know, I know. I just...we're so close but we also have nothing. Just a lot of loose ends."

Rory shrugs. "That's the fun of it, babe."

I glare at her and she lets out a laugh.

"Come on. Let's scroll through more tape until your man gets let out and you can go back to his bed."

And really, who am I to argue with an offer like that?

FORTY-TWO

Suspect list for Daydream resorts based on current intel:

- Tanya
- Carter

FORTY-THREE

JOSIE

I leave Rowan's room at the ass crack of dawn to take a morning yoga class with Rory, our eyes and ears open for any whispers. We realized that Tanya often is on the standby list for these classes, and considering these days she seems to be our number one suspect, we make sure we're there. Unfortunately, it's a packed class and she isn't in attendance, but I can't be too mad at the way the slow, languid movement makes my body feel, especially considering my new nightly activities have me feeling sorer than I'd like to admit.

Not that I'm upset about it, of course.

I'm tying up my bikini top for another morning at the pool while we try and figure out next steps when there's a knock on the door. Rory answers it, and I hear Rowan's deep voice greet her.

"What are you doing here?" I ask, walking over to him. He looks casual for once in a thin T-shirt and a pair of swim shorts. I don't miss the way his eyes move to my full breasts in my small top. Despite the number of times I've had him in the past week, it doesn't feel like enough. I wonder if, when we're both home, if it will be different. If, once we're free of paradise, the need will be less.

My gut tells me no.

"We've got plans."

That makes my head pop up. "Plans?"

"You and I are going on an adventure today."

I want to be excited. An adventure with Rowan, especially in this paradise of a place sounds amazing. But...

"I'm here for work, Rowan. I can't just go off on an adventure. It's not fair to Rory," I say, giving him an apologetic look.

"Please go, I'm begging," Rory says exasperated.

"What?" I ask, turning to her.

"Go. I want to stay in this room in peace and quiet for six hours. I'm going to start sifting through the cameras around the time of each incident, look into Tanya, that kind of thing. Plus, we have all those new cameras in the staff areas I want to screen."

"I could—" I offer, but she shakes her head.

"You could enjoy a day off like a normal fucking person," Rory says with a glare.

"And you?" I counter, putting my hands to my hips. "*You're* not taking a day off."

"This is be the equivalent of my taking a day off. I'm going to pop in the raunchiest audiobook I can find, then dig through these files. Basically, my version of bliss."

She's not wrong, but it still makes me uncomfortable.

"I don't know, I feel like I should stay here. I could go to the pool and talk to some people or—"

"You also got a lot of intel yesterday." She reaches for my hand, and I know I'm not going to like whatever she has to say next. "I also think you should lay low for a bit," Rory says, looking at me.

"Excuse me?" I ask, my eyes wide. I've *never* stood aside or laid low.

"Just for a day or so while we dig further into Tanya and check to see if she could be behind this. Where has she been during, before, and after each sabotage? I'm going to keep moving through the cameras and, now that I have access, check all of her scans, see where her card has been used and what times."

"And while you do that, I could—"

"She thinks that if it's Tanya, she could target you," Rowan says, concern in his voice, and my words cut out.

"You guys have talked about this?" I ask, looking from one to the other with a hint of betrayal I know is silly. Rory sighs.

"He came to me with the same concerns I was feeling. I don't want to raise an alarm or anything, but we can never be too sure." She looks at me. "Plus, you just went out with Daniel, and she saw it. If you're out today, flirting with any man you think could give you intel—"

"But maybe I could—"

"You're going to start bringing attention to yourself, and you know it if you don't just enjoy yourself like a normal person." My jaw tightens and I glare at her, but then Rowan's hand is on my wrist and I'm turning to look at him.

"We can do some extra inspections while we're out. Now make a beach bag, and we'll go," he says, then presses a kiss to my forehead. "But it's a hike to get there. Wear sneakers." I stand there, confused and elated, warmth sliding through my body as he sits on the couch to wait for me. I look from him to Rory who is smiling approvingly.

"The man has spoken."

BREAK

He takes me hiking, which at first, I argued against, considering what happened the last time we went. I've been assured that, although the hikes are discontinued for guests until everything clears up, a team has thoroughly swept the area for any other booby traps. They did find another one, a trip wire that lifted its suspect into the air by the foot like in old cartoons, but nothing else. Still, we keep a vigilant eye out for both traps and for any additional evidence.

Nearly an hour into our hike, we make it to the other side of the property, which turns out to be a small, secluded beach with light sand, a few palm trees, and miles of a bright blue ocean. In the distance, I see a dolphin jump up and out of the water, and I gasp. It's so picturesque, I might think it was fake if I weren't actually here.

The entire back of it butts up to the woods, but the beach itself is clear.

"This," Rowan says, looking around with a proud smile. "This is why I chose this location."

"A wooded beach?" I ask with a smile of my own.

He nods. "A wooded, secluded beach. When the excursions aren't stalled, we do super exclusive trips out here. A couple, maybe two, pay extra to be here by themselves, no one else around for the whole day. We cater to it and sometimes even send a masseuse out here for couples' massages. Very expensive, but the guests love it. It's like their own private beach. They don't even have to wear suits if they don't want to."

"Are you telling me this is a nude beach, Rowan?" I ask, my eyes wide. "I'm super cool and like to think I'm pretty progressive, but sand in my bare crotch is not for me. Sorry to break it to you."

He lets out a deep belly laugh, tugging me into him and pressing his lips to mine. When he pulls back, his smile is wide and carefree, and suddenly, I can't find it in me to feel bad about taking some time to myself while on a mission.

"I would absolutely have warned you ahead of time if that was something I expected, but just for the record, sandy crotches don't do anything for me, either."

"Phew," I say in exaggerated relief as I toe my sneakers off and step into the warm, soft sand. I expected it to be filled with rocks or twigs, but it's not; it's perfect and luxurious and pulls a soft sigh from me.

Rowan grabs my hand and walks me to the center of the beach before dropping his own large bag he brought with him. I dig through mine, setting things aside on the beach blanket he's laid out to find the sunscreen I already know I'll need a second layer of.

"Uh, is that a taser in your beach bag?" he asks, and when I turn, I see my sparkly pink taser is sitting on the blanket. His look of utter concern makes me smile.

"Oh, Betty?" I reach and grab it, pressing the button once, then twice to spark it to life. Rowan sits back further, and I laugh at him. "Yeah."

He opens and closes his mouth a few times before asking, "How did you get that on a plane?"

"Don't question my methods, Fisher," I say. He glares, and I giggle. "I put it in my big luggage, my god. Did you think I was bringing a taser on a carry-on?"

"If anyone could manage it, it would be you."

I pat his cheek and smile. "I love the confidence you have in me. "

"I have all the confidence in the world in you, Josie."

"As you should," I say, standing up and stretching. The sun feels glorious on my skin after we walked through the shaded trees, but the water looks even more inviting as we stand beneath the beating sun. I shrug off my shorts and start making steps towards the water, looking over my shoulder to see Rowan staring at my ass. I smile wide and wink before speaking again. "Come on. I want to go for a swim."

"I never want to leave here," I say on a sigh later, after Rowan fed me the most amazing sandwiches and fresh, homemade chips that he had the kitchen make. We're lying on our backs side by side on the beach blanket, letting the sun dry us off, and it feels like absolute heaven.

But the reason I never want to leave has so much less to do with the sun and sand and more with the man lying next to me.

We've spent the last few hours *talking* nonstop. I've learned that, like me, he has no pets because he's not home enough, but he would like one eventually. He learned to ski as a kid but hasn't gone in years, though he might find a few chances with the new Aspen location opening soon. He always knew he wanted to be in business, though luxury hotels were something he fell into during his undergrad when he got an internship with Daydream. His favorite food is Japanese, his favorite color is navy blue, and while he doesn't watch much television or movies, when he does, it's mostly eighties action films.

In turn, I told him I desperately want a cat, though not until I can make sure I'll be home often enough to care for one. I've never been outside of the Americas, nor have I ever been skiing; however, once on an assignment, I learned to surf while investigating a guy who owned a surf shop.

It's been...easy. Shockingly so. I keep waiting for the other shoe to drop, for him to drop some kind of lore that makes me get the ick, but everything he tells me fits him so well and just...*fits*.

We fit.

"Yeah, me neither," he says, reaching for my hand and squeezing it. I give him a smile, but it's tinged in worry despite trying to fight it back. Inevitably, the incredibly attentive man notices it.

"What's wrong?" he asks, brow furrowing as he sits up to look down at me. He leaves a hand on the beach blanket beneath us before using one hand to brush back some stray strands of hair. I let out a deep sigh before confessing.

"It's just...right now, like this, it's perfect. We're stuck together, with minimal distractions, because our work is kind of the same. But it won't be like this in a week. And we both have admitted we work a ton, much of it traveling around, I just..." I feel so silly spilling this out right now during this perfect afternoon, especially since everything is so *new* with us, but I also know that bottling things up never ends well for me. When he gives me a soft, reassuring smile, some of my nerves ease.

"We'll figure it out, Josie," he tells me, not a hint of doubt in the words.

"Will we?" I ask, and I can even hear the nerves in my voice. Nerves because the reality is, I *like* Rowan. I like him, and I like what we have right now, right here. As we get closer to solving the case and closer to the end of our stay, the reality that this bubble will burst soon feels suffocating.

"Of course we will. You get vacation time?"

"I never use it," I admit.

"Well, sounds like we're a perfect pair because I've been told if I don't start using mine, my boss is going to lock me out of the system."

I let out a laugh, this one a bit easier, and he smiles down at me before his face goes serious. "Vacations together every other month, at least four days. Besides that, I work in Hudson City a lot, and that's where I live." I smile before telling him something I already know.

"A lot of my assignments are near home."

"So when we're both home, we spend the night in one of our beds." I squint at him.

"What size is yours?"

He chuckles at that. "King."

My mind moves to my bed, that, while comfy, is only a full. I've never really needed much room for more, what with my never taking a man home.

"How do you feel about sharing counter space if I double up on my toiletries?" His smile turns to a full-blown megawatt grin that makes my belly go warm.

"I have double sinks and only use the one. More than enough counter space for your mess."

"My mess?" I ask pushing his shoulder. He laughs then, light and happy, before his hand moves to my hip as he falls back, tugging me up and over onto him until I'm straddling his waist. My hair falls in a curtain around us, and he gently shifts it all to one shoulder.

"I don't think even you can argue you're a bit of a mess, Josie." I can't and we both know it, especially when it comes to my vanity and bathroom sink. He sees that he's won this battle, but he doesn't push. Instead, his hand cups my cheek reverently before he speaks again, his voice low and filled with care. "We're going to make it work, Josie."

I bite my lip, nerves taking over again. We talked about assignments yesterday, and he seemed okay with it here, but when we're back home in Hudson City, it's different. He's bumped into me on assignments, and each time, he knew who I was in some way, shape, or form. It's a big city, but not *that* big. I guess now is as good a time to tackle this as well.

"I, um," I roll my lips between my teeth before I speak. "I can't stop. The dates." He doesn't speak so I keep talking, hoping to explain, hoping he'll understand. "I know it's a lot, your...girlfriend out with other men, much less ones you might know in some way. One day, I can talk to Gabriel about expanding beyond Hudson City, taking things out of town or something, but not for a while and—" He moves then, cutting me off as he rolls me to my back on the large blanket and pinning my arms down, forcing me to look at him.

"Are you mine?"

His words take me aback. "What?"

"At the end of the night, are you mine? It is my bed you're going to crawl into when I'm home?"

"I mean...or mine."

A small smile plays on his lips as he rolls his eyes before sighing. "Am I the only one invited into your bed?"

I lift a hand then, cupping his cheek, rough with a five o'clock shadow. He looks good with the scruff, though I love his clean-shaven face just as much. "Yes, Rowan," I answer.

"That's all that matters." I open my mouth to argue, but he continues speaking. "The rest we can figure out as we go, Josie. Am I going to love avoiding whatever restaurant you're at that night, because if I bump into you, I won't be able to resist coming over to you? Absolutely. Do I get a little hot thinking about you playing men for a living but sucking my cock at the end of the night? Abso-fuck-ing-lutely." I smile because I never really thought of *that perk,* though I should have. I fucking *love* when Rowan gets all jealous. He sees my look and mirrors it. "We'll figure it out, Josie."

"How are you so fucking perfect" I ask, confused because there are very few men in this world who would respond that way. He smiles again before using his hand on my jaw to guide my lips to his, pressing there sweet and soft before whispering against them.

"Because I was made to be yours, Josie. It just took us a while to figure it out." My heart skips a beat. Still, I don't respond, the remnant of concern and worry still lingering. He senses them, as he seems to do often, and sighs, moving and shifting us so I'm sitting in his lap.

"Are you going to get mad when I have to work?"

"What?" I ask, confused.

"Are you going to be annoyed if I can't take you out to dinner because I have late calls across the world? Are you going to be mad when I basically ignore the world right before and after an opening? I'm telling you right now, during that time, I'll be a ghost in your life, barely reachable through anything but a text or email to prove I'm alive. Are you going to question my loyalty because I have to schmooze some board member, flirt with her to convince her to trust that I know what I'm doing?"

"Of course not, Rowan. I mean, fuck with my job—" I start, my brow furrowed.

"Exactly," he says like that's all the explanation he needs. He pauses then, waiting for me to understand, and slowly, I do. Then he explains, so it's crystal clear. "Our jobs are different, but they're the same. We both work a lot. We both aren't going to stop that completely. We both love our jobs and, at least for me, that has been a big obstacle in finding someone in the past. We get that. We understand that. We are going to make it work." Finally, like he can't help himself, he wraps an arm around my waist and holds me closer to him, pressing his lips to mine. When he breaks the kiss, he rests his forehead against mine. "Got it?"

"Yeah, I got it, Rowan," I whisper.

And for once, I think I do have it: the job, the life, the man. All of it.

BREAK

Reluctantly, hours later, we pack up our things and head back into the woods to move through the trees and back to the main resort. We keep a firm eye out for any more saboteurs, though we see none, thankfully.

That is, until a gust of wind blows, moving the trees and making them sway and, in turn, filter the light through them slightly differently. That's when I see it in the distance: a flash of light, like a slight reflection off of metal. Without a word, I veer off the trail and through taller grasses in the direction I saw it. Another glint helps me narrow the area down, but it's still a hundred feet of rocky and potentially dangerous terrain away. I'm grateful I wore sneakers instead of sandals.

"What's that?" I ask, tipping my chin towards the spot.

"What's what?" Rowan doesn't catch what I saw, but I move towards it regardless, ignoring him. It's deep in the woods, but even now, even on a day when it's just Rowan and me hanging out, doing nothing, my mind is still on work, still processing the case.

As I approach the area, I almost lose track of the spot, since it's hidden really well, and the only reason I *did* see it was a perfectly timed glinting of light on metal made possible by the fortunate sway of a tree. I move slowly, never shifting my eyes from the spot now, as if I'm a predator and it is my prey.

"Josie, what are you doing?" Rowan asks, but I don't respond, instead waving a hand to indicate he follow me. I'm going with my gut, and that's never led me astray, but I don't have time to explain that.

"Josie—"

"I saw something," I say. My heart starts to pound as I see another flash of metal.

My hands are shaking as I reach for it, trying to ignore the ick that covers the item. I push away that fear, swiping away leaves that were covering what I see is a towel of some sort, before I unwrap it.

And there it is.

The missing surveillance camera.

"Saw what?" he asks as his steps slow beside me. I point then and smile up at him.

"That."

Beneath a swatch of tall grass and a few palm fronds that I believe must have slipped, is the charred camera from the rental shack.

"What is that?" Rowan asks, leaning forward but not reaching for it as if he's nervous it might bite.

"This is the biggest piece of evidence we haven't been able to find," I whisper, then reach into my bag for the towel I dried off with. The universe has been in my favor the last few weeks, but my *god* is she working with me today with this find. If the trees hadn't moved at *just* that moment, if we hadn't taken exactly *this* trail, if we hadn't left when we had, the sun wouldn't have hit just right to catch my eye.

"That's a security camera," he says finally as I pull it up and inspect it. It looks to be in pretty good condition despite the char marks and grime on it. I'm hoping that the chip is preserved as Rory said it should be, and that it will contain some usable footage on it.

"There was that big storm last night. Maybe it was better hidden and now it's revealed?" Rowan asks, and I nod.

"Probably. Rory might be able to salvage some footage on this, so now we have to get it back to her asap. She's going to absolutely lose it," I say, almost giddy at the new find. It seems my afternoon off was productive after all.

He smiles at me wide and shakes his head before grabbing it and putting the package into his backpack. "Then let's get this back to her."

FORTY-FOUR

JOSIE

Josie

"Welcome back, love birds," Rory says when we walk in, and I smile at her, my body light with happiness. As much as I hate to admit it, she was right: I so very much needed an afternoon with no work, without having to dig into the minds of people. Now I'm refreshed and excited to close this case.

Finding a huge piece of evidence helped.

"How was your afternoon off?" she asks.

"Amazing, actually. We have a discovery," I say, reaching into Rowan's bag. She looks at us, exasperated.

"I don't want to know about your sexcapades, Josie."

Rowan chokes on his spit before coughing, but I ignore him.

"No sexcapades, you freak." My fingers wrap around the equipment before I grip it and lift the heavy equipment out. "But how about a camera?"

"Is that...?" She whispers, eyes wide as she takes in the charred camera in my hands.

"The camera from the rental room? I hope so."

"Oh my god," she whispers, then reaches for it. "Where did you find it?"

I hand the wrapped camera to her.

"Luck, really," I admit. "We went to some hidden beach, and when we walked back, it just happened to catch the sun. I went to look at it, and there it was. The hikes were cancelled after the booby traps, so I'm assuming our culprit hid it there, thinking no one would be out that way for a bit."

Rory moves across the room, moving to the table in the room, laying out the towel, and then going to her small tool kit. "I hate to do this, but I do have a call in..." Rowan looks at his watch, "...forty-five minutes, and I need to look slightly less beach bum than I do right now."

I smile wide before nodding.

"Go, go. We're going to be working on this," I say, tipping my head towards Rory, knowing I'll probably spend the time she's working on it to go through more files.

"Keep me updated?" he asks.

"Of course. Let me know when you're done."

He grins. "I'll bring dinner."

"Good, we're going to be here all night," Rory says, unwrapping the camera and reaching for her toolkit. She looks like a kid on Christmas and doesn't even bother to look up at Rowan. "Now go. Josie has files to look through as well, and you're distracting her."

"I do?" She looks up at a time with a glare.

"I segmented the files for us to go through while you were gone. I'm good, but I can't comb through them all that quickly."

I nod, slightly relieved she's going to let me help instead of hunkering down with eight energy drinks and zero sleep as I've seen her do before.

"Okay, well, I'll let you ladies get to it," Rowan says, then steps closer to press a kiss to my lips. "Let me know if you need anything." And then he's out the door.

We sit in near silence for long hours while Rory references manuals and videos to try and figure out the best way to open the camera without damaging any evidence. Unfortunately, with the fire, there were no prints as we had expected, and some of the actual camera casings were melted to the interior. This means Rory has to get creative in opening it without damaging the internal mechanisms.

Meanwhile, I've been scanning carefully through the dates and times Rory took out of the system, trying to find something our suspect didn't wipe, some kind of evidence they didn't carefully cover up.

Finally, we catch a break on hour two, and I let out a soft, excited breath. Rory's head snaps up to me, the microscope glasses she's wearing making her looks ridiculous and bug-eyed. She knows what that sound is, though. "What did you find?"

I shake my head, unsure. "I don't...I don't know," I say, turning the computer towards her as she takes the glasses off before I hit play. It's a clip of an employee looking in a room while in a hallway, clearly panicking and then running in a different direction. After a few more clicks, I show him running into one of the many hidden storage closets, though unfortunately, I don't think it's one we bugged, inevitably. He walks out nearly ten minutes later, a bag slung over his shoulder and a phone to his ear.

"Who is that?" she asks, staring at the screen.

"I think it's Carter," I say, flipping through the photos we've taken of employees, then turning it towards her. "He's an assistant manager in landscaping."

"He's the one who said Tanya was ruining the job he got her by hooking up with Daniel, right?" I nod. "But why is he running away? Was he scared?" Rory asks. "When is this clip from?"

I turn to her fully and smile.

"I think he might be our security breach," I say.

"What?" Rory asks, but she's already shifting the camera to the side and grabbing her computer and starting to type.

"About three minutes after this, someone hacked into the camera feeds to erase the previous footage and create an inconspicuous loop after the rat incident. This was from one of the side halls, one that wasn't wiped. Can you check where he was before and after every incident?" I ask, my pulse pounding.

"On it," Rory says, then starts typing, two screens running at the same time. Over her shoulder, I see she has set up some kind of system to crawl the keycard system before and after it was used, then she inputs the times and areas into another screen which should pull details from the cameras Rowan gave us access to. Then she moves to her other computer and opens up a tab to run a background check on him.

There we find out he's 25, has an older brother, and has lived in Florida his whole life. He started at Daydream when it was opened, so his story of getting Tanya the job tracks.

"He has a juvie record," Rory mumbles to herself.

"He does?"

"It's sealed, but let me..." She scares me with her talent, but somehow, she cracks into the system in just moments before reading aloud.

"Oh fuck. When he was 17, he hacked into the school records to change his grade. He was caught, but the school didn't press charges. Just made note of it, essentially."

"So he has the skill and the ability," I say, and she gives me a grim nod.

Her other computer dings like it's done running its search, and she shifts her focus. More typing and clicking occur before she sits back in her chair, crossing her arms on her chest. "I'd have to compare more closely, but from what it looks like to me, his breaks coincide with either right before or right after each sabotage was reported."

My pulse spikes, adrenaline racing through my system, but I'm still able to think logically and tactically.

"He's visible right as they occur, so he's not the one actually doing the incidents?" Rory asks as she pulls my computer closer to her, speeds through the clip for the thousandth time, then pauses and zooms in on Carter's face.

"No, I don't think it's him. See his face when he saw the mice? He looks absolutely petrified and panicked. He didn't know that was happening."

"But he's definitely involved. Maybe he's covering up for our true culprit?" I ask.

"Or he's probably working with someone," Rory says.

"Working with someone?"

"Either way, I think we've got our security leaks, it seems. An accomplice," I whisper.

"But why? And for whom?" Rory asks aloud. Not knowing the answers to that is really starting to piss me off. "Fuck, I wish we could just grab him and put him into a room and question him." I shake my head, knowing that's not the right tactic for a case like this one.

"No. Not yet. At best, he is the mastermind, with someone else completing the tasks for him and covering it up. At worst, he's being used by someone, and if we go after him, we lose our real target. We need to have all angles of this to nail it. Right now, it's far too circumstantial. Plus, he looked shocked when he saw the mice, so my gut says he's trying to save someone. A friend or a lover…" I sigh, knowing that while we're getting closer, it's not close enough.

"I'll see what I can find while you work on that?" I ask, tipping my head towards the charred cameras she's holding like a baby.

"Well, actually," she says with a smile. "Right before you found this, I almost…." She moves back to the camera and fiddles for another moment before lifting something in the air with tweezers. It's surprisingly clean and in one piece, and my excitement ratchets up.

This is my favorite part of the case. When it all starts to fall into place. When I can feel just how close we are to solving this case once and for all. My body feels electric, supercharged, and excited.

"Is that—" I start, but Rory cuts me off with a pride-filled smile.

"A microchip that hopefully holds the footage of the last moments of the rental building before it was torched? Yeah."

"Oh my god," I whisper excitedly. Rory smiles and pulls out a chip to slide the smaller one in before putting it into her computer. I hold my breath as we wait for the computer to process it, and then a screen pops up with files.

"There's a recording of the last ten minutes before it was burned down," she whispers, pointing to the last file on the screen. It looks like they're saved in thirty-minute increments, but this one was cut short. She clicks it, and we watch. It's dark, but night vision cameras help us see. I smile when a turtle passes the screen, and Rory lets out a laugh, remembering how Rowan caught us the first time we went to check the place out.

And then we see it.

There's no sound, unfortunately, but in the corner of the screen, a man in all black and a mask moves towards the shack, clearly on a mission. Then he turns, throwing his hands into the air. Our guy takes another step, and another face comes into view, this one not covered. Clearly, they're arguing. It's a woman in a white tank top and black biker shorts, carrying a large, long-handled tote with a gym logo prominently displayed on the side.

"Do you recognize the woman?" Rory asks low, that same hint of discovery excitement in her words.

"No," I whisper, because although we can see the interaction, the quality isn't amazing. She nods as we watch the rest, as he tugs out of her grip and she clearly stomps off, annoyed or irritated. Then the person in all black pulls some items out of a backpack, including lighter fluid, before liberally dousing the place with it. He sets fire to the shack, and a few minutes later, the camera goes out; clearly, the heat of the fire is too much.

We sit there for a moment, taking in what we just watched.

"And then...what? They came back? Took it?"

Rory shrugs, but nods all the same. "Must have, and then tried to stash it." She opens another window and, after checking the exact time on the shack footage, she leaves the camera screen, spending a few minutes working her magic. I watch as she moves through the resort cameras, attempting to track the woman's departure through various cameras, trying to work around the missing footage. Right as

the cameras went back online, when she checks the employee park-
ing, we see the woman's back once more, in the same outfit and bag
slung over her shoulder step into a car and drive away, though we still
never get a good look at her face. Rory takes a screen grab of the
vehicle.

"License plate," I whisper. Rory nods.

"I don't have the equipment to clean this up enough to get some
numbers, but Demi..." she says and I smile, grabbing my phone
without another word and dialing our coworker.

"Hey, man-eater," she says when she picks up on the first ring.
Demi is also great at flirting, but even more, she's basically a human
lie detector, something that I'm sure she's using on her current
mission with our other coworker, Lana.

On the video call, she's sitting in a hotel room bed, her auburn
hair pulled up into a loose knot on top of her head and her glasses
perched on her nose.

"Hey babe, real quick: I've got a photo for you—any chance you
have a sec to work your magic? There's a license plate we'd love to
identify."

"You caught me at a great time," she says, smiling. "Lana just left
for practice, and I'm here all alone, bored out of my mind. Send me
the file, and I'll see what I can do. I'll run it through the MVC, too. I
just had the system open."

"You're an angel," I say, then shift the camera to Rory, who is
sitting at the computer, sending over the photo.

"Hey Rory!" Demi says.

"Hey girl, I just sent it." Demi nods and pulls over a computer,
obviously transferring the call to the laptop as the angle changes, and
she begins typing.

"Where are you guys again?" I ask, sitting on my bed.

"This week we're in Minnesota. Far cry from the Florida Keys."

I laugh.

"Can't say I envy you," I say. "You guys are doing that monster
truck case, right?" She nods vigorously. "Is Lana in the truck?"

"Yeah, you couldn't pay me to do what she's doing right now. You've got to see it; it's insanity," she says. "Okay, the image is processing. Hold on, I'll send you some pictures." My phone vibrates, and I switch screens to see multiple photos have been sent from her.

Scrolling through, I fight back a laugh as I see Lana dressed in a full-body racing suit in colors of pink and purple, her helmet resting on her hip with a unicorn horn on it. Behind her is a giant, sparkling, unicorn monster truck painted in pinks, purples, and whites. When I swipe again, there's a video clip of the car going up and flipping in the air on a dirt mound before landing on all four tires.

"Holy shit! Lana's in there?" I say, eyes wide, and Rory shifts then watches my phone in similar awe.

"I'm telling you guys; she was born for this. It's insane. She's beating all the boys in the rankings."

"Boys, huh?" I say with a smile.

"Oh, you should *see* the one Lana has to work with the closest," Demi says, then starts waving hand at her face. "An asshole, but fuck, he's hot."

"A suspect?" Rory asks, and she shakes her head.

"Target." I cringe because a case where we're working closely with a target is always complicated. "A real piece of work, hates that a girl is beating him, thinks he's too good for the job. He used to be in F1, but never got very far."

"Oof," I groan, knowing the type. "Good luck with that one."

Target cases, where one person is being targeted either physically or emotionally, are some of the hardest to figure out because we have to take human emotions into account. Motivations become blurred when someone is trying to hurt another person. Even more so when you're trying to protect an asshole like that.

"Yeah, it's been very entertaining to watch them fight. Okay, done," she says finally. "Okay, so the car is owned by a....Tanya Renard. Ring a bell?"

I look at Rory, whose eyes are wide.

"No way," I whisper.

"I'll take that as a yes." There's a knock at the door on Demi's side, and she stands. "That's my food. Need anything else? I'll send you what I've got." I shake my head, and Rory answers.

"No, that's it. Thanks, Demi. You're a godsend."

"You guys stay safe, okay?" I say.

"You too. Drinks when we're all done here?"

"I'm begging," I say. "I'll call you when we're home!"

She nods and drops the call, and I turn to Rory, nearly jumping in excitement. Rory, as is her way, has already pulled up the ID cards for the employees, and it becomes even clearer that we've found who our arsonist was fighting with. "One of the sabotages before we arrived was in the spa, right?" I nod.

"The irritant in the mud." My mind continues to run circles as I attempt to place it into our list, since she obviously could have had access to the spa. She was on our suspect list, but I'll admit I hadn't actually thought of her as a viable candidate until recently. A mistake, obviously. But...

"But she wasn't the one who burned it down," Rory says.

"She was in the vicinity when it happened, though," I say with a tip of my head, trying to put the pieces together. "Could her hooking up with Daniel have been some kind of distraction?"

"Can we check where she was each time there was some kind of sabotage? I know the cameras have been tampered with for most of the issues, but where was she when, say, the break-in happened?"

"I can look. But I think we're going to need some more info on her." I nod, agreeing. "Where do we get it? She very much does not like you, so you can't work your magic on her."

Just then, my phone beeps with a new text from Rowan, saying he's done with his calls and headed up with dinner. I smile wide at Rory, a brilliant idea coming to mind.

FORTY-FIVE

JOSIE

Josie

"It's her," Rowan says after we show him all of our newly discovered evidence. Rory and I give each other a disbelieving look before I give him a small smile and shake my head. "Seriously? You two don't think it's her?"

I shrug and feel the urge to pat his hand.

"We've done this a lot, Rowan. Trust us. She's involved, don't get me wrong, same as Carter is. But it's not her." He sits back in disbelief, but I continue to explain our reasoning. "That clip of her before the fire? She was angry. She told our perp not to do it. It's not her, but she knows who it is. She also didn't come forward to tell on him, so there's loyalty there, some connection. I'd go as far as to say our perp is doing it for her."

His eyes go wide at that.

"For her? Why would someone sabotage a hotel for someone?"

"People have done crazier things to get someone's attention."

"You think he's trying to get her attention?" I shrug. I have nothing really to go on for that theory but a hunch, but still, I explain what little I have. "Many of the sabotages have occurred in the spa," I remind him.

It's still fresh on his mind, of course, since when he walked in he told us that part of why he was busy so long was because a massage table collapsed as an employee was prepping it for a guest. When he looked at it, he found it was missing three screws, the exact three that would've made it almost inevitable to collapse during a service. Thankfully, there was no service at the time and no one was hurt, but it was another clear sabotage. Rowan shakes his head and lets out a sigh.

"That's one way to get someone's attention, I suppose."

I smile and grab a French fry from the room service container he brought up, chewing thoughtfully before speaking again.

"We need to talk to her," Rory says, beginning to pace the room. This is her least favorite part of a mission: when we're close, but not there, and there's just one piece missing before we can solve our problem.

"Good luck with that, because every time Tanya sees you, she looks like she hopes she chokes," Rowan says with a laugh. I roll my eyes, but then I look over at him, taking in my boyfriend, all broad shoulders and rumpled hair, and I grin.

"Why do I feel like I am absolutely not going to enjoy whatever you're about to say?" he asks with one exasperated sigh. I look from him to Rory, who smiles as well, already knowing where I'm going with this.

"Have you ever considered being a super cool undercover spy?" I ask.

BREAK

. . .

The next morning, we have the cameras in Rowan's office running and are watching attentively. Last night, after we convinced him this was our best option and he totally could pull it off, Rowan sent Tanya an email requesting she visit his office bright and early, and she is due in his office any moment.

"Do you feel it?" I ask, my voice low.

"Yeah," Rory replies, and a chill washes over me with her confirmation.

There's a moment in any given case where you feel it: the tipping point approaching, the moment where all of the pieces fall into place and everything makes sense. It's in the air, and while I still don't think Tanya is our culprit, she knows who is, and she is going to give us just a crumb of what we need to solve the case.

Today.

I can feel it in my bones, as sure as I know my own name.

Before I can say anything else, a knock comes from the monitor and Rowan straightens. His shoulders go back, and he takes in a deep breath before he calls, "Come in." Even though this moment is incredibly important, I can't help but steal a single moment to take in my man and how good he looks in a dark navy suit and a white button-down shirt with no tie, the top two buttons undone intentionally to really amp up the hot factor and get Tanya off her game.

But I can't focus on that long because the door opens and in walks Tanya, a strut in her step as she smiles too wide for my liking and pushes her chest out as she approaches his desk.

"Down girl," Rory mutters, and I realize the grip around the pen in my hand is turning my knuckles white. "He's absolutely bonkers for you, no need to get jealous."

I want to argue that I'm not jealous, that I just don't like the woman, but Tanya speaks, and I have to focus, forcing my own personal emotions back into a box and turning on my professional interpretation of her every move.

"You called for me?" she asks, putting her hands on the chair and leaning forward, a cat-like smile on her lips. If I hadn't gotten fucked over that very chair just a few days ago, I might be jealous. But alas...

"Yes, yes, I just want to chat with you for a bit. Please sit down." She makes an exaggerated show of pulling the chair out, popping her ass out as she does before she sits in the chair.

"There was another incident in the spa yesterday. A massage table collapsed while an employee was prepping it for a guest. No injuries, thank god, but it's the fourth issue of its kind in the spa department that we know of."

To her credit, Tanya looks shocked and concerned, eyes wide and her lips parted. We did our best to make sure she was not informed of the issue before she made her way to Rowan's office, and it seems we were successful.

"Oh no! It collapsed? Was it faulty?"

Rowan tips his head before explaining.

"Initial investigations show that screws were removed or loosened to ensure a collapse." Her eyes go soft and innocent, and for a moment, I almost feel bad.

And then I remember the piling evidence as to why I should not feel bad, most importantly that she knows who has been creating all of these issues.

"Did you call me in here because..." her eyes widen, and a hand moves to her chest. "Do you think I'm doing this?" Her voice goes a pitch too high. "I don't know anything about any of this mess."

"There it is," Rory says, noting the same thing. "She's lying about something. Panicked."

I nod in agreement, and watch as Rowan smoothly shakes his head.

"No, no. I just wanted to tell you personally so you didn't hear it from anyone else," he says. Relief washes over Tanya's face and she reaches over, touching his hand on the desk and pushing her cleavage together in a way that is far too vulgar for work.

"I really do appreciate that," she says in a terrible impression of Marilyn Monroe that makes me roll my eyes. People thing being the man-eater is easy: bat your lashes, perk your tits, pout your lips and you'll have them eating out of your hand, but it's about reading your target, knowing what they want, and giving them just that. It's about reading the room, about tempting without giving, and forcing the chase.

It's clear to me Tanya thinks she has the skill, but she doesn't.

"Though, actually...I was happy to have an excuse to call you in here. I feel like we never have time to talk; we're always too busy with the resort." He leans back, a small smile playing on his lips as he tilts his head to the side, crossing his arms across his wide chest.

"Oh my god, he's actually good at this," Rory says in an awestruck voice.

"Too good," I grumble, especially when Tanya dons her own catlike smile before leaning farther into his desk and pushing her breasts closer together. It's a move I've done a million times, but she clearly doesn't have the same ease, making it too sexual and far too obvious.

"You know, I've always felt a bit of a connection between us, you know. We have the same work ethic," Tanya says while fluttering her lashes. I tighten my jaw, but Rowan just smiles and nods.

"Have you always worked in hospitality? It seems like you were made for this industry?"

She lets out a flirty laugh and waves a hand, shaking her head.

"Oh, you're too sweet. No, no, I worked in a med spa in Miami before this. But a friend of mine told me there was an opening here, and I applied and was shocked when I got the job."

Rowan raises an eyebrow, and my heart starts to beat a bit faster, my veins filling with endorphins.

"A friend?" Rowan asks.

"Oh, Carter over in landscaping." For the first time since she walked in, my eyes leave the monitor and look at Rory who is staring at me with the same excited look. Carter, who we caught running to a storage closet moments before the cameras were tampered with.

Carter, who said Tanya was throwing away the job he got her.

She's leading up right where we need her.

I expect him to take the easy route, to ask another question about Carter or how she knows him, but he doesn't. Instead, he picks up her hand and holds it, and that familiar jealousy rolls through me. His thumb brushes over her index finger and a wide smile spreads on his lips.

"A tan line, huh? Seems like it at least used to be exclusive." The smile makes me wonder if he's remembering that night in the bar when I told him my tan line trick, the way I am now.

"Oh, well, I was engaged up until recently," she says, a hint of embarrassment or hesitance in the words. My heart stutters, and I turn to Rory, whose body has the same tense hold as mine. That never came up in our investigations. Immediately, Rory moves to her computer and starts digging.

"Oh? What happened?" Rowan asks, and Tanya waves her hand.

"Oh, you know, the normal thing. Girl meets boy, girl falls for boy's shit, boy gets far too possessive and controlling." She shrugs as if she doesn't care. "Girl gets dragged around for a bit before she realizes she needs to get out."

"That's too bad. I hate to see a good woman locked down," Rowan says.

"Cool it, girl," Rory says, looking at me as she types away.

"What?"

"You look like you're about to break a tooth."

I roll my eyes once more but loosen my jaw, not bothering to argue because she's...not wrong. I focus on breathing as I watch the screen some more, as Tanya sighs in a way that tries to get sympathy. Her free hand moves to her necklace, playing with the small charm there absentmindedly.

"You know, it's been really hard. I moved out of the place we shared, and he's been contacting me nonstop. I feel like I can't get away from home. I could really use a friend." My body stills, not because of her obvious come on, but because of the hint she dropped.

"Rory," I say, not moving my eyes.

"Already on it," she responds.

"Oh? Where are you living now?" Rowan asks, leaning forward. I don't miss how he pulls his hand back from hers, resting his fist under his chin. Tanya doesn't notice the brush off and shrugs.

"Oh, Daniel has been kind enough to let me stay with him for a bit while I figure things out." She pauses, then shakes her head. "We're not an item or anything, though. I'm totally single."

"Do you feel safe?" Rowan asks, giving her a soft, worried smile. "I want to make sure you feel safe." Her eyes go wide and dreamy, and her lips form a soft smile before shrugging.

"I mean...he's been a bit overbearing. Always has been, but lately it's even more. Reaching out, trying to keep in touch with me even though I told him I'm done. I just...I worry, you know?" She looks side to side before her voice lowers again.

"Sometimes I think he's keeping an eye on me." My pulse speeds.

"Why do you feel that way?" Rowan asks, looking genuinely concerned, and in a way, I'm sure he is.

"I just...when we were younger, he would always get really possessive. If he saw me even talking to another guy, he would make a big thing about it. That's why we broke up. He said he saw me talking to Daniel, but I swear, we were just talking. We work together, you know?"

I roll my eyes at her exaggeration, but stay focused.

"The listed address in her employee file is a rental. I'll have to hack into the system of the housing company to see who is on the lease," Rory says. I continue to watch Tanya and Rowan on the screen, endorphins racing.

"That's hard," he says.

"Well, you know, I'm grateful I have such a great support system here at Daydream. Like you," she says, reaching out to touch his hand.

I don't even care, not now. Not when Rory whispers a little yes, not when she smiles because she just got into the system she needed. Not when she starts speaking.

"Tanya's last known address was in an apartment complex called Seaside Meadows." Rory keeps clicking, doing what she does best. "The least was signed with a Randy Short."

"Short?" I ask, the name ringing a bell, but my brain can't move nearly as fast as Rory's can.

"It looks like Carter Short is his younger brother."

"No way," I whisper, then tip my head. "How tall is he?"

Rory types a few more times before answering.

"Driver's license says five ten, so probably five eight."

I can't help it: even in a serious moment like this, I have to laugh.

"And Tanya?"

Rory looks up at me with a wide smile on her lips.

"Five five."

"So that would give a good three-inch gap, right?" I ask, thinking of the video of Tanya arguing with our mystery man. When Rory smiles, a chill race through me.

"Did we just find our guy?" She shrugs.

"I mean, I'd venture to say yes. It makes sense. If he's as posses-sive as she says, making the hotel look bad and, in turn, Daniel would make sense if he thought she was cheating on him with Daniel."

"We need to set up a trap," Rory says. I nod then, reaching for my phone and texting Rowan that we've got something and he's cleared to wrap things up. On the monitor, Rowan pulls his hand away from where Tanya is slowly creeping to him and checks his phone.

"Sorry, I've got to take this," he says, back to all business, any flirting gone from his tone. It makes me smile, knowing it was all a mask to win her over. I fight the childish urge to giggle when I see her face drop with confusion at his sudden change. Then he stands and moves around his desk, walking to the door and opening it. "Thank you for taking time out of your morning to meet with me. If you have any insight on the happenings, please let me know."

Slowly, she stands and then walks towards the door. "We should—"

Rowan cuts her off again. "I'm sorry, I really do have to go. I have a meeting to get to."

He ushers her out the door and closes it behind her. Then he turns to where he knows the camera is, smiles and gives it a thumbs up. I shake my head and laugh, then text him to say to come up to our room as soon as he can.

"What if Carter isn't trying to help, but cover up his brother's fuck ups?" Rory asks contemplatively, continuing to dig through files she shouldn't have access to. "It looks like his brother may have helped to raise him. Single mom, latch key kids, super close. Their social media channels show they spend a lot of time together. It would explain him trying to cover up for his brother."

"And possibly why he wouldn't want Tanya to turn him in? Why he's annoyed at Tanya for flirting with Daniel?" It's all falling into place in my mind. "He would of course think Tanya continuing to date Daniel would be bad: every time his brother got wind, he tries to sabotage Daniel's hotel."

Rory nods, mirroring the wide smile on my lips.

"Now we have to catch him," I say with a smile. Rory groans in exasperation, but my own smile widens further. "My favorite part."

FORTY-SIX

JOSIE

Josie

I knock on Rowan's door after Rory and I finish setting up last-minute details for tomorrow. Rowan came up and spent most of the day helping us, contacting different people to try and get our idea rolling before he had to leave for a meeting and told me to meet him at his room when I was done. There's a good chance this is our last night in paradise—or at least, the last one where we won't be celebrating a closed case and Rowan won't inevitably be doing major damage control to decide how to deal with the employees who had a hand in all of this, and I desperately want to spend it with Rowan.

It's our last night in this bubble before life goes back to normal, or whatever the new normal is, and despite Rowan's reassurance that we'll make things work, I can't help but feel a twinge of nervousness.

"Coming," the voice behind the door says, and I smile, looking down the hall once more to ensure no one is around. Rowan's suite is down an empty hall, though, so I don't have to really worry about anything. When the door opens, Rowan standing there in a casual pair of shorts and a Daydream T-shirt, I smile, but then my brow furrows in confusion. The lights are off, though there seems to be some flickering behind him and maybe...fairy lights?

"Wha—" I start, but his hand moves out, wrapping my wrist and tugging me into his dark hotel room. "What is going on?" I ask as I take in the living room of his suite, which has four tables scattered about, each filled with food and drink, though each area has a clearly distinct vibe. One has white linens and tapered candles and champagne flutes, a salmon dinner on each plate. On another low table, there's some kind of fried noodle dish and a bottle of sake. A third table has what I think must be mozzarella sticks, pizza, and beer, and on the final table is steak and what looks like truffle fries, a bottle of wine, and big goblets.

"What is this?" I ask with a laugh. Somehow, he's put together this big...feast, yet I can't rack my brain through all of the conversations we've had to figure out what he's doing or why. He moves closer to me, putting a hand to my lower back and I look at him and see there's...nerves on his face. My unflappable man is *nervous*. His hand lifts and he tucks a piece of my hair back before resting his hand on the back of my neck.

"This is four of the twenty-one dates I should have taken you on." My body stills, and I continue to stare at him, confusion mixing with eager anticipation in my veins. Whatever is happening right now, I know to my bones I'll remember it until the day I die. Cherish it, even.

"What?"

"I bumped into you twenty-one times before I had a drink with you in the bar." Goosebumps erupt over my arms, and his hand moves down, rubbing them away absentmindedly before continuing to explain. "Twenty-one opportunities I could have tried to take you out, to win you over." My stomach flutters as I start to understand, start to put the pieces together. "If I hadn't been such an idiot who let his bruised ego get in the way, I probably would have been more persistent." The hand on my back presses, tugging me into his chest, and my hand moves around his neck instinctively. He looks down at me with warm, open eyes, and I see the truth in every single word he's saying.

"I'll still owe you at least seventeen more after this, not including all of the other dates I plan to take you on." My breathing hitches with his words. "This is just my way of saying I know we should have been this...me and you...a lot longer, but I was too stubborn to take a step. It's on me, and I'm going to make every effort to make it up to you."

I shake my head then.

"You don't have to do this, Rowan," I say with a soft laugh. "I also am to blame."

Now it's his turn to shake his head, but with less humor and more fierceness.

"As far as you knew, I was an asshole for no reason."

My hand moves, cupping his cheek. "And as far as you knew, I wasn't into you and lied about not dating people."

He shrugs.

"The difference is, if you told me that right now, if you said you didn't date, it wouldn't stop me. I'd keep asking. Five times, ten, twenty-one times until I convinced you to give me the smallest shot, to let me in."

"That's kind of obsessive," I say with a laugh.

"That's because I'm completely obsessed with you, and even though I couldn't admit it to even myself until recently, I've been obsessed with you for some time. If I paid attention for just a single moment, I would have realized the world was throwing me a million chances to find my person finally."

I swallow emotion before giving him a small smile, my thumb grazing over his sharp cheekbone.

"You're such a romantic," I whisper in awe.

"No, no. I'm not."

"Look around, Rowan. This is a romantic grand gesture at its finest."

He gives me a soft chuckle and shakes his head. "I'm not a romantic. I'm just wild for you."

My heart thumps, but because I can't let him think he *totally* won me over, despite us both knowing the truth, I smile and tip my head.

"You bumped into me twenty-two times, but I only get twenty-one dates?"

He smiles wide. "The twenty-second time I bumped into you was a date. We drank, we talked, I dragged you into an office and made you come. It was our *first* date, even." My jaw drops and my eyes widen. He laughs at the shock on my face before his head dips, pressing a kiss to my neck. "That's exactly how you would have wanted that date to go, and you know it."

I roll my eyes, but he doesn't miss the shiver that rolls through me.

"I would have preferred you fucked me, but—" I start, but he cuts me off.

"Then we'll recreate it the right way when we get back."

I let out a loud, free laugh, my heart full and light at the same time, the way I find myself always feeling when I'm around Rowan. Even when I used to see him out and dread him coming over, dread the fact that he could blow my cover, I also anticipated it. Wanted it. Craved the back and forth of it. Craved *him*.

God, I am so gone for this man. And I think I always have been.

"Promise?" I ask in a whisper.

"Promise," he agrees. We stand there for a moment, and I contemplate forcing him to take me to his bed and fuck me, but then I remember the intricately planned date—*dates* around us.

"So, these dates—you gonna explain them?"

He grins down at me and nods, leading me around the room, starting at the table with no tablecloth and paper plates.

"This would have been After Hours. Pizza, mozzarella sticks, cheap beer," he says, referencing the restaurant on campus that pretended to be a restaurant but was really just a dive where students could eat junk and hang out. There's a *Go Raven*s pennant on the table, cheering on our school team, and my chin wobbles, understanding this wasn't a spur-of-the-moment decision of his.

"Where did you get that?" I ask. "*When* did you get that?"

"Ordered it the day after you explained what happened all those years ago. That you didn't even remember turning me down, and I'd been holding a one-sided grudge like an idiot."

"You knew you wanted to do this then?" I ask with a laugh.

"I knew I needed to."

Something in me melts, but I can't focus on it because he leads me to another spot in the room.

"This is the restaurant where I technically had dinner with you and Stephen. You ordered the salmon and potatoes with green beans." I laugh and shake my head, remembering that was what, in fact, I ordered that night, mostly because despite being excited for it, Rowan being there and the nerves that accompanied it made me lose my appetite.

He moves us to the low table, pointing out that when he bumped into me there, I was in a red dress and barely even said hi to my date because he couldn't keep his eyes away from me. Then he shows me the final table, a steak house where I took a man who was embezzling, and Rowan was so mad about it because he already knew the man was a piece of shit.

"How do you remember all of this?" I ask after he shows me each table. He shrugs, a light blush on his cheeks.

"I can't seem to forget a single detail about you, Josie, no matter how hard I've tried." I turn to him and smile up at him softly, my hand moving to his cheek as it all comes over me. The past few weeks, the revelation that has been Rowan, the fact that we both want this to work outside of this mission... It hits me with such clarity, it makes my throat tighten.

"This is going to work," I whisper.

"What?" His brows furrow, not understanding.

I shake my head and smile wider before explaining. "After the assignment, you and I. We're going to work."

He returns the smile now, pressing his lips to mine gently. "I'm going to make sure of it. I'm not losing something this great, Josie," he whispers. I have to fight back the lump in my throat. He must see it because he changes the subject. "Now, where do you want to eat tonight?" I look around the room, around the five-star meals that were created specially for me, for this moment.

"You know, I could really go for some mozzarella sticks," I say, and he lets out a loud laugh. But he doesn't question me, doesn't try to sway me towards any of the other more luxurious meals; instead, he grabs my hand and leads me to have dinner like we're young lovers in college.

And even though I do end up tasting *all* of the meals, our first missed date was my favorite.

FORTY-SEVEN

Rowan

I wake with Josie in my arms and take in a deep breath, reveling in the relaxation of being with her.

After all these years.

All those missed opportunities.

All those stupid fucking assumptions I made.

And yet, somehow, she's here in my arms. Somehow, she gave me a shot, and now she's mine. She's so worried about what will happen once we leave here, and I know there's nothing I can say that will ease those nerves, but I can try. And I can show her, long term, just what she means to me.

Josie's body starts to awaken, and her drowsy eyes open slowly before she smiles at me.

"Morning," she says, all sweet and sleepy. I smile at her.

"Morning."

"What time is it?" She asks with a soft yawn. I look over her shoulder and check the bedside clock.

"Seven-ten." She groans, then moves to press a kiss to the underside of my jaw before rolling out of my arms and out of bed. She stands and stretches and my eyes track her every move , roaming over her naked body. She smiles at the clear intent in my face, but shakes her head. "No time. I'm officially on the clock." I glare, then begin my own effort of rolling out of the bad, and I miss how she has to fight her own urge to watch me.

I can work with that.

"How does this clock determine time?" I ask, my voice low. My cock is already hardening as I move towards her.

"It's self-appointed. I make my own hours," she says softly. I pull her into me with an arm around her waist, and the feeling of her skin on mine is phenomenal.

"What about a shower? Everyone has to shower," I murmur, my morning stubble grazing the skin of her neck and making her shiver. "We should just...do it together."

She breaks just like I knew she would.

"A great idea," she murmurs. "Honestly, it's just responsible. Save the fish and whatnot." And then my lips are on hers and I'm dragging her into the bathroom to get our day started with the distinct thought that I wouldn't mind doing this every morning for the foreseeable future.

BREAK

"So can you explain how this works again? Because I trust you guys, but it kind of feels like we're setting things up so this guy can potentially hurt a lot of people," I ask that afternoon as she gets ready in a slinky dress and full makeup. She looks over at me and smiles.

"You gotta trust the process, babe. That's the key." She bends over, roughing up the roots of her her hair in a way I know is to make her have full, sexy hair I'll think about wrapping around my hand all night, and despite myself, despite the serious topic, I can't help but stare at her ass. From this angle, wrapped in her fire-engine red dress, it looks practically diabolical, and instantly, I remember her bent over my office chair the other day.

She keeps talking as if I'm not over herethinking completely filthy things about her and her ass.

"We have three more days here, though I have high hopes about tonight. An opportunity like this is almost a sure thing for a guy like this."

We spent the morning with the girls while they placed the final dominos for the plan this morning before I had to run off and do *my* part, which included greeting out guests and having a huge staff meeting, where I told everyone how vital it was that everything go perfectly tonight.

Harper and Wes Holden arrive this morning, a year after their original honeymoon stay, and for one night we will be allowing paparazzi in to take photos of them together and squash the newest rumors that Harper is already pregnant with the rockstar's baby. Somehow, we were able to convince Leo and his clients to participate in a setup, with extra undercover security from Wilde Security on site, posing as paparazzi.

While tomorrow is the actual day for the paparazzi to come and snap some shots of the couple, we've informed nearly everyone at the resort that the couple is arriving today, and the paparazzi will be capturing their every move. Staff have been told to prepare for them to attend a big party we're throwing tonight for the guests. Rory and Josie are convinced the news will reach our suspect quickly, and he won't be able to resist trying to sabotage something there. Rory and a few of the Wilde Security guys will be carefully monitoring both our cameras and the ones the girls planted, while Josie moves around and does her thing on the ground. I was a bit shocked when Leo agreed so quickly, despite his owing me about a dozen favors at this point, but it seemed the rockstar's fashion designer wife loves drama.

Our hope is that throughout the night, there will be at least a handful of situations where we can catch Randy in the act. Rory spent last night connecting to the video feeds for the boat that takes staff from the mainland to the island every day as well as planting her own cameras on the docks, so we'll know the moment he steps foot on the property. She's going to stay in the room where she has created what looks like a security headquarters with four different screens showcasing four different cameras at any given moment, as well as a fifth computer that is scraping the hotel's security for any strange changes that might mean Carter is accessing the feeds. It's all very detailed and a bit over my head, but the Mavens seem convinced it will work, and I trust that they know exactly what they're doing.

"You seem absolutely giddy about this," I say, looking over Josie who is, in fact, nearly jumping with unreleased energy.

"This is the best part of any mission," she says, moving across the room to sit on my bed, heels in hand. She starts to put them on, her tight red dress absolutely stunning, and I notice then that she's wearing light colored thigh high stockings and fucking *garters.* It takes everything in me not to stalk over to her right there and fall to my knees. Instead, I try and focus.

"What part?" I ask as she slips on her second black heel then stands, brushing he dress down with her hands before striking a pose I think is supposed to be a spy pose.

"Threat level midnight," she says, her voice low. I burst out laughing.

"Threat level midnight?" she nods and smiles.

"Yeah. You wouldn't get it; it's a super hot spy girl thing."

That's what does it, what has me moving toward her and tugging her into me. My hand moves to twine in her hair, to angle her face how I want before placing a kiss to her lips, careful not to mess up the makeup she just did so studiously.

"All right, super hot spy girl, are you ready to get this thing going?"

That smile goes absolutely devious before she nods. "Let's go."

BREAK.

"Any updates?" I ask two hours later, sidling up to Josie as she stares at the party, a bit of an annoyed look on her face.

"No. I'm starting to think tonight isn't going to be the night."

"No?"

She shakes her head and sighs heavily.

"Rory's watching the feeds of his apartment driveway, and his car has been parked there all day. From what she sees, he hasn't gotten on the boat in at least three days, which is how far back we've been able to see with their system."

Since we outsource the operation of the boat that takes employees to and from the island, their security footage isn't on our cloud, but Rory was able to hack into it remotely last night for this reason.

"So he's not here." She shakes her head. The frown between her eyebrows is so fucking cute, the disappointment that she won't be able to enact her big plan tonight plain.

"I think we might be clear tonight. We're still staying vigilant, but..." she shrugs like this is a huge disappointment to her. "I think we'll have to reconvene and try to figure out a new plan."

I look around the room, watching all of the guests enjoy themselves, including Wes and Harper, who are dancing to a slow song together, her head on his chest and the most serene look on his face, like he has his entire world in his arms at that very moment.

Up until recently, I didn't understand that in the least, the way your entire world can shift to be about one person and their happiness, especially not when you can have such a seemingly fulfilling life from just your career. But since Josie fell into my life, I get it.

Looking around, I take note that no eyes are on us, and I step back, pulling her into my arms and walking with her. She doesn't hesitate, wrapping her arms around my neck and melting into my body, letting me sway her and following my lead.

My whole world is in my arms. What a wild 180 from when I first got on this island, thinking my world was this resort, this job.

"Sorry, we didn't catch him tonight," she mumbles. When I shift a hand to tip her head turned up to me, I catch sight of the nearly indiscernible earpiece she's wearing that looks like a piece of glittering jewelry, and a nervous look on her face.

"What?" I ask, confused.

"I wanted to get this done, solve the case so you have one less thing on your plate finally. Sorry, it's not going to happen tonight."

I shake my head, then dip to press my lips soft to hers.

"It's going to happen, Josie. I know you and Rory have about a dozen ideas of how to get this guy to show himself so we can nab him," I say, and she smiles softly, confirming my thoughts. "If we don't get him today, it just means I get another day of watching you do your thing. Midnight Spy Girl or whatever."

She lets out a laugh and shakes her head. "Threat level midnight,"

"Ah, yes, of course. I wouldn't get it. I'm not a super-hot spy girl."

Her smile widens, the disappointment melting from her eyes, if only temporarily.

"Exactly," she whispers, then moves to her toes to press a kiss to my lips. "I'm still annoyed that tonight isn't the night." I let out a loud laugh, then continue to sway with her, laughing and chatting until the song is over.

Her brow furrows, and she looks at her feet for a moment before I realize she must be listening to something in her earpiece. Then she sighs and rolls her eyes.

"It seems Tanya and Daniel are missing." My eyes widen, and panic fills me because, despite both of them irritating me for different reasons, I don't want anything to happen to them. Confusion also hits because she doesn't look concerned in the least; she looked annoyed. Before I can ask, Josie shakes her head. "No, no. No one is hurt. Yet." I raise an eyebrow in confusion. "They're fucking in the staff room on the third floor."

My jaw slackens. "You have got to be kidding me," I groan.

"Rory says she wishes she was, but unfortunately, she is not. She has a full view of Daniel's ass as we speak."

I cringe at the mental image and step away from her. Frustration fills my veins as I take in the reality that my employees are ignoring the direct order for everyone to be in attendance at this party in order to make it run smoother, and my general manager is off fucking around, literally. I was hoping I would be able to find some kind of reason to keep him on board after this all died down, just give him some more training and a slap on the wrist, but it's seeming more and more likely that won't be an option, not with how recklessly he is acting.

"God fucking dammit." I look around the busy room, noting a few staff looking around, a bit overwhelmed. They're probably looking for their *fucking boss*. "All right. I'll go break it up," I grumble.

Josie lets out a laugh. "Have so much fun with that. I'll be here, bored out of my mind, praying something exciting happens."

I roll my eyes and shake my head despite the smile I'm wearing, then move through the resort to get my idiotic employees handled.

Twenty minute later, I'm trying to clean the image of Daniel fucking Tanya and wipe the sound of her fake screams from my memory completely while trying to weigh what to do with Daniel tomorrow. Obviously fucking an employee during work hours when we have a high-profile guest being celebrated and I *specifically* told everyone all hands on deck today is absolutely grounds for a firing. But also, in the next few days, our culprit will be found and, at the very least, I'll have to fire our spa manager and the landscaping assistant manager. Having to also fire the GM probably wouldn't be great for employee morale.

I'm on my way back to the party to fill Josie in on all of the new updates when I pass the lookout, the one Josie dragged me to on her first day here, the one where I almost kissed her. I smile at the memory, thinking that before we leave, I should make sure I get the chance to recreate that moment right there.

But my mind is quickly diverted when I see a dark form folded over near the railing. I step outside with concern, only to see it's not someone who collapsed, thank god. Instead, it's someone messing with the railing. Some kind of alarm bell goes off in my mind, something familiar flickering in my mind. But instead of heeding it, I step further outside to the lookout.

"Everything okay over here?" I ask. The man's head pops up, and the world goes still.

This is Carter Short's brother, Randy.

And he's currently messing with the railing in some way. My mind flashes back to the spa massage table, the way Josie and Rory agreed it was meddled with precisely to collapse under the right pressure, and panic builds.

If he did the same here, it wouldn't be someone injured on a broken massage table or tripping in the woods.

It would be death, certainly, with a drop that has to be at least forty feet onto the rocks below.

For a moment, when he looks at me, he's panicked, like he has been caught, but then he looks around and realizes it's the two of us before his shoulder goes back and a menacing grin comes over his face. He turns back to the railing, grabbing out the last screw and slipping it into his pocket.

"You're the VP, right?" he asks before standing casually. He looks rough, not just like he hasn't had much sleep, but like he hasn't bathed in a week or so. There's a thick layer of hair on his face that we didn't see in other photos; his hair is unkempt, and there are patches of sunburn on his face that feel like he's spent an inordinate amount of time outside lately.

"I..." I hesitate, unsure of what to say, but I also know being too suspicious right now would be bad. "Yeah. VP of Operations."

The man straightens and takes a step towards me. On instinct, I take a step back and over, trying to keep as much distance between us and inadvertently moving towards the railing.

"Mind if I ask what you're doing over here?"

The look in his eye is a little unhinged, a little too far gone, and my heart rate picks up.

"If something happens to *you*, Daniel will definitely lose his job," he says, his eyes nearly feral. For the first time since this all started, I don't feel anxious or worried. Instead, I feel genuine fear.

Up until now, most of the things this man has attempted have been indirect, as far as we know.

"They might not even suspect anything, just that he hasn't been doing the regularly scheduled maintenance. You came out for some air, you leaned on the railing, and *poof!* Gone."

Keep him talking. Get some answers. I can't remember if Josie and Rory bugged this area, but if they did and something happens to me, at least they'll have the evidence they need.

"So that's what this is about? All of the sabotage?" He doesn't speak, but I'm determined to get him talking. I could overpower him: he's a good bit shorter than I am, but he also has a wild look in his eyes and there *is* a cliff a foot behind me that he could easily push me over if he really wanted to. As I moved to gain space between us, I realize belatedly that I had moved closer to the railing than I would like right now.

"I saw you flirting with her, too. Double duty, really. You're not special, by the way. She does it with everyone. But she always comes back to me."

Jesus Christ, so he also sees me as a threat.

And I'm alone with him.

Next to a forty-foot drop.

With a wild look in his eyes.

He starts to move to the side and back, and I turn to keep my eyes on him, realizing my error as he lifts the screwdriver in my direction and takes a step toward me. Without thinking, I take a step back, and then my knees hit the railing gently, and even with that, I can hear the creak. Now this man is before me, clearly threatening me, and my back is to a railing that wouldn't take much for me to fall over.

I sure up my stance, trying to prepare myself. My eyes move from his face to the screwdriver in his hand and back as I try to make a concrete plan that won't end in my falling off a forty-foot cliff, and decide that, from the look of him, I can probably take him. I just need to get that fucking screwdriver away from him.

And, of course, not fall off the cliff.

I make my decision, my plan of action, and take a step forward, ready to reach for the screwdriver.

But before I can do a thing, he falls to the ground.

FORTY-EIGHT

JOSIE

"Did you just tase him?" Rowan asks like an idiot as I stand behind where Randy Short lays in a heap, my pink bedazzled taser still in my hand. Sliding the safety back on, I slip it back into the holster of my garter.

"Yeah, now can you step away from the edge, please?" I ask, kneeling on the ground beside a knocked-out Randy. He really did fall to the ground like a sack of potatoes, hitting his head on the way down. If I weren't so stressed by the fact that Rowan might trip off a goddamn cliff, I'd be squealing at a job well done and my first successful use of Betty.

Thankfully, he does as I ask, stepping forward and then away from the weakened railing, then moves over to me. Together, we roll Randy onto his front before I reach into the small bag on my other garter and grab some zip ties.

"What the fuck else is in there?" he asks, tipping his chin.

"You don't want to know," I say with a smile, moving to to his feet and zip tying those, as well.

"Did the cameras go down?" Rowan asks, tipping his chin to

where there's one installed by the hotel. "If not, we have a confession." I give him a small grimace and nod.

"About five minutes after you left. Once Rory gave me the update, I went to find you, but you weren't in that staff room, and when I bumped into Daniel, he said you had headed back to the party."

Rowan's brows furrow with confusion.

"How did you know where I was?" he asks. "This isn't the normal way I'd take back to the ballroom and Rory didn't put her own camera out here."

I cringe before answering, not sure how he's going to take this news.

"Don't get mad, but I put a tracker on your phone," I say as if I'm telling him I spent too much on a pair of shoes.

"I'm sorry?" he asks, stilling. I decide to lean into it as I wrap Randy's wrists with a hot pink industrial zip tie.

"A tracker. It's in your phone. Just in case. It was the only thing that Rory agreed to, just to quadruple check you had nothing to do with anything. She wanted to bug your room, but I planned to get railed in there and—"

"Jesus, Josie," he says with a groan. Regardless of how he might feel about my late admission, it's something I'm insanely grateful for, considering we lost track of where he might be and the only reason I knew where to go was because of that tracker.

Five minutes after Rowan left to talk to Daniel, all camera footage went out completely. That's because Randy destroyed the alarm control panel after storming into the security office and knocking out Jonas. He's with one of the Wilde Security guys and should be fine. On the bright side, because Randy seems to have simply lost it, he didn't bother to hide his actions, so we have incredibly clear evidence that he's the one behind the issues. We don't need the confession the cameras apparently missed: we have more than enough evidence on our side to seal this.

"Do you think hog-tying him is too much?" I ask, tipping my head as I finish off Randy's feet.

"What?" he asks, looking me to me. I gesture to the still-out-cold Randy, though I assume he should be coming to soon.

"Hog-tying him," I say, sitting on my knees, my hands on my hips as I take in my handy work. It's a mix of hot pink and bright purple plastic holding his hands and feet together, and honestly, it's kind of a cool look.

"I..." Rowan starts, taking everything in, and for a moment I wonder if he's going into shock.

"I know, I know. It's a lot, getting saved by a five-four hottie in heels, and all, but I am going to need you to snap out of it."

We don't have time for him to be fish-mouthing at me, not when this dude could come back to this world at any moment. I could give him a second zap if needed, but I'm also not entirely sure about the long-term impacts of something like that. Back up shouldn't be far out, and Rory is aware of the updates via the earpiece and on her way over now, but you can never be too safe.

"It's less about who saved me and more about the fact that my girlfriend is hog tying a man with ease in front of me after tasing him and not even blinking an eye," he says as I zip the last one in place before looking up to him and smile wide.

"I'm your girlfriend, Rowan?"

He shakes his head in confusion and my smile widens.

"I thought that was kind of an accepted fact at this point."

I shake my head, then decide a hog-tie is never a bad idea, grabbing another zip tie and fashioning it to attach the hand and foot ties.

"No, you definitely have to ask. It's a rule."

Happy with my handiwork, bright colored lines across our culprit's hands and feet with both pulled to his back, I stand, wiping off my hands and knees in the process before putting my hands to my hips. As I do, Randy groans a little, coming to.

Perfect timing.

"What the fuck?" he mumbles into the floor, his head turning to the side and glaring at us. I wiggle my fingers in a wave to him, before stepping towards Rowan, more important things to worry about.

"You were saying?" I ask, redirecting my attention to Rowan. He shakes his head with a small laugh before pulling me in tighter. Down the hall, I hear a commotion and realize the Wilde Security guys and Rory are nearby.

"I have to ask, huh?" Rowan asks, ignoring everything else.

"Oh yeah. Full send, grand gesture, the whole nine." My hand lifts to wrap around his neck.

"Not really my style," he says, voice low as he lifts a hand to rest on my jaw, his thumb brushing over my bottom lip. The touch moves through me, the endorphins that are already flowing through me making me feel every move intensely.

"I don't know if you know this, Rowan, but I'm kind of high maintenance. A man-eater, some would say. If you don't give me what I need, I'll just chew you up and spit you out."

His smile goes wide and cocky. "Oh, I give you what you need, Josie, and we both know that."

Now *that* goes right between my legs.

"What the fuck is going on?" Randy yells from the ground.

"Shut up, we're busy," I say, eyes never leaving Rowan's. "You still haven't asked."

Rowan smiles then, shaking his head gently like he's thoroughly entertained by me.

"Will you, Josephine *Man-eater* Montgomery, be my girlfriend?" he murmurs, and it's like I'm fourteen, and my crush is asking me to prom; the butterflies in my stomach are going a mile a minute, and the smile on my face spreads into a wide grin.

"Did you really have to ask?" I say with a smile before I move to my toes and press a kiss against his laughing lips. We stand there as he deepens it in this spot, the same one I wished to high heaven he'd kiss me in not long ago.

Our culprit thrashes at our feet when back up enters, and Rory's laugh fills the area.

God, I love my job.

EPILOGUE

After Rory stopped laughing at the sight of Rowan and me making out next to a hogtied Randy, we got our culprit to the police, who got a formal confession out of him. It turns out, we were dead on with our assumption: Randy found out that Tanya was cheating on him with Daniel and started doing things to try and jeopardize Daniel's job, thinking that if he could get him fired, Tanya would no longer be interested in him. When his small efforts didn't work, he upped his game with the almond oil in the mud bath and the fire. The video we found from the shack was Tanya confronting her ex and a halfhearted attempt to stop him.

Also, as we assumed, his younger brother did what he could to cover for him while also trying to convince him to stop, hacking into the cameras to clear any footage that would show him in the act. Unfortunately for Carter, as his brother escalated and had more and more incidents, he forgot to cover his *own* missteps, like any footage of him stealing the camera from the ransacked room.

We didn't see him get on the boat because he never returned to the main island; instead, he lived in the forest for weeks while carrying out his sabotage. Some of the missing food deliveries were actually just Randy needing to eat, it seems. When, as planned, he heard that the resort needed all hands on deck for the arrival of the Holdens, he took his opportunity, both of employees being distracted and to cause a major issue. Rowan had two dozen handymen conduct a thorough inspection of every railing, as well as the other locations Rory had caught him tinkering with, such as wall hangings and light fixtures, as well as a team to come in and repair the security system. After that was completely, guests were once more allowed to wander the hotel safely.

But once he was locked away and we could ensure that the hotel was safe again, we *partied.* The hotel party that was thrown for the Holdens (and the paparazzi) was the first time I've seen Rowan let go in public, and it was a *time.* With the pressure of the sabotage done, he was free to spend the night dancing with me, although he refrained from drinking, and after, we said goodnight to Rory and our new friends Wes and Harper before continuing a party of our own late into the night before Rowan, Rory and I left the island in the early dawn hours.

After we got home and wrapped up a few loose ends, Rowan and I did, in fact, take a vacation after: the full two weeks in a little beach house we rented in Seaside Point at the recommendation of his assistant, Sutton. I don't know if Annette actually followed through on her threat of removing Rowan from the server, because to my knowledge, he never checked. Instead, we spent two weeks together, lazing on the beach, spending nights on the boardwalk, knocking off a good number of those dates he thinks he owes me, and getting to know each other without the pressure of work hovering over us. It was perfectly blissful.

Six months later and things have only gotten better. The only real difference is that many of my most recent assignments haven't been local since I've started a serious relationship, instead driving a bit out of the way, often to Philly or New York if need be to ensure there won't be too much crossover. When I do have an assignment in Hudson City, I make sure I let my boyfriend who, as of two weeks ago, moved me into his fancy high rise condo, know so he doesn't have to break a tooth gritting his teeth while watching me flirt with some asshole he knows right in front of him.

All that to day, life is good.

Even better when Rory and I are given another mission in paradise. Aruba, this time.

"Maybe we should go on an excursion together while you're here," the man across from me says, watching my finger play along the rim of the wine glass in front of me. I've had three, though he doesn't know that after the first one, I was quietly switched to sparkling cider to keep my mind clear.

He, on the other hand, has not and instead has been served stronger and stronger drinks each time. His eyes are hazy, his smile sloppy, which is exactly how I need him.

For reference, this is *not* a situation where I feel bad for potentially ruining this man's life.

"That would be so fun. You know, I've always wanted to swim with dolphins," I say with a smile and flutter my lashes. Although he returns the grin, it's barely a moment before his eyes go back to my ample cleavage on display. *God, men are so easy.*

"Let's book it. Tomorrow," he says before looking around as if the hotel restaurant will have some kind of guest services lingering around where they would help him book an excursion for tomorrow. "I'll pay for it, of course."

"Oh, that's so generous," I say, sugar in the words. Then I let my smile falter just a bit before turning into a pitying pout. "But aren't you hurt? I doubt they'll let you go with that." I tip my chin towards the leg in an air cast.

"What?" he asks, confused as to my one of questioning, just as we assumed.

He doesn't even remember he's wearing it. What a fucking idiot.

"Your cast," I say. "You can't swim with that on." His gaze leaves my breasts for another brief moment, moving to his leg before he smiles and waves a hand at me.

"Oh, no need to worry. It's not broken." My eyes widen, and my lips part and I make sure my hand is on top of the table to ensure all three wearable devices I have on catch his words clearly.

"It isn't?" He shakes his head, then leans in closer.

"Can you keep a secret?" I grin, something genuine for the first time all night, the excitement of a win building in me.

"I'm an amazing secret keeper." His eyes go *back* to my tits before he nods.

"I bet you are." He motions me to lean in again before saying in a stage whisper, "It's not broken." I gasp at this complex and totally new concept to me, not seeing it coming in the *least. Cue eyeroll.* "I fell at work and had a doctor buddy of mine sign off on it being worse than it is so I could get Workman's comp." I let out a girlish giggle and a wide smile, and he returned a gleeful smile. He thinks it's because he's *so smart*, I'm sure, but it's really because I just won.

And in record time, nonetheless.

"Oh, that's diabolical."

"The best men are the ones who know how to play the system." He lifts his glass and motions for me to copy. "To working the system."

"To working the system," I concur. Then my eyes drift across the room to where Rory is sitting with our newest Maven, Isla. She gives me a thumbs up, indicating our mission has been accomplished and in record time. We were booked at the Daydream Resort for a week just in case, but we're only two days in and already hit our mark.

Which means we just earned ourselves a nice little vacation.

"Mr. Martin," an employee says, coming up to my dinner date at the perfect time. "We have someone at the front desk who is trying to get in touch with you. They say it's an emergency." I know the emergency is fabricated and that he won't be coming back to finish this meal, but I still pout all the same as my date lets out a deep sigh.

"Alright. It should only be a minute. Then we'll find the best time for our dolphin swim."

"Can't wait," I say with a smile, knowing damn well I won't be here when he gets back, an "emergency" of my own taking me away.

As I watch him lumber off with a smile over his shoulder at me, I sit back, the pleasure of a completed job washing over me as a new, *real* glass of wine slides before me.

And then Rowan slides in across from me, a smile spreading over his full lips.

"Job well done?" he asks with a raised eyebrow. I nod and grin back at him before taking a long sip of my new drink, the exact brand he knows I love.

"Easier than expected."

"What are the chances you can take off for a couple of days and spend them lazing with me? I've got five days here, after all, all expenses paid." I smile

"I don't know, my boyfriend is pretty powerful," I whisper, and he shakes his head, smiling. Rory comes over then, giving me a thumbs up.

"You did good, kid," she says and I roll my eyes.

"I *always* do good."

"Yeah, yeah," she says.

"Do they always... just fall for it that easy?" Isla asks, clearly equal parts confused and impressed.

"Every time," Rowan says as he sits back with a smile.

"Wow," she whispers. I smile and shrug.

"Men are stupid and simple."

"I'm right here," Rowan says, and I turn to him, an eyebrow raised.

"And?" He stares before smiling and shaking his head.

"As much as I love to see Josie take Rowan down a notch or seven, I'm planning to give the report to Gabriel tonight so we can enjoy the rest of our trip." I nod, then move to stand, giving a wink to Rowan, but Rory shakes her head. "No. You two stay. I'm going to show Isla how to process the footage and data. You're going to be bored and start chatting and distract me." I fight a smile because she's not wrong.

"Are you sure?" I ask, feeling bad because we are on a job. She nods and turns to my boyfriend, pointing at him.

"You owe me one," she says with a stern face. Rowan gives her a smile, and I can't help but think this is pre-planned.

"There's an unlimited credit for spa services and room service attached to both of your cards," Rowan says to Rory and Isla. "On me. Enjoy yourselves."

"Rowan, you—" I start, but Rory cuts me off.

"Perfect. Later, Josie! Lunch tomorrow." I try to argue, but then she's grabbing Isla's hand and tugging her out of the restaurant. When I turn back to Rowan, he's grinning wide.

"Is this one of your dates?" I ask, though we've gone well past the 21 promised to me months ago at this point. He smiles wide, leaning over the table to press a kiss ot my lips. He never answers, but I guess I didn't really need him to anyway.

BREAK

"I love you, you know," Rowan says two hours later as we walk along the empty shoreline hand in hand, the soft ocean breeze wrapping around me as he says those words for the first time.

Out loud, at least. Rowan's been showing me he's in love with me for months now. Years, maybe, in his own strange, Rowan Fisher way. I thought when we finally said it, my heart would pound and butterflies would fill my chest, but instead, it's like warm, soothing water is coasting along my skin, filling my body. It makes sense, though. I think that's what love is, after all: comfort and desire and friendship wrapped up into something so precious, I can't believe I once convinced myself I would never want it. Need it.

"Hmm?" I ask, though I heard him loud and clear. With my words, he stops walking, turning towards me and tugging me into him.

"Don't play dumb," he whispers. "It's not cute."

"I'm always cute," I argue, because even now, I can't seem to find it in me to just give in to him. It's been six months, and I still love to get under his skin.

"Are you going to really argue with me when I'm telling you I love you for the first time?" My heart lifts and spins just a bit at his words.

"I wasn't arguing! I was just saying I'm always cute. That's a fact, not an argument." He closes his eyes with exasperation, letting out a long breath, an action I've seen so many times. One I hope I'll see a million more. For the rest of my life.

"So the answer is yes, then," he murmurs to himself.

"You haven't actually said the actually thing, Rowan," I say, grinning now. He rolls his eyes but returns that wide smile before he puts a hand under my chin, pressing his lips to mine, slow and sweet. There's none of the normal heat that is typically in our kisses, and it makes the moment more magical. "I love you, Josie." The waves crash behind us, reminding me of the Keys, where everything changed for us, our twist of fate that I'll never stop being grateful for. "My troublemaker." He presses another soft kiss to my lip. "My maneater."

"But always yours," I whisper.

"That's all I'll ever care about, Josie," he replies. That warmth moves through my veins.

"I love you too, Rowan."

"I know baby." He kisses me again, lips moving over mine before he presses his forehead to mine. "A while form now, we're going back to the Keys resort and I'm taking you to the private beach. One last date. I'm going to tell you something else while we're there." I look up at him and move a hand over his cheek, stubble already forming despite the fact that I watched him shave in the mirror of our room this morning while I stood beside him doing my hair.

"Yeah?"

"It'll be a question," he says so low I almost don't hear him. My pulse starts to pound.

"Will it come with jewelry?" He lets out a small chuckle.

"Yeah." I smile again, because even though we've talked about this, about our future and where we want this to lead, I'm filled with giddy excitement. "Any idea what you might say? So I can prepare?" I pretend to think for a moment.

"You love me?" I ask.

"More than anything." My chest swells.

"Then I think you'll get the answer you're hoping for," I whisper. His laugh fills the night air, free and happy, and even though I hear it often now, it still fills me with joy.

"I think I may have won over the maneater," he murmurs against my lips before kissing me, hot and deep. And even though I'm too preoccupied to respond, I completely agree.

Made in the USA
Middletown, DE
03 August 2025

11159976R00208